the wilderness

the wilderness

A LESLIE STONE NOVEL

karen novak

BLOOMSBURY

Published by Bloomsbury Publishing, New York and London
Distributed to the trade by Holtzbrinck Publishers

All papers used by Bloomsbury Publishing are natural, recyclable products
made from wood grown in well-managed forests. The manufacturing processes conform to
the environmental regulations of the country of origin.

Library of Congress Cataloging-in-Publication Data

Novak, Karen.
The wilderness : a Leslie Stone novel / Karen Novak.—1st U.S. ed.
p. cm.
ISBN 1–58234–483–3 (pbk.)
1. Older men—Crimes against—Fiction. 2. Women private investigators—Fiction. I. Title.

PS3564.O893W55 2005
813′.6—dc22
2004016083

ISBN-13 9781582344836

First U.S. Edition 2004

1 3 5 7 9 10 8 6 4 2

Typeset by Hewer Text Limited, Edinburgh
Printed in the United States of America
by Quebecor World Fairfield

For my daughters

Because hate is legislated . . . written into
the primer and the testament,
shot into our blood and brain like vaccine or vitamins . . .

I need love more than ever now . . .
I need love more than hope . . .

Walter Benton, *This Is My Beloved*

I know. You have heard this before—
But for this woman, this rock and field,
this blur of body's suggestion, matter shifting
as she would shift; here, everything begins.

Amy Small-McKinney, "Snow Blind"

seeing

solstice

I had been thinking about the body since morning. More accurately, I had been trying not to think about the body and its former inhabitant, how his last hours had been spent alone in the cold night. The story—DEAD MAN IDENTIFIED—had been boxed on the second page of the local paper, lower corner, near the fold. When measured against the headlines that the discovery of his body had rated earlier in the week, I took the placement as an indication of diminishing interest. It wasn't a murder, after all. Nothing remarkable. He had been no one.

Skiers trekking the fields around Willet had stumbled upon the body, frozen, beneath a knoll of heavy snowfall. Authorities determined that he had been an itinerant trying to ride out the cold snap at Happy Andy's, the abandoned petting zoo and defunct cut-it-yourself tree farm. Preliminary coroner reports estimated the victim to be in his late eighties or older; this advanced age had only hastened the effect of the below zero temperatures. The body showed no indication of foul play. No alcohol or drugs in his system. That blankets, clothing, cans of food had been scattered around Happy Andy's empty caretaker's house, that the woodstove there had been stocked with kindling but gone unlit, that the body was naked, curled fetal several hundred feet from any structure implied he had wandered away from his shelter. Whether this was due to confusion, dementia, or the outright courting of his end was not pertinent. Officials were calling the death an unintentional suicide.

The unintentional now had a name. He was—had been—one James Kendrick, this according to a homeless shelter ID card found among other papers squirreled away near a "graffiti-covered wall" in the caretaker's house. It was hoped that someone would recognize the name and aid authorities trying to locate the man's family. The paper again offered a brief description of the lanky, toothless remains and noted a forearm tattoo that was not described in detail beyond "unusual." Kendrick's name was familiar to me in the way that names in newspapers always seem familiar, but it was the details—the cold, the aloneness, the naked body beneath the snow; these nagged at my thoughts. Poor old man.

Not counting a few mean-spirited spates of wind-driven slivers, it had not snowed since Kendrick had been found. The snow we had was now hard, icy and dulled under grime. We wouldn't be getting any more soon. Too cold. The forecast in the paper had arctic air slicing south for the holidays; we would be hovering at the zero mark through New Year's, and it was only the twenty-first. Outside the clock of the northern sky was striking nadir: longest night, first of winter, the climatic shimmer on our tambourine panic that the sun's attentions might have drifted beyond recall.

I carried the paper with me all that morning into the afternoon, feeling pursued. The shadows stretching across the windows and floors had taken on a sense of hunger. This was how my illness announced its return, unease percolating through reality, investing even inanimate motion with a palpable intent to grab and swallow. The illness had a name of multiple syllables that came no closer to describing it than I could beyond this sensation of exterior hunger. Like any prey, I did my best to keep moving. To stop would mean I had admitted that I could not outrun the appetites of my madness, and would have no choice but to admit that sense of encroaching menace to my husband, Greg. That was my half of our reconciliation bargain. I was not to harbor ghosts in secret. If *it* started up again, he was to be told. His half of the bargain was that until told otherwise, he was going to believe everything to be fine.

My bargain keeping leaned more toward the spirit rather than the letter of our deal. It was our first Christmas back together after a four-year separation that had not worked out any better than the marriage. Forces beyond logic joined Greg and me, our essential selves melded on the molecular level so that we were just as unstable apart as together. We were each other's irresolvable, the *why?* that pride and stubbornness could not leave alone. There was love here, without question, but for Greg and me, love without question was not to be trusted. We poked, prodded, split up, and fused back together if only to keep proving love's existence to our own satisfaction. We were one of those couples with a half-life, more interested in the glow we gave off than in the long-term implications for the health of those around us.

This year, however, was going to be different. This Christmas was to be the demarcation line, the moment we could point to from a vantage in the happy future and say, "That was the beginning of better." In deference to our agreement, in hope for that future, I waved the newspaper in Greg's general direction while he, on the other side of the room, was trying to find which of the tiny twinkle lights had burned out on the decidedly nontwinkling Christmas tree.

"Do we know anybody named Kendrick?"

"Who?" He pulled his hand from deep inside the stiff-branched pine and lifted it to his mouth to suck on a bleeding scratch. "It would be a big help if someone actually checked these lights *before* I put them on the tree."

We went through this every year. Greg, not remembering the ordeal from one year to the next, saw the tree lights as just another annoyance to cross off his current to-do list. I saw the whole exercise, from finding the unmarked box that held the lights to the moment we finally had twinkle, as a tradition as vile and nutty as the fruitcake I was obliged to make but no one ever ate. Even during our separation, when we only pantomimed our way through a semblance of a family holiday for Molly's and Emma's sake, we had had this fight. We had to have this fight or it simply was not Christmas.

"Greg, I *did* check those before you started—"

"All of them?"

"No. I only checked every other—of course, I checked all of them. I always do, don't I? They were working."

"Well, they are not working now."

"Maybe one of them got knocked loose when you—"

"It's all right, Leslie. I've got it under control."

"No one said you didn't."

"Why do we hold on to this cheap crap? Next year we're getting brand-new everything. I'm amazed we haven't burned the house down."

"You say that every year—"

"So why do we still have these?"

"—And then you hold me responsible. Every year."

"If you're so up on what happens *every year* then maybe you could have bought the damn new lights?"

"See? Why is it my responsibility? You put them up. You take them down. If *you* want the damn new lights shouldn't *you* be the one to go buy the damn new lights?"

This was my traditional ploy of trying to end the discussion with a persuasive mix of the obvious tinged with just enough sarcasm to come across as both insult and threat. Anger thus ignited, he'd shut down, shut up for fear of setting off something larger.

Determined, willfully silent, he would go back to twisting bulbs in and out of sockets. I'd grouse under my breath about how he had to stop treating me like an open keg of nitro; if he was pissed at me, he should say so; it was the quiet that made me crazy. He'd continue as though I were not there, inches away from his ear, yelling at him in whispers. The tree would not light. Greg's movements would intensify, his body bending away from me; my complaints would grow louder. Our daughters would hightail it to their rooms, taking cover before the inevitable combustion of my superheated frustration met their father's airless nonresponse. Hark! The herald angels sing . . . *Kaboom.*

But this year *was* going to be different. We had promised each other we would do whatever we could to try to be different. In the name of trying, I clamped my mouth tight. Our eyes locked in mutual pleading to not go where the ritual demanded. Greg broke the gaze first to examine his scratched knuckles. "Yeah, you're right. I should have taken care of it."

"No, you're right. I'm the one who remembers. I should have done it. Still can. The stores—"

"Don't bother. More of a pain to take them off at this point. I'll find the uncooperative bastard—" he noticed the paper "—you wanted something?"

"Never mind." I crumpled the newsprint in both hands, twisting it, the ink smearing on my damp palms.

"You asked me if I knew someone?"

"No. It was nothing."

"New lights next year, then?"

"Absolutely. Next year." I tossed the paper into the fireplace where it caught on the lazily flaming logs and was gone, flared to ash in an instant. Nothing burns that fast. I had blanked out and come back. Flames clutched at the charred bits of paper caught in the updraft. How much time had I lost? Ten, fifteen seconds?

"Leslie?"

I should have told him what had happened. But how could I explain it? That time was getting as unreliable as light? Anyway, when this sort of thing started happening, it was too late to do much about it. I smiled at my husband. "It was nothing."

Night came on thin and quick, edged by a shrill icy wind. The tree was dark still; Greg still checking bulb after bulb and swearing softly in time, in tune to the carols lilting from the stereo, both refrains drowned out by the occasional shriek of wind in the chimney. Molly knelt at the coffee table in front of the fireplace, book open before her, reading, her face flushed from the heat of the now-dying flames. Emma was in the kitchen giving gingerbread men fashion statements of colored icing. I, who had been growing increasingly restless, was wandering the house, unable to settle my body, let alone my concentration for having to admit to the sense of whispers just beyond my hearing. I shuffled about in my bedroom slippers, annoying my family with cheery inquiries as to whether they were hungry, if maybe they wanted cocoa or cider or anything at all.

Greg kept eyeing me as I passed him in my anxiety-driven circuit. "Les?" he finally said. "Why don't you sit down?"

"I'm fine." *Fine* was what he wanted to hear; *fine* was what I wanted to be true. I could not tell him, could barely tell myself, that since burning the Kendrick story, *it* had been getting worse: Time was hiccuping fast, slow, skipping moments in which I, outside of time, was seeing the shimmer of movement, quicksilver running through rooms I knew to be empty.

Even if I could have told Greg, what would I have told our daughters? The scary stuff is back but don't be scared? They'd heard that one before. My selfish insisting that they endure my uncertain presence often appalled me; it would have been more selfish to explain to them why I needed it so.

An ember in the fire snapped. I startled as though it had been a gunshot. *Run.* "Going out to get wood," I announced to no one, turned, and headed for the kitchen. I thought to grab my gloves but not my boots or coat before dashing out the door, down the back porch, and into the trench of a path we'd worn through the snow trekking back and forth to the woodpile. The wind hit sideways, thrusting into the collar of my shirt, under and up the hem of my sweater. My feet, bare in thin flannel slippers, ached with the insult of the cold. Pointless to turn back, I was already halfway to where I was headed; I pulled the collar closed around my throat and hurried on to the side of the garage where the wood was stacked. The motion sensor of the light fixture had already been tripped by the wind. Sparkling filaments of powdery snow danced tornado ballets through the spotlight. I quickly filled my arms with a bunch of hardy branches and wheeled about to run back for the warmth of the house.

The wind built, gusted. I tried to hunker into myself, make the thump of my footfall thump faster. The floodlights Greg had installed over the girls' basketball hoop were blazing, the sensors there tripped, too. Into the light swirled a sheet of newspaper. I would have ignored it as an errant piece of litter, but it was followed by another sheet and then another. I stopped to watch them—dozens now—tumbling and twirling toward me, giant curling planes of translucence just above my head. I dropped the branches and tore off my gloves so that I could better grab at the sheets when they passed, but the wind attenuated, wilted like a dying breath; the sheets fell, not far away, and slid in a lazy jumble on the ice crust. I took off after them, my numb feet punching knee-deep shafts in the snow, moving farther and farther from the shelter of the light. Aware of nothing but the repeated crunch of punctured ice and the throb of my breathing, I did not feel myself fall out of time. I reached the pages, began gathering the ones I could. I heard Greg shouting from behind me: *Leslie, what are you doing?* I was about to shout back, but when I turned to show him the papers, my voice retreated. In front of the woodpile stood a peacock. The bird's thickly clawed toes ticked on the icy crust; his broad, night-blue breast heaved. The tail draped out heavily behind him in a massive train of plumes twelve, maybe fifteen feet long. He took no notice of me at first, but in a moment his head bobbed about, sending a vibration through his crown of spurred frills. He turned toward me, and with a flourishing snap, he fanned his tail upright, an arc of a hundred blind, burning eyes, staring out red and gold, unblinking, still, even in the once-more-building wind. All those eyes directed at me. It was an accusation.

Greg called my name. At least, I thought it was Greg. The moment was disrupted; the bird vanished and the world resumed. I looked down at my hands clutched tightly around nothing. The paper had been unreal as well.

Greg met me on the path and helped me collect the wood to carry back to the house. He asked if I was all right, and I told him that I was fine, that I had chased off a raccoon or bear or something. He wrapped his arm hard around my shoulder, pulling me against him, saying we should get me inside where it was warm. I told him I wasn't looking forward to that. He noted my snow-clogged slippers and said something in my ear, his breath hot where I could feel it. I lost the sound of his words in the whine of the gathering wind. Greg urged me toward the house. I kept shifting my gaze, turning my head to look behind me where the peacock had been, turning back to where I could see the shifting patterns of tree lights now in play as patterns on the windowpanes.

The next morning, in full sun, I went out to check the woodpile. Maybe I was hoping to find one page escaped from the girls' school bags or a newspaper insert, a single fragment from my current willed-to-center life that could have triggered the hallucination. I found none, of course. The trigger had been that reference to *papers* in the Kendrick story. The part of my mind too slippery for words had wanted to see those papers and so had made its request in dream-speak. Until I saw them, I wouldn't know why the pages were important to me. Or what the hell that peacock was supposed to mean. I might not even know then. But until I saw them, the hallucinations would continue, intensify. My subconscious, having no self-awareness, had no self-control either. What the illness wanted, it got. Better to surrender up front.

I stood in the snow and considered the windless sky scoured to a gleam by the cold that was now steeling itself in my head as a too-bright idea. I could call Andrea Burnham, my detective friend on the Swifton police force, to see if she might call up to Willet and finagle copies for me. Apply police logic to uncertainty, isn't that what I always did? As a child, I had assessed the forces of the world as oppositions embodied by the quiet constants of the resolve of my father, the police chief, and the continually dissolving variables of my mother's carnival impulses. My mother ended up lost inside the violence of herself and left us to avoid hurting anyone. We never heard from or of her again. My father lost himself in the violence of the world and tried to will peace through his fists and a two-by-four. I had watched him try to kill a man he feared might kill us. And so I was lost, although I did not know that yet.

I ran away to the city where I joined the police force. I thought that being able to name chaos was the same thing as creating order. It wasn't until I was talking to shrinks, bleary between dosages in the dayroom of the institution and going all third-rate Lady Macbeth about the blood on my hands, that I started to understand everyone in my family was running different frequencies on the spectrograph of crazy. I, the introspective cop, the family mediator, had lost it completely and, like my father, killed a man; like my mother, abandoned my daughters. Because I was scared. See? My madness was nothing if not reasonable.

For obvious reasons, I had to call Andrea, and appeal to the hierarchies of law to graft order into my thoughts. The simple imagining of the chain of events this might set in motion sent a wave of warmth though my chest, as though a deep breath had at long last reached my lungs. My posture straightened, the curl of a genuine smile tensed the muscles of my face for the first time in days. Maybe I could be of use tracking down Kendrick's family? Calling Andrea might lead to work. That was what I needed. I needed work, a purpose other than proving myself sane.

The nature of my work, however, would only accelerate the illness. Tracing effect back to cause necessitated imaginative thinking, and my imagination was a dangerous place. I longed to have my husband and our daughters see me as safe. The effort had failed. It always failed.

The initial glow of happiness cooled; icy air replaced the warmth around my heart. To even contemplate returning to a search for the missing was an untenable risk to my family's security. To pursue this Kendrick fixation, which had already put my mind in jeopardy, was selfish and foolhardy. I knew that. I also knew I had to see Kendrick's papers, that if I did not see them my waking mind would be overtaken by the depths of shadows spilling out from beneath it. I had no choice.

Before heading back to the house and the telephone and the call, I scanned the yard one more time. Maybe, just maybe, I was hoping to find traces of peacock claw in the snow. If it had been real, I could forget it, leave it behind the way real things get left. I didn't find anything, no scratch nor puncture in crusted snow. Nor could I seem to find those gloves.

greg

Leslie is out prowling the snow for the third time this afternoon, retracing her steps. She tells me she is looking for her gloves. She's looking for something, all right. The color in her face is up, berry-flushed from cold and excitement. Syllables trip over themselves in the rush to get out of her mouth. Her eyes blink as though adjusting to a new level of lighting. She plays with her hair. Turned on, the air around her crackles with energy. Over a lost pair of gloves? Yeah, I believe that. I offer to help her look. No, no. Don't bother, she says.

Missing gloves. Calling Andrea. Signs rise like a crest of fire on the horizon. What reads to me as a clear alert that an enemy is approaching, mesmerizes Leslie as though it were the crown of the aurora. We're seeing the same thing and yet cannot make each other understand what it means.

The first time it went to hell, Doctor Edelstein—who would become to all of us simply "Frank," our stooped Buddha, as Leslie calls him, the quiet, myopic bachelor uncle every family adopts—Frank took me aside at the hospital, into an austere office that was too small for its spare furnishings. He had been fatigued beyond measure, yawning mid-sentence, pinching at his earlobe, lacking the resources for the niceties that would have blunted the impact of his words: psychotic break.

My wife, in the course of her work, had killed a bad guy whom most of us were happy to have taken off the planet. That's what the police were supposed to do, right? Get rid of the bad guys? The shooting had been impulsive, Frank said, but it also had a deliberate quality, a kind of panicked severing of her last tether to this world. Leslie had shoved herself somewhere outside reality; it was up to her to want to come back. When she did, if she did, reentry was going to be hard for her and even harder for those of us who could do nothing but watch. Once back, in order to stay here, she'd have to figure out what she'd been trying to run from in the first place and then convince her self from moment to moment, day to day, for the rest of her life that running was no longer necessary. I'd asked the obvious: how exactly she was supposed to do that. "Hell if I know," Frank had answered. "Drugs. Talk. Whatever helps when it helps, and sometimes nothing will."

He had warned that the coming months would reveal how much the marriage could withstand. Limits, he had said, were not the same as failures. I was not to feel failed for admitting to resentment or anger or helplessness. I ought to be on watch for the symptoms of despair. Other than that, take care of myself, my daughters, do what was necessary to keep going. That was my job. He gave me his card in case I wanted someone to talk to.

Talk? I could not find sound in my body to describe what had been taken away. For the first few weeks, when Leslie was nearly catatonic, the best I could do was send Frank articles from the newspapers, what the reporters had written about Leslie, about us. It was the only way I had to convey the reality of the shooting, her illness, our loss. I'd cut out the story, put it in an envelope, and mail it care of the hospital. No letter of commentary. It seemed enough, more than enough, to show it to someone else as proof that, yes, this was really happening.

Had happened. Five and a half years ago. Always on the brink of happening again. Is still happening. What is time anyway but infinite angles on the same two stories? What I knew then and what I know now. Nothing happens to Leslie except what her life allows. Someone needs to watch over her, to keep her from throwing open the gates to yet another marvelous, disaster-laden illusion. I can always tell when she's *seeing* something; she's never looked at me that way. Is it possible to envy an illness?

I love her. Of course, I do. No one questions that, and I'm glad because those words, that word, can no longer contain its meaning. I am the last sentry on the wall of an already defeated city. The damage is done; the ruins smolder behind me. Nothing that happens from here on out could be any worse than what has already happened. I get up every day, climb to my post, and watch for fires on the horizon. That's my job. That's all I know.

edge

Light falls upon the eye, triggering photoreceptors that send chemical and electric signals, via the optic nerve, to the brain. The signals are then relayed through the visual areas of the cortex, where they are converted into finer and finer perceptions of color, angle, shape, movement. Meaning is assigned as a function of context in terms of previous experience. What has been seen before? What did that mean? All of the visible world is transmitted and read in fractions of a second. All of it is happening inside the head.

The point at which the optic nerve leaves the retina, the boundary between out there and in here, is called the optic disk. That disk contains no photoreceptors, transmits no light, and therefore produces an unavoidable blind spot in the visual field. It is not a mere pinpoint loss either; as neural measurements go, it is a rather good-sized void. The reason we are not constantly aware of our blind spot is a source of much theorizing. Some hold that blindness can't be seen; the brain cannot process information it is not receiving. We don't see it because there is nothing to see. Some argue that in the need for a complete visual field, the anxiety of the blind spot causes the brain to make an assumption about what is missing and fill in the blank. An ongoing hallucination, essentially. We see what we need to see. Mapping the boundaries of an individual's blind spot is not only interesting; it's downright prudent. Frank explained this before sitting me down before a computer to map mine. He had me focus on one of two dots, move close and away from the screen, then click the mouse when the other dot vanished. The good doctor was proving a point: Any trick of perception did not in and of itself indicate a person was ill. Or special.

When I was a kid, I didn't know anything about optic nerve heads. What I knew was that my mother could make the moon disappear. She taught me to do it that last summer before she left, as she had taught it to my sisters during summers before: Fix my eyes on the moon; cover my left eye with my hand while I shifted my right eye slowly up and toward the left. The moon became a halo as though at full eclipse and then vanished, snuffed out of existence. It took some practice to hold my sight still and let the moon be gone, to move my eyes at all brought everything back. I couldn't help myself; my mind went after what it knew should be there.

I knew there was something to be seen in Kendrick's papers, and I had staked myself to the house for three days waiting for word from Andrea, willing her to send them to me. When she had not called by the morning of Christmas Eve, I resigned myself to the likelihood that the call would not be coming any time soon. So, of course, I was at the mall, fighting my way through last-minute shoppers, when Andrea and Kim stopped by the house.

They had not stayed long, Greg said. Long enough for Christmas cookies—the homegrown zucchini of winter—to be exchanged. Before they left, Andrea had tucked a manila evidence envelope under the tree. The envelope had been decorated with a stick-on bow of green ribbon and big block letters of silver glitter: HO! HO! HO! Greg pointed it out to me without saying anything, his face skewed into an expression between reprimand and worry. I didn't offer him any reassurance, just took the envelope and, hugging it to my chest, trying not to run, went upstairs to the sewing room, where I had stashed the boxes of supplies and files from my old office in the city.

I was a cop no longer, but like the zealots for whom proving that the moon landing was faked is a more impressive feat than actually having landed on the moon, my mind was fixated on the notion that—in spite of hard evidence to the contrary—sanity was itself a function of human law. My viability as a public servant might be null, but still, upholding the law is the basic work of all good, sane citizens, right? This was the argument I'd used with Greg when explaining why I was setting up shop as a private investigator. The powerful shall defend the helpless. Who was more helpless than the lost? What could be more insane than hurting a kid? I'd used that argument with the bubble-gum-snapping clerk who'd processed my license. I would be doing good, sane work, I'd told my landlords when signing the lease for my office at the Reeves building; I would be putting families back together. None of us had believed a word of it.

Breaking my lease at the Reeves had been as much my landlords' idea as my own, disheartened as they were by the disquieting behavior of my often-distraught clients. People tend to look for their missing children with an escalating urgency of dread. My practice with bad news was to tell my clients the truth quick and let them grieve. The tax accountants and interior designers who shared the floor were not unsympathetic to the occasional wailing cries, but the intrusive necessities of human emotion could curdle a business transaction in seconds.

Diplomatic complaints were registered and diplomatically ignored until the mother of a long-lost baby showed up in the lobby with a gun. I paid for the damage and the cleaning; Reeves management suggested that should I wish to move, they would happily let me leave.

I shoved aside boxes to get to the window and raise the shade. Cold winter sun knifed through the shadows; pricking sparks off the dust. When we moved me back here, I had packed my professional life into this little-used room, finding floor space between and on top of the broken television and nonworking treadmill, the roll-away bed and shorted-out lamps. I'd shut the door on it and had not been back since. Now, in the sparkled sunlight, I found myself running my hands over the smooth paper skins of those boxes and files as though they were old lovers. Memory sleeping. I was wary of waking what lay inside, anxious that it might never wake again.

I leaned against the windowsill and carefully opened the seal on the envelope. The sheaf of pages inside was not thick; I guessed—hefting the package—around twenty, twenty-five sheets. The sun played over the foil of the ribbon, the glitter. I took Andrea's big, bad Santa laugh as ironic. It would be her way of admonishing me: Proceed with caution; this will not be fun. I was hesitating to be sure, but not because of what I might find in the envelope as much as what I might find in myself. To consciously begin this was to admit that I had reached the end of something else. I waited for wisdom, the swirl of dust-sparks slowing and settling down about me. Wisdom wasn't coming. I exhaled hard and took the pages from the envelope.

Andrea had clipped everything together with a note typed on half a sheet of yellow legal paper: MERRY, MERRY. YOU HAVE NO

IDEA HOW THESE GOT TO YOU, RIGHT? I pulled the note free and reached instinctively for the shredder before remembering where I was and that the shredder was packed away in the closet. It would take but a minute to set it up; I should get myself organized. Unpack and make a proper space for work, but then my eye caught the first lines on the photocopied page beneath Andrea's note:

Dearest,
I write to you from the edge of eternity.

Frail, looping letters, but the meaning and intent were distinct enough. I was vaguely aware of setting Andrea's note aside as I continued to read.

The boy is here now. Light still in the sky, and yet he is here. He knows. He knocks. More are coming. He incites them. The bell rings and the doors rattle mightily with their demand that I acknowledge him. How little it would take to make this child happy. How great his fury that he is still denied.

I will deny you nothing now. In the pages below, I have set out finally what you have so long wanted, the whole of the events as I can best recollect. I count on your good judgment to guide the future with these words as justice might demand. And I do most fondly hope that in sending this forth into the world that you find peace. I expect none for myself. I must go to the door now. I anticipate a long night with no morning. Faithfully yours in deepest remorse,
J.

An old man's farewell; talk of ghost children; implications of old crimes and madness addressed to an unnamed correspondent—and that was only page one. I understood now why Andrea had cautioned me; I also understood why she had wrapped the thing as a gift. Never underestimate the value in a stocking full of coal; it could keep a bad girl warm all winter. I flipped through the rest of the pages, pretending I had a decision yet to make. On the bottom of the last page was a Post-it note from Andrea: WELCOME BACK, BABY!

Years after Mom took off, my sisters and I would still have contests to see who could keep the sky moonless longest. They always beat me by minutes. I didn't understand how that came so easily to them; trying not to see was like trying not to breathe. It did not occur to me until a much later age that my sisters might be lying about their records. What they were claiming was impossible. The sky moves continuously. The moon moves itself out of the blind spot. The world insists on being seen.

Merry, merry, indeed.

molly

Molly angles the mirror of the medicine cabinet to reflect back the full-length one on the door and stands between them so that she can check the part between her braids. Perfect, finally. The pale line of scalp bisects her dark hair, centered, straight down the back of her head. She tightens the elastics on the end of each braid and leaves the bathroom only to find Emma blocking the stairs. She's got a bowl of popcorn balanced on her knees and is eating it in that way that makes Molly want to scream: piece by piece, nibbling off tiny bits of the white fluff and then returning the wet, shorn kernel back to the bowl.

"Move, Em."

"Go around. I'm waiting for Mom."

"Where is she?"

Emma rocks her head back, using the almost stripped piece of popcorn between her teeth to point toward the closed sewing room door.

"Still?"

Emma nods and spits the kernel back in the bowl. "I'm supposed to help with dinner." She slides over toward the banister to let Molly pass. "Go around."

Molly sits down next to her sister. "Want me to wait with you?"

"I don't care."

"She'll be done soon."

"Maybe she's wrapping presents."

"She'll be done soon, Em."

shred

The physical fact of how words fill a page is full of meanings beyond those held in the words themselves. Penmanship, precision and width of margin spacing, level of line will convey emotional information in a grocery list, let alone a suicide note. On my first pass through Kendrick's pages it was the rendering of form that I studied if only because the variance between pages demanded it. Kendrick would be all over the place on one with illegible annotations and doodled ghouls only to haul it together within a clean, straight line on the next. Nothing was dated. The change up and down in control at first glance indicated work completed over different sessions spanning who-could-say-how-much time. The divergence between thickness of stroke and slant of letters in a single sentence lent the appearance of years passing between dependent clauses. But that seemed unlikely. Instinct, informed by experience of my own writing under different stresses, told me Kendrick probably had been dealing with some form of psychosis. The changes might have occurred spontaneously over one sitting as his mind shifted through its fractured facets. If that were the case, the meaning in his words would have to be filtered through personal references to which I had no more access than the clues presented in the words themselves.

*. . . each person who enters our lives possesses in secret
an aspect so foreign and troubling it remains outside the*

bounds of imagination. If fate is kind we will sense the shape of it before we love, and should we love too soon, fate will provide that we never have cause to sense that aspect ever. Fate was not kind to you, and so you came to see what you could not have imagined . . .

After the topographical read of surface features came the more careful sounding of depths and density in the texture of the language. To pace the reading, to give Kendrick's words time to settle and sink, I went about the long overdue unpacking of my office. I'd read a paragraph aloud, then open a box as I concentrated, repeating in refrain, those of Kendrick's phrases that seemed to signify pattern. It would not occur to me until much later that exhuming my old life as I dug through James Kendrick's was significant patterning in itself.

. . . memory undoes itself even as it knits together. I have undone myself, you see. Having once created fiction, I can no longer authenticate any image in my mind . . .

I tore the tape from a box marked STUFF and found cellophane-wrapped packages of notepads, boxes of ink pens and highlighters, the stapler, tubs of paper clips, tubes of Wite-Out, blank computer discs. I freed one of the notepads and opened up the pens. Ran a band of yellow highlight over Kendrick's phrase; rewrote it for myself: *Having once created fiction????*

. . . the weather mills on, grindstone cruel. Too cold for snow, the wind pierces this frail armor. Death attends me.

I used an old pillowcase to wipe the dust off my computer. Cleared space on the desk; set the machine up; plugged it in. It whirred and beeped itself into electric alertness, while I highlighted and copied. *Death attends me.* These first pages had been composed recently. The writing bore the same deliberate formality of the note he'd written before his death; the description of the weather was accurate to that time as well. It sounded as though he had reached his decision prior to beginning this. A confession was coming. But confession of what? *Death attends me?* If he had added the qualifying *now*, I'd have felt better about where this path might lead. *Death attends me.* When? Occasionally? Always?

    . . . so you and I go alone into this night with an untrustworthy tale of Memory's making . . .

I stood in the middle of the room, coax cable in hand, looking for the hookup. Didn't have one in here. For a second, I entertained asking Greg to help me set up a jack, knowing he'd do it but with the grimacing optimism of scheduling a root canal during a world-wide Novocain shortage. The prospect of his expression at the mere request was enough to convince me I could live with dial-up for a while. I switched out the modem hookups. *Untrustworthy tale. Memory's making.* Kendrick was explaining what he was about to explain. A spiral thinker, like myself. I took up the pen and drew a coiled line in the margin of the notepad. Was this down with the rabbit hole or up with the cyclone? Same difference. I was being led away from this world into a reality distilled down to a particular intent.

    Let us begin in fact, then . . .

27

The modem went through its alien whale song. Connection made, I called up the search program. I typed in "James Kendrick," hit Enter. Rather than wait for the data to churn through on the landline, I went to the closet to disinter the shredder and dig my file cabinets from beneath the piles of summer clothes we'd dumped on top of them.

Appropriate to our grieving, the summer had been wet, the days draped in mourning swags of fog.

Inside the file cabinets I had stored the pictures of my former clients, their losses, their happy children, as they had once been, some children lost forever, some children lost only to themselves, each photo slipped into its own glassine envelope, the hazy paper like a pane of quartz, trapping them as though captives to a fairy tale. Once upon a time: *Let us begin in fact.* I began the slow task of resurrecting them, taking each photo from its translucent case and pinning it onto the bulletin board I'd hung over the desk, fanning the photographs in an arc, making again my hallucinatory peacock's tail, those iridescent and unforgiving eyes.

The connection here was obvious: The bird stood in as guilt for my failures, sorrow for the failures of the world. Even when I found the kids, even when reunions were realized, I couldn't make the mending seamless. Lessons learned in fear could not be unlearned. The restoration of innocence I wanted from my work was impossible to achieve, which made me work for it all the harder. But why had Kendrick's death manifested in such a vivid picturing of my psyche? Had the trigger been Kendrick himself or the location where his body had been found?

Happy Andy's petting zoo and Christmas tree farm had been a standard outing for my family when my sisters and I were kids— whether or not we wanted to go. Countless times, my sisters and I had been carted out to that miserable Willet playground during our summer vacations. Back then it had been the only official amusement available. Asshole Andy's, we called it among ourselves. Nothing like ninety-degree July heat and humidity spent with stinky, pellet-addicted livestock. Amid the pens of goats, emus, sheep, miniature ponies, et cetera, the owner had allowed motley gangs of birds to wander at will and shake down kids for handfuls of feed. The geese and roosters could be mean. The peacocks with their threadbare tails dragging in the dust, their reptilian toenails, their shrieking lunges at the back of a kid's exposed knees or relaxed elbows—the peacocks had been just freaking evil.

Funny, I had not thought about those peacocks in years. I glanced at the computer monitor. The Kendrick search had produced several thousand hits. In an effort to refine them down to more a manageable number, I added "Willet" to the search phrase, hoping the broadest intersection of coincidence in our lives would produce a cross-reference more exacting than my sympathy for the old man's death. The animated hourglass let me know the cyberwizard was processing my request. I went back to reading.

. . . before making my escape from the suffocating confines of the house and Mother's insistence on quiet. Father was already at breakfast. Starched white collar pinched his neck; black vest buttoned; watch fob gleaming. He grinned at me and said, "Today, my boy, we tackle the stables."

Theories of parenting changed; the needs of children did not. James had been, I sensed, a lonely child at the best of times.

Father felt it a requirement of manhood that he spend some time away from his duties of moving large amounts of money and devote himself to those efforts "God intended for the sons of Adam, labor that put shit beneath their nails and sweat upon their brows." Mother felt it a requirement to escape the suffocating closeness of the city heat. The staff would come down the first week of July to open the house and make arrangements to lease the horses and livestock for Father to tend and butcher. He also enjoyed hunting with some of the local men, bringing in quail and rabbit. Father had not the patience for fishing and so paid the more accomplished anglers in our area to pick from their catches. Since the end of last winter, he had not much patience for me, either.

The suffocating closeness of the city. This had been their summer place, "camp," as they so quaintly put it in these parts. That word—*escape*—troubled me. *Suffocating* troubled me even more. *Appropriate to our grieving.* What had happened at *the end of last winter*? The repetition of that phrase lent an aura of dread to the page, the wavering sensation of heat before combustion.

Where I was concerned, he had a newfound dedication to teaching me the responsibilities of my sex: strength, purpose, and the enduring virtue of hard work. My days became my own only upon completion of whatever chores he had designed to further my education. I understood that when he said "we tackle the stables," he meant I would be the one doing the shoveling, the sweeping, and the breathing in of flies. He would be tackling the inaction of my wasted rainy days of repose, saving me from sloth, himself from accusations of inattentive stewardship. Laziness of execution or complaint would be answered calmly, his belt on my bared flesh. "Pain makes a man think," he would say, striking in rhythm with the meter of his words, "Thought makes a man wise."

I wanted to set the page aside. Kendrick had told me enough. It was necessary to go on though; it would be wrong to leave this child alone in his suffering. If he were brave enough to tell it, I had to be brave enough to be told.

In wisdom thus acquired, I said, "Yes, sir," and sat down. We ate together without speaking. Never a loquacious sort, my father was uncomfortable with idle conversation. Since the end of last winter, that silence had deepened, was deepening, rushing downward in a manner that made the space around him breathless—

From downstairs, Greg was calling me to dinner. I had not noticed the hour or the dimming of daylight. It was night and I was reading by lamplight, although I had not been actively aware of unpacking desk lamps or plugging them in. Had Greg tried to interrupt me earlier? Molly and Emma? I'd given over hours to this already. And it was Christmas Eve. *Put the papers down,* I told myself. Put them down and go to your kids, your husband. I could not. I could not leave James alone with his hurt in the decades-removed clutter of my mother's old sewing room. Greg and the girls would have to wait for a minute more; they'd have to understand. This boy was trying to tell me something.

I gulped down my meal in silence, and left Father, his grin still fixed upon his face. He thought himself a cheerful man. I did not wish for him to think me a dawdler.

Dawdle I did, however. I tramped on out toward the stables, planning to take the most indirect route I could devise: round the front of the house, out past the pond, along the creek bank, under the paddock fence. The day was as thick with heat and steam as the kitchen when Cook did her canning. Along the way, the ground was puddled and muddied. The rain-glazed trees sparkled, but the leaves hung tired, already sagging toward autumn and another winter. The grasses lay flat. Mother's pots of geraniums, pansies, and impatiens, which she insisted on in lieu of a proper garden, looked battered, fearful, as though they blossomed for fear of what might occur should they refuse.

I ran my fingers along his words. *Battered, fearful.* "I bet you were, sweetheart. I bet you were," I said to the page. He had a way with a sentence, this one. Way too artful. Not false, but practiced, forced. The words seemed encrypted. One set of information embedded in another. Maybe this was an affect of his inner dissonance, his illness. I added another question mark and a triple underscore to the *Having once created fiction* line in my notes. Then I typed "fiction" after "Willet" in the search engine. Hit Enter. The hits were down to less than one hundred. Greg shouted my name again; I heard his footsteps on the stairs. "I'm coming," I shouted back at the closed door. "Just a minute."

I reached the pond and ducked under the heavy rustling skirts of the old willow tree that reigned over the border between the yard and the pasture. I hoped for some shade, but the heat was denser, smelling green and vaguely corrupt. A tickling sensation traipsed across the back of my neck. Startled, I leapt away, turned back to find myself eye-to-eye with the bottom arc of a peacock's—

I backed up to make certain I'd read it correctly.

. . . peacock's tail. The bird was perched on the branch above me, mumbling in throaty garbles, unheeding of my presence. Mother had purchased the pea chickens from a local breeder several summers earlier. Her stated intent was that they might add a touch of elegance to the rustic appointments of the farm. But they'd proved more a nuisance to her than pleasure and she found their childlike screams [I highlighted, underscored] *in the night beyond her endurance. She requested of Father that he make a hunting expedition of them, but one of the local women informed her that the peacock is a great killer of snakes. Astounded by the usefulness of such a gaudy creature, stricken by the prospect of slithery fanged silence, Mother decided that the fowl should be chased away from the house and then ignored as best as possible. So ignored, they bred at will and hid in the trees and screeched horror*

when approached, charging, threatening to peck one to death . . .

I sank into the desk chair. The way it worked, the way it had always worked, was the hallucinations drew from my existing data bank of symbol and sense. I wasn't clairvoyant; I was merely screwed up. I could not *see* anything of which I had no previous knowledge or emotional investment. My illness was driven by the sublimely convoluted self-interest of my subconscious; it projected onto my blind spot what was relevant to its needs, to its questions and fancies. I saw things for the benefit of that part of me that had no sense of its existence beyond the appetite to know everything and save everyone and hence find peace. My doctors' strategies, my family's fears, my own desperate need for stability, nothing had been able to convince my illness that peace lay in the exact opposite direction, in accepting the unknowable and surrendering responsibility for lives other than my own. It was not a weakness, we had all lectured, to admit that reality is bigger than I am and to work on saving myself. In rebuttal, my underworld defense would summon droves of the lost as if to say "damn straight it's bigger." The hallucinations were my mirror-shield against logic's Medusa stare; if the child who was lost was lost inside my head, the illness argued, then saving him, her, them, is the same as saving me. So many get lost. The madness saw sanity as accepting failure; it wasn't about to budge. Reality is bigger than all of us.

Reality would hold that the shimmering-feathered image to which both Kendrick and I were attending had to be coincidence. The sole viable logic was that the peacock apparition I had encountered out in the snow was one from my past, and part of the reason why I was fixating on James. The trigger for the hallucination had to be Happy Andy's. Kendrick had taken shelter there until his strength and resolve gave out. Yes, they'd kept some ragged, ornery peafowl about the place, but the place was long deserted, the animals long dead or relocated. The birds were nothing to hang a theory on, and yet—there was the peacock's fan of children's faces on the bulletin board above me. I did not understand what I was seeing and that lack of shape in the invisible twisted my nerves upward toward frantic. When my subconscious perceived itself thwarted in attempts to get through to the upper levels of my mind, it raised the amperage on the communiqué. The peacock had been surprising but not threatening. The threats were gathering. I could sense them as a dull ache behind my eyes. Greg called again, angry. I angered back: "Go ahead without me."

    . . . *the bird's pitchy scream of "help-me, help-me" rose through the willow, and I continued on my path to the stables, my thoughts now on the ordeal ahead. The heat. The stink. The buzz and awful bite of horseflies. The blisters from hefting the pitchfork that would soon welt my palms. Father's promised judgment. How much did I loathe the very idea of what awaited me? I reached the paddock fence; the quartet of horses that were ours for the month ambled toward me expecting apples or oats. I thought suddenly of the painting in Father's study back in the city. In my mind, it was not an image rendered in static or silent oils. I could see the stallion, huge and dark, its eye burning with terror as it was brought down in the wild by a mighty striped tiger. The detail was lucid and*

35

precise; dimensional: the shrieking fear of the horse, the roars of the cat as its claw and teeth brought forth blood. Excitement surged in advent of an inspiration. I turned from the paddock and ran, ran with all my might, away from the farm.

Make no mistake; I understood that the abandonment of my chores at the stables would be seen as defiance akin to satanic treason. Every foot of distance I put between my father's order and myself was adding lashes to my punishment. I was escaping nothing but hope of mercy.

I thought of Kendrick's conviction in the visitor, the boy knocking at his door. We really had only two options of dealing with the unknown when it came knocking in the middle of the night. We could assume its intentions malicious and make haste to check the locks, reinforce the barricades, load the guns. Stay safe but stay afraid. Or we could throw the door wide and invite the unknown in, risking destruction for the chance of understanding more and thereby fearing less. Either way we learned something. I typed "peacock" behind "fiction" in the search engine. Hit Enter. Opened the door. And got nothing for the exercise except an error message indicating that no documents anywhere on the entire Web contained the elements of James Kendrick and Willet and fiction and peacock together. That meant nothing more than I'd tried the wrong entry. There must be other doors; I could still hear this thing pounding in an attempt to get in. I went with the common denominators of certainty between us: Willet and Happy Andy's and peacock. I admit to hesitation here, for the most part because I was pretty sure I was right. I hit the Search button. One result. It was a real estate agent's site listing of a commercially zoned property. I clicked on the link. The photos would take eons to download, but the text came up quick enough. Happy Andy's Petting Zoo and Christmas Tree Farm was for sale, had been for a long time given the dates on the description. The list of acreage and structures didn't interest me—except perhaps the "peacock pen" item—and I had no idea what I wanted from the pictures, which were resolving into view with the speed of glaciers. I went back to reading the pages of James's confession.

I went the way I went. What other way could I have gone given where I was? But here, at this late hour, facing the very end of the tale, I find myself fighting the inevitability of story's backward-looking juggernaut into nothing. What once I thought my creation has it seemed turned about into the thing that created me. From here I proceed in my telling as I did from that meadow, enslaved to the notion that where I was must, by necessity, lead to an elsewhere—

Greg was now at the sewing room door, calling to me, demanding to know if I was okay; I ignored him; I was . . .

—lead to an away, a later, a more and eventually, eventually emergence of larger purpose.

. . . involved.

I had fallen into the gravity of story. Not God, but the force that pulls gods into being. Salvation and every justification we tell ourselves when we are not saved. The growing realization that I had—

"Goddamn it, Leslie! Open the door!" Greg rattled the knob. When had I locked it?

—lost myself was met by the odd effect of lightening my heart. The farther I wandered in confusion, the happier I became until it seemed clear that I was not running away but being drawn toward a great destination.

Greg jimmied the lock somehow. His expression was dazed with confused panic. He began to take in the room, the stack of flattened boxes, the file cabinets, the bulletin board of children, and he began to register comprehension and then anger. I felt ashamed, annoyed as though he'd walked in on me spending quality time with a vibrator. His voice went low, protecting our daughters who were no doubt hovering nearby. "What are you doing?"

I looked around the office and shrugged.

"You promised, Leslie. You weren't going to go back to this. You weren't going to bring this here. You promised."

"Yes, but . . ." I trailed off for wanting not to have to tell him more and hurt him further: The hallucinations are back; the hunger is back; you and the girls are not enough to stop it. I couldn't bear to keep my eyes on his, and so I looked away. He took the opportunity that provided, strode across the space between, and yanked the pages from my hand.

"Hey!" I jumped up and grabbed at the papers.

"This is what Andrea left for you, isn't it?" He jerked the

papers back farther out of my reach. "I asked her. I asked her point blank if this stuff was *safe*."

"What did she say?"

He inhaled, held it, got on top of it. His shoulders fell. "It's Christmas Eve, Leslie."

"I know," I said, my own anger deflating, and sat down. "I screwed up." I held out my hand, thinking my retreat would be met halfway. He did not offer the pages. I lowered my head a bit and risked a conciliatory smile. "Time gets away from me."

"Time and everything else," he said, accepting my admission with an indulgent smirk. "I worry." He didn't need to say it aloud; the gray in his hair and the fatigue in his face said it for him every day. I ached with regret for the drain I represented to his energies. He loved me, but he loved the *me* he hoped his love would somehow force into being. I would never ever be that woman, and even as I grieved that failing, I hated him for constantly reminding me that I had failed. At the same time, I wanted his forgiveness for having failed him again. And I wanted those papers back.

I hooked my finger in one of the belt loops on his jeans and pulled myself to standing, pulled him to me. Before he could question my intentions, I had my mouth on his mouth, my tongue forestalling his tongue, my free hand at the back of his neck holding him there. He worked his arm up between us, prying me away by a few inches, and forcing an end to the kiss. "This isn't going to work, Les," he said, laughing for the transparency of my tactics. But I knew him better than that. I pulled my finger along the level of his jaw line, down his throat, tapped my way along the buttons of his chambray shirt until I reached the one on his jeans, which I undid and slipped my hand inside. My smile went from conciliatory to evil. "Oh, I think this is working just fine."

His mouth gave in and up to a reluctant grin. He set the paper down on top of the computer monitor in a haphazard pile—pages sliding to the floor—and put his arms around me. "Emma and Molly are listening you know," he whispered in my ear.

"That's why God invented those things," I whispered back and pointed to the still-open door. I kissed him again, bit his bottom lip before slipping out of his embrace, trying not to hear the knock, knock, knock in the back of my head as I pulled down the window shade and then went to shut the door on our vigilant daughters. "Don't you think it's bizarre that we're okay with them hearing us fight but—" The thought was cut off by a whirring hum. I turned back to Greg. He had gathered up most of the pages and was holding them suspended above the shredder's rotating teeth.

"Don't."

"Leslie, I get that this is important to you. I really do. But you have to understand that you can't have it both ways. I can't live like that again. None of us can—and you know it."

"You want me to choose?"

He shook his head. "I wouldn't ask that."

"Then what are you asking?"

He shook his head again and switched off the shredder, said nothing more. What was love anyway but the word we use for the moments that the vast and unfathomable complexity of another person's life moves through our own?

I double-checked the latch on the door before pulling my sweater over my head. I took off my jeans, my underwear, my socks, until I was standing before him naked. I went to him then, took the pages from his hand, and said, "You haven't asked me for this," before hitting the switch on the shredder again and feeding the sheets in one by one. When the papers were gone, I pulled him out of his jeans, pushed him down in the desk chair, swiveled it around so that the back was braced against the desk edge; I was straddled on him, my hands locked around the top rail of the chair back, my legs locked over the arm rests, to stabilize myself as he thrust upward into me, his fingers death-gripped on my hips, his mouth on my breast; I kept my eyes on the computer monitor, the pictures changing, revealing, kept my eyes on the apparition of a naked old man wandering among the empty, rusting animal pens, his posture becoming more and more crouched until he was on all fours elongating, strengthening, metamorphosing into a creature of size and claws and teeth. "Oh," I said; I shook and rocked, trying not to make too much noise, my body locking onto my husband's and my mind locking onto comprehension and the part of me that belongs only to myself in a quiet chant of certainty: *He didn't get them all; he didn't get them all.*

quest

We clambered back into our clothes, giggling under our subsiding breath like a couple of horny kids who knew they were about to get caught by the terminally uncool prudes downstairs. Greg kissed me hard before leaving, shutting the door behind him to allow me privacy to finish getting myself back together. The second he was gone, I was collecting what few pages—only four, dammit—had escaped the shredder for having slid behind the monitor. Not wanting to risk another confrontation or worse, losing what little I had saved, I folded the pages as small as I could and shoved them in the pocket of my jeans. I ran my hands through my hair, practiced smiling with nonchalance, and turned off the monitor before hobbling my way to join my family.

Molly and Emma were installed at the fireplace, roasting marshmallows on wire hangers that Greg had straightened for them. They eyed me with shifting regard, curiosity and disdain, that told me they'd figured out enough. Children have a vested interest in their parents' intimacies: Fighting might affect their security through dissolution of the kingdom; sex might affect their supremacy through the arrival of competition for the crown. Molly's and Em's insecurities were compounded by the fact their mom's reign alternated between calling for heads and believing six impossible things before breakfast. It was hard to judge which was the less appealing, but I knew they were angry with me for sending tentacles of doubt slithering among the tinsel. In return for their stares, I bestowed one of my practiced smiles upon them. They gifted me with practiced smiles of their own. The marshmallow Molly was toasting caught flame. She withdrew it from the fire, blew it out, and offered the charred remains aloft, smile unfaltering. "Want one?"

"Sure." I pulled the blackened lump from the wire and popped the molten sticky sweet in my mouth, burning my tongue in the process. My smile was unfaltering, too.

After the girls were sleeping, Greg and I placed their presents beneath the tree and filled the stockings hung on the mantle. We shared a bottle of beer at midnight, wishing each other Merry Everything. I told him I had a few little surprises yet to look after, and he went up to bed alone. I sat at the foot of the stairs until I heard him snoring.

We had turned the thermostat down for the night; the house was getting cold. I went back to the front room where the fireplace was still radiating soft warmth. The Christmas tree was twinkling, throwing strobe shadows against the ceiling and walls. At the hearth, I took up the poker and tried to stir some life into the dimming embers in the grate before putting on another log. Then I wrapped myself in the old quilt we kept on the back of the sofa, settled on the hearth and, as the log began to crackle and catch, I pulled the pages I'd saved from my pocket. The plan was to finish reading and burn the evidence; a Christmas present Greg would never know he'd received. Besides, Andrea could get me another set of copies, I was sure. Nevertheless, I had to have more; that image my mind had thrown onto the monitor of man becoming tiger to prowl the grounds of a children's park was not to be set aside for a more convenient hour or the blessings of my family.

. . . had moved between me and thoughts of my father with such distracting beauty that I can state in full truth that as the hours and miles wore on I had forgotten that return is the inevitable outcome of every successful quest. Almost forgot. Every so often, the ache in my legs or the emptiness in my belly would whine for relief, for home. That whine would darken my heart and in rapid succession, my head would be gripped in the multi-limbed imaginings born of memory: Mother unmoving, her pale face an oval of stone mounted on a stiff black collar, her mouth pursed, eyes shining with tears she would never cry, silent; Father's brow growing red with exertion, dripping sweat as the belt descended, his voice rising and rising. Pain makes a man think.

And stop thinking. I would of a sudden be aware of needing a name for the precise blue of the sky, a name for the tiny yellow blossoms hidden in the grass. Back in the present where the unknown would once more arise, the veil of delight descended and reenergized my awareness that this world would continue to exist as long as I continued to journey into it. We are as happy as we make up our minds to be. Lincoln said that. The Great Emancipator. I made up my mind; and made up my mind; and made up my mind; and walked and walked, both on and away, until at last, I crested the breast of a ridge and saw before me in the distance, a mountain. My destination had found me and it was . . .

I slipped that page through the fire screen and watched it ignite. On returning to the reading, I was disappointed to discover the pages that had been spared Greg's ultimatum were not consecutive. Then again, given Kendrick's mid-sentence personality shifts, it might be hard to determine sequence of thought one way or the other.

. . . what we are. It is what we are able to see. It is what we want to see.

I think over these matters often, in full knowledge that they are sinful. How like a serpent's tooth, the ungrateful child. That was another of Father's favorites. Pain makes a man think about pain. About how to make it stop.

And so I stopped when I reached the mountain, which I now recognize is no more than the clumsy resting place of convenience for boulders and slabs of broken rock. Still, in the haze of defiance and exhaustion, my boyish knack for fantasy allowed for a certain looseness of definition; it looked like a mountain to me. I scrambled up the rocks for what I told myself was a view of the distance; I may confess now that having reached a destination of any sort, it seemed rather pressing that I locate the eventual point of my return.

My survey was sidetracked, however, by the sighting of a person, the first I'd seen since I'd started out. A boy was standing by the edge of a small pond at the base of the slope. He was dressed quite formally for the day and circumstance, a tweedy suit with knickers and stockings. Touring cap on his head. He was skipping stones on the surface of the pond. I found myself wondering how he should have come to be out here alone.

In honesty, I don't recall perceiving dread, but must believe, now, it was present. That may be the human need for order rearing its head to strike at the majesty of randomness, over which it stands no hope of besting. God will not be denied.

I started down the mountain. Ungrateful child who should have been heading for home. Prodigal son that might have been, I would now be the thorn in my father's thigh. Wound never healing, like that of the Fisher King. A serpent's tooth is no more than a thorn. Put two thorns together and you have a snake. Your snake.

I reread this page, several times, each successive pass leaving me further off balance. It still felt as though I were reading a foreign language I did not understand, but coincidental arrangements of letters had tricked my brain into recognition. I had not enough context to figure out if the perception of significance was accurate or imposed. Instead of sending this one into the fireplace, I set it aside, intending to go back to it, and moved on to the next.

. . . successfully skips a rock across water is a moment of simple, joyful triumph over the rules of the world. The stone does not sink; the water has an impenetrable skin. It is an illusion of power, Christ stepping out upon the sea, but not one that can be conjured without skill and the proper materials. The rock must be rounded and flat bottomed; the water must be reasonably still. Much practice must go into perfecting the split-second flick of the wrist that sets the proper spin. One can become obsessed in

the pursuit of distance and number of jumps. It wasn't until I grew older that the lesson became apparent: The only way to learn a skipper's potential is to lose it. The ones that work best jump farther away and sink deeper. Fortunately, the world is full of rocks and water.

I avoid. Yes, I avoid. Simply then: I scrambled my way down the escarpment, calling to the boy who was as intent on his skippers as I had ever been. His technique was dreadful, however. Throwing rock after rock with its edge perpendicular rather than parallel to the water, his arm cocked back over his shoulder as though playing at pitch. An entirely different game. The boy was either inadequately schooled in the art or a poor pupil. It occurred to me that I might offer some pointers and that might prove the basis for a friendship. These thoughts of how to make overtures to one who seemed determined not to notice me, plus the care needed to get myself off the boulders in one piece, had so tangled my attentions that I didn't notice you until I was almost at the edge of the pond. By then it was clear that the boy was not entertaining himself with defying nature but busy at the work of covering your body, rock after rock, piling up against your silt-dark skin, weighing you down beneath the water . . .

That was the end of what I had left. I crumpled the page tight before tossing it into the surging flames. The Christmas tree was blinking on and off, apparently random, but if watched for a while the pattern in the flashing emerged. I wondered if that's what the inside of my head was like, the on-and-offing of neurons, chaotic at that instant, on the precipice of an order that I would only see as shadows dancing along the solid surfaces of the world.

I did not know what to make of Kendrick's images. He stated outright that he was not to be trusted; he did not trust his own telling. *Having once created fiction.* Were these just shadows for him? Some metaphorical rendering of his internal agonies? I found myself hoping that was the case; I also found myself doubting that hope. The page I'd set aside troubled me more than any of the others I'd read that day—the grandiose philosophizing on God and the implications of a fracturing of his identity into two personas was a textbook response to the religion-justified abuse he had endured as a child. But. But. There was something else in the wording that provoked, annoyed really, with a sort of pebble-in-my-shoe effect. I studied Kendrick's phrasing again, growing more frustrated. Finally, I decided to put these thwarted energies toward something useful. No way would I be sleeping that night; might as well get started on the traditional gauntlet called Christmas dinner.

I took the page out to the kitchen where I turned on the lights as well as the oven to heat the place up a bit. Greg's grandmother had given me, as a wedding gift, her recipe for Vandoka, the Christmas bread that was shaped and braided to resemble the baby Jesus in his swaddling clothes. I couldn't quite bring myself to make edible infants, so I'd reworked the thing with elements of my grandmother's Christmas poppy seed cake. I called my version a *stollen* because it fit both the definition of this type of bread as well the hijacked source—this was my traditional bad joke that induced traditional cringes. The filling, over which the bread was braided, called for honey and lemon and almonds and a short ton of poppy seeds that had to be mashed together with a wooden mallet. I rooted around the cabinets for the ingredients. My mind kept being yanked back to Kendrick's words, turning them this way and that, believing I could make the sides line up in solution like a puzzle cube.

I scooped a handful of poppy seeds onto a sheet of wax paper, spread them flat with the back of a spoon, and covered them with more wax paper. I tamped them with a rolling pin, crushing as I went—I didn't have a wooden mallet. Kendrick's language set up a meter, and I fell into the rhythm of the work: *We see what we are; how like a serpent's tooth; I reached the mountain, which I now recognize; on the surface of the pond; all alone; I started down the mountain . . . which I now recognize . . .* I stopped, rolling pin halted in midair. ". . . the mountain, which I now recognize . . ." I set the rolling pin down gently on the wax paper and went to look at the Kendrick page, reading out loud, "I reached the mountain, which I now recognize is no more than the clumsy resting place of convenience for boulders and slabs of broken rock." *Now* recognize? *Is no more than?*

I left the kitchen and walked carefully, quietly back to the sewing room, trying to maintain an aura of control but for what audience I could not say. I shut the door but did not turn on the light. Navigating by the tiny green stars on the computer's CPU, I found the monitor button. The screen faded up into brightness. The Happy Andy's screen came into view. I scrolled down through the photographs, taken at various locations throughout the facility: the stables, the aviary, and then toward the bottom of the page, the one I wanted. A picture of the tree farm, with the hill sloping upward to the Castle. That was Happy Andy's name for the pileup of earth, of "boulders and slabs" of excavated granite and slate . . . *which I now recognize* . . . Kendrick had not been merely seeking shelter up in Willet; he had returned to the scene of some terrible event.

I shut the monitor off again and for a few minutes pretended to debate the options on a decision I'd already made. I did not leave a note; I planned to be back long before any of them would wake. I did, by accident, leave Kendrick's page on the kitchen counter with the poppy seeds and honey and almonds. Greg would find it later when he couldn't find me. He would read it with increasing concern and then see the Happy Andy's site on my computer. He would call Andrea, waking her and Kim. He'd let Andrea know exactly what he thought of her giving me access to this sort of material. Andrea would argue that I was a big girl and could take care of myself, but then, guiltily, she would volunteer to call up to Willet and have somebody run by the property to see if I was indeed up there. And call she did, sending a deputy out of his warm station house to trek up to Happy Andy's just as the sun was cresting the horizon, another frigid white star in the frigid white Christmas dawn. He would arrive in time to summon an ambulance and save my life.

ice

I would never be able to remember very much of the drive up to
Willet that night, and what I did recall may have been quilted
together from previous experience: the asphalt winter-worn,
frost-heaved, and potholed; ice; the old turnpike road cutting
through fields cloaked in snow. The moon was a few days from
gone, a cold fingernail crooked above the cold landscape. Willet
was nearly an hour from our house; I would have been thinking
about getting there and back before dawn and so would have
driven faster than I should have. The farms and few roadside
homes I passed would have been dark within but lit up on the
outside with multicolored bulbs and wreaths and plastic figures
of the season.

I would not recall reaching Willet itself or driving through
town. The first distinct memory was that of reaching the turn
and the sad-edged tug of nostalgia that I felt at finding the sign,
faded and listing, still there: HAPPY ANDY'S PETTING ZOO AND
CHRISTMAS TREE FARM. I did remember making the turn. After
that and up until the very end, events are clear, vivid, as though
recorded on film. I remember thinking that not much had
changed since I'd last been down this narrowing road a decade
earlier, pregnant with Emma, morning sick, and cranky, when
Greg had indulged me by bundling up three-year-old Molly in a
snowsuit and mittens while I packed a lunch, hot chocolate, and
a saw. It was the first Christmas after my father died, and I had

insisted we drive all the way from the city to Happy Andy's to choose our own Christmas tree—the way my father had hauled my sisters and me out there each December. We arrived to find the place had gone out of business, apparently years earlier. The trees that remained were shaggy with age or stunted, weak and rusted from acid rain. Rusted, too, were the cages and pens. My father had doled out a fortune in nickels for us to plug into the feed machines that had long since been knocked down, battered by vandals. Greg, to his lasting credit, had simply said, "Sorry, Les," turned the car around, and taken us home.

I pulled alongside the field that Happy Andy's had always kept clear for parking. It went unplowed now, but the snow at the edges was packed flat where tree seekers and cross-country skiers—not to mention the emergency personnel that the Kendrick situation would have required—had tramped paths. I buttoned up my coat, got out of the car, and took the big lantern from the trunk. The beam was wide and bright. I swept it about, getting my bearings before heading toward the entrance to the petting zoo itself. The admission booth was still there, but its roof had collapsed. Remnants of yellow crime-scene tape fluttered from the post that had once supported the entry gate. The animal pens and cages beyond were sagging in disrepair. Although, oddly, the doors on each of the enclosures were flung wide, as though someone had rushed about recently setting the animals free.

The flashlight beam stretched and depressed shadows of chain-link fence and posts onto the snow. I thought of the peacock in my yard; that image drained down my neck and into my chest with a palpable sense of forces coalescing. It was the aura of arrival, an accelerating certainty that I was looking directly at something I couldn't see. My subconscious, frustrated by my peering ineptness, was willing embodiment into view. I clenched my nails against my palms. *Remember why you are here.* Still alert for movement on the periphery of my senses, I continued toward the little house at the rear of the yard. I wanted to see where Kendrick had made his decision to die.

It was a two-story cottage, a Mother Goose sort of affair, with an asymmetrical ski-jump roof. As a child, I had imagined this as Happy Andy's own home, before I'd learned that Happy Andy was but an invention of the no-nonsense spinster who had owned the place. The storybook quality of the house was a decidedly pragmatic marketing façade. The structure sat stolid and heavy, fieldstone foundation and rough wood clapboard traced over with the skeletal threads of dormant vines.

The front door was unsheltered, though the discoloration and splintering of a few clapboards suggested that a porchlike roof had been recently removed, perhaps brought down by the weight of snow. A wind-up key was set into the broad board of the door frame. I knew it was one of those old spring-action, wind-and-release doorbells, but it gave the appearance that the house was a mechanical toy. A corroded brass knocker, a ring in a lion's mouth, was affixed to the top of the door and a Realtor's key box was padlocked to the knob. Despite these implied requirements of invitation before entry, the wood of the door-jamb had been ripped apart, broken into. Something had gotten in. I pushed at the door lightly. It opened without resistance. I stepped one foot over the threshold and ran the light across the interior. The place was run-down but in decent shape. Small rooms, plank floors, staircase intact.

The gathering wind whistled softly around the windowpanes

and buffeted the shutters so that they bumped against their latches. Kendrick's knocking children? I hesitated before venturing farther into the house; the sense of apparition in approach was getting stronger. I did not believe in the supernatural or the any-other-natural outside the one we have; if an event was experienced by human senses, it was as natural and as explicable as any other experience of being. Ghosts—those pictures for which I did not yet have words—did not frighten me; what those ghosts might eventually reveal about the truth of living in this world scared me witless. As well it should. After you've been here, in this place, consciously alive, alone in the universe and knowing it, how could the release of death possibly scare you? Perhaps that is the real terror behind ghosts, the implication that there is no release.

I went inside. The woodstove, potbellied cast iron, hulked in the corner of the front room. The flashlight showed the sticks of kindling and wads of newspaper readied for the match that Kendrick would never strike. I went over to the stove, laid my hand against the cold metal. The newspaper he'd used as tinder might provide a date as to his resolve. It was not important in any evidentiary sense, but I wanted to know how long he'd been in the house, stood here before the stove, a match in hand. I shifted the sticks aside and pulled out the newsprint. The pages, from one of the local freebies, were dated December 10, of this year, two days before he'd been found. He'd reached his decision quickly then. Probably loaded the stove, seen his ending, and sat down to finish whatever writing he could. I took up the papers to return them to the stove, when the flashlight caught, half-buried in the ash of the firebox, the rounded edge of a photograph.

I took the photograph by its edges, wiggled it free from its bed of ash, and blew the fine gray dust off the surface. It had been undamaged by fire. The photograph was quite old and the oval shape was imperfect. It looked to have been cut from a larger picture. The image was grainy, indefinite, but I recognized the subject as the boy Kendrick had described in his writing. He was about ten, in knickers, jacket and cap, all of a matching tweed-type material. The boy filled the better part of the oval, but it was clear he was being held by the shoulders from behind by an adult male in a dark suit; only a portion of the man's torso and his hands clamped on the child's shoulders were visible. The boy had the brim of the cap pulled low over his eyes, his head slightly lowered so that his features were obscured except for the line of his jaw. A faint shadowy defect marked the upper-left curve of the oval as though the picture taker's finger had darted in front of the lens or a mistake had happened during development. Perhaps that was what had been trimmed out. I turned the photograph over and saw that it held part of an inscription. The lower letters were indecipherable and faded, but one section was legible, written more recently in a different hand: WILLET 1913.

This was Kendrick as a boy—it had to be—apparently Kendrick had planned to burn it. The metaphorical suicide to proceed the actual? The ashes I had disturbed in pulling the photo from the stove had been picked up by an invading wind; they swirled about in the light, trying to resettle on the photograph, sucked in by the static. Frustrated, I turned my back on the stove, to find myself being glared down upon by the glittering dark eyes of a giant peacock. I stepped back before realizing that this one was really there, drawn in shimmering color on the wall opposite the stove. This would have to be the graffiti mentioned in the newspaper account. Kendrick's work?

The bird's tail, painstaking in detail, dense and vibrant—oil pastel?—arced the entire width of the wall. The bird's beak was lowered; it was looking down. I shone the light to follow its gaze. Beneath the drawing of the bird, Kendrick had written in the now familiar uneven hand:

I SAW A PEACOCK, WITH A FIERY TAIL,

I SAW A BLAZING COMET, DROP DOWN HAIL,

I SAW A CLOUD, WITH IVY CIRCLED ROUND,

I SAW A STURDY OAK, CREEP ON THE GROUND,

I SAW A PISMIRE, SWALLOW UP A WHALE,

I SAW A RAGING SEA, BRIM FULL OF ALE,

I SAW A VENICE GLASS, SIXTEEN FOOT DEEP,

I SAW A WELL, FULL OF MEN'S TEARS THAT WEEP,

I SAW THEIR EYES, ALL IN A FLAME OF FIRE,

I SAW A HOUSE, AS BIG AS THE MOON AND HIGHER,

I SAW THE SUN, EVEN IN THE MIDST OF NIGHT,

I SAW THE MAN, THAT SAW THIS WONDROUS SIGHT.

I ran the beam of light over the lines again. I knew this. I had not seen those words in decades, but I had learned the rhyme as a child. How? My sisters? My mom? Didn't matter, but it had been part of my memory long before its formal introduction as poetry by my sixth-grade English teacher. Giselle Mordon was her name. She wore bangle bracelets, peasant blouses. Her long, frizzy hair always smelled ever so faintly of pot. She had written the words on the board, using the lines to show us how meaning rises and disappears depending on how you choose to see the words. The poem had a trick to it; even though it was written vertically, it worked like a combination lock. The descriptive clauses could be moved against the nouns, changing the images into twelve possible arrangements. The poem told you to do this, gave you permission to do this, because (chalk scraping the blackboard, bangles clanging) if you dropped each description down a single line, you'd get the version that unlocked sense. *I saw a blazing comet, with a fiery tail*; that made the *cloud, drop down hail*, and so on, until *I saw the man, even in the midst of night* forced the final description to circle back up to the top.

The question (sandals slapping her heels, skirt swishing at her ankles): Which was the better poem, the sense or nonsense? For homework, we'd had to write down the arrangement of lines we thought the better poetry and explain why. I was the only one in the class to choose the logical version; I liked it because only that arrangement made the endless rotation of the words stop. Miss Mordon had handed back my paper, remarking that she was a bit disappointed in my lack of imagination.

"I saw a peacock—" I read the sensible aloud from memory in order to get out of the memory "—that saw this wondrous sight." I felt dizzy, as though Kendrick's madness had taken up waltzing with mine. I wasn't sure which one of us was leading the other. Why this nursery rhyme, James? What sort of farewell did you intend here? Beneath his lettering of the poem, Kendrick had written, THE WILDERNESS. "Wilderness," I said, louder, taking a certain comfort from hearing my voice against the wind. It occurred to me I ought to make sure of my sight. I reached out to touch the drawing, make sure it was real. Before my fingers reached the wall, the air around me chimed brightly with a bell sound. The doorbell? I whipped the beam of the flashlight over to the entryway. "Hello?" After a few moments, I laughed at myself. The wind had found a way into the bells. Or it was mice. There had to be hundreds of mice in these walls. One of them must have hit the mechanism. I was here alone. The bell rang again. "Stop being an idiot," I ordered myself, and strode over to the door to prove to myself that an idiot was indeed what I was being.

He was standing beside what had been the llama pen, maybe thirty yards away, too distant to get distinct focus. I recognized him all the same, knickers and cap pulled low, lit from within, as though he'd walked off the screen of a black-and-white film, two-dimensional, flickering. The longer I stared, the more he seemed to draw from that, filling out in depth, stabilizing in solidity, until he was fully formed. He raised his hand and motioned me forward, then turned and headed off toward the raggedy little forest of overgrown Christmas trees where he disappeared, dissolving into the darkness. I knew where he was going.

I headed after him, up the rise toward the steep outcropping of the Castle. Up here, the trees had filled in densely, deformed and stunted in the slow-motion battle to sustain growth among the rocks. Those who had come up here to chop down what they wanted for the holidays had etched the snow with narrow trails. I followed those needle-studded paths, my flashlight casting needle shadows on the snow. From below, the tree line blocked any clear view of the top of the Castle, but beyond them the entire public part of the farm, as well as the surrounding fields, was readily visible.

The going was tricky. The wind was honing the predawn cold ever sharper. The rocks were slicked with ice and where shaggy evergreen limbs had blocked the snowfall, fallen pine needles blanketed the ground, disguising the security of each step under a spongy layer of rust-colored slivers. I pulled my way up, going slow, relying on the trees to steady me; I had no gloves and the roughness of the branches became harder to feel as numbness set in. It wasn't much further. The trees thinned quickly up against the massive sheets of slate pitched among wedges of granite in a violent upward thrust as though something beneath the earth had tried to escape here.

The wind wove and slid through the crevices in the rocks, providing the night with soft sighs and squealing whines. I was not going to try to get to the top. I wouldn't need to, the view here was sufficient—darkness all around except for the eastern horizon where a dull band of lavender pressed upward. I had to get back to Swifton. I walked out to the precipice my sisters and I had called Ralph's Nose in honor of our neighbor whose face had inspired that sort of awe. The Nose jutted out into a sudden drop of earth—sinkhole, meteor crater?—that served as the reservoir for runoff rain and melting snow. It was winter; what water had collected there froze straight through into the earth. Why would Kendrick, whatever the nature of his delusions, have come all this way to end his life? I imagined him trying to crawl up here in vicious cold, surrendering the effort, and laying himself down, his letter of confession replaying itself in his head.

Dearest . . .

He had come back to Willet to deliver the letter. He could not put it in the mail because the recipient was no longer living. Because . . . because the recipient was still here?

I shone the flashlight down into the darkness below me. A little girl in a white dress and boots, her skin dark as sleep, looked up at me and smiled. I could not see the whole of her, only what the beam of the flashlight hit. It danced off her eyes, her smile, the ribbon in her hair, tiny little braids; each tied with a different color like a peacock's tail. And then I knew, and upon knowing the image shut down, sinking into the murky ice at the bottom of the pit.

My memory became murky here, too. I would not remember climbing down there or when I picked up the rock I used. I remembered striking at the ice, over and over, calling to her, telling her that I was coming. *Hold on. Please. Hold on.* I was yelling, shouting so that she might hear me way down there in the frozen earth. It was my shouting that the deputy from Willet heard from the yard. That's how he knew where to look for me.

That's how I came to be in the psych ward at Swifton Memorial on Christmas afternoon, my frostbitten, rock-torn hands bandaged. Andrea, exhausted and sad, her electric red curls squashed beneath a knit cap, showed up to tell me that although the frozen earth had made the digging difficult, about fourteen feet down they found the top of a pile of rocks, and beneath that, wedged into a protective crook in the broken slate, they had found the skeletal remains of a child. The coroner's first assessment: prepubescent, female, of African descent.

"That's her," I said, the medications they'd given me slurred the words into a single syllable. I showed Andrea my hands. "Didn't get there in time. What's her name?"

"We don't know that yet." Andrea smiled. "It will take a while. How did you know she was there, Leslie?"

I shrugged. Only had the truth. "I saw her."

the peacock and the comet

gift

The child's remains forced a redefinition of my placement in the apothecary cabinet of the medical establishment. For a few hours they were uncertain of exactly which box to stick me in. The staff had contacted Frank Edelstein, my shrink from back in the Big Breakdown days. After his consultation it was decided that I had suffered a posttraumatic episode of limited duration; the crisis had passed and I was stable, if a bit bruised and emotional.

They took me off the sedatives, which cleared my mind enough to fully perceive the sorrow and hurt I once more dragged in the wake behind me. I would have wept, but did not want the added shame of appearing to need comfort when others were far more damaged. Greg, who had been briefed by the doctors, seawalled his disgust and fear and frustration behind a front of tired detachment. He spoke gently, without smiling, coming to visit several times but never staying more than a few minutes. He delivered my Christmas gifts at Molly's and Em's request.

"Tell them I want to wait until I get home," I had said when I brought in the first round of wrapped presents. "I want us to do Christmas together."

"I told them you'd say that. They insisted."

I took one of the boxes between my gauze-swaddled palms. It was from Emma. The paper was a print of blue and purple ornaments on gold, held in place by yards of tape and a purple bow tied in shoestring fashion. The scent of lavender around the box was strong.

Greg sat down at the foot of the bed. "They're kids, Les. You can't expect them to understand."

"They understand plenty. I've let them down. Again. On Christmas."

"They also understand you went out to help a person you thought might be in trouble and you're feeling very sad because you could not help."

"Someone's been talking to Frank."

"Someone needed advice on how much to tell Molly and Em."

"And he advised you so well that they don't want to see me?"

"It's not you. It's the hospital."

More Doctor E., that. "So, did you ask his advice for what should be done *after* the hospital?"

"Yeah." He looked at his own palms, nodding to himself. "Sure you want to do this now?"

"Better now while we have access to the really good pain-killers."

He exhaled. "We're already getting calls from media types."

"Refer them up to the police department in Willet."

"I did and then I went one further. I unplugged the phone."

"Smart man. Look, we know how this works. We ignore them until they get bored and take their pointy sticks off to poke at fresher wounds."

He nodded again but said, "I don't want to work it any more, Leslie. You promised you wouldn't take on any of these cases for a while."

"I didn't take on a case. I didn't know *this* was going to happen. You think I go looking for this sort of thing?"

"Who called Andrea and asked for background on this James What's-His-Name? Why did you do that? Why did you put us at risk like that? Yourself? What—" He must have heard the growing urgency in his voice; he spread his hands as though slowing his thoughts. "Last night? I told you I would not ask you to choose. But you know eventually you are going to have to."

I crossed my arms over my middle and looked away from him. The strained muscles of my neck and back and shoulders protested that simple effort. "It's not as though I choose these events."

"No. You choose to feed the system."

"Sign me up for the elective lobotomy then, Greg, because merely being awake feeds the system."

"That's not what I meant."

"Or maybe it *is* what you meant. Maybe it's you who has some choosing to do."

He reached down the length of the bed and took Emma's present from me. He looked at the gift tag. "Already have."

"I can't switch off this thing in my head, you know that, don't you?"

"I know you wouldn't shut it down even if you could."

I glared at him. "Why would you say that?" My huffy, offended tone was too theatrical. He wasn't buying it; he knew me too well. He could list the ways in which I kept the madness running: refusing medication, canceling shrink appointments—

"I have a right to my work. Don't need your permission or approval to work."

"No, you don't." He pulled at the loops of the bow Emma had tied, tightening the knot. "I keep thinking about what you did up there, Les. I keep thinking about you trying to hack your way through that ice, how if you had told me what was happening, I could have gone with you, helped. But you don't think you need help, so now there are pictures in the paper, pictures of people you pulled away from their families on Christmas morning. Pictures on the television. The Willet cops, Andrea, the guys who run the hydrovac. They showed it on TV, the steam of the hot water blasting away the ice and the frozen soil made a cloud so thick no one could see. All that, their work, their inconvenience, ours, it seems like so much nothing compared to finding what they found because you need answers, you need to see . . . well, I keep thinking about how awful it must have been for that girl's parents, her brothers or sisters, aunts and uncles for so long. Andrea said that the bones had been buried there fifty or more years . . . I mean to not know for that long. And now, because of your *work*, they have an answer—"

"If we can figure out who she is."

"We?"

I lowered my head. "Remember what you just said about needing answers?"

"I was talking about the cost of those answers, Leslie. The cost of being a person whose *work* looks a lot to me like an ongoing campaign to level hope wherever she finds it."

"That's what you think I do? I kill hope?"

"I didn't say *kill*. Not because you want to. I meant—"

"If I'm such a plague, why the fuck would you want stay married to me? Do you want to stay—"

"It's probably not a good day to ask me that question."

"Humor the lunatic."

"Like I do anything else." He got up and bent close to brush my hair from my eyes before kissing me on the forehead. I gave him my best snotty bitch face in return. He laughed without warmth and offered Emma's gift back to me; I didn't get my bandaged hands around it securely enough. It slipped, bounced off the bed—Greg tried to catch it—and it hit the linoleum with a shattering crash. He lifted his eyebrow. "That wasn't a sign or anything, okay?" he said as he picked up the box, shaking it in order to hear how completely everything inside it had broken before handing it back to me.

I rattled the box again, wincing for the sound, and managed to nudge aside the ribbon, tear free the paper. The scent of lavender was quite pronounced. I opened the box to find a pale purple candle surrounded by the remains of the frosted-glass container that had held it. Greg leaned over to see. He lifted the candle by its wick. "She bought this at the drugstore. Kim extended her a line of credit."

"Think Kim might have another one?"

"I'm on it." He set the candle on the table beside my bed and then took the box, carefully reclosing the lid before setting it down in the wastepaper basket. "I'll tell Emma you loved it."

"I did. I do." He had already gone. I tried to gather the candle up in my bandaged paw and succeeded only in knocking the thing over. A paper label had been affixed to the bottom: SCENT THERAPIES / LAVENDER / TRANQUIL DREAMS. I closed my eyes and inhaled lavender, picturing fields of the flowers, Emma dancing in garlands, Molly stripping buds into medicine jars, Greg thatching the roof of our house with stems of blossoms, and I make my way toward them, my steps crushing lavender down to oil perfuming the day, the night, the distances between stars until my foot hits an obstacle and I look down to find I have been walking over children's bones.

greg

The doctor meets me out in the hall to say that Leslie will be released in the morning. I round up Molly and Em from the hospital cafeteria where they have been hanging out while I visited Les. The cashier had kindly agreed to run a tab for the girls; I pay the bill for french fries, sodas, and creative efforts made at the self-serve sundae bar, very little of which have been consumed. We walk out to the car, the cold wind stinging like alcohol on razor burn. The girls are in pretty good spirits, comparing and competing over the gifts they've received. They do not ask about their mother, not because they do not care but because their worries are too large for words. What I feel I can tell them is insufficient as comfort, but it is true: "Your mom's going to be fine, guys. Her hands are hurting, but everything else is great. Frank says—"

"Frank?" Molly whips her body around, walking backward, the wind blowing her hair into her face. "Frank was here?" Her expression falls, keeps falling. Apparently, Leslie does not hold a monopoly on the hope-killing business. I cannot believe I said such a terrible thing to her. *"Truth" is what I meant, Les. You insist on digging up the truth. It's truth that kills hope.* Sworn already to be true to my daughter, I try to make it quick, to mitigate her pain. "I talked to Frank on the phone. He's not worried."

It is not happening again. I want to tell that to Molly, now stoically rigid in the seat beside me, braced, tell it to Emma, yawning in the rearview mirror, eyes drooping, sinking into the safety of sleep. I want to tell them it isn't happening again and have them believe me. I would need to believe it first.

My father, the lapsed Catholic, never shook the notion that faith is acting as though our beliefs were fixed in certainty. Faith requires that we must live as though what we wanted already existed. Done with enough deliberation and attention to detail, the acting as-if would pull the longed for reality into being. Acting as-if, I smile with faith at my daughters and take them home.

The kitchen is as Leslie had left it. Bowl and pans on the counter, the flour and yeast and sugar sitting on the table, a mess of poppy seeds spread between wax paper held down by a rolling pin. I should have heard her. This house conducts sound like an amphitheater; rattles and confusions are funneled up and out. Pans banging about, ceramic bowls clattering seem louder in the middle of the night. Had I heard her, I would have known to come down and redirect her energies. When Leslie starts baking at two in the morning, she is announcing disruption as plainly as if she'd written BRIDGE OUT across her forehead. If asked, she will say that she is thinking, that the measure, mix, knead, the watch and the wait help her to settle her mind, help her to figure things out. I have seen her at work this way, her arm muscles flexing and giving way, her hips rolling as she kneads the dough, all the while her mind focusing itself into a needling fineness, surgically bright and sharp, riddling through her reason. She *thinks* things through the way a junkie *thinks* about the next fix. She'll lose track of what her body is doing. She'll knead and throw more flour, talking to herself, arguing ideas one way and then the other. Her voice changing timbre and volume, probably unaware she is speaking aloud, she will filibuster on where a particular course of action might lead. The arguments chase each other through the house without resolution. She avoids sleep, avoids bed, twisting herself up into that knotted state of overanalysis where her thoughts get stuck and stagnate, the natural process of corruption takes over, and her eye tricks itself into making demons out of swamp gas.

Molly and Em begin cleaning up, as much to sweep away what has happened as the need to do *something*. They putter about, keeping their voices low, shutting cabinets softly. Leslie's grandfather built those cabinets out of pine boards he planed from trees he cut down with his own ax and saw; the hardware he'd purchased from a roadside sale of goods salvaged from a farmhouse fire. The work shows no great artistry—the doors are marred with knots and pins that could easily have been trimmed out—but he was precise and careful in his carpentry. Everything still closes square, stays shut. He sealed the wood with several coats of shellac that have grown deeper in orange and ugliness over the years. The cabinets should be stripped, allowed to breathe for a while, and then resealed. There never seems to be time for that.

In the door of the cabinet beneath the sink, the center portion of a large knot has fallen out, giving the effect of an empty eye socket. This happened, according to Leslie, when she was a very young girl. Her sisters once told her that the "Eye" could look up her dress when she was doing dishes. She became so terrified that the only way her father could get her to even come into the kitchen was to cover the knothole, both sides, with pieces of tape. The first night after she'd moved back in with us from her apartment in the city, she got up from the table, went to the junk drawer, took out the roll of duct tape, and proceeded to cover up the Eye. She laughed it off, saying, "The problem with seeing things, is that you begin to wonder what things are seeing you." That night she baked bread, and came to bed near dawn. She woke me and we made love, Leslie crying and clutching, her voice knotted, as though she were trying to tell me she is dying in a language only she spoke. Her fear was plain, but communicating reassurance back to her was impossible.

The girls move wordlessly around me, sweeping, wiping down, erasing. I could imagine Leslie here, only hours ago, preparing. The oven beeping preheated long before she needed it. Leslie would have been chatting to herself about something or with someone who was not really there. Her plan would be for us to find loaves of bread waiting for our breakfast, heavy, sweet, glazed shiny with egg yolk and milk, still cooling on the counter. A gift, an artifact of how hard she is trying. She would have made much more than we could possibly eat, so she'd wrap the leftovers and put them in the freezer with all the others she has made since moving back. Stockpiling her concern, her understanding of love, enough to tide us over for the inevitable hour when her interior world overwhelmed her and in order to survive it, she had to take off again.

count

I wasn't able to do much with my hands for the first week or so that I was home. The thickly wrapped bandages gave way to ointments and fading bruises, making it easier to use the computer, drive the car, take notes as I cast about for leads on the child gone missing from Willet decades earlier. It was as though the natural progression of healing in my tissue were some sort of confirmation I was on the right track even though no track had presented itself. At night when I was alone with the images and the thinking, I had to content myself with poring through cookbooks and deciding what bread I would be making if kneading with my injuries did not constitute a health code violation.

The doctor at last gave me the okay to get back in the kitchen, saying that working with dough would prove excellent physical therapy for my stiff joints. Since then, I'd been on a five-night baking spree. Pretty much Frank's official definition of the onset of a manic episode. He used to ask how many loaves I'd turned out. I'd ask how many patients he'd seen. "Who is the patient here, Leslie?" "Why, Frank? Don't you know?"

I was thinking about Frank, how I was supposed to have called him. I finished washing out the bowls, rinsed them under the steaming tap, and set them on the drain board to dry. Four lovely plump loaves of whole-wheat bread lay on their sides cooling. The kitchen was clean, the counters wiped, the floor swept. The sun was coming up in colors of metallic intensity that gilded the edge of the windowsill in molten orange. I used the edge of my hand to clear the condensation off the window over the sink. The sky was cold-scoured, a pure and brightening blue. I gave it a few degrees above zero at best. A still, frigid Thursday three weeks into the new year.

Molly and Emma had departed for school a few minutes earlier. Above me, floorboards creaked and footsteps thudded down the hall toward the bathroom. Greg was up. I set about making a fresh pot of coffee, putting my mug under the coffee filter to refill myself before shoving the glass pot in place. I tore off a hunk of bread, grabbed a paper napkin. I wanted to get out of the kitchen, out of Greg's way and the inevitable questioning over what I was going to do. I wasn't quite fast enough. Already dressed for work, he was at the top of the stairs, heading down as I started up.

He leaned against the banister blocking my escape. "Did you sleep at all?"

"I'll catch up tonight. Or I'll take a nap later. I have a few things that have to get done today."

"A few *things*?"

The hunk of warm bread collapsed, squished in my clenching fist. "Yes, well, there's the grocery shopping. And I want to touch base with Caroline McCreedy; I saw her last week—don't think the chemo did her any good this time. And then—"

"And then you're going back up to Willet to see if you can, after weeks of finding nothing, find out who that little girl was."

"Somebody has to."

"You don't need to rationalize it for me, Les."

"But I'm so good at rationalizing."

"It's that talent that worries me most."

"Yes, I know." I laughed weakly and offered him the mug.

He took it and sat down on the step above me. "Want some advice you didn't ask for? Let this one go. Let this be the one where you figure out how to let one go."

"Is Frank feeding you these lines, Cyrano?" I ran my hand through his hair, over his ears, as though checking for wiring. "It's Emma who has gone missing, Greg. Do you want whoever finds her remains to stop trying to find out where she belongs?"

"You know, Leslie, I can't even begin to think like that."

"The difference between us, then."

"The little girl you found has been gone over fifty years."

"More like eighty. Carbon results came in yesterday."

"Then whoever would be missing her is most likely gone, too."

"That makes it even more important. That pain, that unanswered questioning, that doesn't go anywhere. It gets passed on down the line, Greg. You get sad, frightened people generations removed who have no idea what they're mourning—or what they're running away from."

He took a swallow of coffee. "Whose family are we talking about here?"

"Right now, two. Kendrick's and this child's—all right, three counting mine."

"Four, counting ours."

"Let's stop counting."

"Good idea. But Leslie, if you're going to insist on swimming into the deep end of this, I'm going to insist on a lifeguard. Call Frank Edelstein. Today."

"I will. Promise."

"No more promises, Les. Understand me. Either you start seeing Frank again regularly or you leave the house."

"So this is the one where *you* figure out how to let go?"

"Somebody has to."

I bent over and kissed him softly on the side of his mouth. "Somebody will."

It had become ritual: the stop at the convenience store to top off the gas tank; the broken fence post at which point the classic rock station I'd tuned to in the car would begin to fade and buzz into static; the sad pair of tilting wooden crosses that marked the site of a collision; Willet rising, broadening on the horizon; Willet's desk duty officer's scowl when I asked for new information—had anyone called about identifying Kendrick? The child?—No and no; double-checking on the promise to call me should any new information arise; the drive out to Happy Andy's to climb up to the Castle and look down into the earth where the recent excavation had frozen solid in ruddy brown ridges like scars on dark skin. Then to the house to stare at the peacock drawing, take another set of Polaroids of the colors and the words. Then tramp about the yard, closing up the pens and gates that would be, without fail, upon my arrival the next day, thrown wide again.

Other than providing the idea of doing a useful thing, these trips proved useless. It was a meaningless circuit of activity that I'd established as a way of holding my place while waiting for . . . what? I had tried to forestall the momentum. Released from the hospital on the day after Christmas, I had planted myself on the couch in a posture of serene resignation. Emma had stayed close by my side, quiet except for the occasional burst of point-blank questions as to the experience of being bonkers and how could I be sure that the kids I saw weren't really ghosts. Molly ambled into view every so often, pausing as though perhaps this time she'd let loose the words she held behind her bitten lip only to retreat in silence. Greg worked on taking down the tree, smiling at my bandaged applause as he dumped the knotted cords of twinkle lights into a garbage bag. I was getting better. We were going to get through this.

Monday morning, without second thought of risk to anyone, without thinking at all, I drove up to Willet to see if I might con my way into another look at Kendrick's papers. The clerk repeated the go-away litany of "Sorry; can't help you; the papers are lost." I then went over to the county records office to search down death certificates. After that to the library to try to find newspaper accounts. Anything that would have alluded to a direction other than *away* from Willet.

In the late 1940s, the petting zoo property had been deeded to one M. N. Hoffman and apparently had not changed hands since. I found no references to missing children from that area in that time frame; no reference to land in Willet owned by anyone named Kendrick. It might have meant they had only leased the place as summer property, if they had been there at all. I could find no reference to such a family or person by that name even passing through. I asked the clerk if anyone else had been asking for the same materials, if perhaps papers had been removed. She couldn't help me there. I left the library in late afternoon. Antsy, unready to go home to what would surely be Greg's disapproval, I'd gone to the morgue. I asked the attendant to see Kendrick's body under the pretense that one of my elderly uncles had gone missing, and I feared the worst. My hope was that the attendant would misread my very real anxiety and circumvent due procedure. He had been sympathetic, but police forms were required. He explained with gracious concern how I should go about obtaining those forms and sent me off with wishes that my uncle turned up safe.

If not for the digging conditions of winter, they would have interred Kendrick's remains already, and the family, should they show up, could pay to have him moved to a site of their choosing. Right now it was cheaper to keep him in deep cold storage. I imagined him as frozen inside himself, waiting to thaw and awaken. I wanted him to wake up, to tell him that we had found her, for him to tell us who she had been and how she'd come to be in her own cold, dark place. I decided not to pursue the forms or the viewing; I could not allow the man to be beyond retrieval, yet. I went home empty-handed and complained about a futile shopping exercise to my family. Not exactly a lie.

The child, however, was another matter. If not for her, I might have been able to admit defeat. The question she posed and my lack of progress in finding her definitive answers became a compulsion for the one definitive fact I could get to. I had to see her as she was, real and outside my memory of imaginings. Her current location was, according to Andrea, in the forensics lab that the county ran out of United General, a rambling complex of consolidated hospitals in the city. The forensics intern, as much out of pity as curiosity, had been spending what time they could spare on attempting a computer-generated reconstruction of her features. I did not want to wait for a mechanical brain's programmed attempt to call forth what had come to me unbidden.

I had waited, made myself wait, until New Year's Day when

the staff would be sparse and probably hungover. I left my family sleeping, long before daybreak and drove for hours, slowed by icy roads, into the granite and glass canyon of the city with its darkly glittering walls. I reached the labyrinth of old brick and limestone that was the General. Steam bulged out of power plant stacks, basement vents, and manhole covers sunk into the surface of the parking lot. I walked in the main entrance and waved my bruised hand at the security guard as though we did this every morning. The elevator smelled of antiseptics and roses. Down it dropped and opened onto a hallway, a desk manned by a female security officer watching music videos on a tiny black-and-white set.

"The Jane Doe," I said. "The one they found up at Willet."

She did not look away from the television but pointed at the registration book on the desk. "Sign in." I dashed out an authoritative signature and carefully printed the time. She didn't look at these either, just gestured down the hall. I thanked her. "Make sure you sign out," she said. "Everyone forgets to sign out."

I found the remains on a tray beneath a blue sheet. I forced my hands into a pair of latex gloves—not wanting to confuse whatever efforts were being made on her behalf with my prints—before rolling the sheet back gently, as you would from a dozing child. Her bones had been laid out in proper skeletal formation, on her side, as she'd been found. Dirt and age and the fact that you are not left alone by life even after you've left it had contributed to the discoloration and pitting of the bone surfaces. Char ran over her lower ribs in a narrow but definite arch, a scythe-shaped evidence of burning. I knew enough to recognize the fragile slenderness of her foundation as a sign of malnutrition as much as one of age. Still, she had been a tiny thing. I ran my fingers over the length and curve of the ribs, up the now disconnected vertebrae to the clean snap line at the base of her neck. That was the how of her death.

I tried then, desperately, to see her whole again, as I had exactly a week ago, not realizing until that moment that I'd expected to find the peacock array of ribbons, the tattered scraps of white lace from her dress. Those had been my personal additions. For the first time it occurred to me that I had *seen* her without any suggestion other than Kendrick's writing. That had not happened before. The hallucinations had always been a function of visual cues. Had I become even more suggestible? What mattered was that she had been found. I had rolled the thin sheet back over her, the fabric draping into the empty spaces. I had promised her, out loud, that I would do whatever I could.

As it turned out, so far, all I had been able to do was drive every day to visit the empty space that had been her grave and repeat the promise by repeating the visit. It was all I could do for Kendrick to keep asking if anyone had asked for him. It was all I could do for the third lost soul, whoever or whatever had been lost at the end of that last winter, the source of grief that had set these events into motion. I didn't try to explain any of this to Greg. Wouldn't try to explain it to Frank. They'd only say they worried about losing me. The fourth one lost. And Molly? Five. And Emma? And Greg? By that point, all I could do depended on not counting.

molly

Molly looks up from her book and checks the clock. Lunch is almost over, and she's yet to even take her sandwich out of the bag. The cafeteria is crowded and loud. The laughter and voices and calling across tables rushes together and crashes against the hard surfaces, bashing back into itself and making it one endless blast of noise. The cold weather is keeping them inside, making them more chatty and restless.

She's sitting at her usual table, the one closest to the fire exit, the only eighth grader at a table of seventh-grade losers, who, being ignored themselves, know how to ignore her. It gives her the satisfaction of choosing to be alone. Plus it is a good place to read. Maybe a little too good. Her vision is blurry and her head hurts. She hopes this is due to the noise and not a sign she's going to need glasses. Because that? Would suck.

She closes her eyes and presses against the top of her nose, an index finger at each side. Their technology aide calls this acupressure. He says that it helps with eyestrain, releases the focus lock from staring too long at the monitor. Molly opens her eyes again to see if the same exercise works for reading. The clock over the door is clear, but the words in front of her are soft, and the letters bump into one another. Her head hurts less if she keeps her eyes fixed on the distance. She doesn't want to be caught looking around or looking at nothing, so she raises the book like a wall in front of her face and stares again at the pink slip of a "Please See Me" office pass. Miss McCreedy, the school shrink—who signs her full name with a happy face dotting the "i" of Caroline—wants to see Molly *immediately after lunch*, which will be ending in five, four, three, two . . .

The class-hour bell begins its electronic *bong, bong, bong.* Molly shoves a piece of sandwich into her mouth, chewing fast so that hunger won't overtake her later. She needs to be able to steer her concentration straight in these meetings with McCreedy. Keeping her expression steady is as important as keeping her GPA up. Smile enough; get enough As and the questioning drops to bearable levels.

The chaos of the cafeteria has moved out into the halls. She scarfs the rest of the sandwich, gathers up her things, and slides off the bench. The tables and floor are strewn with bags and crumpled napkins, chewed up straws, the standard debris from dozens of standard lunches. Everyone is gone. The late bell *bongs.* Molly runs out of the cafeteria; being on time is important, too.

Miss McCreedy is waiting by her office door. She is a very skinny woman who is always drinking special canned nutrition drinks that promise to build curves. Her clothing tends toward short dresses in bright colors that look like she bought them in one of those 'tweener boutiques. Today she's in a lime green sweater dress that hangs limp around her bony frame. A bad color on her under the fluorescent lights; her skin looks gray. Her hair is bleached to an unnatural blond and she's clipped plastic green barrettes in at her temples to keep the hair out of her face. Her earlobes sag with the weight of her big, gold hoop earrings that bobble when she moves her head. Her voice is chirpy-cheerful, cartoon chipmunk, as she says, "Well, hello there, Molly. Happy New Year. How are you doing?"

How am I doing? Look around you. My mom is losing it again; my dad doesn't eat or sleep; no one talks to me anymore. How do you think I'm doing? She doesn't say that; doesn't show it. Ever. She's got to hold herself together; if she doesn't, what's Emma going to do? Someone has to take care of Emma. "I'm okay," she says in as flat a tone as possible. She drops herself in the chair opposite McCreedy's cluttered desk, holding her book to her chest, and focuses on the picture of the comet in a BELIEVE IN THE UNIQUENESS OF YOUR EXTREMELY SPECIAL SELF poster on the wall.

Miss McCreedy closes the door, takes her seat, and sighs. "Your mom called this morning."

"What for?"

"For the same reason she always calls. She's concerned. The holidays were a little disrupted, I hear."

"You didn't see it in the paper? Or on TV?"

"I was away visiting family. Believe it or not, what is big news here in Swifton doesn't seem like such big news to the world as a whole. The real news is that your mom and dad love you very much and they know this is hard for you."

"I'm fine."

"Always were. Always are." Miss McCreedy laughs her chipmunk laugh; her earrings sway. "May I tell you a secret, Molly? Well, not really a secret, but not the kind of thing you can say to just anyone. Here goes. I hate Christmas. Well, not Christmas itself, but I hate having to pretend to be happy when I'm not. Hate it."

"Really?"

"Really." McCreedy nods. "Christmas makes me sad. Makes a lot of people sad."

"Why?"

"That depends on who you ask. I'm asking you. Did this Christmas make you sad?"

"No."

"Scared?"

"No."

McCreedy's smile shifts. She points at the book Molly still has pressed against her chest. "What are you reading there? Yes, I can see it's a book, Miss Stone. Show me the cover." She laughs but not unkindly. "Again? You ought to have that series memorized by now."

"They're good," Molly says, hugging the book once more against her heart.

"But those fantasy books are the only thing you're reading."

"Not true."

"Yes, true." McCreedy takes a sheet of paper from the file folder and passes it across the desk.

"You're keeping a list of the books I take from the library?"

"The computer tracks the students' borrowing—calm down; we do it so we know where to look for books that aren't returned."

"Right."

"The point is, Molly, that I think you could branch out a little. I can recommend several authors who write about teenagers who are facing down personal challenges—you know, problems with parents and friends; that sort of thing."

"Why would I want to read about what I'm already living?"

"So you might not feel quite so alone?"

"Who says I feel alone?"

"You do. Every inch of you says it. But feeling a thing doesn't make it real." McCreedy taps her chin with the tip of her perfectly painted nail. "What you also tell me is that these fantasy stories about young adventurers whisked away to heroic events in strange lands are a means of escaping from your difficulties. They allow you an excuse to avoid contact with your peers."

Molly slides her stare hard onto McCreedy's cheery face. "You think?"

McCreedy raises an eyebrow. "I think you should try something new—just to try it. In fact, I have one I know you will like." She swivels toward her book-crammed bookcase and runs the perfect nail over the spines on the sagging shelves. "Here it is." She pulls the slender volume free and shoves it at Molly with such force that Molly has to take it to keep it from colliding with her nose. The title *Oswald and Octavia* is embossed into the gray-green cover among curling vines and lilies.

"It's old," says Molly.

"I found it a few years back in a used bookstore called Smedley's. Little downstairs cave of a place. I spend hours there whenever I go to, um, visit my family."

"At Christmas?"

"Whenever. Give it a try. Just to be different. I want a book report on that by next week."

"What?"

"Book report. My desk. No later than Monday morning."

"But you can't—"

"Just did. The book, too. I'm fond of that one."

"Fine." Molly stands. "I have to get to science. I'm missing a quiz." She doesn't wait for McCreedy to write out a hall pass; she bolts from the office, charges down the hall, passing the girls restroom from which creep soft giggles and the smell of cigarette smoke. She dumps *Os-what?* and *Octa-who cares?* in the gray plastic waste barrel outside the restroom door.

seep

Greg and I agreed on a plan of containment. I would keep my work in the biohazard box of the sewing room and away from the rest of them. I could be the madwoman at the top of the stairs but on a swing shift that organized itself around the girls' school hours and Greg's job. When they were around, I was to be Leslie, mother of two, wife of one, keeper of a cluttered, noisy house, gatekeeper on the dam against her own thoughts. I did what I could, but obsessions, being fluid, tend to seep; they find their own level, and within days mine had filled the sewing room and started to spread and rise into areas deemed off-limits. These things have to go somewhere.

Because I had used up the largest wall of the sewing room trying to replicate Kendrick's peacock art with cheap oil pastels, I had to set up my white board for brainstorming in the front room where the other computer made it too efficient a space to coordinate research with thinking. The good light combined with the flat eggshell paint in the dining room became the excuse for taping up a gallery of dozens of dated Polaroid photographs from the petting zoo: the painted peacock and the animal pens—open and shut—along with close-ups of frozen, overturned earth. Having encroached this far, it seemed logical to accept that the refrigerator made too functional a palate for trying out different combinations of the clauses in the peacock poem. I'd printed out the lines by their parts—along with THE WILDERNESS as title—in large letters and affixed each to a peel-and-stick, cut-to-length strip of magnetic tape. I was on my knees pushing magnet words around the front of the fridge and pretending I'd forgotten, yet again, to call Frank, when Molly came in from school.

"Hey there," I said and sat back on my heels.

She dumped her book bag, coat, and scarf on the table. Her braids were coming loose and static had played havoc with her fine, dark strands. Her cheeks and nose were scarlet from the cold. The ice in her stare was not to be thawed by my welcoming smile. "Emma went to Rita's house."

"And so the sun will continue to rise in the east."

"What?"

"I meant some events are always going to happen." I shoved THE WILDERNESS up against ALL IN FLAME OF FIRE and squinted at the juxtaposition before separating them again.

Molly came over and opened the fridge door bumping it hard into my legs. "Sorry."

"Yeah. Anything of interest happen at school?"

She pulled out a can of orange soda. "I know you called and told McCreedy to check up on me."

"That's not exactly how it happened," I said, as I tried the next description BIG AS THE MOON AND HIGHER. "If I wanted you to see Caroline, you'd know about it first. Don't I always tell you when I'm going to call her?"

She reached over my shoulder and guided one of the word sets toward the bottom of the door. "That saw this wondrous sight" has to go at the end. It's the only one with a period."

"Very smart, Mol."

"You should get one of those fridge poetry sets. You'd have more words."

"I have too many as it is." I pushed the next phrase in line up to replace BIG AS THE MOON AND HIGHER. "I called Caroline to find out how she's feeling, she told me a little about the hospital, and then she asked about you. If she called you in, it was only because she—"

"What do you mean, 'hospital'?"

Distracted, I had said too much. I looked up at my daughter. "Nothing for you to worry about."

"Don't do that *nothing's wrong* thing. Is she okay?"

"We hope she will be. I don't think she wants the students to know."

"You mean she's going to die or something?"

I dropped my head. "Molly. I—"

"Well?"

"Caroline is sick. She has been for a long time. The medicine that worked doesn't seem to work anymore. She's going into a hospital in another city next week. Monday evening, I think that's when she's leaving. The doctors there have some procedures they want to try."

"And that will make her better, right?"

"No one knows. No one ever does, really. So we hope for the best."

Molly sank to the floor next to me. "I did something awful."

The folding lattice of the security gate kept us out of the hallway, but we found a custodian of grandfatherly demeanor who took pity on Molly's plight, unlocked the chains, and let us in. Molly sprinted to the waste barrel where she said she'd tossed Caroline's book. The barrel was empty. The custodian helped us dig through the stuffed plastic bags he'd loaded onto his cart. We came up with graded papers and wads of chewing gum and pencil shavings, but no book.

"What's the title?" asked the custodian. "I can keep an eye out for it."

"I can't remember," said Molly, her upper body deep in a bag of refuse we'd already searched once.

"The author?" I asked, as I reached in and took her arm, gently urging her away from the futility of her digging.

"I don't know, Mom." She sniffed her fingers and winced. "I don't know."

"No title and no writer." The custodian started closing the garbage bags. "Going to make it difficult to find another one, then."

"The store," Molly said, sniffing her fingers again, "She got it from a store when she was visiting . . . it was called Smelly's—no, Smeld—no, Smedley's. That's it. I'm sure. We can find the store and ask them if they have another copy. I can describe what the cover looks like, maybe that will be enough."

I exchanged a glance with the custodian. "You find another copy and then what?"

"I pay for it."

"And?"

"I tell Miss McCreedy what I did."

"Caroline McCreedy?" The custodian cleared his throat and hefted another bag onto the cart. "Ah, man. Damn shame about that poor woman."

Molly looked at him, her face registering the full scope of what he was damning. "Please, Mom. I have to find her another one. I bet I could get it to her by the end of next week."

The custodian and I exchanged another glance, one that said to each other what we dared not say in front of Molly: Caroline McCreedy might not be with us by this time next week.

We drove back to the house. I set about making dinner and Molly dashed upstairs to use the computer in my office. She said that she didn't want to deal with the interruptions of dinner or family or phones or any of that "crap." What she meant is that she wanted to panic in private. I sent my best wishes behind her, that she would be able to recall at least part of the title. She needed to be able to fix this one. If she could not locate a replacement copy of Caroline's book on her own, I'd take up the search later after she'd gone to bed by calling Caroline and getting the needed info. I'd have the book shipped out overnight, in Molly's hands again by tomorrow or Saturday. My father would have scowled at my wimp-out parenting, but I figured we'd reached the point where Molly's sense of impending abandonment and confusion threatened to overwhelm any lesson to be learned. The last thing this family needed was yet another girl child who believed that when she got angry, the people she loved got gone.

I took the roaster from the plastic wrap, pulled out the soggy paper bag of gizzards, and rinsed the bird under cold water from the tap. Outside, the sky was pulling down into night. I turned on the oven to high heat while I washed the red-skinned potatoes, which would be mixed with garlic, lemon, rosemary, and olive oil before being stuffed inside the chicken. My sister Joanne's recipe. We'd also have salad of spring greens and a caramelized apple tart I had picked up at the bakery. Quite the upgrade for a clan who thought that having the ketchup in little foil packets made supper fancy. I could hear Frank laughing as I patted the chicken dry with paper toweling: "Overcompensating, are we?" Just a little.

I heard Greg's truck pull up in the drive. A few seconds later, Emma bounded through the back door. "Rita cut my hair! Look!"

I didn't see a bit of difference except the dark, normally tangled curls had been combed and flattened with styling gel. "Rita did a nice job, sweetheart."

"Where's Molly?" Emma used one foot to force the snow boot off the other. She didn't wait for my answer; she ran out of the kitchen shouting. "Molly! Rita cut my hair!"

Greg stamped the snow off his work boots before coming inside. "You may not have heard, but Rita cut Emma's hair."

"No!"

"It's true." He came up behind me, wrapped his arms around my shoulders, and rested his chin on the top of my head. He smelled of wood and sweat; his late-day beard prickled my scalp. "I'm dreading the day when Rita pierces Emma's tongue. Because you know that is coming."

"Yeah, but it might keep her quiet for an hour or two."

"You're all about the optimism aren't you, Les?" He kissed my hair. "Gauging by the size of that chicken, I'm guessing that someone is going to tell me something I won't be happy about."

"Molly's had a rough day. Another one. I had to tell her about Caroline."

"Poor kid. And you? Get a chance to talk to Frank?"

"Technically?"

"That's what I thought." He released me. "I'm going to grab a shower before we eat." He left without saying anything else but his disappointment was plain in the silence he left behind him.

The heat of the oven was burning off weeks of pizza grease and casserole boil-over, sending smoke through the vent stack beneath the rear right burner. I switched on the fan, grateful for the white din against the hum of Greg's absent condemnation. I went back to slicing the potatoes, losing myself in the nothing noise of the fan and the rhythm of the rise and fall of the knife; I didn't hear Emma come into the kitchen, didn't realize she was there until she grabbed at my elbow. I dropped the knife and pivoted, startled. "Don't do that."

"Molly says you have to come upstairs. She says she found something."

I smiled, relieved for my daughter's sake. "Good. Tell her I'll be up in a minute."

"Go now. She won't let me see it until you do."

"She can wait five minutes."

"No, she said to tell you to hurry."

"Then let's hurry." I took a towel from the counter and wiped potato milk from my hands as we went into the dining room, where I saw that Greg had stripped my Willet photos from the wall and piled them, neatly enough, on the table. Tiny flecks of tape speckled the wall. I scooped up as many of the photographs as I could carry; he might have time to think while in the shower, decide that he should have thrown them away. Emma was already up the stairs.

"Hurry up, Mom."

I cradled the photographs against my middle, feeling a few slip away as I made my way up to where Emma was waiting outside the sewing room door. I could hear the water pounding in the bathroom down the hall.

"I got Mom," Emma shouted through the door. "Let me in."

Her voice came muted from the other side. "You really there, Mom?"

"Open the door, Mol."

"It is open."

Emma tried the knob and gave the door a push. Molly was standing away from the computer; she was studying the giant peacock I'd sketched out on the wall.

"You found your book?" I asked, as I let the photographs fall onto the bed.

She shook her head. "I found yours." She hitched her thumb over her shoulder. On the screen was a photograph of a very old book, the cover an embossed version of my peacock—Kendrick's peacock—drawn exactly as he had up in Willet. Here the bird was perched on the center *e* in *The Wilderness*. The breadth of its fanned tail stretched from opening *T* to closing *s*.

"How?" I said, breathless.

Molly came to the desk to show me how she'd found it at the Smedley's Rare and Collectable Bookstore Web site: With no idea of the title she was looking for, she had gone page by page through the small number of listings for children's books offered by Smedley's online, each detailed description, each photograph. She had then moved into the far more extensive Private Collector Requests section. A few pages in, she'd stumbled on it:

SEEKING PICTURE BOOK *THE WILDERNESS*. PUBLISHER UNLISTED. CIRCA 1928. AUTHOR UNKNOWN. ANY CONDITION. CONTACT BOOKSTORE FOR FURTHER INFORMATION.

Beneath it had been the thumbnail photo of the cover, which could be enlarged for better viewing. Molly had enlarged it, and then sent Emma down to summon me.

"Is that it?" Molly said moving to stand behind me.

"It would have to be."

"It wasn't like I meant to help."

"But you did." I swiveled the chair around and took her hand, kissed her wrist before she could yank herself out of my grip. "Very much." I then told the girls I needed a few minutes to think and that Molly would probably find her search less frustrating on the cable modem downstairs.

"Yeah, I can *not* find it much faster that way."

"Well—" I hit the prompt that would take me back to Smedley's homepage "—you could just see Miss McCreedy in the morning and 'fess up."

She groaned softly. "I'm going." Emma departed behind her. "Did you see my hair, Molly?"

The homepage ran down the celebrated history of the bookstore, how it had served as a hangout and underground library for the anarchist set of the early 1900s. Raided, closed, reopened, burned, flooded, changed in ownership many times, it was still proudly Smedley's in honor of its original proprietors, Florence and Harry. I wrote down the 800-number and operating hours for the bookstore. With the difference in time, they would have been closed for a couple hours already; that did not mean they would not answer the phone.

I found my cell phone under a stack of papers and dialed Smedley's line. The ring repeated without a voice mail response. The line rang twenty, thirty times before an automated operator broke in to suggest that perhaps the party I was trying to reach was not answering the phone; for a small fee the phone company would be happy to redial the number, every hour until they could relay my message. I hung up and paged back to the collector's request for the book itself, clicked on the e-mail link, and wrote:

IN REGARD TO YOUR REQUEST POSTED AT SMEDLEY'S BOOKSTORE (#074599):
MAY HAVE LEAD ON FIRST EDITION OF WILDERNESS BOOK. CALL OR WRITE.

I provided my cell phone number but gave no name. The screen told me the mail had been sent. For the countless hours I had spent trying to find threads within cyberspace that might connect Kendrick to a nursery rhyme, it had not occurred to me that the connection had been one of mere affinity or nostalgia for a relic of his childhood. Myopic as I might have felt at the moment, the coincidence of Molly's stumbling over this was unsettling. Too easy for so obscure a reference. Even if the picture book itself was a rarity, demand for it might have been widespread. I distilled the Smedley's request down to its key words—Wilderness; 1928; Unlisted; Unknown; Contact Bookstore—and plugged them into the search engine, hit the Go button, and went back downstairs to finish making dinner.

We ate late; the food was overcooked. Greg carved the chicken in quarters and spooned potatoes onto plates while I shoveled the salad. The girls, famished, ate in quick suspicious bites broken by intervals of chatterbox talk of hairstyles and dismissive rolling of eyes. Their father questioned them about homework and upcoming exams; he said nothing to me outside polite requests to pass along the bread or salad from my end of the table. I busied myself with trips to the fridge and sink to refill water glasses. No one wanted dessert. After a contentious round of negotiations, it was decided Emma had dish duty, but Greg would dry and put away. Molly escaped the table to get back to her "project." I shouted after her to work downstairs; I still needed my office. I got a surprisingly agreeable "Okay" in return—along with a stern glare from Greg.

"I have some phone calls to make," I said, trying to imply acknowledgment of a promise still not kept and my intent to rectify the matter.

"What sort of phone calls?" His expression did not soften.

Emma, her gaze shifting between us, said, "I can start cleaning up now?"

"Yes," Greg answered her, "Go ahead." I took this as my cue to exit before he had a chance to further pursue specifics.

The monitor in my office had switched to sleep mode. I tapped the space bar to bring it back to light and dropped into my chair to consider what had faded up onto the screen. The search engine had coughed up more hits; page after page of requests for *The Wilderness* at other bookstores and each one worded exactly the same as the one at Smedley's. I moved through the links: the same photograph of the cover. I started calling bookstores. Some were closed for the day; some had gone out of business, their numbers assigned to other parties. Some my cell phone could not connect with. When I did get an answer and found myself speaking with a person who could help me, I was told that the request had been made with the instruction that interested parties leave their contact number. The collector or the collector's agent would get in touch.

"But how do you contact them to let them know you've been approached?"

97

"I don't know. Says here on the form 'collector or collector's agent will initiate all communications.' I guess that means they'll call us to see if anyone's called us."

"Handwritten or typed?"

"Stapled. The instructions came in the mail. When we get one of these anonymous things, we staple it to one of our regular request forms. Why would it matter?"

"It doesn't. Is it dated?"

"Not the request itself. But the form is stamped May of ninety-nine."

"That's a long time ago. Any notation of when you last heard from him or her or them?"

"Nope. Are you the police or something? Is this stolen material we're talking about?"

"Nothing so dramatic. I just really want a copy of the book."

"As far as I can tell, we've never found one."

That was how the calls went. No one was deliberately secretive, but no one had any information to offer, either. In between the calls, I would check my e-mail, trying to will a response to my Smedley's lure. Who knew which of these bookstores was legit or which might be a front for the collector? Only one way to find out. I copied my note to Smedley's into an e-mail for each of the bookstores the search had pulled up. I couldn't mass mail or blind copy because each store had its own system for requests. It was worth the effort; I wanted whomever it was to know I'd figured out enough of the game to counter the opening move.

It was nearing two when I decided, with many pages of results still waiting, that I'd put out enough bait. The girls were long asleep; they had knocked around ten and said their *good night*'s through the door. Greg had gone to bed without saying anything. Downstairs, light shone from the front room and the sheen on the dining room furniture told me the over-the-sink fixture in the kitchen was still burning. He'd left these on for me. No doubt a courtesy, but it was also his way of determining if I'd left my office that night. I went down to shut the lights off, and thus reassure him.

When I reached the kitchen, I saw the bakery box, the tape securing it unbroken. I ran my thumbnail through the tape, grabbed a knife from the drain board and cut a hefty slice of the thin, gooey tart. I switched off the light and stood in the dark gobbling down overly sweetened apples and too-thick caramel in a crust beginning to go soggy from fruit juice. It was delicious. I rinsed my hands under the tap, drying them on my jeans as I went to shut off the desk light in the front room.

The light had been positioned so that it shown directly on my white board, producing a glare that blotted out my squiggly Web work of facts and possible connections. A few sheets of paper were scattered on the floor beneath the desk; the printer had a way of spewing work right out of the bin. I didn't want the call from school in the morning from one daughter or the other begging to have a forgotten assignment rushed to their grasp. I gathered up the sheets. They belonged to Molly.

DEAR MISS MCCREEDY:

I THINK I HAVE LOST THE BOOK YOU GAVE ME. I AM SO SORRY. I TRIED TO FIND ANOTHER COPY BUT I CANNOT REMEMBER THE AUTHOR. IF YOU WILL TELL ME THE NAME,

I PROMISE TO GET ANOTHER ONE FOR YOU AS FAST AS I AM
ABLE. I CAN SEND IT TO YOU WHEREVER YOU ARE.
I AM REALLY, REALLY SORRY.
YOURS TRULY,
MOLLY STONE

The pages held different attempts at the same confession, one draft going as far as to admit she'd been angry about the assignment and thrown the book out. I wondered which of the versions she'd chosen to give Caroline. I put the sheets of paper back on the floor, as I'd found them. Then I picked up the phone, dialed Frank's office number and left a message for him to give me a call when he got a chance. I hung up, shut the light out, and went back upstairs to see if my husband would make room for me in his bed.

the cloud and the oak

halt

My days began to take on the dull drag of lethargy that comes at the end of a binge when you realize that you are going to have to stop because your gluttony has sapped all the energy required to keep going. Except for auto responders and an occasional clerk's acknowledgment of receipt, my e-mails concerning *The Wilderness* went unanswered. Except for a spurt of "private" calls to my cell phone that disconnected after I'd said hello, no one phoned. I made appointments with the good doctor Frank's secretary only to call back and reschedule. What would we have talked about? Nothing was happening. No one was going to claim Kendrick's body. No one was going to identify the child whose bones were now numbered and stored among other anonymous remains. I wasn't going anywhere with this but around in the same circles, running myself into the ground. Even my madness had forsaken the cause. The hum in my head had gone silent; the hallucination station had signed off the air. I'd had trails go dead on me before, and I tended to delay the inevitable vastness of loss by flogging myself forward with accusations of failure. This time, between the unraveling of the Willet cause and Caroline McCreedy's death, I had no defense against bottoming out in sorrow and helplessness. I came to a halt.

The days lengthened, which only seemed to make my depression worse. The snow dirtied in lumpy heaps that mimicked the cloud-covered skies. Grumpy February hauled its listless hulk onto the calendar, lugging along with it those indefinite hours through which nature fought the tug-of-war between seasons. On the first Saturday in February, we had taken Molly to Caroline's memorial service. Crocuses were thrusting Easter-egg optimism through the grimy slush that morning only to be buried under a fresh four inches of resignation that afternoon. Around here February was the month of fever and ash, wallow, self-pity, and repentance, shored up at its midpoint with a spun-sugar heart that began to dissolve at the first touch of the tongue.

Midpoint in February was where we were. I had yet to see Frank but abandoning the Willet trips seemed to have alleviated Greg's larger concerns. My worries for Molly and Em pressed with more urgency than deciphering Kendrick's meaning in an old poem. I found myself seeking out their company, looking for excuses to stay close to Greg. My stability was righting itself. Although worn down and mournful, I could look out a window and see the world as being real.

It was late morning, Friday, the thirteenth, and I was busying myself by helping Greg sort and stack a delivery of rough lumber, cherry planks that he would eventually use to build the cabinetry for the kitchen remodeling gig he had contracted. The lumber had to spend time acclimating to the workshop, during which period it would warp in accord with its interior stresses. Cup, bow, crook, or twist, it warped one way or the other because that's what wood did. Once the contortion process was completed, Greg would flatten each plank by running it through the jointer and the planer, choose the grain line he wanted and rip it to spec on the band saw. I envied his faith that he could straighten out even the most severe distortion.

It would be several weeks before he could begin this part of the work—acclimation takes time—but he was, he told me, patient. The metaphor was about as subtle as a kick in the shin. He had been insulted the one time I suggested in jest that he saw me as just another board length. He'd asked if maybe that's why I spent so much time out in his workshop. I now kept my mouth shut over the obvious; he kept sharpening his blades and checking on the humidity.

On this Friday, except for his occasional "Watch out; that edge is rough," or "Other side up, Les," we worked without talking, letting the radio's prattle and the clatter of the workshop's heating system fill in the silence between us. Mostly I stood around watching as he graded each board, chalking off scarred sections, gauging its dryness with a two-pinned moisture meter. He had a system of color-coded stickers that he used to tag particular grain patterns and defects that were the hazard of using kiln-dried lumber. Once the plank was coded, I would carry it to its proper bin. I had yet to replace my work gloves, so Greg had given me a pair of his. The gloves were too big and I worried because my grip on the boards felt faulty. Not that any real harm could be done if I dropped a board, but I wanted, given how things were going, any opportunity to prove myself reliable to him.

It took me a moment to realize Greg was speaking to me. ". . . you expecting someone?" He was running his hand along a plank, but he was scrutinizing me. "Les, I said I think someone is here."

A car door banged shut outside. I brushed the dust off my jeans and took off the gloves, laying them aside as I headed for the door. The morning had gone gray; the cold had whetted a bite. I pulled my jacket tighter, trapping my hands under my arms for warmth. Andrea Burnham was pounding on the back door. I called to her and she waited for me on the porch before opening the door to let us both into the kitchen. Inside it was pleasantly warm and still redolent with breakfast smells. Andrea was dressed in wool trousers, a fleece pullover, and her white knit cap that forced her curls down so that the ends barbed and jutted out at odd angles about the cap's edge. She took a seat at the table, pushing aside Emma's half-eaten bowl of cereal. The sudden change in temperature caused the lenses of her glasses to fog up; she pulled them down her nose to regard first the poem fragments stuck on the refrigerator and then me over the top of the thick frames.

"You have competition on the Happy Andy front."

"They can have it. I'm done." I sank into the seat beside her. "Who?"

"Some reporter chick."

"A reporter?"

"Yeah, and apparently she's been asking around town about you."

"She's writing about the little girl? Or Kendrick?"

"I don't know." Andrea pulled a prescription slip from her pocket. "Kim got a call from the pharmacist at the Willet store. Young woman was in there asking if the pharmacist knew you. She wants to interview you. Said you and she were old friends." She looked down at the note. "Sophia Mallory."

"Can't recall anyone by that name."

Andrea grinned. "There you go. Something new to work on."

"I can't work on this anymore," I said, leaning in to whisper the word *work* in case Greg had bugged the kitchen.

"But you want to," she whispered in return. "And it's what? One day? You wouldn't have to tell *anyone*."

"Oh yeah. That's a good idea."

"You don't have to lie. Simply say that you're going out for the day." She handed me the script. It was Kim's pharmacist-careful block print beneath a slug for a prescription cough remedy. The note read: INVESTIGATIVE JOURNALIST. INTERVIEW. $$$. CALL. The phone number had a Willet exchange. My disdain must have registered broadly because Andrea laughed. "Try not to pull a muscle being grateful or anything."

"I don't talk to reporters."

"Normally I'd say blow this off, but I think she may be trying to lock down the story of what happened up there. Like you are."

"Were."

"Will be again. You might actually be of some use to each other. And it's money. Play it right, and you could turn this into a paying job."

I leaned back in my chair. "You've already spoken to her. All that crap about pharmacists in Willet. What did you do, have Kim fake this thing?"

She grinned. "You're so good at cutting right through the BS."

"Have to be when so much of it gets dumped on my doorstep. This Mallory reporter person called you because you were involved with the find. And then she got you talking and you dropped my name and—"

"Give me some credit, honey. She asked about you; I said I would pass the request along. I think you need to do this. You aren't going to be able to walk away from it. Besides, it would be sanity-making to be a part of resolving the details of whatever

107

befell this child. You can see that. Your shrink would see that. Hell, even Greg would have to see the sense in that. And if it became a more involved position . . ."

"I don't see how that would be possible."

"Investigative journalist? You're a private investigator? See how that would work?"

"I look for people, Andrea. Remember? Living beings, not historical factoids."

"Not recently, you haven't." She flattened a ridge of spilt sugar with the tip of her little finger. "I told Kim you'd argue. She's worried about you, you know. Said you were in the store a couple days ago and you looked so tired and seemed so distracted. Kim felt it was, quote, 'time we kicked Leslie's escape pod into gear before that depression she's circling sucks her into the next dimension.'"

"Remind me to buy my drugs from another pharmacist. One who lives on this planet."

"Do not dis my girlfriend." Andrea put her hand on my shoulder, narrowed her eyes. "She's your friend. We're both your friends. We're tired of worrying about you. We'd much rather be fantasizing once again about how good it would be to throttle your sorry, pain-in-the-butt, stubborn-bitch self."

"You left out 'paranoid.'"

"When you talk to Mallory, I'd probably change 'paranoid' to 'imaginative.' But that's just me."

"Reporters are not among my favorite people, you know? I'd be terrible to work with. Even for a day."

"I do know. That is why this is so perfect. Rebellion is the original Prozac." She patted my cheek, a bit harder than necessary, and got up to leave. "Call her."

"I'll think about it." I walked her to the back door. "I really will."

"You think too much, my dear." Andrea waved farewell. I closed the door behind her and looked at the phone number for a few seconds before crumpling it in my fist. I threw it on top of the carrot scrapings and wilted lettuce leaves in the meant-for-compost bin under the sink. I then went to the fridge and pried off the magnetic words—nearly worn to nothing from my handling—and dumped them in the trash can beside the pantry door. Done. Satisfied with my resolve, I began to clear the cereal bowls and happened to glance again at the sink, where the latest duet tape patch over the Eye was slowly peeling itself away from the wood, rolling down to expose the ovoid of darkness. I thought about Molly, digging through the trash at school in her vain attempt at finding a second chance, the note card now pinned on her bulletin board—

Dear Molly, I appreciate your honesty and your kind apology. You know something funny? I cannot recall the author's name either. Not to worry. It was, after all, only a book . . .

—the replacement copy of *Oswald and Octavia* Molly had paid for and carried to the memorial service, believing there would be someone to return it to. She had been too intimidated to approach Caroline's family members, and so she had handed it to one of the teachers she recognized, saying, quickly, almost in a whisper, "This isn't mine." The teacher, having no idea what was going on beyond the fact of a shaken kid, had accepted the book and assured Molly she would deliver it to whomever it belonged.

Molly had seen an obligation of her own making through to its conclusion. I had obligations as well. No one may have yet claimed Kendrick's body. No one may have found the family from which that child had been torn. That did not mean they didn't belong to someone, somewhere. I opened the cupboard with the empty eyeball that stared straight through to the center of my fear, retrieved the crumpled notepaper from the carrot shreds, and went to the phone.

greg

Leslie comes back to the workshop, takes the push broom from its corner, and begins to sweep. "That was Andrea," she says, her eyes on the area of floor ahead of the broom. Her expression reads as uncertain, but the truth is in the tone of Leslie's voice as she tries to complain, to sound weary and resigned as she lists the reasons why she has to go up to Willet one last time—just this one last time. She means it, of course; she believes she does, but forces stronger than her belief have snapped into place, her secret circuit breaker is back in On position. The dragging out of her explanation and the fatigued regret dulling her voice are artificial, an insulation meant to protect us and herself from the electrical current powering up the arc lights in the outlands of her mind. If she would look me in the eye, I would see her shining.

"Are you okay with this?" she asks the floor in front of the broom.

"I'm fine." Now we're both dishonest, but any other response would only start up the same old useless fight. She's going to do what her illness wants anyway. It lures her in deeper by chasing her with accusations of failing to stand before it. She is crossing the open throat of a sea monster on a bridge that both falls apart and comes into being with each step she takes. Can't stop. Can't go back. Wouldn't if she were able to. This is what Leslie needs to know she's alive.

"When would you be going?"

"Tomorrow. Early."

"And back?"

"Early. You're sure you're all right with this?"

"I'm all right."

She sweeps and sweeps, waiting for me to try to dissuade her. I go back to my work without saying anything. It would be easier for her to do this if she's angry and thinks she's proving something to me. I won't give her my blessing, but I won't make it easy, either. Not that it matters what I do. No one can help her now. I can only hope that this is one of those times she gets across the bridge before the monster snaps its jaw and traps her. I hope that after tomorrow she finds herself back on solid ground, heart beating fiercely, laughing for the near miss as she wanders on back home. She sweeps. I say nothing. I don't want to fail before my fears either.

interview

I'd called the number Andrea had provided; Sophia Mallory had been too busy to speak to me. A man named Nate had said she was not available until after three o'clock the next afternoon. He began to give me directions but then caught himself. "I suppose you already know how to get there." Yes, I assured him, I knew where I was going.

On the car seat beside me was the yet unopened envelope addressed *To Leslie* in Greg's spiky, blueprint-practiced lettering. The card was tucked into the red satin ribbon on a small heart-shaped box of chocolates that still bore the price tag from the drugstore. He'd handed it to me on my way out of the house so that he wouldn't have to watch me read it. I'd left a similar box and envelope on his workbench in the garage. Ritual thus met, we were free to scurry back to our opposing sides of awkward.

I had not lied to him, although I wished I had. Lying would have been less a burden of guilt than his flat acquiescence. My throat felt constricted from swallowing that much silence—give me an air-shattering, earth-quaking shouting match any day. We had attempted to feign normalcy for Molly and Emma when they came home from school. They were old hands at unscrambling the cryptogram of stilted solicitude and forced smiles. I talked to them; Greg talked to them. Everything's fine, we said in perfect unison when we tucked them in. Then we slept in separate beds, he in our room, I in my office. Just for convenience, right? What with me getting up and away so early.

I did leave early, which left me hours to use up before my appointment. I walked around Willet, an exposed-brick fantasia of antique shops and tiny boutiques that served formal teas. The main street was lined with ornamental plum and crab apple, bare-branched but sprouting the first nubs of new life. Between the trees, faux antique streetlamps arched their palely glowing hexagon heads on swan necks of molded black aluminum. All this meant to replicate, no doubt, a sense of Willet's past. But I remembered coming through here as a child, pinned between my sisters in the back seat of the station wagon, on our way to or from another benighted family outing. Then, the streetlamps had been single-lens eyes staring straight down from plain steel standards. The buildings had housed hardware and feed stores, catalog depots, a fabric shop, a five-and-dime, and a diner, called Terry's, where we would sometimes stop on the way home for pot roast sandwiches and made-as-we-watched potato chips.

Terry's was long gone. Like the other businesses, it had been overtaken, scrubbed down, reimagined to the point of theme park artifice. Thus gussied up, Willet was predictably drawing more and more outsiders in search of safety and abundance. As though one proved the other. I gave it five years at best before these artfully charming storefronts were boarded up, bankrupt to the "lifestyle centers" that were already pouring foundations on the edge of town.

Killing a few hours in pretty little Willet—butterfly balanced on a mounting pin—did not help to lighten my already dismal mood. I could not help but examine the sidewalks and window displays for evidence of what may have been covered up generations ago. Back in my cop days, I had been acquainted with *cleaners*, men and women who made damn good money setting to rights the aftermath of crime. They bleached and scrubbed and vacuumed away the traces of rampage and wounding, but only those traces. Those returning to homes or businesses would find sections of floor or wall cleaner than the surrounding areas. So, the reality of the crime was made more palpable by virtue of its being so carefully excised, and the room from which reality had been taken made into a stage set for pretending you could not see what was written on the walls in antiseptic neon. Survivors went straight out and bought cans of paint in new colors they had always wanted to try. Pragmatic reconfiguration of surface arrangements was an attempt not to get through but to get away from what had occurred. Willet suddenly had me thinking of the witnesses who arrived at an interview with day planners open and phone numbers ready in anticipation of a need for alibis. I got back in my car and headed out to the farm.

The road cut through fields where the snow had melted enough to expose—February mange—moist, stalk-stubbled earth. The sky sank lower and lower under the weight of clouds too lethargic to threaten anything more than a gray damp discomfort. Close to the roadside, I saw a hawk, its gaze fixed on the distance, its talons locked on its prey, which was struggling in such a manner that the hawk rose and fell with the exertions, as though the bird were perched on a beating heart. My car neared and the hawk took wing, a soft dark mass wrestling but held tight in the bird's grip.

I passed the usual lumbering earthmovers and concrete mixers at work on Willet Crossroad Center Shoppes, made the turn to

Happy Andy's, and crested the final hill that would descend to the parking area. Once again, I felt myself cross the barrier between the crowded busy world of the real and the dim hollowness of events waiting to happen; it was the empty-theater feel the petting zoo had evoked the night of the ice and the bones. I was a pretend Leslie who was going to meet a pretend writer and discuss the fantasy scenario of fanciful imagery that had led her, in flashback, to the resting place of the plastic skeleton of a child who had never really existed. Having once created fiction, it got easier each succeeding pass.

The yard had been plowed and shoveled; what snow remained was piled up inside the cages and pens and melting. Drip and trickle rhythms dabbled music about the wet yard. I made my way around puddles to the cottage where Nate had told me Sophia would be waiting. My assumption had been that we would merely be meeting here at the unoccupied house. It did not appear unoccupied any longer. The shutters had been opened, the windows washed and draped with curtains that had been pulled wide. Smoke lugged itself out of the chimney and hung, drowsy, above the trees. Parked next to the hemlocks that served as a break on the windward side of the house was an SUV of European make. Tinted glass and polished chrome, this year's model. It likely cost more than I would pull down in a year of steady work. My appetite for income reawakened, I set aside my hesitations and went to keep the appointment.

At the door, I noticed the Realtor's lock box was gone. I twisted the key on the doorbell and heard the chimes trill. Before the reverb from the bells had died away, the door was yanked open by a woman whose expression was serious, bordering on anger. On seeing me, she leaned against the frame, her brow relaxed and her slight build became even smaller as her posture drooped. The oversize cabled sweater she wore seemed to swallow her, the delicate blue of the yarn stark against the umber undertones of her very dark skin. Her long skirt of deeper blue brushed the threshold, covering her stocking feet. She tugged at one of the countless braided strands worked into her shoulder-length hair. "I was afraid you were one of our little jokester neighbors, who have been playing ring-and-run day and night. I swear I'm going to catch those kids—"she had raised her voice to a yell suitable for a much larger audience "—and shut them up in one of the cages until they learn some manners!" She smiled, extending her hand. "Leslie. Sophia Mallory. At last we meet."

At last? I took her hand. "I talked to Nate? He said come at three. I'm a little early."

"You're very early, but that's fine. Three is when I usually quit for the day." Sophia motioned me into the house, the air of which clutched at my lungs with the parched and smoky grasp of an overfed woodstove. Sophia was still at the door. "Nate tends to be more protective of my time than I am. You saw him on your way in?"

"I saw no one."

"That's strange." She went up on her toes and scanned the yard before coming inside. "I very much appreciate your helping me out here. Considering." She held out her arms to take my coat.

"We'll see how much help I am." I slipped out of the wool, grateful to get one less layer of warmth away from my body. Another look at her heavy sweater, and I had to wonder which one of us was out of whack.

117

She went to hang my coat on one of the hooks by the door, missed, and the coat landed in a heap on the floor. She whimpered in self-contempt before picking it up, brushing it off and securing it on the hook above which was a shelf lined with prescription bottles. "I can offer you coffee or I can offer you booze."

"What are you drinking?" I asked.

She motioned me toward the back of the house, laughing as she went. "You know, I can't remember. I haven't been sleeping. Idiot kids ringing the doorbell all hours."

"Annoying, I'm sure." I wasn't ready to volunteer my experience with the doorbell; I was unsure still whether I would volunteer anything. I followed her into the kitchen, which was small with sloping floors, lopsided cabinetry, and one massive freestanding sink of chipped white enamel that stood between the propane range and the shuddering refrigerator. The door of her fridge was covered with the tiny words from one of those magnetic poetry sets.

"You do that, too?" I said.

"Do what?"

I censored myself: *Find out first how much she knows.* "Nothing." I moved toward the round pedestal table and two ladder-back chairs that took up most of the floor space. The miniscule counter area was finished in worn, undressed granite and was piled in papers weighted in place by the phone. A second kitchen entry connected the main living room. The potbellied stove radiated ferocious heat, proof at least that the thing worked. "I'll have water, if you don't mind."

"Hope you don't mind the store-bought," she said as she pulled a glass from the cupboard and then opened the fridge, pausing for a second to read an arrangement of the magnets. She switched out a few words, her sudden smile holding the quality of private codes deciphered. Then she brought out a plastic jug of water and poured the glass full for me. "Nate and I are still trying to figure out the problem with the well. The water seemed fine when we came out here with the rental agent. Now it tastes like sulfur. So we're having to buy our water."

I took the glass and a deep swallow. "Probably needs to be shocked."

"Come again?"

"The well. If it has been standing unused for any length of time, you're going to get sulfur bacteria. The distribution lines need to be flushed out with chlorine." I peeked around the corner into the front room; the peacock was still on the wall. "You know? Shocked."

"But the water was fine. The agent himself gave us a glass."

"Did you see him take it from the tap?"

She frowned. "I can't recall."

"The ideal of good country folk dies hard, don't it?"

"Actually, in my case, that ideal has been dead and in the ground for generations."

"You mean the little girl?"

"Her and many, many others." She took a large silver barrette from the windowsill and used it to gather her braids at the base of her neck while she gazed out the window. "Still, it's more of a comfort to think we were scammed by the rental agent than to consider the alternative. You know, problem with the ground water. Or someone tampered with our well."

"Who would do that?"

"Those idiot kids have parents. Uncles and aunts. Cousins.

We aren't exactly welcome around here." The February light cast a thin pewter sheen on the curves and creases of her face, muting the richness of her complexion, exaggerating the bone-deep weariness I recognized from my own experience of sleep deprivation. I figured Sophia no older than her early thirties, but I sensed also a long-term fatigue that added years. She shook herself out of her thoughts. "What would you like to know about the project?"

I leaned over my knees to stretch my back. "How much you'd be paying me."

She turned from the window and gave me a smirk. "Why don't we go upstairs and I'll show you what I'm working on."

I followed Sophia down the entrance hall, this time noticing the framed art—watercolors, pen-and-inks, pencil sketches—hung in regular intervals on the wall. Several were of Sophia, and I, trying to be ingratiating, made a general comment that I liked them. Because I did like them. She said she'd pass that along to Nate, who was the artist. She paused to straighten one of the frames that had tilted, and sighed. "That's probably where he is. He goes out drawing. Loses track of the time." She said it as though she were reassuring me.

We climbed the stairs. She, ahead of me, recounted the New Year's Day drive out of the city in which she and Nate first saw this place; how on impulse they had decided to move up here. It was quiet and removed, perfect for both their work, and anyway, how often does a writer get to live at the epicenter of her material? I responded that I had no idea. At the top of the stairs was a truncated corridor, more of a large landing than a hall-way, flanked by doors that would open onto rooms to the front, left, and rear of the house. The heat had pooled there seeking to further its access upward. On the right wall under a museum spotlight was a framed photograph of Sophia, her shoulders bared, entwined in the arms of a young man with a long face and large, pale eyes under hooded lids. He was bare chested, his lips parted in the sort of smile that told me they'd just gotten out of bed for a breather and planned on heading back shortly. This had to be Nate. His hair, unkempt, fell about his stubbled face and the back of his neck in thick layers. Because the photograph was black and white, I could only make a guess at his coloring, brunet leaning toward muddied blond. His eyes would be pale blue. I bet he burned in the sun. The photograph had been taken outside somewhere, but the focus had been pulled so that the background—rock or water—blurred beyond recognition. Sophia and Nate, their contrasting skins yin and yanging in embrace, young, impossibly beautiful in the shelter of their egg-shaped pose. I understood then the delicate fortitude implied in Sophia's "we aren't welcome around here."

"Who took the picture?" I asked, aware she was watching me.

"Nate. We did together. Self-portrait." Her hand rested on the knob of the door that would open onto the room at the front of the house. "Our, well, not-honeymoon. Our post-deciding-to-live-together trip. Whatever *moon* that would be." She laughed. "Do you find it uncomfortably warm in here?"

"A bit," I said, gasping a laugh. "I think you're overloading the stove."

"That's Nate's doing. He claims it's always freezing in the house. He says it's colder in here than outside." Sophia pushed the door open and the landing flooded with chilled air breezing from the open windows in this other room. "He is, of course, an artist and therefore completely insane," she said in such

121

deadpanned earnestness that I had to grin. She grinned back as she ushered me into the blissfully cold room. "You do understand I say that with love?"

"Love and no doubt much respect." The sudden cooling sent a brisk shudder of relief across my shoulders along with the implicit threat that soon the relief would be too much. The sill-length sheers billowed against the incoming air. Sophia closed the door and the curtains fell to lazy ripples. The room, an architectural hodgepodge of nooks and dormers, was spare in décor with water-marred floorboards and walls painted a once cream color now yellowed with age. Between the windows stood barrister bookcases crammed with texts and papers. A bulletin board with notes and clippings took up most of the narrow space at the far end of the room. A big old desk that looked like the survivor of a schoolhouse took up most of the wall beneath the slanting line of the eaves. A computer monitor sat in the center of the desk, the screen saver scrolling royal blue text against black: GROWN-UPS PAY FOR THEIR OWN SINS. Sophia sat down in the old-style swivel chair, creaking wood slats and squeaking springs. I pulled up a tapestry-upholstered armchair, turning it so that it would best protect me from the cold.

Sophia pursed her lips for a moment and then said, "Truthfully? I didn't think I'd hear from you."

"Truthfully? I didn't think you would either."

"It's very *brave* of you to come out here, let alone talk about it on the record."

"Brave?" I shrugged. "The question is more why would you want *me*? My background doesn't lend me a lot of credibility as a source."

"I know your background, Leslie." She swiveled in the noisy

chair and hit a button on the computer's keyboard. The screen saver switched to that of a search engine listing. I could see my name in link after link. Sophia sat silently as I read down the electronic archiving of my happy little history: the shooting, the institution, the cases of missing kids I'd been involved with since. She gave me a few more seconds before turning the monitor off. "Remember who you're talking to here."

"Am I supposed to know you?"

She clasped her hands against her chest and narrowed her eyes before smiling warmly. "No. Not at all. I just thought you would have—"

"I apologize if you are big-time famous and I haven't recognized you."

"It's not a problem, really. Probably better this way. What *do* you know of the project?" She was obviously trying to suppress her delight for my confusion.

I, on the other hand, made no effort toward suppressing the suspicion rising in my awareness. "I know only what *Nate* has told me. And what you told Andrea. You're writing a book, and you want an interview for which you're willing to pay."

"What do you want, Leslie?"

"I want to know what you aren't telling me."

"Detective Burnham apparently did not share how I came to call her instead of approaching you directly." She made a face that told me I was not going to like what I was about to hear. "Does the name Phil Hogarth mean anything to you?"

"*Phillip* Hogarth?"

"That's the one."

Phillip Hogarth, my never-ending mistake. The man, who the first time we met, had told me that my name meant "from the gray fortress," and the way he had said "Leslie," the tone inside the tones, the implications, his voice on my name had unlocked every security gate between the moat and the keep. I had tried to hold him among my hallucinations; no real being should be allowed that overwhelming a presence in another's life. Being Phillip he refused to stay put. Or gone. Although our affair had battered my marriage to Greg, it had also preserved it. Inside the marriage I was safe. Phillip's unwavering interest in my darker nature was terrifying. He did not want to conquer or fix me; he wanted to know me. I did not want to be known. I hid and he hunted. Every so often he caught me outside the blind, and we *saw* each other so clearly that the fact of the other burned itself into our individual understanding of who we were. It wasn't love. Or sex. It was our mutual, unspoken certainty that we had already been buried alive and that fucking each other into oblivion was the only way to not feel the earth weighing down around us. Simply saying *his* name, here, after all these months had sent a surge of primal currents so massive through my body that my pelvic muscles clenched and my brain nearly shut down.

I smiled at Sophia. "Phillip Hogarth is who the devil wants to be when the devil grows up. What does any of this have to do with Phillip?"

"This project? Nothing, really. When I was in grad school, I picked up a few extra dollars doing research for him and some of the other lawyers at the firm. The Donald Oliver scandal?"

"Phillip has a knack for scandals."

"Boy, howdy." She laughed. "It was during that particular one, you and I spoke on the phone. Several times."

"Did we?"

"No reason you should remember me. I recognized your name

in the papers and called Phil because I knew you two were, ah, friends. He suggested I take the more indirect tack to contact you. He said you startled easily."

"Such a helpful guy."

"He said to say 'Hello.'"

Heaven help me, I could hear him say it; feel him say it. *Hello.*

"So, I feared that if Detective Burnham had mentioned Phil, you would not be quite as willing to participate."

"That there is a horse worth betting on."

"Well, you're here now, and whatever you can tell me about that night last Christmas may prove helpful in tracking down the full story of what happened here. That's the important thing, yes?" She took a manila folder from the desk and handed it to me. "This is what you found?"

Inside: the oval-cut photograph of the boy. "In the woodstove. I assume this is Kendrick. How did you get this?"

She ignored my question. "Assumptions are not the same thing as facts. That's what I'm trying to find out up here. The facts? I think we may assume, given what he left in his papers, that Kendrick and this boy in the picture had something to do with the girl's body. I understand you've seen his confession."

"Some of it. I tried to get more copies, but somebody went and lost—wait. You have the originals. And the picture. Phillip."

"He owed me one. What matters is that you have seen the way James went about confessing."

"Not enough to get the whole story."

"James could have written thousands of pages and we'd never get the whole of the story, what with the digressions and philosophizing and fantasy he hid behind."

"Couldn't hide the important stuff." I looked down at the photograph.

"He could. He did. I've gone over those pages for hours trying to figure it out. Gone over it so often, the writing is etched into my retina. The horses. The tiger. Those giant spiders on the bridge."

"Spiders? I didn't get that far."

"Be glad of that." Sophia shook her head. "The spiders arrive after James leaves the boy covering the girl with stones, which never quite gets finished. He crosses a bridge over a pit of live embers where hundreds of very phallic spiders are spinning webs of molten iron. The bridge itself happens to be one of the webs."

"And James is trapped. Sounds like guilt."

"I should hope so. It gets more gruesome and confused from there with flayed horse flesh and decapitated tigers and comets that rain down blood until God arrives, stark naked and erect in a crown of peacock feathers—"

"I saw a peacock."

"—and then the words disappear in a morass of scribbles. The whole of it reads as a bunch of wild nonsense until you take into account that a girl's body was located exactly in the sort of place Kendrick alluded to it being. If that is fact, then what is the rest of it?"

"A front-row view of how the events looked from inside his brutalized mind."

Sophia lifted her chin. "As described, those events lead one to believe that James was far from the most brutalized individual in the tale."

"He was a child at the time, too, you know. Obviously, that nursery rhyme down there on the wall is some attempt to organize, get some control over whatever horror took place here."

"Perhaps." She lifted the photo from my grasp, lightly, sharp, and fast, like a fly fisherman lifts the lure from the water. "But that is my problem, so let's get my few questions for you out of the way. Then you can leave this place and never think of any of us again." She took a small cassette recorder from the drawer in her desk. "Do you mind? This protects both of—" Her thought was stopped short by the trembling chimes of the doorbell. "Those kids." She bolted up and dashed to the window, held onto the sill, stuck out her head. "You can stop now! I know you're there!" Her posture relaxed and she pulled back inside. "Determined little things, aren't they?"

"'Little' is the operative term." I smiled; relieved to be on top of some information here. "It's mice, Sophia. In the walls. To make it stop you're going to have to disconnect the bells. That or learn to ignore them."

"Is that what you believed was going on the night you were up here? That the doorbell was ringing because of mice?"

"That was my first, best theory—wait, I never told anyone the doorbell had rung."

"Not until now, you mean." She tapped at the tape recorder.

I nodded in reluctant acknowledgment of her finesse. "You're good."

"Yes. I am." Downstairs the doorbell rang again.

molly

Dad takes Molly down to her weekly two-hour volunteer job at the Swifton convalescent home. Mom and Dad think that, given how alone she feels right now, it will be comforting to be useful. Every Saturday she helps with the recreational program that is supposed to exercise the minds of the patients, keep them alert and aware. Molly is of the opinion that if she were in a diaper and could no longer feed herself, alert and aware is the last thing she'd want to be. Molly keeps her opinions to herself.

The rec events are run by a rotating series of staffers. Some of them are kind and good-humored; some are bored and inattentive. Molly finds her attitude tends to mirror that of whoever's in charge. Usually they play bingo—which is usually a huge mistake. It never fails to collapse into a noisy fight caused by old people shouting out "Bingo!" too soon and arguments about what numbers were called and accusations of cheating and lies on the part of the bingo caller. It's worse than any baby-sitting job she's ever had. Old people swear like gang members. It's "fuck this" and "crap on you" and "drop dead you old cocksucker!" Someone always cries. Molly is supposed to go around and check their cards and reassure them that everything is as it's supposed to be, which is next to impossible. They think she's in on the conspiracy.

The regulars are in the dayroom watching a movie about gauzy Victorian girls lounging around a big rock. Molly is happy to learn from the desk attendant—a new one, named Zeke; the one who was here last time has quit; no one stays at this place long—that today they won't be playing bingo! Instead they'll be opening and sharing Valentines from families who live too far away to come visit. Molly's task, Zeke tells her, is to write out cards the staff has purchased in bulk, signing the names of family members who either forgot or couldn't be bothered to send anything. She is given a list of family names, grandchildren's ages. Just like grade school, everybody gets a Valentine. The feeling behind the card isn't as important as not feeling left out. Since she understands that particularly well these days, Molly tries to compose a little note for each card, imagining what the family news might be. The notes get longer and more complex with each card she signs.

Zeke comes by every few minutes to read over her shoulder and tell her that she's "truly cool" to give them that much attention. She wants to tell him that his interruptions are annoying, but he's new, so she figures that maybe he's nervous and trying too hard. She smiles a quick sharp smile and tells him thanks. He smiles back, bigger. There's a gap between his two front teeth, not huge but distracting. Even though he must be twenty or older, his face has a softness to it—not pudgy but no angles, as though his bones are still growing to fit him. The same thing with the rest of his body. He sort of reminds Molly of her mother's bread dough when it is rising. Pillowy. He has the longest eyelashes she's ever seen on anyone ever, although his eyes are kind of hard to see because the front part of his very shiny blond hair keeps falling across his face. Molly thinks he looks like a golden retriever puppy. He acts like one, too. *Play with me! Play with me now!*

"I'd better finish these cards." She points to the pile with her pen.

"Sure," Zeke says, still grinning, not moving.

"Yeah." She turns back to the desk, checks her lists and then writes on the open greeting card: *Happy V-day Grandma Mary, Hope you are feeling better. I'm doing good, but there's this guy in my class that's driving me bonkers because he will not leave me alone . . .*

And Zeke is back. This time to offer her candy from the box of stuff patients have received but cannot eat. She says no thank you because the taste of chocolate does not mix well with the smells of pine cleaner and old people. Besides, anyone who sends a box of caramels to someone who has no teeth is probably buying the cheap, crappy stuff, anyway.

"They're good," says Zeke, popping three in his mouth, working his jaw as his face sets in concentration against the rock-hard caramel. "Good."

Molly realizes the guy is stoned out of his head or high or something. People leave pills lying around all over this place. "Yeah."

"You're cool, Molly."

"Yeah."

"Want to do something tonight? Like a movie or something? Back at my place?" He leans in, breathes caramel into her face. "I can show you stuff I bet you've never seen. Best Valentine's Day ever."

Definitely out of his head. She doesn't answer him but goes back to the card: *I mean he's really, really bugging me.*

When Dad picks her up he hands her a bag from the drugstore; in it is the new paperback she wanted. He has also bought a tiny red velvet heart with stubby pink legs and arms open in embrace. The heart has a face with googly eyes and a ridiculous big-bad-wolf grin of white satin teeth. She pulls it out of the bag and shakes it so the eyes go around. It makes her think of Zeke and she sticks her tongue out at it, and then grins at Dad. He half smiles. She is just about to ask if maybe they could get a dog, a puppy, when he says, "We need to talk about your mom."

Molly puts the book and silly toy back in the bag. "Okay."

When they get back to the house, Emma is at the dining room table with her markers and scissors. Molly asks what she's doing. Emma tells her it's a surprise for later. "Now, go away!"

"I'm going." She takes the bag upstairs, intending to go to her bedroom, but she stops in front of the closed door to her mother's office. When her mother was sick, the first time, Molly had been almost ten years old, like Emma is now. She'd hated closed doors back then. At the hospital where they had kept Mom, you couldn't open a door without somebody first pressing a button. There'd be a terrible buzzing sound and then a clank; you only had a few seconds to get through. Back then, those sounds and the sense you had only one chance to make it had scared her so badly that she couldn't let any door stay shut. When a door was closed, it felt she couldn't ever stop paying attention, waiting for the buzzing and clank—her chance to get out. Dad would often wake up to find the front door standing wide open. He'd have to rush around making sure both Molly and Emma were still in bed, still there. He'd be angry and make Molly promise not to do that again. Back then.

Molly lays her hand against the sewing room door and then pulls it away, leaving it shut. She reaches for the switch and turns on the hall light before sitting down to read the new book, her back braced against the door.

juice

Sophia, interrupted by the occasional trill of the doorbell chime, gave me a quick outline of her book project. She had acquired a grant—with Phillip's help, she made a point of adding—to write about the ways in which our culture perceived and handled violence against children of different races and what that told children as a whole about how they were valued in that culture. "When your school is falling down around your head and your government decides to build a new football stadium rather than fix your school, what does that tell you about what's important to them?"

"Football players?"

"Exactly. So what does it tell you when four of your friends turn up dead one after another in the same vacant lot? They have the same sort of wounds. Number five is your brother. What does it tell you when no one thinks to put together a pattern of predatory homicide until victim six is found and victim six is white? So is victim seven. When they catch this beast, right after number eight, he says he moved onto white kids because he, the killer, wanted to have his work recognized."

"I remember that one. It was around the same time as . . ." I lowered my head. "Your brother?"

She shrugged. "I never knew him, really. I wasn't even two years old when it happened. But I've lived my entire life with the aftermath. I'm writing this for him, to honor his memory—not that I expect anyone to come away happy from the reading. When this story about Kendrick and the child broke, it seemed like a useful way to frame the subject."

I told her everything I could think to tell up to and including my admittedly half-assed connecting of Willet with the ardent seeker of *The Wilderness* picture book. "Kendrick probably had the book when he was a kid. He may have been fixated on it in later years—a stage of dementia, maybe, like the one my grandfather went through at the end when the only thing he wanted to talk about was how you couldn't get decent pineapple-orange ice cream any longer. For hours, the man would bitch about ice cream."

"Could be," said Sophia. "Did you ever find out who the collector was?"

"No, but then I didn't try very hard. Many of requests were made years ago. The interested party or parties may have found one and left the other requests standing. Or not. It doesn't matter. That nursery rhyme has been in print forever; I did learn that. Since the seventeenth century, at least. A person could make herself crazy trying to make it make sense. Believe me. I know what I'm talking about there. With the weather warming, they're going to bury Kendrick soon, anyway. So, it's over."

"For you, yes." She turned off the tape recorder. "I'll write you a check."

"Consider my ramblings a contribution."

Sophia shook her head and took a checkbook from the desk drawer. "By accepting the check, you are vouching for the accuracy of your story." She wrote and ripped the check off the pad. Wanting to be seen as trustworthy, I took the check without looking at the amount and thanked her. She thanked me. There seemed nothing left to say.

She walked me down the stairs to the front door. We chatted about the dreariness of the weather. I set the check on the shelf above the coat hooks—under the pretense of wrestling on my boots—I intended to accidentally leave it behind. To not deposit it or to tear it up would leave her with bookkeeping hassles. No matter how generous her budget, I could not accept money for my insignificant part in what was to this woman a mission of real personal consequence.

Sophia took a long scarf, striped in shades of purple, from one of the hooks and wrapped it around her neck before tugging on a pair of mud-streaked green galoshes. I protested that she need not make the trip out to my car. I could manage fine. She said of that she was certain, but she needed to find Nate. She then took one of the prescription bottles from the shelf above the coat hooks and tucked the bottle in her skirt pocket. "Don't forget that," she said, motioning to the check.

"I won't." I had one arm in my peacoat when the doorbell chimed. Sophia yanked the door open. No one was there.

"Fast is one thing," I said.

"But this is ridiculous?"

I walked to the door. "Look for yourself. If it were kids there'd be prints in the mud." *Ridiculous.*

"Mice then," she said. Her expression softened but more toward indulgence than agreement. She turned and strode out into the yard, closing up the dilapidated cages, slamming the gates, and yelling "Nate?" Then irritated, "*Nathaniel!*"

I, not forgetting, left the check where it was and went out to join her. "It's a big place," I called above her shouting. "He could have wandered without realizing how far."

Sophia let her hands fall to her sides. "He's late for his medication."

"Is he all right?"

"He's better with the meds." Her concern was straight-forward even if the information was not.

"Do you want some help tracking him down?" I swung shut the gate on the pen where once—I remembered—a straggle-coated, dull-eyed bison had languished. The latch caught with a bang. "My sisters and I used to run from one end of this place to the other. I know it pretty—"

"You do, don't you?" Her head tilted in conversational curiosity, but the urgency in her voice was unmistakable. "Yes, please, if you would . . ." The request trailed off into anxious silence and she started off toward the edge of the zoo where the pony stables still stood, although now weathered and listing toward collapse. I assumed she was heading to areas she knew Nate frequented. That left yet another trip to the Castle for me.

I made my way up the slope, pulling myself along with a now unconscious sense of path through the trees and wondering, again, how I had managed this in the dark without breaking my neck. The warmer weather had started the sap running, and my hands grew sticky. My fingers would smell of evergreen for days. Once on the other side of the pines, I decided that in keeping with the theme of finality, I would not risk another trip out to the precipice rock of Ralph's Nose. I made my way around the first craggy edges of the Castle, using them as a stair-step boost to a better view of the property. We used to climb all the way to the top of it, to sit in the sun, eat snow cones and spy on Dad with his latest girlfriend. No way would I attempt to scale the boulders to the very peak, even outside these slippery conditions. I picked my steps along the lower rocks, pausing every few steps to survey the bleak gray horizon. Except for a herd of deer grazing at the ambitious grasses taking advantage of the thaw, except for the endless circling of a pair of hawks, I saw nothing but empty, open fields. I could hear Sophia calling for Nate; the dampness enhanced the carrying distance of sound. A hawk's screech punctuated the heavy, quickly dimming afternoon. Dark was approaching, and although I didn't have an itemization of Sophia's concerns for this Nate person, I too felt a growing sense of necessity that we find him before night fell.

Two thirds of the way around the Castle, I saw, wedged between slabs of stone, a large sheet of paper. It had been caught by its corner and was waving in the breeze like a flag of surrender. Its position suggested it had been windblown and the snaggled edge told me it had been torn from a spiral-bound pad. Drawing paper. Nate, the artist, had been through here. I studied the rocks for the least foolish route of ascent and chose the pebble-packed rift where I could at least wriggle my toes and fingers into small spaces for something that approximated a grip. The secret to this sort of climbing was to think only of where you're headed and forbid thought of what might happen to you on the way there. I wriggled and went up until I was close enough to grab the paper without throwing myself off balance. I tore it free, clamped it in my teeth, and basically slid back to where I'd started.

The drawing, a miniature that took up less than a quarter of the page, was a faint pencil sketch of a boy and girl, dressed only in their underwear. The children were holding hands and staring directly ahead. Realistic in detail, but odd; the angles were off. The girl's braids uneven on her head. The boy's shoulders were drawn so that one was much higher than the other. The page itself was dry and unsullied—except for the marks left by my teeth. The drawing had been recently pulled free from the pad. Below me, I saw more pages, flapping against tree trunks, held in place by the breeze.

I worked my way down that slope, collecting the drawings as I went. Each a portrait of a child or children, varying periods of dress, each drawing off-kilter in a manner I was beginning to believe I should recognize. Down the hill, seven drawings in hand, I got through the trees and found Nate. He was seated cross-legged on a shelf of rock that was exposed in a downward run of earth that bottomed out in the recently refilled excavation. Much more water had gathered there, as to be expected from the thaw; it was now a pond. Nate had the drawing pad propped against his left arm as he drew with his right hand; his head bent low to the page. Other sheets of torn pages pooled and drifted about him. It seemed like he had been here for quite a while, oblivious to the cold, which would be quite the feat of concentration, as he was ill dressed in a cotton sweater. No hat. No coat. High-top running shoes of ragged blue canvas. When I got a few steps closer I could see he was shivering. Not wanting to startle him, I kept my voice soft, "Nate?"

"Hey," he said without looking up, his words chattering through his chattering teeth. "You see them?"

I picked up a few more of the discarded sheets. "They're nice. From what I can make out."

"They said that if not for the plates of rock under there, she would have sunk so far into the earth, she never would have been found."

The young man was obviously struggling with his emotions. I thought of those prescription bottles on the shelf. "It's getting a bit dark to work isn't it? We should probably be heading back."

He stopped drawing and gazed up into the sky. "Sophia's going to be ripped."

"She struck me as more worried than angry."

Instead of getting up though, he waved me over, down next to him. I kneeled in the stiff, cold grass. He spoke in a whisper. "You haven't answered me. Do you see them?" He fixed on my face with an intensity of need so naked that I had to look away.

"See *what*?"

He pointed down toward the shallow runoff pool; the water was opaque with mud and the last of the ice crazed with branched cracks. "Them?" He nudged at the sheaf of drawings in my hand. I got it. The fractured angles. I got it.

"You see these kids under the ice?"

"Not see. Feel. But I thought that since you *saw* her under the ice—"

"Excuse me?" I offered him my brand of intensity.

"It's okay. Leslie. I may call you Leslie? I thought that if you could see them, you could tell me how close I am to getting them right."

"I see no one down there, Nate."

"They feared there might be more. They searched for others. The authorities."

"That's standard procedure. Why do you think there should be more?"

"There are always more, right? If they were here, you would see them."

"Nate, I can honestly tell you that I don't see anything here but a guy who's going to be stuck in bed for three weeks with pneumonia if he doesn't get himself into something warm and dry now."

He shook his head. "It's warmer out here. Quieter, too."

My confusion blurred to a generalized alarm. "Warm or not, Sophia says you have some pills to take."

"I guess I missed a dose."

"You have allergies or something?"

He added a few quick strokes to the drawing. "Wouldn't it be easier to risk offending me by asking what the meds are for?"

"Yes, and it would be even easier if you volunteered the information without my having to ask."

He laughed. "I suppose that is true." He closed up his drawing pad and pushed himself, stiff jointed, to standing. Not as tall as I first thought, one of those bodies that's long of torso and short of leg. "Time to go," he said and offered me his hand to help me up. "You really do not see them?"

"I'm sorry, Nate, but I'm not accustomed to discussing my—"

"Epilepsy, my meds are for epilepsy." He took the drawings I had collected and stuck them in the sketchbook. "I have absence seizures. Do you know what those are?"

"You don't have to tell me."

"No. I don't," he said with the confidence of one who understood that the sharing of scar tissue was founded on competition. "Absence seizures are self-descriptive, I guess. I *disappear* every so often. For a few seconds. A minute. My brain shuts down or freezes up and I'm just not there."

"All right."

"Absent. What about you?"

"You already have some idea, Nate, or you wouldn't be asking."

"Sophia researches the facts like a scientist. I want more than facts about the phenomenon; I want the phenomenon itself. I want juice."

"Juice?" He sounded like a thirsty child. "All right. Yes. I saw someone that led to the discovery of her body. I see stuff—sometimes. Not so much anymore."

"You have visions."

"No, not *visions*." I gave up trying to make it sound sane. "No matter what you want to call it, I would not be able see these kids you're drawing because I have no idea who they are. It has to be in my head before it can be projected outward. Understand?" I could hear myself struggling to convince us both.

Apparently Nate heard it, too. "I don't know who any of them are, either. Yet they're here and they want us to know it."

"You're telling me that these kids you've drawn are connected to Happy Andy's?"

"Didn't Sophia tell you about her project?"

"Enough, but maybe not in adequate detail, huh?"

"Yeah, the detail. That's where the trouble always starts." With that he strode off for the trees. I took off after him.

We hurried. Darkness was swallowing the horizon, heading for us fast. Nate seemed sure-footed along the rocks. We made it down without incident, and as we reached the yard, I decided that I would forego any attempt at excusing myself. I started to veer my course toward my car. Nate slowed.

"Who closed the cages?"

I turned around, walking backward. "Sophia and I closed them."

"But they don't like it."

They? All those times I'd returned to Happy Andy's to find the gates flung open. Sophia's truly panicked voice rose from beyond the stables.

"Damn it, Nate! Where are you?" Sophia came around the stables, saw him, and broke into a run toward the young man, who hung his head in childlike sheepishness. Happy to leave them to their reunion, I pivoted in mid-step and picked up my pace, glancing at the long narrow pen that marked the edge of the zoo. The peafowl had been kept in there during the night. I'd halted before I realized it and found myself staring. Memory turned me on my toes. The shape of Sophia and Nate in embrace was a shadow outside the rectangle of yellow light shining from the house. That's not what held my attention, though. Around the cages and pens, around Sophia and Nate, strutted at least a dozen peacocks. Luminescent as though in full sun, they preened and clawed at the earth, their eye-studded feathers fanned and fell. Not a dozen. Fifteen. Twenty-three. And I understood that the more I tried to count the birds, the more birds would appear. So many. There were so many. *There are always more, right?*

Do you see them, Leslie? Yeah, damn it all, I saw them. I forced myself to take a step toward the house; the peacocks vanished. I kept moving forward, picking up momentum. I passed Sophia and Nate. "Forgot the check," I muttered, not certain who I was more annoyed with, either one of them or myself, but if the hallucinations were coming back on account of these two, then yes, I could damn well cash that check. The door was unlocked. I pushed inside and grabbed the check from the shelf. I felt pulled further into the house by the need to see Kendrick's drawing again, touch the oily chalk, carry the colors home on my fingers. I was halfway to it, when the doorbell rang.

"Extremely funny," I said coming back to the already open door, expecting to find Sophia and Nate laughing for the joke. They were still in the yard, speaking in hushed affection. They had not moved. And the cage doors were thrown wide. All of them, from what I could tell. Hallucination. Had to be. But then Nate lifted his head and looked about.

"They don't like it when you close the gates," he said.

"What keeps doing that?" I asked, not really wanting an answer.

Sophia pulled away from Nate; hands on her hips, she studied the yard and shrugged. "I don't know. The mice?"

love

The drive home had been unnerving; I had to turn on the interior light to make certain I was alone in the car. It was after seven when I finally pulled up to our house. I parked beside Greg's truck, got out, and tried to clear my head before facing my family. The night had turned colder, crystallizing the moisture in the air so that the exterior light fixtures wore halos. I could hear Greg working in the garage, hammering along with the beat of the rock station he had tuned to on the radio. If I were lucky, he'd already have eaten and would spend the better part of the evening out in the workshop. He was probably figuring his luck along the same lines.

Beyond the exchange of tokens, neither of us had mentioned the significance of the day. We'd cocooned ourselves in our familiar shelter of mutual disapproval, work, and skepticism to better buffer personal history. Greg had proposed on Valentine's Day, seventeen years earlier. I had said yes without hesitation. An hour later we were in a long quiet fight about church weddings that had me tearfully withdrawing my acceptance, only to be exchanging "I – do"'s the next morning at city hall. My acid to his base, the resulting turmoil between us always ended in equilibrium, which he saw as desirable and I saw as dull. Seventeen freaking years, we were still trying to figure out how to make it work either with or without the other. Ah, chemistry.

I stood outside, motionless so that the motion sensor lights would go dark. I listened to him work, listened to the rush of my own chemical nostalgia. The winsome affections between Sophia and Nate had tempered my disdain for the forced romance of the Valentine holiday. I could remember bending before those same simple emotions; the tensile wonder that had laced between myself and this man, who was at this moment actively avoiding my avoidance of him. I hated like hell that I couldn't will certainty into being. I would have, at that moment, accepted its illusory presence. I seemed able to conjure up all manner of other lost souls. Why couldn't I conjure up my own?

I made my way to the kitchen entrance, thinking to hide out the rest of the night in the sewing room. When I reached the back door it became clear that I might have to amend those plans. On the window was a large heart cut out of poster board and inscribed with Greg's and my initials wrought in girlish curlicues of Magic Marker bisected by a construction paper arrow. Emma, with her nine-year-old's obstinacy before reality, had apparently ignored our long, carefully worded talks about the predictable difficulties of reconciliation. It was Valentine's Day, we were back together, and that meant *Love*—naysaying adults be damned.

I let myself into the kitchen to find Emma, an apron over her best dress, futzing at the stove over a skillet full of her one specialty, grilled cheese sandwiches. "Mom! You're just in time. I made supper for you and Dad." She lifted one of her creations with a spatula. "See. They're heart-shaped."

"Oh Em, you didn't have to go to all that trouble."

"It's not trouble." She flipped the heart onto its soft uncooked side. "And I made tomato soup. See? I set the table in the dining room. Go sit down."

"I need to do a couple things in my office—"

"You can do that later. Go sit down."

Cupid had spoken. "I'll go sit down then." I left my coat on the clothes tree by the back door and pushed through into the dining room, which was awash in candlelight. Emma had placed every candleholder she could find on the table, which was set for two with the good china and decorated with a drinking glass vase of tissue paper roses on pipe cleaner stems. Molly, in jeans and sweatshirt, her hair caught in a loose knot and shot through with pencils, was seated at the far end of the table, reading—or trying to by the unsteady light.

"Hey," she said without looking up.

"Hey, yourself. Would it make any difference if I told you yet again how much your eyes might appreciate adequate illumination?"

"I could be watching TV," she said, ending the discussion. "I'm supposed to go get Dad when you come home. This is a surprise, you know."

"Well, it would appear that I am now home."

"Yeah. Surprise."

"Your father?"

"I'll go get him." She rose from her chair without taking her eyes from the page. "I told Em this wasn't a good idea."

I took my place at the table and saw the foil-wrapped chocolate kisses Em had laid out on the rims of our plates. "It's not exactly a bad idea." Molly gave a snort of dismissal and pushed out into the kitchen, book in hand. I shifted, restless against the sullen thrum of hunger in my belly; the buttery aromas of the grilling bread only making it worse. Desperate, I peeled the foil from a few of the chocolates and gobbled them down. I heard Greg come in, Emma's ordering him to wash his hands. She then yelled at Molly to leave the soup alone. I looked at the rim of my plate and quickly rearranged the remaining kisses, in case Emma might be offended that I'd disrupted her efforts.

Greg came into the dining room buttoning the cuffs of his flannel work shirt. "Emma Stone: Romance Nazi."

"Poor little thing. How could we say no to this?"

"Who said we wanted to say no?" He sat down and set about deconstructing the origami swan Emma had made of his napkin. "We have to eat, right?"

"Right." I followed his lead and took up my napkin as well. We fumbled with our place settings. Greg rearranged the candleholders toward the empty end of the table, away from the tinder of the paper roses. He then folded his hands in his lap and avoided looking at me. The candlelight blunted his displeasure with me, softening the set of his jaw and the lines that his life had worn into his face, giving him, even in repose, the expression of a man hell-bent on solving the puzzle before him. But the candlelight also deepened the shadows in such a manner that his increasing leanness—pounds dropped due to the physical demands of his work—took on a mournful quality. As though he sensed my broach of his privacy, he cleared his throat and said, "So, what about Willet?" with the same strained interest you'd ask a rival about that winning lottery ticket.

Any hint of my morbid sense of inevitability would have had us fighting again in seconds. I tried to sound indifferent. "It was interesting enough."

"Interesting?"

"She told me about her project. I told her my happy little Christmas story. Got paid." I would not have told him about the hallucination under any circumstance; I didn't see much point in mentioning Nate's strangeness—let alone Phillip's involvement.

"How much did you get?"

"Forgot to look." I pulled the folded check out of the pocket of my jeans and handed it to Greg, who leaned over to see it better in the candlelight.

He laughed—"Holy Christ"—and handed it back to me.

I saw the amount, the lovely little zeros, and gasped. The pleasure of easy money gave over fast to a recall of the nature of bribery. Sophia was assuming that by giving me this extreme amount, I would be able to infer the possibility of more. Good living in Grant City.

"So, you're done now?" Greg lowered the check from my gaze.

"As done as I'm going to get."

"Wrong answer."

"Yes, I'm done." Too late, I realized I was leaning into the denial; I leaned when I lied. What a poker player would call my tell.

"Leslie?"

"For Chrissake, Greg—" I straightened my posture. "I'm not going back."

Emma pushed into the dining room. "Are you fighting?" she said in a tone that bore a hazard of tears. Greg and I exchanged a glance and shook our heads. "Okay," she said as she held the door for Molly, who was carrying our dinner, her face set in a grimace of concentration as she managed the tray overladen with steaming soup bowls, a platter of sandwiches, and champagne flutes brimming with cola. Emma served while Greg and I made the appropriate sounds of delight and anticipation. She set our glasses before us. "Now you can make a toast."

Greg lifted his glass by the stem, trying not to slosh soda over the rim. "To our talented chef."

"No, Dad. Make a toast with Mom."

Molly sighed heavily. "Let it go, Em; they aren't—crap, don't start crying."

"It's all right, Emma." Greg turned to me and smiled the knowing smile of a longtime trench mate. "Happy Valentine's Day, Leslie."

Perhaps this was the best we could hope for, this sense of united resistance against those forces that would tear us apart, none the least of which was ourselves. I raised my glass to meet his. "Happy Valentine's Day, Greg."

"Did you know," said Molly, pulling a pencil from her hair, "that Valentine's Day marks the *death* of this guy named Valentinus. We learned it yesterday in language arts. He, Valentinus, had something wrong with his brain—what did they call it—oh yeah, epilepsy—"

"Excuse me?"

"You know, Mom, the thing where you jerk around and you can bite off your own tongue?"

"The word is 'seizure,' Molly."

"Well, yeah. So when Valentinus died and they made him a saint, he became the official saint guy of people with epilepsy—why are you looking at me like that?"

"Nothing." I wasn't about to confide Nate's medical concerns to my kid.

"Let's drop it," Greg said with traffic cop authority.

"Now Dad is angry." Emma could barely get her voice through her tears. "Why do you have to ruin everything, Molly?"

Molly glared at her sister before turning on her heels and hurrying, head down, out of the room. Emma fell to her knees in sobs. "Nothing ever goes right around here."

Experience had taught us to let Emma's epic tragedy play itself to conclusion without audience response, or we'd be getting curtain calls and encores for a week. Greg picked up one of the congealing grilled cheese hearts and ripped it in two.

"This," he said as he handed half to me, "would have to be love."

I bit into the thin cold sandwich. "Yep," I said, mouth full, "would have to be." We ate. Emma wailed.

We went to bed around eleven, both pleading extreme fatigue in advance of whatever the other might have had in mind. Greg was asleep in minutes, turned on his side away from me. I would begin to drift off only to hear Phillip's voice in my ear: *Hello.* I pulled the pillow over my head trying to block him out, hating myself for the disloyalty of Phillip's unbidden presence in my mind, in Greg's and my bed, hating him for refusing to stay in the past where he belonged. Who the hell did he think he was?

It was after midnight when I knew that I would not be sleeping. I wanted to bake something complex and time con-suming. Croissants, maybe. All that folding of dough and work-ing of butter—but then I might wake Greg and he knew what sort of work really went on in my night kitchen. I'd asked him to deal with enough in the last twenty-four hours. I crept out of bed, trying not to send any undo movement through the mattress springs, grabbed my robe from where it had fallen on the floor, and made for the sewing room.

After my eyes adjusted to the sudden blare from the overhead light, I took Sophia's check from where I'd stuck it among my other banking papers and sat down on the floor to study it. It really was way too much money; she wanted something more from me, but what? The check number was 1011, drawn on Willet First National Savings and Loan. Brand-new account. Why go to that much trouble for a temporary residence? Chance to chat up the locals maybe. The imprint gave only her name: Sophia Mallory.

I studied her handwriting, her rendering of numerals and letters, her signature; she had the sort of schooled penmanship that indicated a pride for such matters. I turned the check over, endorsed it *for deposit only* with my slash-and-dash scrawl, and placed it out of the way on the bed behind me. I went to the computer to find out what I could about Sophia herself, her brother's death, thinking it might be possible to reverse engineer the larger logic of our meeting.

The dial-up number was busy and so began the auto repeat process. I waited, chin propped on hand, elbow propped on desk. I had been one of the last holdouts when it came to the Internet. The word *web* in World Wide Web was not reassuring; I had seen how fast my kids' minds had gotten caught up in its infinite threads. They sat rapt before it, this spinning oracle that spoke for a suspect deity; it would answer all their questions without once asking why they wanted to know. One simple query could have you free-associating your way into hellish corners of cruelty or boredom. One's friends were abbreviated text without context. The box of light, so compliant, so untiring, so willing that it seduced trust, loyalty, love within minutes because it made us forget that behind that bright, cool subservience roiled the usual dark, hot human desires to possess and control. It was important, I told my daughters, myself, to remember that every pixel, every bit of datum, everything we saw on that screen had been put in play by active choice, by someone who wanted something. *Having once created fiction.*

Finally, the connection found its handshake; the modem sang. Not having Sophia's brother's name or the exact dates, I would have to refine down from general references. I typed in "Mallory, victim, fifth." I could not bring myself to type the more descriptive words for the nature of that victimization. Hits came up in the thousands. To be expected. Molly had once, for my benefit, repeated an experiment they'd conducted in her social studies class to show me that a search on "war" would turn up three times as many links as came up for "peace." This is the sort of information that surprised a teenage girl. I'd been kind of relieved to learn the gap had not been larger.

The first link promised a thoroughly detailed account of the crimes. I didn't want detail at this point, just a name to contemplate. I did, as I had told Sophia, recall the coverage of these murders, which had occurred on the other side of the country. By the time I heard tell of them, I had already been balming the sting of my own family trauma with massive infusions of true crime. The more horrible, the better the effect. I numbed my new knowing of the world through descriptions of violence that kept me afraid and therefore unable to think. Everyone thought that I was showing an early interest in police work and that I had decided to follow my father's path. What no one understood at the time was that no decisions were involved. I had to become what he had been in order to stop what he had done. That I could not do so was the sort of information that surprised me still this late in life.

What I had *not* told Sophia was that of the coverage I remembered poring over so enthusiastically, I only recalled the three last victims: the three white boys. That realization had left me with queasy dissonance between feelings of shame and wanting to protest my innocence. I could not know what had not been told. But I also knew that someone had chosen not to tell. *Having once created . . .* The only logical reasons for such a choice made me heartsick: The first five did not count enough to cover. *Fiction.*

I braced myself for impact and clicked on the link. There was a long introductory section on the case history and a detailed biographical profile of the killer, who had been found sleeping in his car at a truck stop. I remembered this part. The murder weapon, a hunting knife still bloodied—I remembered—on the seat beside him along with some toys, which authorities suspected had something to do with the way the victims had been lured into the car. The victims themselves were listed, each with one of those blue-background school portraits, last name first, in the order of their deaths, without any information other than age, date of disappearance, and date and location where their bodies had been found. No profiles on these boys. No mention of favorite foods or music or movies. How had they been doing in school? What would they have watched on television if they had come home as expected on the day they went missing? We had only the most rudimentary details. It was that war and peace phenomenon, so much easier to generate language about violence than it is to find words for what that violence has obliterated. I read down the list, saying the names, the ages aloud: Simms, John Darius, 10; Jordan, Thomas Owens, 13; Barterson, Tobey, 10; Jones, Clayton Samuel, 10; Mallory, Joseph Stephen, 12. And then the ones who had generated national interest: McGregor, Edward C., 10; Gates, Gordon Matthew, 12; North, Charles William, 12.

Sophia's brother had been broad of cheekbone and narrow of chin, like his sister. His coloring was not quite as dark as hers. His head was clouded by an Afro style that only added to the head-too-big-for-his-body look boys get as they enter the first growth spurt of puberty. He held his slender shoulders back, his eyes shining with laughter as though the photographer had just ordered him—and every kid before and after—to sit up straight and settle down. Joseph's easy smile revealed a need for a future date with an orthodontist. A relaxed, happy kid. I wondered if Sophia's expression had ever been as careless as her brother's here. Probably not. That's what she meant by "aftermath."

Suddenly I was seeing too much. I scrolled the screen up, away from any of the boys' photographs, but I could sense Joseph's presence being added to the repertory troupe of unavenged kids in my head. *There are always more, right?* The screen was set up as a stack of file folders, with menu options listed across the top of the tabs: Overview, Case History, Profiles, Evidence, Photographs, Media Links.

I clicked on the Evidence tab. This brought up an array of thumbnail photographs detailing different angles of the truck stop parking lot; the car—a sun-faded turquoise behemoth—inside and out; the knife; the toys. A descending order of intimacy. I'd seen most of these before; I'd gone looking for them in the pages of tabloids and my father's police magazines. I clicked about, enlarging the washed-out images at random, seeking the old numbness of overload, more sensation than my mind could handle. I hit the picture of the toys, which brought up a set of thumbnails of individual evidence shots, sets of differing angles. So much detail. What was it Nate had said? The trouble starts in the detail.

I remembered the toys—or remembered remembering right then as the images increased in resolution: the windup puppy dog, the paddleball game, the music box radio that ran illustrations through the dial display as it played "Old Macdonald," and the picture book. Toys for toddlers. Why had these boys fallen prey to trinkets so beneath their years? I remembered asking that of my father. Why would baby toys appeal to teenagers? How had the killer *known* these toys in particular would work? My father had no answers. No one ever would, he said. Who could know how many boys had walked right past the trap? Who could say why these kids had walked into it? That nonsolution had not placated me. I was a kid; I wanted absolutes like gravity and homework and vanishing mothers. So I had gone back to staring at pictures of the toys, trying to figure it out. And here, remembering, it still bothered me. Even though the external features of his victims were different, his victims were essentially the same kid: the helpful good boy who, although well-warned away from offers of candy and money, would not think twice about retrieving the plaything left on the curb for the man in the turquoise car. I went through each picture, enlarging each detail, studying each, trying to figure it out. The mechanical dog. The paddleball. The music box. The picture book.

The picture book. How could I have forgotten? More

important, how could I have not caught the memory before now? Or had I deliberately avoided it by stopping my search? I studied the photograph of the book's cover, the same one that had been posted at those bookstore sites. The one I had replicated badly on the wall behind me from the replication on the wall up in Willet. The last photograph was a close up of the back inside cover, the left-leaning script in faded ink, in the upper corner: *James Kendrick*.

I could not remember having seen Kendrick's name in connection with any part of this case before. Did memory have a blind spot, too? If so, it would have to be a different sort of blindness because unlike the exterior world, memory does not move of its own accord. Memory chooses what is seen, and if given reason enough to not remember seeing the moon, memory could make the moon stay gone forever.

Driven by a sort of amnesic panic to find this newly seen part of the past, I hunted around the site and then for other sites, trying to locate pictures from inside of the book, to see the illustrations, the text. None to be found anywhere. But I must have seen Kendrick's name in the studying I'd done as a kid. That would explain why—the only rational explanation why—I had been seeing peacocks. I had been remembering *The Wilderness* since Kendrick's death without letting myself see it. This would be the rational explanation as to why Sophia Mallory had taken up residence in the final refuge of a man who, with or without knowing, had played a part in the undoing of her family. The epicenter of her story.

the ant and the raging sea

rain

Over the next couple of weeks, I read every piece of Sophia's writing I could locate. Lots of magazine articles, essays pertaining to culture and race that ranged in tone from academic detachment to deliberately provoking anger by generous applications of salt and vinegar to old wounds. Sophia anticipated how her audience read. In none of these articles, however, had she mentioned her brother, Joseph. She'd been saving his story for when she could tell it fully. Her reticence on the subject demanded a sense of propriety stronger than my curiosity; it would have been wrong to go poking though her family history, one that she held so private, without invitation. I would not pursue this connection between her brother and Kendrick unless she asked. Sophia did call several times to clarify points of my interview. We chatted about Nate, their well water, the research. I engaged her in any topic that would signal my continued interest in her project, but she offered no more work. Still, she called often enough to make me think she intended to keep my interest active.

Other calls came in as well. Those listen-and-click-offs to my cell continued at irregular intervals. The caller's number always showed up as "private." A nuisance, but compelling, as whoever it was was waiting longer to hang up. My repeating "hello?" had given over to reassurances of "I'm here," and then to sitting silently with the silence on the other end. No voice had yet been offered, although I did make out the occasional environmental sounds of traffic or cash registers before the connection was terminated. I could have tracked down the source with minimal effort, but the thought that these calls were somehow related to Kendrick with his legacy of questions was a comfort. I wasn't ready to give up the sense of purpose that came with the implications of the lengthening of each call. Someone wanted to tell me something. The best of it was that I didn't have to explain or justify or rationalize anything to Greg because, hey, this guy was calling me.

Sophia phoned the night of February 28 to let me know that Kendrick had been buried earlier in the day. She had attended the interment. I didn't volunteer that I understood why she would need to do that. The next afternoon, I'd driven up to Willet alone to see the grave. An appropriate use of the oddness of a twenty-ninth day in February, I thought. The grave, raked smooth, flanked by rolls of sod waiting to be laid, was marked with a simple white cross of weatherproof fiberglass. The marker was so they could find him again should his family ever show. I stayed longer than I'd expected, taking in the quiet on that bright, warm day. I was waiting for something, one of my peacocks or one of the lost children of my mind or maybe Sophia and Nate. When it at last occurred to me that what I was waiting for was some sign that my part in this was not over, I'd left the cemetery and gone home.

Bereft of things to do in the days that followed, I concentrated on looking after Greg's bookkeeping and stock in the workshop. On a sandpaper and glue run to the hardware store, I noticed a Help Wanted sign posted near the cash register. I asked about the work and was hired on the spot for part-time customer service in the garden center. We were well into the mud pit of March; most of my work was filling out orders for delivery of truckloads of mulch and gravel. We sold a lot of phlox and pansies and hanging baskets of impatiens. Weed prevention and fertilizers. I discussed the merits of one shrub over the next as I helped customers load their carts with future hedges. I liked the physical work and was gratefully tired at the end of a shift. Fatigue made a reliable inoculation against fantasy. The job was keeping me busy thirty-some hours a week; we had a little extra income, and Greg was benefiting from my employee discount.

Newbie to the payroll, I pulled lots of time with the weekend crew when we were swamped with do-it-yourself types. Traffic would slack off on Monday, and staff would be scaled accordingly. My weekday hours were often solo, which was fine with me. I off-loaded flats and priced seed packets, transplanted root-bound young plants into larger pots while reciting that old poem on an endless loop: *I saw a peacock; I saw a blazing comet; I saw cloud* . . . And the sturdy oak and the pismire and the sea. It was more entertaining and took longer than it might first seem, what with all the permutations. Each turn through, I shifted the descriptive clauses both in and out of the rhyme scheme. I played with anagram structures. *The Wilderness* as anagram in the poem didn't work; the title had thirteen letters, the poem only twelve lines. Still, the title had to point toward something in the verse. Besides, the wordplay gave my mind something to do, the meter of the poem set a rhythm to my day.

On the days it rained we were welcome to work indoors until summoned by a customer's needs, but I chose to station myself in the small shed of the garden center's office, where I answered phones and checked for requested inventory on the computer—

in between idle searching on "Kendrick" and "Wilderness." Which is what I was doing on this Monday, two days past the official arrival of spring. Rain was slugging the earth, a downpour so dense that it veiled the clear view of the parking lot. I was soaked through from dragging tables of annuals under the shelter of the awnings to keep the onslaught from shredding the flowers.

Back in the shed, I tried to avoid dripping on keyboards and catalogs. The roll of paper towels they provided for us to wipe our hands was of little use in drying my hair or clothes, but I squeezed what water I could into the toweling, leaving a soggy heap of paper in the wastebasket. My wet clothing wicked away any warmth from my skin. I began to shiver. Chilled, miserable, certain I was getting sick, I decided that since I could not possibly feel worse, I might as well call my sister.

Joanne answered with her honey rich, inside-sales, "how may I help you?" voice, which acidified fast. "What's wrong, Leslie?"

"Why do always assume something is wrong?"

"It's you, isn't it?"

I took a beat to let that one roll by. "I was calling to see if you'd found it."

"Refresh my memory, Les. What did you want again?"

"The poem thing? The nursery rhyme I sent you last month? You said you were going to look through our old stuff."

"Oh. That. What the hell is a *pismire*?"

"It's an ant."

"Well, it sounds vaguely obscene."

I repeated the definition for her, exaggerating my pronunciation: "It is an ant." Joanne was only half-listening. I could hear her typing away, multitasking. She hated it when I called her at work. She barely tolerated me calling her at all. "Say it with me, Jo. Pismire. Piss. Ant. Pissant."

"Lovely."

"*Pissant* is a word. It means *insignificant*." I doodled with the pen, putting black ink insects into the margin of an order form. "Can't spell *insignificant* with out *if I can't*."

"Or *separate* without *a rat*. What do you want, Leslie?"

I couldn't help but laugh. "I'm not asking you for a kidney, here, Joanne. For the third time: Did we ever have a book with the pismire rhyme in it?"

"Did you ask Denise?"

"She said to ask you."

"We had a lot of books, Les." That we did. On top of our ever-late library borrowings, my family had possessed its own eclectic stacks of trashy paperback thrillers, textbooks, and *Readers Digest* abridgements. My father held most of these off-limits; that only made them more appealing for late-night shelf raids. We learned Dad's prohibition had possessed a double reverse logic. He had told us years later that he knew we'd read them on the sly. He also knew that one Harold Robbins sex scene could scare a kid into celibacy for decades.

My sisters and I had our own books, of course, but those had been divided up and shared as the sons and daughters and cousins proliferated. When Dad died, Joanne and Denise had gone through his shelves hoping for first editions of worthy titles. What they had determined of no value went to the church rummage sale. Everything else had gone with Joanne. De facto curator of our family mementos, Jo remained the one rooted most firmly in our Swifton past. Even though hundreds of miles and dozens of years from here, she had the best recollection of the minutiae of our childhood.

"Maybe we did have it in one of the books. I have a big book of poetry. It was Mom's. I'm not giving Mom's things to anyone."

"I don't need the book. I just want to know if the poem has a title. Do you remember if it had a title?"

"I don't even remember the poem, sweetheart. I didn't get a whole lot of reading time back then."

I rolled my eyes and made a face at the phone. Joanne was the eldest, four years older than I. After Mom took off, the maternal responsibilities had defaulted to her; at ten years of age, she had been supervising much of the household. Denise, who was eight at the time, could be counted on to help, keep herself quiet and out of trouble. I, on the other hand, had been moody, obstinate, given to tantrums. Joanne, overworked and frightened and grieving for Mom in a way I never would, had resented much of her life and me in particular. Unlike Mom, however, Joanne had seen no need to even try to protect me from the knowledge that I was the defining element in her sense of being trapped. She had shared her misery with me through determined silences, frost-skimmed stares, skin-breaking pinches, dead arms, and the occasional shoe to the shin. At times my legs were so bruised, I had to wear kneesocks in summer. But bruises fade. We'd survived each other, our selves, the emptiness. Distance and the flow of years had eroded some of our furious mistrust of each other. We'd learned to be civil. Sort of.

"Could you look through what you have at your house? Please?"

"When I get a chance. I really have to go, Leslie." She hung up without saying good-bye. *Pissant* really did sound a lot like *piss off.*

Even if Joanne could find the poem, I doubted it would give me any new information. I'd scoured the local libraries and bookstores, sources online and off-, trying to figure out why, in this one instance, the old anonymous parlor trick of a rhyme had been called *The Wilderness.* In every other printing I could find—including references to its very first publication in something called the *Westminster-Drollery* back in 1671—the piece, if given a title, went by its first line: "I saw a peacock with a fiery tail." If anything changed, it was in the punctuation, some versions used commas, some did not; almost all insisted on the period at the end of the final line. Kendrick had written it out on the wall with the commas; that was the version that I took as correct.

The rain started coming down harder; I drew more ants along the order form; those gave over to a rain of commas and semicolons. My teeth were chattering. I had heard only the occasional slam of a car door and the squeals of young children as they dashed with parents for the store's entrance. No one had come out to my area since I'd started my shift. I had less than an hour left; it was time to make my own dash for the warmth of the store. It took a few minutes to close up the computer and shut down the customer service windows. I grabbed the padlock for the door and stepped out under the shallow ledge of the shed roof. My foot sank into a puddle that came up to my ankle. The whole yard was inundated. Rain cascaded from planters and the bowls of the bird-feeder display. The pallets supporting the plastic bags of mulch and topsoil were sagging beneath the weight of waterlogged loam. It was twenty yards of open deluge between me and the doors, automatic sliders that let customers come and go from inside the store to the garden area. I snapped the padlock closed and took off in a dead run, splashing, feet close to floating in my flooded sneakers.

The automatic door did not slide open to receive me. I pressed my face to the glass—rain running down the back of my neck, under my sweater—and rapped with my knuckles until one of my fellow employees wandered over and pointed down. I was standing in close to two inches of accumulated rain. The doors couldn't be opened. He motioned and mouthed to go around front to the store's main entrance. I was already as wet as I could possibly get, so I turned and walked—waded—toward the garden center gate and the parking lot.

A tall figure in a pale coat was making haste in my direction. His black umbrella was lowered against the pummeling rain. I shouted at him, gesturing. "Go in the front door!"

He didn't alter his direction. I shouted, louder. "You can't get in this way!" He kept coming as though he had not heard or did not care. I pushed the rain and wet hair out of my eyes, saw, and stopped where I was, waiting the way one waits for impact in the unavoidable collision.

"Mr. Hogarth," I said, trying to get the upper hand by getting in the first word.

"Mrs. Stone." He tilted his umbrella to divert the rain from my face and gave me his best con-artist smile. "Hello."

"Good-bye." I tried to push past him.

"This is business, Leslie. Can we go somewhere and talk?"

"We are somewhere. Start talking."

He stuck his hand outside the shelter of the umbrella, let his hand fill with rain, and then dumped it to the ground. "Sophia Mallory called a couple hours ago. Nate's missing."

"I'm sorry to hear that. How long?"

"He wasn't there when she got up yesterday morning. She doesn't know what to do."

"Call the Willet police. In Nate's case, I'd call the hospitals— at least alert them to his condition. You know how this works."

"We need to handle this quietly. Can we please go inside?"

"I'm rather enjoying the rain."

"You're shivering." He made a movement as though he intended to take off his coat and give it to me. I shook my head, meaning to say no to any offer or request.

"I'm fine with things as they are now. Thank you."

He fixed me with a cold courtroom-honed assessment, running odds on angles of approach. His staring made me shiver harder. Prey senses when it has been targeted. He tilted his head. "May I have one question?"

"No." I lifted my chin, met his gaze just as hard. "I'm smarter than that, Phillip. Finally."

"What you are right now is scared. You really want in on this, but you're scared; that's why you can't deal with even one little question."

"A dare?"

"Double dog."

"All right. One question."

"What is Nate's full name?"

I remembered Sophia yelling into the night. "Nathaniel. His name is Nathaniel."

"Nathaniel what?"

167

"Don't know; it never came—" I jumped, backward, into the full fall of the rain. "He's a Kendrick."

"That's what she tells me. Nathaniel Kendrick."

"Why would she hide that?"

"Are you sure she's hiding it or did you just not ask? Oops. That's two questions. Sorry."

"If he's family, how could he let Kendrick's body go unclaimed?"

Phillip tapped the side of his nose. "That would be question three." He took a step toward me so that I was under the umbrella again and flicked a drop of water from my ear. He let his hand come to rest on my shoulder. "Can we go now?"

I picked up his hand and let it fall away from me. "You can go now."

"Wow," he said softly. "I'm impressed." He jostled the umbrella. "Can you take this for a second?" I grabbed the umbrella's handle. He let go, flexed his long thin fingers as though he were arthritic. He took me by the upper arms and gently—pushing backward—straightened my posture. I had been leaning into my dismissal of him. "Okay then, Leslie." He turned and headed off into the rain, leaving me the umbrella.

Did he think that since I was already drenched, I would take pity on him, wolf turned mongrel puppy in the rain, and run to give him back his umbrella? Yet the farther away he got, the harder it became to watch him go. I tried to look beyond him at the headlights of the traffic passing on the street. I looked up into the sky and then down at my feet, obscured in the rising water, but my eye kept finding its way back to his retreating presence. Damn it. He was not going to do this to me again. Neither was I. I shouldered the umbrella like a weapon and pivoted, watchwoman at the gates of temptation, so that my back would be to him.

There in the rain, not five feet in front of me, was the boy from the photograph, his tweed suit untouched by the wet, his head down, face hidden by the cap and his unkempt hair. His hand was working, gripping and releasing. He was holding a rock. His head began to come up, slowly, he was going to show me his face and I knew I would not be able to bear seeing.

I threw the umbrella aside and ran for the parking lot. Phillip, who was taking one last cruise past the garden center, nearly ran me down. I fell against the hood of the Jag, catching myself with both hands spread flat against the warm metal. We stared at each other through the swath cut clear by the wipers. I held up four fingers and mouthed, "Why do we have to keep it quiet?" The auto locks on the Jag's doors disengaged. I pushed myself to standing and got in the car. He didn't say a word, but tossed me the towel he had wrapped around his neck. We pulled away, and I risked a peek at the spot where the boy had been. He was gone, of course. The umbrella was floating, upended, spinning in the wind.

greg

The rain doesn't let up all day, slowing the dry time on joint compound. The day seems a waste, but no one complains. The job originally contracted was only a kitchen remodel. That has since expanded to the entire downstairs, although we have nothing in writing. The project is going to take months; what's another day. They're both professors; one is in mathematics, the other is in science. The house, one of the old farm properties on the edge of Swifton, is a wreck of a place, but the owners speak in terms of potential.

They have a child, a toddler, who has a problem with his eyes and is trying to adjust to thick lenses, which are held in place by an elastic strap that fits about his head. He hates the glasses and fights to pull them off. He has to be constantly distracted. I hand over planed wood curls from the floor, the broken ends of shims, chunks of wallboard, old drawer pulls. I sand down scraps of two-by-fours that he can use as blocks. He and I spend a lot of time together. The wife, his mother, is pregnant again, but not that far along. She is having a rotten stretch of nausea, and is housebound because of it. I hear her running to the bathroom several times a day. Her presence in the house hums with what Leslie's obstetrician called "second-child syndrome"; she knows what is waiting for her, knows there's nothing she can do about it.

They never mention how much time I spend with their son;

instead they tell me they appreciate my craftsmanship; they are in no rush for me to finish. Time is infinite, the woman says as she unconsciously rubs at her swollen belly the same way Leslie used to do. She takes a piece of chalk I use to mark up boards and proceeds to work an elaborate equation on the unfinished wallboard of her slowly reconfiguring kitchen. "See," she says as she underscores one of those sideways eight symbols, "Infinite. It never fucking ends." I nod in enlightened agreement, my ear to the telephone. It's after dark. I've called every number I can think of; I can't find Les.

It is only back at the house that I find out Leslie has no idea where she is or when she'll be home. I learn this from Emma, who greets me at the door, Les's note in hand, which is hard to process because Em is gushing with news, trying to tell everything at once: Mom is working and Em needs poster board and the dentist called about her braces appointment. Em hands over her mother's written explanation, hoping for a more optimistic translation than her fears are giving her.

"One thing at a time, Em." The note is the usual list of promises and apologies, to be stuck on the message board beside the phone. Emma waits for further reassurance. I point out Leslie's writing on the calendar. "Already have the dentist thing on the list, see? And we're bound to have one piece of poster board somewhere in this house. Where's your sister?"

"Up in her room being mad. What about Mom?"

"She'll call."

"When?"

"When she gets a chance."

"Will you tell her I need poster board?"

"We *have* poster board, Emma."

171

"But you will tell her."

"Yes, Em. I will tell her." And as I say it I know that what I really want to tell Leslie is to not bother coming back, to pack up her one-woman freak show and take it to some other town, because if she's so intent on leaving us alone, she can just leave us alone. The phone begins to ring. It's Leslie; I know it from the ring. The woman possesses authentic genius for knowing the precise moment she's gone too far. I can hear her breathless explanations in the space between the bell tones. She will be astonished by her own actions, regretful, giddy.

"That's Mom!" Emma makes a grab for the phone and nearly shouts into the receiver. "I need a piece of poster board."

It never fucking ends unless we end it.

indenture

I asked Emma to put her dad on the line and heard her say,
"Mom wants to talk to you," as though he were close by. The
receiver buzzed with a hushed anticipatory static. Then I heard
Emma again. "Don't you want to talk to her?"

I was calling from the pay phone in the lobby of the Aberdevine Motel, a roadside place about ten miles out of Willet. We'd
arrived less than an hour earlier, in separate cars. I had insisted
that Phillip take me to my car in the employees' part of the lot. I
wanted to go by the house to change into dry clothes. The last
thing anyone needed was to spot that red Jaguar in our driveway. I left a note for my husband and daughters, so it wasn't as
though Greg had no clue that I'd gone. Emma again: "Dad?" On
the floor beside me, a plastic bucket was catching a slow leak
of rain through the drop-ceiling panel. The bucket had been
emptied recently, and each drop of water that hit it thudded
loudly against the bottom. Greg still didn't come on the line.
Maybe he'd gone to pick up one of the extensions so he could tell
me what he thought of me without Emma's audience. He was
furious; I already knew that before I called. I had planned what
to tell him: I would not compound this breach of his trust with
falsehoods—nor was I about to say "Yeah, hi, Greg, I'm up here
at a motel with Phillip Hogarth."

Phillip was back in the room tending to Sophia, who had fled
the house in Willet and stationed herself in this roadside motel

on the other side of town. She had told Phillip already she could not go back to the farm property, though she would not tell him why. It had taken us nearly ten minutes of convincing to get her to unlock the motel room door and let us in. One look at the woman and I could tell it would be unwise to leave her alone no matter what was happening with Nate. That was what I was going to tell my husband. Greg needed to know only that Nate was missing and that Sophia was in no state to handle this on her own.

I heard him exhale into the receiver. The first apology was out of my mouth before he'd finished saying my name. "I'm sorry—"

"You always are."

"This is real work, Greg. I've been on the clock since I was contacted about Nate's disappearance. Every minute here is billable." Phillip had told me to forward my invoices to his firm.

"That's nice for you." His tone was level.

"For us. Em is going into braces next month."

"Yes. I know."

As always his nonchalance troubled me more than his rage would have. We should fight at moments like this, slash at each other with accelerating ferocity until the pain of the moment had our full attention and the fear we held for each other's safety was out of mind. This was the Greg I expected and yet, every time I got this Greg, his effortless disinterest felt like the thump of a failing engine. "Take care of yourself, Leslie." He hung up without a word about wanting me to hurry home or asking where they could reach me.

I left the lobby and hurried through the chill of the open-air corridor. The rain had settled into a sulky drizzle. Moths and flies, slowed by the cold, bounced in lazy glances off the overhead fixtures and the lit windows of the other occupied rooms. Television sound traveled through the doors, as did voices both in conversation and in the stifled cries of more physical communications. The room we were in, at the end of the row, gave off no hum of inhabitation. I'd taken the key so that I could get back without having to convince anyone of my intentions.

Neither Sophia nor Phillip remarked on my return. Sophia had not moved since I'd left. She had propped herself against the headboard of one of the double beds, the farthest side of the one farthest into the room. She clutched her knees to her chest using them to hold the pillow she'd pressed to her middle. Her flannel pajama pants were ruched up to her knees; she had pulled the sleeves of her thermal undershirt over her hands—this is what she had on when she left Happy Andy's. Phillip was seated in the desk chair, straddling it backward, talking on his cell phone, quietly persisting on the necessity of some piece of information. He would straighten and fall with his intonation. Sophia was watching him talk, her body shifting as his shifted. She knew how he moved. It was clear that research had not been the only endeavor in which she'd assisted him. *It doesn't matter now*, I told myself in spite of the sudden descent of my stomach; *he doesn't matter now.* I told myself this the way you might tell someone that with the ship sinking and the sea raging, it was time to drop the goddamn margarita and get in the lifeboat.

Phillip, still grousing to some associate about a brief, saw me and waved me into the room as though I needed an invitation. I stayed where I stood. He rattled off a list of instructions, muttered a curt good-bye, and tossed his phone onto the bed where it landed near Sophia's feet. She sighed and shook her head. "I'm not going to do that."

Phillip sighed back at her. "Then I don't know how you expect to find him. Everything okay at home, Les?"

"Everything is just freaking okay everywhere."

He rested his chin on his hand and grinned at me. "So this is going to be a long night, huh?" He didn't wait for an answer but took his car keys from the desk. "I need to eat. We need to eat. While I'm gone, Leslie, see if you can talk some sense into Ms. Mallory, here." He squeezed my shoulder as he pressed by me. The door closed and a few seconds later the Jag revved to life.

Sophia inclined her head to the sound as it pulled away; she looked at me. "Do you want the official Phil and me story or would you rather parse it out in your imagination?"

"You wouldn't want my imagination working unregulated on any part of your life."

"Eleven and one-half times, then. Well, maybe three-quarters."

"Three-quarters?"

"Conference room. Lunch hour. We got caught. By clients. I was fired—or rather the partners told human resources that they, human resources, had determined that my services were no longer needed. That's how that song goes."

"Phillip feels obligated to you."

"I can't speak for anyone's obligations but my own. Phil is an ally."

"To women everywhere apparently—and he hates being called 'Phil'; he must have told you that."

"Many times." She gave me a tight smile.

"All right, now that we've bonded over girl talk—" I sat

down on the edge of the other bed. "—Now that we're *sharing* . . ."

"You did not need to know about Nate's family." She freed her hand from the shirtsleeve and bit at her thumbnail. "Not pertinent to your involvement. Or anybody else's for that matter."

"Because it is kind of tricky to explain how you come to be in *love* with a guy so closely tied to the source of your own tragedy?"

"Everyone has a tragedy, Leslie. Nate and I share the same tangent of specific vocabulary."

"Like the name 'James Kendrick'?"

"Look, bringing you here was Phil's idea. I don't owe you . . ." She closed her eyes. "Forget I said that. Whatever you can do, I would appreciate. I need to find Nate. I need to focus on finding Nate."

"What was going on right before he took off? Did you argue?"

"We've been arguing since we moved in up there. What we argue about is the house itself. Whether or not we need to keep the woodstove going all the goddamned time. Should we take a longer lease on the place or continue the month-by-month."

"Which does Nate want?"

"Nate? Nate wants to buy the place. He wants to live up there; never, ever leave."

"But he has left."

"Yes." Sophia twirled one of her braids around her finger and tugged the braid with a hard, sudden jerk. "He has left."

"The house? Or you?"

"He doesn't see a difference. He's troubled."

"That's our given. What say we be smart about this? Let's start checking in with area hospitals—not because anything has happened to him, but with Nate's medical situation it's best to make sure everyone is on the lookout. And then, I can poke around the back channels though Andrea Burnham."

"No. I can't take this to the authorities." Her gaze fell to the far corner of the room. "You saw what Nate was like the day you came out. He's even more fragile now."

"Does he at least have his meds with him? Does he wear a Med Alert in case he has a seizure?"

"It's a complicated situation, Leslie."

"You're afraid of him."

"Afraid of Nate? No. Never." She tugged her braid again and then let it unwind from her finger. "Not Nate."

"Then why aren't you at the house? Shouldn't you be there in case he comes back?"

"Too noisy."

"The doorbell? You were going to disconnect that thing."

"We did. That didn't stop them. The cage doors slam all night. And the knocking. They're always knocking."

"Oh, Sophia, sweetheart, you need some sleep. You're exhausted. That's the wind messing with your fear. You know that."

She smiled at me with sad indulgence. "I didn't say I was afraid."

"Then we're going back out there. In case Nate tries to—"

"He won't." She raised the pillow a bit higher on her knees and laid her head against it. "No way he's going back there on his own. Nate is the one who is afraid." Her voice was muffled against the bulk of the pillow. "At the end of November Nate got a phone call from his Uncle James, his great-uncle, to be genealogically correct. As usual, James wanted money. The man was an itinerate most of his adult life. No one would hear from him for months and then, out of the blue, he'd choose some relative to contact and request funds. Always very specific amounts. He'd ask for say, forty-three dollars and eighty-five cents from a cousin. A year and a half later, he'd want six hundred and two dollars and seventeen cents from a niece. I know this from trying to find James when I started my research, back when I thought I was looking for the chain of ownership on a children's book."

The rain had picked up again, thumping at the roof, slapping at the pavement. I pulled off my shoes and lifted my feet to rest on Sophia's bed. "What do you *think* you're looking for now?"

She raised her head from the pillow to consider my deliberate invasion of her space. "I'll let you know when I find it."

"So, James calls Nate and . . ."

"James calls Nate and says he needs thirteen hundred and forty-seven dollars. Even. As usual, he won't say why. Nate agrees to go to the bank. He tells me he is going to give James a couple hundred dollars tops—if anything. Can't let the man starve. James tells Nate to meet him at a particular coffee shop down near the mission where he had spent the night. James is iffy about an exact time, so Nate goes down early and waits. And waits. James doesn't show. Nate waits two, three hours and then gives up, gets up to pay his tab and go. He says that right then, right as he's leaving the coffee shop, a little girl runs up to him and asks if he is Nathaniel Kendrick. She gives him a scrap of paper on which James has written, 'Sorry, my dear boy, I'm so sorry. Fondly, Uncle J.' At least that's what Nate remembers as being written. He lost the paper on the way home; he thinks he must have left it at the bank when he returned the money to his account. Almost two weeks later, we see the story about the old man's body found up in Willet."

"And then they find the papers at the house."

"Nate was sure before the papers. But he wouldn't go to make the ID. Refused to discuss the idea. He would become distressed at my even vaguely suggesting his responsibilities here. I try to get in touch with Nate's family and they hang up on me."

"Why didn't you come up here and do it yourself, then?"

"I might have but then *you* happened. The discovery of the child's remains hits the press and Nate starts to come undone for real. I tell you, Leslie, I could hear that boy's cables snapping under the strain. He starts saying that girl you described seeing up at the pond that night is the same girl who brought him James's suicide note out on the street."

"Retrofitting memory."

"And then the seizures started."

"His epilepsy is that recent?"

She scrubbed at her forehead with her fingertips and then laid her head down again, her face away from me. "Nate doesn't have epilepsy. The doctor said the events are pseudo seizures; part of a dissociative disorder brought on by trauma. What sort of trauma? When? Doctor couldn't say. The meds are antipsychotics. *James* was the diagnosed epileptic. He kept losing his emergency information tags; he tattooed the word *epileptic* on his forearm so people would know what to do if he had a seizure. It was the tattoo reference in the paper that made us certain it was Nate's uncle they'd found. *James* had absence seizures."

"Nate is copying his uncle's illness?"

180

"Worse than that. Nate believes James is taking over his mind. That's why Nate left. Because that's what James does. He leaves."

"You have to call in the authorities now, Sophia. Remember what James did in the pursuit of leaving? Nate requires medical attention *stat*."

"Yes. But if they pick him up, he's going to tell them what he's *done*. That he killed the man in the house. Marched him naked out into that freezing night and watched him die. Nate will tell them that once James was dead, it was *he*, not James, who drew the peacock on the wall." Sophia raised her head and faced me. "He confabulated all this the night after James was buried. We had gone out that afternoon to see the grave. I wanted Nate to see that James was really gone. It was there that Nate told me that he had killed the man in the grave. For me. To avenge what had been done to me."

"He's avenging your brother's murder?"

"My murder. Nate is now convinced that not only is he becoming James, but also that I am becoming that little girl. I am that child whose bones were found."

"Grown up? Reincarnated?"

Sophia shrugged. "Who knows? He absolutely believes that she and I are the same person. Although he can't seem to recall what my—her name is. Was. He believes it the way he believes that he has epilepsy and that he killed—how could Nate kill anyone? I've told him it's impossible. Reminded him over and over that we slept together every night that month; he wasn't away from me once. Plus, I have the bank statements. Nate withdrew the whole of James's request, the whole thirteen hundred forty-seven dollars on the day he was set to meet his uncle. He never put any of it back in the account. There was no suicide note. No little girl running up to him on the street."

"You think Nate did meet with his uncle?"

She shoved her braids behind her ears. "I took Nate back to the coffee shop. The cashier told him she remembered him sitting with a skinny old man. She remembered Nate yelling that the old man was 'fucking insane' before he ran out of the place, that the old man had no money and there had been a nasty scene with the manager. Nate denies not only what the cashier told us, but also that such a scenario could have taken place. According to Nate, James never showed up."

Outside, the low growl of a car engine grew in volume. Phillip was back. I lowered my voice as though he might hear us through the walls and the rain. "So, what really took place?"

"I believe Nate gave James the money because I believe James may have finally told his nephew what he needed the money for. James provided Nate with the missing pieces of the family history, some story so awful that Nate's first response was to pretend he had not seen the man at all. That was easy enough until James died and you led them to the child's remains."

I pulled my feet off her bed, moved to sit beside her. "You know, I'm somewhat of an expert on 'too far gone.' Please, let me get some backup on this. Your guy sounds in serious trouble. So what if some cop picks him up on a corner and he confesses? People are always confessing to crimes that they had nothing to do with."

"No." Sophia squared her shoulders and fixed her eyes on the door, where Phillip was now knocking. "Too much has been lost. You could not begin to understand how much has been lost. Entire generations hacked apart and scattered. If James

Kendrick told Nate what part *The Wilderness* holds in this, if he told Nate that child's name, I'm going to hear it first. I'm going to take that child's story back to her people. They deserve to hear it from someone who authentically appreciates and shares the full scope of their grief."

Had I missed something or was Sophia, careless in her exhaustion, letting new information slip? "You appreciate their grief because of your brother? Or are your families somehow—"

"I appreciate, I grieve, because of shared history, yes." She lifted her hand and turned it back and forth in display.

"All right, you are African-American but how is your brother and that little girl and the book—"

She sighed. "So much unspeakable history in that one hyphen; I mean, have you ever noticed how odd the term *African-American* really is, all things considered?"

"I wasn't considering all things."

"That's because you don't have to. The way that child died and was discarded leaves much of history to be considered."

"And while we're considering history—" I shoved myself off the bed to go open the door for Phillip "—we'll just forget about Nate?"

"That was unfair." Her voice went flat with anger. "I don't expect you to understand."

But I did understand, perfectly, right at that instant. "It was your idea, wasn't it? After James's body was found. You moved Nate up there to get him to remember what James had told him. You pushed him closer to the edge. You think he's located a copy of that book."

"I want only to locate the truth. Both his and mine. Nate and I have different investments in history. His is personal. Mine is founded on hundreds of years of suffering and oppression and theft and terror and murder justified solely on the basis of differing levels of pigment in human skin. I love Nate, but I have larger obligations."

I got up and went to open the door. "There's that *obligation* word again."

"Why are *you* here, Leslie? Being that you are such an expert on obligations, shouldn't you be looking after your own?"

"I claim no expertise in obligations, Sophia. My specialty is the lost cause," I said, mostly to Phillip, who had pizza boxes in one arm and a carton of beer in the other. I grabbed a beer out of the box before he was in the room. He followed me in, the aromas of garlic and tomato rushing ahead of him, and set the pizzas on top of the television set.

"So, Sophie, are we looking for Nate yet, or are we still protecting your intellectual property?" He offered her a beer; she waved it away before rolling over on her side and speaking to the curtained windows.

"The night before Nate left, he tattooed his forearm. He used a safety pin and india ink. Tell them to look for the tattoo. Tell them he is upset. He doesn't know what he's talking about."

"Finally." Phillip tossed the cap from his beer bottle across the room, sinking it perfectly in the center of the wastebasket.

"The tattoo, Sophia?" I picked up the receiver to the room phone. "The same as his uncle's?"

Her head moved in negation. "Nate was in a hurry, I guess. Or maybe it hurt more than he expected. All he managed to get written was the word *gone*."

molly

It is now thirteen minutes after three. Molly has killed a whole four minutes since she last checked the time. She throws off the covers, gets out of bed, and goes out into the hallway. The light is on in her parents' bedroom. Apparently Dad cannot sleep either. He's waiting for Mom. Or worried. Both. She knocks lightly on the door. He doesn't answer. Maybe he fell asleep with the lights on. She peeks in the room. "Dad?" He isn't there. Downstairs?

She's halfway down when she hears his voice. He's in the kitchen, on the phone. He sounds upset. She ventures down further, her bare feet silent on the steps. The floor is cold so she hurries, clutching her fists at her belly because as she gets nearer to the kitchen she's beginning to feel ill. His voice is thick and halting. Molly recognizes that voice. He's talking about Mom; he's trying not to cry.

". . . I really don't know if I can do it again, you know, Frank? I don't . . ."

Molly knows only one Frank who takes calls from Dad at three o'clock in the morning. It's Mom's doctor. She pivots her toes and heads back for her room, sick for real. Before she runs up the stairs, Molly unlocks and opens, just a little bit, the front door.

She runs as lightly as she can; she doesn't want him to know she's up; he'd try to reassure her again and she can only do the *fine, fine, we're just fine* crap so many times a day. Back in bed, she stares up at the dark ceiling, her heart is racing with a weird sort of urgency and her breath is gaspy.

Out of bed again. She runs to the sewing room, tries the knob, opens the door. The peacock drawing stares down at her, the oil surface gleaming back the thin light from the thin moon as though mocking the moon's own trick. She reaches up on her toes and runs her hand over its eyes, smearing them shut. Her face is hot. She feels both relief and dread as she smears the colors again with both hands. The smell from the oils is dense and awful; she knows she's making a mess. She's pounding at the smeared drawing, her fist sliding in the muck. She can't stop.

The office light comes on. Dad stands in the doorway, his hand on the light switch. He's still wearing his work clothes.

"What are you doing, Mol?"

She can't answer him because she's crying too hard. He rushes over and grabs her wrists, making her stop hitting, turning her from the murky gray blank she's made of the feathers and words, pulling her gently away through the open sewing room door.

view

Phillip and I called our contacts in the loop, ran down the particulars of a few John Does in drunk tanks and psych wards. Nate had not turned up in the system as yet. We sat about the motel room, picking at our cold pizza, not talking much, waiting for the phone to ring.

Around four A.M., Sophia fell asleep. Phillip and I moved our vigil into the tiny, white-tiled bathroom. We got the two-cup coffeemaker going and put the rest of the beer on ice in the sink. He pulled the room phone out to the full length of its cord and set it on the floor outside the bathroom door. I filched the pen and notepad supplied by the motel—and Sophia's satchel-sized handbag from where she'd left it in the corner between her bed and the window. The bathroom was too small for a full-size tub; I spread a towel in the shower stall and sat down inside it to go through Sophia's things. Phillip took the only seat left, the closed toilet lid, and watched.

"What exactly do you think you're going to find, Leslie?"

"If I knew," I said, "I wouldn't have to search for it." I undid the latch that held the soft leather closed; the bag must have set her back several hundred bucks. I found an eyeglass case and withdrew a pair of half-lenses, tried them over my own eyes—strong prescription—and put them back. "What is her deal, anyway?"

"She doesn't have a deal. Sophia is a very committed human being. Focused."

"You would know." I unsnapped the card section on her wallet, checked out her driver's license on which she still had her city address. I flashed her array of rare metal credit cards at Phillip. He grinned.

"I have a thing for estimable women."

"You have a thing all right, *Phil*." In the cash fold, I found a torn strip of index card on which she'd written a list of phone numbers. I took up the pen and copied down the numbers, ripped the list from the pad and stuck it in my pocket.

"What are you thinking, Les?" He pulled a beer from the sink and brushed it free of ice.

"I'm thinking this woman is more frightened than she's admitting." I returned the index card to where I'd found it. "Not frightened of what is happening around her but of the sense she's losing her grip on forces she can't name. Basic CFP."

"Definition please."

"That's one of Frank's. CFP. Control Fiend Panic." I held up a prescription bottle, shook it. "Xanax. Only ten prescribed. All accounted for and out of date by eight months. Bet you anything she hates to fly but can't take the pills because that would be allowing herself to admit she's overwhelmed."

"Which of you are we talking about now?"

I sneered at him and dropped the bottle back in the bag. I poked about her makeup pouch. "Discount lipstick, but top-of-the line perfume." I spritzed a little on my wrist. The same sandalwood and spices, I associated with our first meeting. "Our Sophia didn't come into her money until she started working."

"She has earned it."

"So, I've heard."

"Yes." His expression grew grim. "I am a bounder and a cad."

"Don't forget selfish bastard."

"You know, darling, for someone who constantly pleads death of affection, you are being quite—"

"Estimable?" I opened a zippered sleeve in the side of the bag and found a bulky envelope held shut by a rubber band. The contents were rigid. More index cards? I pulled off the rubber band and slipped it over my wrist so as not to misplace it before opening the flap. I saw a canceled stamp and the familiar side-by-side address and message setup. I took the stack of postcards from the envelope. The dates on the canceled penny stamps ranged from the early 1900s through the late '30s. The addresses were different, none to anyone named Mallory. The recipients lived in towns I'd never heard of, all over the country. I moved through them, holding them one by one up to the light, trying to pick up a sense of pattern in the addresses. What I did sense was Phillip, moving in closer, crouching down to my level. His hand closed over the top of the cards.

"Turn them around, Leslie."

I turned them around. Back when I was a cop, I developed a methodology for viewing crime scene photos. The secret was in that word *view*, as though from a great distance, the way you view a city from the top floor of a skyscraper. First you fix your sight on the far edge of the horizon, beyond the city, taking in the vastness of the world. Your eye moves inward from that, seeing the tops of other tall buildings, looking down upon the rooftop gardens and sunbathers, who thinking themselves unseen, give themselves naked to the sky. Farther down, venturing closer to the edge, you see the scuttling of cars on the street, the purposeful scurry of people for whom, as hard as you try to come up with something original, really do look like ants. You can't see both the ants and the horizon simultaneously. You have to choose between the specifics and the expanse. Like Alice, you learn to size yourself in accord with the information that you mean to acquire, with what you can manage.

The picture side of the top postcard was that of a crowd of men at night, faces to the camera as though instructed to pose. Their expressions were blank and blared out of detail by the flash used to capture the image; a process the photographer had taken credit for in an imprint at the base of the picture. A small fire burned in the distance, illuminating the eleborate dental work of the front grill of a few cars. The crowd of men and their cars were gathered around a bare-branched tree. The tree was framed off-center, as good composition would demand. Hard to gauge the arboreal species, the flash washed out the texture of bark and foliage, but it was a big tree with long, sturdy branches that did not seem weighed down by the ropes or the naked body of the dark-skinned man hanging by his neck.

I looked over at Philip, who had crowded into the shower stall with me. We passed the postcards between us, unable to speak. Each was the photographic souvenir of a lynching, different locations, different times of day, different number of bodies, different years, but the pictures are essentially the same: crowds photographed in stately posture around bleeding broken human ruins of their making. We cycled through the pictures rapidly, not wanting to see too much in any one of them. I kept coming back to the first one, coming back and coming back until I finally saw the little boy in the tweed suit, just barely, toward the back, at the edge the firelight. I thought at first that it was my mind again, projecting my horror and shame for my own kind in the guise of a child. I ran my finger over the tiny image. It did not alter. He *was* there, had been *there*.

"Leslie?" Phillip asked as I scavenged for Sophia's eyeglasses. I had to work to get the correct magnifying position. It was the boy. I knew it was the boy as surely as Sophia must have known when she first saw the oval photograph. I gathered up postcards—stacking them as Sophia had stacked them—put them back in the envelope, put the rubber band seal back, put it back in the pocket, pulled the zipper shut. I returned her glasses to the case, closed up the handbag, listening for the click of the latch. I stood, stepped over Phillip's legs, left the bright whiteness of the bathroom, and went to return Sophia's bag to the place from where I'd taken it. She was awake and sitting up against the headboard. I held out her bag and she took it, slowly crushing the soft leather to her middle.

"Sorry," I said. "I had the feeling you were holding back something that might help."

"Did *that* help?"

"Those were actually sent, actually delivered by regular post?"

She shrugged and gave me a look that I would never be able to describe. "Consider your vocabulary expanded."

Phillip came back into the room, leaned against the wall, his head down. Sophia tucked her legs to the side and indicated I should sit.

I perched on the edge of the mattress. "The boy in the picture is James Kendrick."

"The date on the photographer's imprint corresponds with the other photograph."

"I didn't think to look at the date."

"Those images do tend to overthrow thinking. You know. *Postcards*." Her voice held an edge, like that of a teacher, who while understanding the responsibilities of her job, still tired of underscoring the same material over and over. "Still, we can't say for certain who the boy is or even if it is the same child in both pictures."

I studied my hands, still ruddy with scars from frostbite and the cuts of Christmas Eve. "It's Kendrick. The kid even looks like Nate."

"How do you know what he looks like, Leslie? You can't see his face in either picture."

"No you can't," I conceded. "But come on. Who else could it be?"

"I'm not saying you're wrong. I'm asking how you know."

"I don't know. How did you find those things?"

"It wasn't difficult. I had seen books that reproduced others. It was only a matter of placing an ad in the right papers and offering money. It was background material for the book but then—"

"Kendrick died and left behind that oval photograph of what looks to be the same boy taken on the same night. Between *that* and his father's beatings, no wonder James had absence seizures. I'd want to be gone, too."

Sophia pressed her palm against the bag and smiled without warmth. "When I show that postcard, I get an instant reaction of either 'how horrible; a child saw that,' or 'how horrible; look at what they did to that man.' Want to take a wild stab at the demographic breakdown of those reactions? Please notice to whom your heart is going out to here."

"I'm not denying the horror of that man's death."

"But you didn't see him. You didn't look."

"Yes, I did, Sophia. Do you have any idea who he was?"

"No. They didn't record these events outside their trophies and vague references to unruly mobs and frontier justice. *Homme, hélas*. What can you do?"

"That lynching and the little girl are connected?"

She balled her fists as though pulling back on her own reins. "Seems plausible doesn't it? My instinct is that he is probably buried not far from her. At least in the area."

"Even if you could prove that—" Phillip slid his back down the wall and sat on the floor "—we've got no way to dig up an entire countryside."

"You'd find a way if it were your family, Phil."

"You want to talk family? My ancestors were nearly wiped out by the Cossacks. Only two Hogarth brothers made it out of that village. That's how we ended up on this continent—"

"Phil? You don't see a difference? The place every one else on the planet gets to think of as sanctuary—"

"—on this continent where they were worked in coal mines until their lungs gave out, worked into their graves by men who never knew their names or cared to know they existed." He shook his head. "I can feel terrible about those pictures, Sophia, but I can't feel guilty. Wasn't there." He raised his eyes to meet her disapproval. "Neither, may I add, were you. This is not your family."

"My family doesn't have the luxury of a clear record of where those lines are. No Ellis Island for us. For me, for us, we're all family."

"Logically—"

"We're beyond logic here, Counselor."

"This argument never takes us anywhere, Sophia."

"Because you know you can't win it." She exhaled in frustration. "I am going to find out what happened to these people if I am able, and I am nothing if not able."

He didn't blink. "I thought we were going to find Nate."

"Same thing, Phil."

I watched Sophia's face shift beneath a subtle agony and understood. "It's not Nate's confessing to imagined crimes you are worried about, is it? Nate's gone after that book. That's why you don't want anyone finding him and bringing him back. Not until he's found it."

"Leslie, I have no idea if any copies still exist."

"But just in case—" I yawned and rubbed at my eyes "—so, what? James was intent on buying up all the copies? Was he looking for the one with his name in it?"

She kept her gaze on the window where early daylight hemmed the curtains. "You can't ever be certain of what is in another person's head."

"Did he know his copy of the book played a part in your brother's, the other boys' deaths. Is that when he started looking for his copy? Wait. James's book? The reason his name is in it?" *Having once created fiction.* "Kendrick put the book together?"

"He had something to do with it. The poem itself is traditional. The illustrations are apparently unsigned. No publisher's colophon. No one knows where it came from or will admit to knowing. Even within the Kendrick family, theories abound; and each has its ardent believers. Different currents of blame. The rifts run deep, parts of the family ceased communications long ago. They're afraid of something. That's the real reason why no one came forward when James's body was found. The Kendricks would prefer that James had not existed."

"And yet in spite of the conflict, the family did support him financially."

"When it came to getting those books back, yes they did actively support that endeavor. Protecting themselves from, well, what shall we call it? Bad memories? What was James's stake in the book? Can't say for sure, but you've seen the cover illustration and what James drew on the wall of the cottage."

"He did the artwork."

"But Sophie—" Phillip banged the back of his head softly against the wall; a habit he fell into when trying to stay awake "—you said that the pictures are unsigned. So how does the book that turned up in your brother's case even come to have Kendrick's name in it?"

"I said they were *apparently* unsigned."

He stopped with his head to the wall. "There's something hidden in the illustrations?"

"If you know how to look. Apparently."

"I hate books." I stretched my neck and yawned again. "In form and principle. All the trouble in the world can be traced back to some book."

"I remember that tone of voice," Phillip said, struggling to get up from the floor. "That's the growl of a Leslie in caffeine withdrawal."

"Make it an IV," I called after him as he went back to the bathroom to start the coffeemaker up again. "Sophia, whatever the book was to James, it's not as though we're looking at the long-lost encryption of God's middle name. It's a kid's picture book. Even if Kendrick is the artist, even if he has laden the images with coded listings of these crimes, the crimes themselves are hardly secret. You've got them recorded on damn post-cards."

"Why a children's poem?" She regarded me as though she were proctoring a test she knew I could not pass.

I opened my hands, a gesture of failure acknowledged. "I have no idea. I have no idea why *that* title. The poem itself is readily available. I've done some research, too, you know. The rhyme preexists whatever happened to the little girl in the pond, the lynching on that postcard. Preexists by hundreds of years. The poem has been in publication since 1670."

"Since 1671," Sophia corrected. "The poem was first put into mass publication in 1671."

"Okay. You're right. It was 1671."

"A lot can happen in a year. You have to understand how insidious slavery was, the beautiful, righteous logic by which it rose up and strangled our souls. Up until 1664, an indentured Negro servant—although slavery had been legal since 1660, no one was using the word *slave* yet—a Negro servant could gain freedom by being baptized and joining a Christian church. But that meant hiring freeman labor at greater cost to the tobacco barons. These were the sons of landed English gentry; they were used to being rich. They had no stomach for suffering. Genius struck: Deny a man God and God will deny him. Maryland passes a little statute saying that Negroes and Indians cannot be baptized to avoid slavery. Virginia follows suit in 1667. Any non-Christian arriving by water is considered a slave. Logically, the more non-Christians you can pack into your ship, the richer the Christians get upon delivery. It was then passed that if you happened to kill a slave while correcting him or her, it was no crime. What was an attempt to escape but a cry for an old-fashioned Christian correction? We do no less for our own beloved children, right? Spare the rod and all that rot.

"Then in 1671, Jamestown enacted a statute that allowed the county courts to dispose of, at will, the Negro servants attached to the children of parents who died intestate. The courts could give the Negroes to the orphan, have them sold at auction for the proceeds, or replace them in *kind* and *quality* when the child came of age. In other words, real estate. Property. Other human beings had become an inheritance. From thereafter you were born either owner or owned, and the 'peculiar institution' had found its grip. So 1671 was a very interesting year for children in the wilderness." She finished with one of her meaningful smiles. She wasn't going to offer; I was going to have to ask.

"Let me guess, the Kendrick family dates its presence on this continent back to Jamestown?"

"I have records of them booking passage from England. In 1671. They brought with them a copy of the *Westminster-Drollery*, the book in which the peacock poem was first published. The book is listed in the ship's inventory. Probably brought it along to entertain the kids."

The coffee machine began its sluggish gurgle. I looked up at Phillip, who had come back into the room. He was considering the carpet, running his foot over a cigarette burn in the nap. "Why now? After so many years? What would be the point of getting James's picture books back now?"

Sophia lowered her eyes. "It is not taboo to go back and fetch what you forgot."

"Thanks, Sophie. That was incredibly specific and illuminating."

197

"To deny the past dooms the future, Phil."

"No one is denying anything, Sophie."

"No?"

"It's in the title, isn't it?" I said. "Something strange in that *Wilderness* title."

She shook her head slowly in response. "You didn't see. You didn't—" The room phone rang and the three of us startled. Phillip leapt to answer it before it could ring again. He turned away from us and spoke quietly into the receiver.

"Nate?" Sophia reached out for the phone.

Phillip hung up and set the phone back on the night table between the two beds. "Leslie, that was Greg."

My mental resources drained, I looked at the phone. "He doesn't want to talk to me?"

Phillip gave me the pitiful stare he used on the slow-witted. "Not anymore, he doesn't."

"Oh no." I could see Greg's expression on, having tracked me down and found the will to talk, getting Phillip Hogarth on the phone. "Oh no." I didn't explain anything to Sophia, just grabbed my things and ran for the door.

sacrifice

Greg, unable to take the constant ringing and re-ringing, finally picked up; I didn't even give him a chance to start. "You have every right not to believe a word of this," I said, my voice pitched in such flagrant contrition that he would have to know I was rolling over and offering him my belly in surrender. "But it's not what you think. It was wrong. I was wrong. But it's not what you think. I'm on my way back. Right now. In the car. Right now." Whether I was actually going to make it was debatable. The far side of Willet was closer to the highway than not, providing a faster route home, and I had reached the access road that channeled the back roads to the interstate. I begged Greg to listen to me while negotiating a heavy run of truck traffic, all of us doing about eighty. I was only truly aware of the gridlock of conflicting regrets.

"I'm not angry, Leslie."

"You'd have to be."

"I'm not. Not angry. Not anything at the moment."

The truck ahead of me hit a puddle and doused my windshield with dun-colored muck; the blades scraped clear double swaths of the equally dun-colored world. "I'm quitting this whole Kendrick thing."

"Again?"

Not anything, my ass. "I have a call in to Frank. Like I promised. We'll talk when I get home, okay?"

"Nothing to talk about."

"Tell Molly and Em, I'll be home soon."

"That's what I always tell them."

"I feel shitty enough as it is, Greg. I feel terrible about everything."

"Whatever you say, Leslie."

"Okay. Fine then." I slammed the phone into my thigh in order to hit every button at once and send Greg's sarcastic martyrdom into silence. It would be all right; I tried to reassure myself. I'd be there in a couple hours. He would have had time to think through the absurdity of his worst imaginings and realize how hard I was working at making us work. Okay, maybe it didn't read that way to him, but I'd given up my office and my apartment back in the city. I had given up my job. I had called my shrink. I'd met every one of his requirements. I was giving up this Kendrick deal, wasn't I? Wasn't I? I was giving up.

Giving up. That wasn't how it felt as I had sped out of the motel parking lot earlier, when shame and panic had me practicing my apologies out loud. Yet, as I had made my way toward the highway, creeping along the wet and narrow two-lane serpentine, into the glowering, overcast day, that resolve had started to sour. Yes, my job had necessitated a no-advance-warning departure; it was my *job*. It wasn't as though I'd run away without word or intention of coming back. Besides, Nate *was* missing, and there were genuine medical concerns, and I had been asked along because it was thought I could be of use in the situation. And we needed the money.

My apologies had systematically realigned themselves as arguments, which were far more satisfying if just as useless. The road wound its way down to the sudden descent of the valley. The trucks braked hard against velocity on the slope, as though those cowboy drivers had no idea it was coming. The pavement was striped with tire marks, the wide shoulders littered with thrown treads. I braked with the rest of them, slowing, encouraging them to pass.

Right before the junction where the road divided beneath a sign that pointed the driver toward the interstate—or back toward Willet—I picked up the phone again. The battery symbol was blinking; not much power left. I did not call home. I dialed Frank's office number and left a vague message with his service about wanting to chat, really meaning it this time; please call soon. The exercise was meant as insurance in case Greg should double-check the time stamp on my veracity. A marriage, after all, is built on trust.

The first twelve or so miles of interstate were through scraggly spring landscapes of wet rock and wet field, gawky young plants crowding the brinks of rain-choked ditches. The sky had gone to a no-color haze over a no-color sun. I kept to the slow lane, lifting the phone to my ear and then putting it back down, checking the dial tone but not dialing. Traffic increased with the push of the morning rush. Road signs let me know the exit for city-bound traffic was next. The airport would be coming up soon. Swifton was well over an hour on the other side of that. The phone started giving the trio of tones that signified the impending death of the battery. I then ordered myself to be an adult, for Chrissake, and hit dial. At the first ring, I found myself leaning into the steering wheel, preparing to lie to my husband about how wrong I was. Because that always worked so well.

The phone rang. Greg may not have been overtly angry earlier but I had a feeling that my having hung up on him had loosened up his resistances; he'd be ready to fight by the time I got home. No one answered. Fine. Let him stew. I tossed the phone aside; it bounced to the far side of the passenger seat. Regret switched poles and what had pulled now repelled. I grabbed the wheel with both hands.

Even though still a distance from the airport, I could sense the big-bellied loom of the jets in the clouds above me. The heated air coming in at the windshield carried the tang of jet exhaust. Up ahead, between the mazelike stretches of self-storage places, runway lights sparked blue and amber. There was undeniable appeal in the idea of the first plane out of here to anywhere else. The phone, somewhere in the dark, began to ring, the weak battery weakening the volume. Greg. Thank God. Without taking my eyes off the road, I fumbled about until I found it.

Not sure how long the phone's battery would last, I cut to where we would end up anyway. "You're right," I said, conceding before he had a chance to say a word. "Whatever you want to say to me, I deserve. You're right."

"Since when?" The caller's familiar affectionate tone broke in laughter.

I didn't wait for him to stop. "Frank?"

"Leslie?"

"This really isn't the best time."

Still laughing, he said, "You called me. Remember?"

I was fast closing in on a van driven by one of those individuals who felt since his tax dollars had paid for the lane lines, he could use them any way he wished. "I'm driving."

"Call me back then."

"I'm on a job, Frank."

"What sort of job? Are you all right?"

"Of course."

"But you've been blanking out?"

"No—hold on." I leaned into the horn to let the line-straddler know I was coming through. He graciously acknowledged my approach with his middle finger. I returned the salute on passing. "Have you been talking to Greg?"

"When Greg needs to talk. He's worried. But that you know."

"I'm really trying, Frank. We both are. Sacrifices are being offered up on both sides."

"It's my experience that relationships are better measured in units of opportunity rather than units of sacrifice."

"Dang, Frank. That deserves to be on a pillow, and me here without my embroidery hoop." *Oh, come on, you stupid battery; die.*

"You are hallucinating again, aren't you?"

"I didn't call about me. It's about this job. I've got a missing—"

"Leslie, right now, I think your *job* is to get safely home to your family."

"How did you know I was gone?"

"Because you only call me when you are coming back." He cleared his throat. "No reputable physician assists in maintaining a delusion, even when that delusion offers paychecks. You want a blind guess as to what you are really working on—" The signal on my phone bristled with static and then the sound cut out completely. It may have been the battery, or it may have been my thumb on the Off button. Whatever the reason, the conversation was over, and I had been spared Frank's getting around to asking about the depths of my concern for Nate. One mention of personality splits or self-induced bouts of absence and Frank would have figured out a way to reach through the ether to whack me in the head like you would a television set losing its horizontal hold.

He would have been right to do so; he was always right. I did need to get home. Tomorrow I could figure out how to get in touch with Sophia. Maybe she and Phillip would have already found Nate. Maybe everything was fine. It really wasn't my problem, anyway. Out the windshield, I caught the wing lights and pale glimmer of a jet coming in for a landing. It was so low, I could make out the landing gear, already down. It passed over me; I lifted my eyes to the rearview mirror to watch it continue its descent, that heavy, impossible grace. How can a thing that huge control its falling? The plane sank behind a row of billboards. Gone. I forced my sight back to the road. That sense of *force* should have been warning enough. I should have expected the apparition.

I saw the shape on the pedestrian overpass ahead. I knew it was the boy even from a distance. He was on the outside of the protective chain-link fencing, balanced perfectly on the concrete ledge. The distance closing, I was coming up on him fast. He lifted his arms outward. Ready to fly. I was nearly there, near enough to see the buttons on his jacket, close enough to count the stitches in the tweed, his eyelashes, his thoughts. *James, no!* Pain makes a man think and a woman see. I saw nothing but stillness when he let go, falling, head first, rock into water, toward the road right in front of me.

The learned responses of driving kicked in. I stomped on the brakes. I felt the wheels lock and skid and the beginning of the spin. The better instincts of survival: I willed my foot from the pedal and started to steer. Behind me I could hear the horns and screeching of other vehicles as their drivers also working on panic swerved and braked, trying to avoid colliding. I got the car straightened out, moving in the right direction. Slowing, slowing, easing to a stop on the shoulder. I talked my right hand into kindly letting go of the wheel long enough to put the car in park and turn on the hazard blinkers; I sat there in that breathless calm that follows a close call, waited for awareness to begin visualizing the *what if's*. Adrenaline burn-off kicked in; I held the wheel tighter to steady the trembling. A vestige of childhood, calming down by holding tighter. James holding his skipping stone. James holding . . . this time I felt it; I knew to be ready. He was in the passenger seat, right beside me. Cap pulled low, looking straight ahead.

"James?" I said, my voice shaking as hard as my body. I made a grab for his chin, to turn his eyes toward mine, so he'd face me, mother to child, and see that I meant business, I wanted an answer. "What have you done?" Hearing my own voice disrupted whatever was patterning him into my sight. He was gone from right beneath my fingers. I waited, expecting him to reappear. He did not. The trembling in my body subsided, leaving behind a sick weariness. I closed my eyes and leaned my forehead against the steering wheel, feeling the car rock every time a truck passed. Plane engines roared above. The arch of my right foot seized in a sudden cramp. It was still hard against the brake pedal in an unconscious effort to stop the bad thing that had already happened.

I slid my foot off the pedal and tried to flex out the muscles. I glanced over at the empty passenger seat. No matter what my rational life demanded, it was undeniable the irrational was not going to be turned away or turned off simply because it inconvenienced those I loved. Frank had once said that in a way, my episodes made perfect sense because how could anyone think rationally about madness? Madness had to be experienced. Since my work took me into the realms of vast madness, I had to experience it irrationally in order to read it. Vast madness is where I was. Those terrible postcards; the self-opening cages at Happy Andy's; the endlessly ringing doorbell; the lives that James—and now Nate—had feared were lost to his *Wilderness*. Including James and maybe Nate. James had been looking for himself, the child who had been crushed beneath the events he'd witnessed. I understood that; it made sense that I would see it. What was Nate looking for? Who were those children he had been drawing, been imagining ice-bound in the pond? What exactly had James told his nephew? *Always more.*

I turned off the hazard lights, put the car back in drive, and pressed the accelerator, to begin building up speed to merge back into traffic. If I took the next exit and refilled the gas tank, I could be back in Willet before eight thirty. I could call Greg from the gas station; I could explain why I had to do this, explain that what was happening here might be much larger than any of us could begin to guess. I had to follow through; I had to go back—yes, "again," Greg. What if it *was* one of our kids? Then, I would beg; beg for his trust; beg for his patience. Beg for real, not for show or penance. It was going to be a terrible conversation, and it was going to be terrible whether I made it from the pay phone at the gas station or I waited until I was back at the motel. May as well wait. Among my many abandoned embroidery projects was the one about forgiveness being easier to get than permission.

venice glass and the well

despair

On the drive back to Willet, I decided not to return directly to the motel. Sophia's complex netting of loyalties and ambitions restricted the flow of information necessary for the urgent nature of the task before us. Nate was in the most severe sort of trouble. The idea of one more innocent lost to this mystery was unbearable. I was convinced of Sophia's love for the man, but love threatened by real loss often plunges into denial of its own existence. Thinking takes over because thinking, even a terrible thought—especially a terrible thought—is easier than realizing profound helplessness. I went back to Happy Andy's to try to get a reading on just how helpless they had become.

The trip from the parking area was an obstacle course of puddles and mud slicks. Patchy islands of grass offered firmer footing, but these too were waterlogged, and last night's rain pooled around my shoe with each step. I went slow and studied the soggy earth for markings. Sophia had not known whether Nate left on foot or if someone had picked him up; that was the sort of information we really could use. The downpour had obliterated everything but the deepest of the tire tracks left by Sophia's SUV, which were now narrow chasms filled with rain.

In the yard, the old cages were open, of course. When I had been coming up here daily, it had occurred to me to try a padlock or wedge a rock into the ground to see if that did not indeed keep the damn things shut. I had allowed the phenomenon to go untested; rather, my perceptions of it went untested because simple answers would have deflated the secret joy in my obsessions. The gates' refusal to stay latched was fascinating in its weirdness, but when we found Nate, the only antidote we might be able to offer him would be the mundane fact of weird old regular physics. It was time to find out exactly what was going on here.

I made my way toward the house, walking backward so as not to take my eyes off the yard, closing pens and cages in my path, checking the flip-down latches to make certain they had caught. And then I waited. And waited. The longer I stood there, the more I knew that it wasn't going to happen with me watching. Whatever this was, it was waiting for me to turn away. It didn't want me to see, could not afford my attention.

"Escape?" I said aloud to the empty cages. "Is that it? You can only run when no one's looking? You're trying to escape?" I closed my eyes, pivoted to face the door. "All right. Go. It's safe; no one can see you." I waited for as long as my curiosity could manage and then peeked back over my shoulder. The cages I had closed remained closed. Thank goodness for that because the last thing my haunted amusement park of a mind needed was to start contending with the notion of real ghosts. Perhaps the rain-swollen earth, the grasses, were preventing the easy swing of the doors? I promised myself to get a video camera up here; find out once and for all.

The key to the doorbell was gone. Sophia had left without locking up. In spite of her protests she apparently held out some hope that Nate might try to return here. Not only had she left the door unlocked, but also ajar. I pushed it open, only to be nearly hit in the face by the dangling remains of the doorbell mechanism. They had not so much dismantled it as ripped it from the wall, gouging a trench through the plaster in the process. The corroded brass domes of the bells were still intact, as were the clapper and spring coil that operated them. Thus exposed to all sorts of movement, it must have made for more ringing than the installed version. No wonder it had driven Nate beyond his limits. Or had that been the point, Sophia? I yanked the bells free from the pull and tossed them aside.

The place was a wreck; so much that at first I thought that vandals had taken advantage of the open doors, that Sophia and Nate's belongings had been ransacked for quickly fenced valuables and cash. I made my way around the lower level; the cupboards were closed and the furniture undisturbed. The prescription bottles were neatly aligned on the shelf where I'd first seen them. Dust filmed the bottle lids. Drugs would have been the first thing grabbed. Nothing had been through here but Nate and Sophia's accelerating desperation. Nate's artwork was gone; some of the framed pieces had been smashed and piled up in front of the woodstove. The floors were littered with wads of paper and tracked thick with mud. The reek of rotting orange peel and sulfur made my eyes water, and there was another smell, a musk, warm and feral, a living odor. It was stronger in the center of each room; I did not care to find out what was causing it.

The peacock still gazed down from the wall, but the colors had dulled under what, upon inspection, I saw were palm prints. I could imagine Nate, pressing his hands against the colors, the words, trying to push through them into what they meant to him, to Sophia, trying to grasp a shape of the history they might share. I could imagine Sophia standing off to the side, tape recorder in hand, playing the roles of both medium and skeptic at the séance.

The sulfur odor was coming from the kitchen sink; they'd never solved the problem of the well. Empty cracker boxes and soup cans spilled out of a trash bag beside the stove. On the refrigerator door, the tiny magnetic words had been pushed around in a jumble. One word stood apart: TIGERS. Another of James's references. The letters were individual, having been apparently cut away from the existing set to make this one word, which had not been provided. So small and forlorn and forced into being, that one little term for the viciously dangerous. Sophia had stood back and watched Nate ravel out, but I knew, absolutely, that she'd hated every second of it.

I went up the stairs to find that the doors to the rooms had been removed, taken right off at the hinges. The lovely portrait of Sophia and Nate had been defaced, literally. Nate, I assumed it had been Nate, had ever so carefully marked over his presence with solid black ink. Sophia was now in the embrace of a Nate-shaped void. Here but not here. Absent. *Gone.* I wondered at what point he had done this. Dust on the pill bottles downstairs? Sophia had stopped giving him his medication.

Sophia's office had been overturned but with a care that led me to think it had been the deliberate erasure of sensitive material. The cover on her computer's CPU had been removed, the memory cards were pulled free, and beaten to uselessness; a hammer lay beside the heap of broken plastic. The bulletin board had been stripped and the file cabinets were open, papers sticking up hodgepodge from file folders. I went to the window to check the yard again. The cages were as I'd left them. The closed ones stayed shut. I noticed then nail heads in the base of the window frame. Sophia or Nate had nailed the windows shut.

The odor of solvent and oil told me that the room across from Sophia's office would be Nate's studio. The studio was the same dimension as her space and its mirror reverse in architecture. They'd probably divided up the space according to the exposure. The studio windows gave out onto the open fields behind the house and would have provided steady, northern light. In this northern light I saw that he'd covered the walls with his drawings of children imagined as beneath ice. The plank wood floor was smattered with dribbles of many-colored paints. Canvases, slashed and stomped upon, had been thrown around the room. A small table in front of the window held a spilled jar of india ink, which had dried over a large safety pin, opened and forced straight. Further evidence of Nate's tattoo work, rusty dried blood spotted the edge of the table and the floor beneath it. If you didn't know, you'd think it was another color of paint.

Here, too, the windows had been nailed shut. A large pad of drawing paper was propped on an easel to which was clamped a gooseneck work light. I switched the light on and turned back the cover on the pad. I expected more children, but what Nate had been doing here was trying to unlock his uncle's *The Wilderness*. Page after page, Nate had written out differing combinations of the lines. It looked queasily familiar. *Anagram* he'd written at the top of one of the first pages and then crossed it out in strokes of charcoal. Below that an elaborate *13* in heavily blackened Gothic script. The thirteen letters, twelve lines problem had stumped him, too.

Why had Nate been looking for a solution? Had James alluded to one or was Nate only trying to make the poem make sense in the larger connotation of his uncle's past? Was he simply trying to make it stop spinning as I had? Why had James or whoever put the book together attached that particular phrase to an old nursery rhyme that had no title? The reason had to lie in the illustrations. I found myself suddenly hoping Nate had gone off in the night to get hold of that book, that he'd bring it home with him. Mine was yet another name on the growing list of those who needed to *see* this thing.

I paged through the rest of the pad. Nate had maneuvered through the same switch-out and switch-around games I had played with the words, probably just as infuriated as I had been, sensing the intended arrangement must have emerged at some point. Without any landmark to let us know we had arrived, we'd kept on going. Nate had dealt with his frustrations by filling the blank spaces of his pages first with squiggly doodles that became, with each succeeding page, more cohesive in form until he was drawing tigers. The tigers got bigger and then took over the words. The last few pages of the pad were angry, heavy thick lines of beasts leaping, jaws wide, from the page toward the one who was drawing them. I closed up the pad and turned off the light.

Between Nate's studio and Sophia's office lay the tiny space they used as their bedroom. Odd here was that, given the struggle manifested in the rest of the house, all was in order. The bed was made and on the table beside it, a vase of what had been fresh tulips, the stems now wilted, the petals fallen to the polished wood. Serene on the surface, the room's incongruity gave off a vibe of sanity's last stand; I could imagine Sophia and Nate going through their rituals of sleeping and rising. Make the bed. Sweep the floor. Fill the vase. See? Everything is fine.

Funny how the noise and chaos of the overwhelming is able to sneak up on a person. I went back to Sophia's office. Had she destroyed records to preserve her ownership or to keep Nate from finding out more than she wanted him to know? Or had Nate done this—in anger or out of the need to protect her—after finding out what she was up to? I used straightening the files as an excuse to read, but they were mostly old receipts of payment, drafts of her articles that I'd already read. I remembered then, the list of phone numbers in my pocket. I pulled them out and picked up her desk phone. No dial tone. I pulled up on the cord. It came free, its end frayed from where it had been cut. The battery on my cell was shot. It would have to wait.

I wandered over to the window, trying to think of the nearest location that would have a telephone. The cages were open again. My stunned awareness pulled back inside the house fast at the sound of something very large hitting the floor downstairs. Not a crash; it was a controlled heavy thump. I stood still, listening. When the growling began, my body locked.

"Stop it." I ordered myself with the last air in my lungs. The growling continued, moving along with slow, padding thumps that circled the lower level. The growl ascended suddenly to a roar; the roar was met with what I was sure was the shriek of a small child. That got me breathing. That got me running. I half fell down the stairs and stumbled toward the front room where the shrieking, roaring battle raged.

"Enough!" My shouting silenced it. The room was empty. "Really." I panted. "Quite enough." The admonishment was now for myself. I had let Nate's imagery amplify what chords his uncle's suicidal fictions had struck in my head. Harmonizing in a minor key. Enough. Let them have their pain. I had plenty of my own. That's what I was telling myself when I noticed the claw marks gashed into the plaster, directly through the peacock's eyes.

I went up on my toes and touched the gashes. Four of them, clogged with pastel, spaced as human fingers would be spaced, but too close together for an adult's hand. I had simply not seen them among the other battering the walls had taken. Rather I had not let myself see them so that I might better set up the Vegas-style magic trick my mind had just razzle-dazzled. The misdirection meant to instruct that what was needed here was to pay closer attention. That's how I decided to interpret it because the alternatives ranged between grim and impossible. Resolved to focus on what was before me, I left the house and went in search of a phone.

At the grocery store I bought a prepaid phone card, coffee, and a box of granola bars. The cashier pointed me to the bank of pay phones; I pulled over a cart to serve as a desk, took one long swallow of cold burnt coffee, and dialed the first, hardest call: home. No answer at my house. That was not a surprise; it was almost eleven thirty; the girls would be in school, Greg at work. Good sign. The answering machine did not pick up. Bad sign. I could call Greg at his job but he'd only beg off until later. I hung up, nearly shaking with relief that I could delay the inevitable. The next call was to the motel. Phillip answered; I didn't tell him where I was or where I had been. They had not heard anything yet. Sophia was growing more despondent as the silence extended.

"Are you all right, Leslie?"

"Me?" I pressed my hand against my open ear to shut out the background music and clanging carts. "Always."

"Of course you are. I meant to tell you, I saw in the paper last week that the Reeves has space available."

"Probably the same office I vacated last fall."

"Probably. I'm not doing anything useful at the moment. I could call, see what they're asking rent-wise."

"You could do that. You know, if only to verify that they'll never have me as tenant again."

"Just to verify that. May as well verify your status at your apartment building while I'm at it."

"May as well." I told him I'd check back in an hour and took out the list of phone numbers. Only a few of the area codes were familiar to me. It occurred to me that one of these, if not more, had been the "private" number of my mysterious hang-up friend. Had that call come from someone who had the book or someone who was looking for it? How many people had a stake in this? James and Sophia and Nate wanted the book for intricately interlocked personal reasons; I understood that even if I couldn't name those reasons. But all these others? One way to find out. I started with the number at the top. An elderly sounding woman with a smooth Southern drawl answered. Only then it dawned on me that I had no idea what I should ask about.

After flailing through an introduction, I went for the direct route. "I wanted to ask you about your copy of *The Wilderness*?"

"Are you from Tyne's Antiques, dear?"

I leaned against the cart to write down the name. "No. But they gave me your number. Tyne's did."

"I told them after the last inquiry to update their records. I sold that piece—it has been years now. Curious, isn't it, how certain items circle back around in popularity? You're the third call in the past year for that piece."

Sophia, of course. And Nate? "Too bad. I was so hopeful that you would have one. Do you think the person you sold it to might be looking for a buyer?"

"I wouldn't know. Frankly, it would not come as any shock to learn he'd passed on. Old, old man. Older than I'll ever see, and that was near ten years ago. Are you, perhaps, in the market for other items of note?"

"No, just the one. Sentimental value, really. It's a family thing."

"That's a shame, I have a very interesting collection. Hoped to sell the lot of it before I go; not leaving this kind of money to my— well, I doubt that should you even find the man alive, you'd get him to part with it. Gave me several times what it was worth. Not a quibble over the price. You expect them to quibble. That's why you start high. But not in his case. The man did not put up a single argument. He merely handed over the cash. He appeared barely able to scrape together the cost of a meal. I remember that."

"It probably had sentimental value for him, too."

"Sentimental. That's an interesting way of putting it, given that particular item's role in the incident—"

"Incident?"

"I thought you said you'd spoken to Tyne's?"

"Briefly. I'd asked about the book; they gave me your number. Frankly, I've been calling bookstores blindly. Hoping."

"Tyne's is not a—"

"Bookstores and places like Tyne's. Places that handle these sorts of *collectibles*."

She laughed, tenuous and throaty. "I could tell you were looking for more than a sentimental trinket. Thought I'd take pity and price you low."

"I'm obviously dealing with an experienced businesswoman."

"You are. The book is gone. Can't offer you that. But from the same collection, I do have—in their original condition, mind you—the glasses from the bathroom, the bed sheets, some of more value than others, obviously, and, the best of the bunch, her slippers. The splatter pattern is quite distinct. I also have one of the knives. I'll be forthright, can't swear to its use in the incident, but I will offer documentation that it is from the set that he employed."

"Excuse me?" I pressed my hand harder against my ear. A baby, unhappy with his lot in the world, was screaming. I knew how the kid felt. "Documentation?"

"Photographic. I have an official crime scene photo of the kitchen where they found two of the bodies. You will clearly see the knife rack on the counter."

"Did your buyer request documentation for the book?"

"He did not ask for any. The staining was authentication enough, I suppose. But as I said, he wasn't the most skilled of negotiators. So, are you interested in individual items or the whole kit and caboodle?"

"Let me think about this. I have your number."

"If those don't tickle you, I have souvenirs of other incidents."

"I appreciate your help."

"Don't wait too long."

"No," I said, and hung up. That made three ghastly events associated with this one little book. The list of numbers now seemed to promise a long trek through a wasteland. I had a feeling where this was going to end up but still had to get there. Picked up the receiver and dialed the next one.

Peacock feathers shimmer because of the distortion of light

hitting the tiny plates that make up the feather's surface; those eyes shine because the lenses are imperfect, essentially broken. The light hitting the facts concerning *The Wilderness* broke without color, a sick pale gleam like the sweat that slicks a fevered body. Each of the copies James had found and bought back had been acquired from sources such as the estate of that murdered family or a junk lot of props confiscated from a kiddie-porn operation or the basement of an abandoned building along with a coil of rope with a noose tied in its end. Over and over I was told of being surprised that James would be willing to pay so handsomely, without questioning the authenticity of the fire damage or rust or distinctive stains on the pages. Apparently, for those who had the book and those who sought to sell it, the reasons distilled down the same as James's and Sophia's: They were fascinated by the pattern of dark ripples it left behind it.

The popular word for this sort of pattern—this repetitive intersection of object and violence—was *cursed*. *Cursed* must have been the word James used that afternoon in the coffee shop to explain the events that descended upon the owners of this book. That's why Nate had changed his mind about the money. Of course, James had not questioned or quibbled over prices. He was trying to get them back, get them out of the world and break the curse he felt responsible for. *Having once created fiction.* He must have returned to Willet because he thought he had found them all; that he could rest at last, and at last, be free of those beleaguered souls dragging along behind him.

The idea of a curse was just another form of make-believe. The only dark forces at work on human lives were imminently human ones: rage and envy and guilt and fear. Whatever symbolic horror ornamented the physical fact of the book, it was that horror that appealed to those forces already obtaining control of a mind. The text of that poem, the illustrations, could not be held responsible for what a person did any more than a rock song could drive a teenager to self-destruction. James had been right about one thing. What we see in the world is ourselves; the voice urging us toward action is our own. We find a means of granting the illusion of necessity to whatever transgression we have already begun. In this activity I was expert.

Before I left to return to Phillip and Sophia at the motel, I tried my house again, knowing there would be no answer. Too early for anyone to be home, but it was enough to hear it ringing.

greg

I wanted Leslie to hear it; I wanted her to hear how ripped up Molly was. I worked backward. Called the number Leslie called from, got the desk clerk, got the room number, got Hogarth. Revenge never works out the way you think it will.

Frank says not to take Molly to the ER; her memory of hospitals is only going to spike her anxiety higher. He says he'll meet us at the girls' pediatrician's office. He also says he's spoken with Leslie and she sounds fine.

"*Fine* fine," I ask, "or fine for Leslie?"

"She's doing as well as she can," he said, Frank-speak for he really wasn't sure.

Emma doesn't want to leave her sister. I let her stay home from school, calling in her absence as a stomachache, which is accurate. We're all feeling ill. We pile into the truck, Molly, color gone from her face, her shoulders shaking, protests that it's okay and she doesn't need to see the doctor. She runs one fingernail under the other, trying to get out the leftover sludge of oil pastel. I haven't yet told her which doctor is waiting to see her.

We get to the medical center, stumble into the lobby. Molly sees Frank, who is playing with one of those beads-on-bent-wire toys. She stops dead.

"I'm not . . ."

"Of course, you're not," I put my arm around her to steady her as I inch her forward.

"Damn this is addictive." Frank glances up and then pushes a row of beads over a camel's hump of track. "I've got to get one of these. How about I don't ask you how you're feeling, Molly?"

She stares at him.

He lifts the bead game, offering it to Emma, who shakes her head, insulted by the little-kid implication. He sets the toy aside. "What I do want to know, Molly, is how you do it?"

"Do what?"

"Goodness, girl. You've been through stuff that would flatten a grown man to the mat, and yet you keep getting up again. I want to know how you do it."

Molly shrugs beneath my arm. I feel some of the tension slide away.

Frank leans forward in the chair. "I can understand you not wanting to give away the secret to your superhero powers out here where anyone can hear you. If I can sweet talk them into giving us a corner back in the offices, would you give me, just me, one or two hints?"

Molly fixes him with a "do I really look that stupid?" stare, but nods. Frank gets up, heavy; we tire him out. He motions Molly to follow him to the examining room entrance. She lifts her arm to force mine away from her shoulder and then stalks off, ahead of Frank. Emma calls after her sister. Frank grins down. "Have her back to you in a minute. You like gum, Emma?"

"I guess."

"You got any?"

"No.

"Me neither. You think you could find us some? Bound to be a vending machine somewhere in this place." He hands her a dollar and off she runs. He turns his gaze up at me and the jolly-uncle façade fades. "And you, Gregory?"

"I don't have any gum, either."

"And you don't want any."

"No."

"You're done, huh?

"I'm done."

"You look it." Frank pats my arm and then heads off to find Molly.

guess

I pulled into the lot at the motel and parked next to the Jag. Sophia's SUV was gone. I let myself into the room. The curtains were drawn. Phillip was stretched out on the bed closest to the door, arm thrown over his eyes, sleeping. He was alone in the room.

I sat down on the bed beside him and lifted his arm away from his face. He startled awake. "When did you get back?"

"The question is when did Sophia leave?" I turned on the wall lamp.

He rubbed at his beard, squinted up at me and then at his wristwatch. "No one called."

"In or out?"

"I don't think so. I've been sleeping only about twenty minutes."

"She was waiting for that. For us to stop watching her. She wasn't telling us everything."

"Sophia is an honorable person, Leslie."

"An honorable person doing an archaeological excavation of her beloved's psyche. With a grapefruit spoon."

"No need to be mean."

"Easy coming from the guy who got some sleep."

He gave me a considered look of amused curiosity. "You're jealous."

"I'm too tired to be anything."

225

"Besides, we're over, right?"

"We are."

"Uh-huh." He smirked before reaching behind my neck to pull my mouth down to his. I put out my hands and pressed against his chest to stop the descent, my face inches from his. "No."

"You sure?"

"You heard me."

"Okay, now make me believe it." He increased the pressure on my neck a fraction before letting me go, allowing me to push away from him, which I did—after only a second or two—or ten. He laughed softly, his chest expanding against my palms. I felt his heart beating beneath my fingers. I pulled my hands back to my chest where my own heart was just starting up again.

He read my face, which—cheeks burning, tears brimming—left nothing for him to guess. The glint of amusement left his eyes, replaced by a sad concern. I broke away from his gaze.

"We should try to find Sophia," I said.

"We should do many things, Leslie. There's only so much we can do. If Sophia wanted help, she wouldn't have gone off on her own."

"I think she may need more help than the rest of us combined."

"You can throw the line out there, Les. Can't make someone grab it."

"She may not understand she needs to grab it; the woman may not know she's drowning. It gets so cold and deep sometimes, you get so tired that you go numb; you lose any sense of yourself or of what's happening around you."

"You?"

226

"Me? I'm treading water hard as I can."

"And you're tired."

"I am tired."

He pushed himself up, swung around so that he was sitting beside me, then stood, offering me his hand. "Okay, Self-Sufficiency Girl. Let's go find *somebody*." I nodded and shoved myself one more time to my feet, without his help.

The man at the desk in the motel office verified that no calls had been placed from the room phone in the past couple hours. He also told us that he'd seen the SUV pull out around thirty minutes earlier. It had turned in the direction that would take it out of Willet; Sophia, we could assume, had not gone back to the house. Phillip paid the bill and left the man with the numbers where we could be reached should Sophia return. He also gave the guy a twenty to help him remember to make that call. We hurried back to our cars. Phillip dug out his road atlas and we set about trying to decide the most efficient means of finding this woman who had thirty or forty miles on us already. I kept watching the road, hoping each approaching engine was Sophia coming back. *Back.*

"How much do you know about her, Phillip? About them?"

He paged through the maps. "Before today? What's to know? They're in love."

"Do you know where they met?"

"Sophia was starting her book—"

"She told me how, but the physical location? Do you know *where* they met?"

He shook his head. "You think that's where she's gone?"

"It may be where she thinks Nate's gone." I looked at the map he had open, the vascular network of connecting roadways and thought of causal links between circumstance and meaning that Sophia had built to get where she needed to go. Skin color and the book's coincidence served to bridge her brother's tragedy with that of another child from another place and time. She had managed to convince herself that the coincidence was in fact the linchpin of reason, that reason being personified in Nate. And Nate? He was gratifying her desire for reasons by becoming the person who could substantiate her belief: James. Nate was trying to give Sophia what she needed, proof of a cause that would serve as solid foundation to the effect she'd already devised. The effort had pushed him farther than he could bear; he had to get away or he would be forced to play out his uncle's path to the end.

No wonder Sophia's terror over not being able to locate him. No wonder his growing panic to remove himself from her presence. Theirs was a huge and spiraling waltz of impossible longings. Not love but grief doing what grief did: bulldozing down one fabrication of reality so we could rebuild it with taller towers, broader horizons. That's what they'd recognized in each other, a soul alone and lost between worlds. Maybe I *was* starting to believe in ghosts.

I ran my hand over the map, expecting a pulse. "They met because of this *Wilderness* book. The location where they met may have some significance to her project. Where else do you go when a thing ends badly, but back to its beginning with hope of starting again?"

"That's a pretty wild guess."

"You have a better one?"

"I haven't any idea where their *beginning* might be."

"Their families would."

"We'd have to find their families first."

The sun made an appearance from behind a cloud, sparking the puddles around us to gold before slipping once more behind the overcast. "She worked for you."

"She worked for the firm."

"But she *worked* with you. You didn't ask about her family?"

"I may have. It was years ago, Leslie."

"All right. Her employment records. She was a grad student? I bet her family information is in her file somewhere. Personal references; emergency contacts. Call your office."

"It would be dicey to ask for that over the phone. Given the fact that she lost her job because she *worked* with me."

"It was, to quote the bounder, years ago."

"And it will be years before it's forgotten. The Society for the Preservation of Decency that is our HR department still thinks I should have been booted along with Sophia."

"And they would be right."

"*Et tu*, Leslie?"

"At the very least you should have been fired."

"They can't fire me."

"You know too much."

"I know enough. You want to drive?"

"You. It's my turn to sleep."

Phillip woke me when we hit the outskirts of the city. I had not so much slept as crawled into the cave of desperate unconsciousness I'd discovered when Molly was a newborn, from which, once emerged, I did not feel rested as much as stunned that you could be this tired and still be alive. My neck was sore from leaning against the window and I could feel the imprint of the seat belt's shoulder strap running along the side of my face.

229

"You were talking," he said, without taking his eyes from the traffic light where we were stopped.

"To who?"

"See, my first question would be about what I had said." We got the green and halfway down the next block made the turn into the parking garage of his office building. "I don't know who you were talking to, but you were apologizing."

"Well, that would be Leslie TV: All apologies, all the time."

We wound our way up the ramps to the level his firm kept for employees. He pulled into the space marked RESERVED FOR P. HOGARTH. "They will survive, Les."

"And isn't that how a person wants to be thought of? Survivable."

"Every one of us is more trouble than we're worth." He shoved the stick into park. "Accept that, darling, and embrace the secret of happiness." He handed me a tissue from the box on the console, and pointed at his jaw. "You've been drooling."

I pulled down the sun visor to use the mirror and saw how awful I looked, unwashed, hair a jumble of rain-styled straggles, circles like trenches beneath my eyes. "Maybe I should wait here. I just scream pro bono, and we know how much you guys love those types."

"No, you need to be there, be my diversion. Charm away their attention while I try to find Sophia's files."

"Charm?"

"Or scare. Whatever works."

We trekked across the parking lot to the stairs, got down to street level, and dodged our way across traffic to get to the entrance. In the lobby of his building, we pushed onto the elevator among men and women in expensive suits, the serious expressions of professional grownups molding their faces as they stared at the ascending floor numbers above the sliding doors. Their eyes slid in my direction as they pressed aside to allow us to make our exit.

The business offices were on the floor below the attorneys' suite and did not boast the mahogany furnishings or original artwork on the walls. Here were the padded cells of the standard hive of the regular drones. The receptionist—young, chic behind her owl-eyed glasses, her demeanor as brisk as her handling of the multiline phones—waved a weak hello to Phillip. He asked—over her ongoing answering and directing of calls—if anyone were free to talk to a potential hire. Her sidelong glances at me became a frank stare. Before she could even signal him to wait while she checked, Phillip headed for one of the corridors formed by the cubicles, saying he'd run on back and see if someone had a few minutes. The receptionist pointed at the chairs that lined the wall of the waiting area. I took a seat, grinning at her as she watched me with steady mistrust, as though I might try to steal one of their out-of-date magazines.

A very tall woman was coming down the corridor Phillip had just taken; she must have been close to seven feet even before adding the sculpted strata of her hairstyle. She came toward me, head high, the drapery of her turquoise, floor-length caftan fluttering out behind her like banners on the prow of a ship. Her approaching presence forced me to my feet; clearly, it was a response she was accustomed to. She extended her hand in greeting, smiling warmly in an I-smile-warmly-because-they-pay-me-to fashion, and said, "You must be Mr. Hogarth's friend." Her intonation left ice crystals in the air, telling me how much she despised him. I knew how to make nice here.

"Phillip has friends?" I said as I took her hand. Her smile became authentic.

"So you're looking for work?" She introduced herself as the head of human resources but made a point of not giving her name, a means of making it plain I was not to contact her again. Still, we proceeded through a half-hearted round of the mating dance of employment: I listed my garden center skills and she told me about working for the firm as a prelude to telling me they had nothing for me at the time, but I might try again in the future. Phillip had yet to reappear, and her entertainment with me was waning fast.

"When in the future?" I asked, stalling.

She smiled. "You'll find a job long before that, I'm sure." She offered me her best wishes and turned to go.

"Do you have a minute more?" *Where the hell was he?* "I mean just a minute. Do you have any advice? I mean for the next time? If you wouldn't mind?"

She stopped, turned back, and shook her head, her shoulders softening. "Oh, honey. Where to begin?" At that moment, Phillip came around the corner. He gave me a quick raise of his eyebrows to indicate success. "So Regina? Can we help Leslie out here?"

Regina gazed down at him, then again at me. "You really want that advice?"

Phillip grabbed my arm and pulled me away. "She's heard it all already."

"Hearing is not the same as listening."

He called back some cryptic gratitude. We rushed toward the elevator, which was taking on passengers and pushed in. The door closed. Everyone's eyes turned up toward the numbers.

Phillip kept his hand hard around my biceps. In the lobby, he guided me toward the street entrance.

Once on the sidewalk, I tugged away from his grip. "What took you so long?"

"Well, first I had to teach myself how to use the HR database, and then—" He held out the hand that had been locked around my arm. "Keys to the kingdom, baby." On his palm were the nine digits of a social security number.

molly

Frank sits on the doctor's round stool swiveling side to side; he's talking about panic and adrenaline and remembering to breathe. Molly sits on the edge of the examination table, swinging her legs, listening more to the paper crinkle than to yet another calm explanation of why her life sucks. Around the top of the room is a hand-painted border made up of the alphabet, each letter worked around a cartoonlike animal. A IS FOR ANT. B IS FOR BEE. They chose easy ones for the little kids, so, of course, P IS FOR PEACOCK. She tries to skip over that one and focuses on poor letter X, no animal for it. Her eyes travel around the drawings, backward, forward, fast, so the letters start blurring, doubling up, changing order. You could start it anywhere, let X go first for once—even though X would still stand alone. You can change the order but PEACOCK is always going to start with the letter P and RACCOON is always going to start with an R, SNAIL with S. Some things cannot be separated. They have to stay together. Coupled. Like rhymes. Frank probably can tell she's not paying attention to him. She doesn't care. She's seeing. Seeing how you could do it. How that stupid, shitty poem could be made to line up as *The Wilderness*.

"What is it, Molly?" Frank has stopped swiveling.

She looks down at the gray gunk beneath her nails. "I'm not telling her."

key

Phillip pointed toward a break in the traffic; we jogged across the street; continued down the block. I hurried to keep pace with him.

"Are you going to tell me where we're going?"

"We need to get her credit report; get that and we have her card numbers, real-estate transactions—"

"And we can trace her backward through time. Yes, dear, I know how that works."

"You really don't play well with others, do you?" He was annoyed with my lack of appreciation for his guile. "Oliver will run this for us."

"Donald Oliver? Your Donald Oliver?"

"Don't make it sound like it's my job to curb him."

"He'll do this? No questions asked?"

"He'll ask questions but we don't answer any of them, Les. Not one. No matter how benign he seems."

I knew little more than the public about the whole Donald Oliver affair, the comfy immunity exchanged for testimony concerning a money laundering operation. The resulting revelations had decimated an international banking firm. Thousands lost everything they had. Except for Oliver. That he had orchestrated both ends of the scandal for his personal profit was well known. What was also known was that Oliver was tuned into networks of information that took ethical investigations years to uncover, if ever. He had exchanged his freedom for the promise of an occasional useful tidbit of data. Oliver claimed to be able to save many times over the lives he had ruined with the well-placed phone call about a chosen flight number or the targeted train station. His magic was that he could make things not happen. What could anyone do but take his word for it?

Phillip had been on his defense team; we were on the outs at the time and hardly saw each other over those months. When I did prod him about the case, he'd turn grim, silent. It occurred to me, now, as I walked along beside him, that conscious or not, Phillip's idiot risk of screwing Sophia in the conference room may have been a deliberate act of career sabotage, knowing that eventually they'd get caught; he'd be fired. Self-destruction had been the only escape available. Had he even thought of what it might do to Sophia? Probably not. Once you decide you're taking yourself out, you really don't care who comes along on the ride.

We walked about six more blocks to a stretch of row houses that marked the latest front of gentrification. Piano scales being run from an upstairs studio were followed by the whine of power tools and the slamming of hammers sounding through the plastic shrouded windows of the next; the silence of abandon in the one beyond that. Phillip and I sidestepped sawhorses and bags of concrete. I thought of my husband; how happy this real-time before, during, and after would make him. Greg believed you could rebuild anything. I believed collapse was inevitable. The tenacity of our marriage had been defined by our need to convert each other. Funny how much damage has to get done before you begin to understand that your beliefs are meaningless outside your own life.

Phillip touched my elbow to steer me up the steps to a door

painted with glossy red enamel and mounted with a small brass plaque that read "D. Oliver." He rang the bell. In short order, a man opened the door. He was in his late sixties, maybe, it was hard to judge; he had the unlined complexion of one who had never spent much time in the sun. His hair was thick, silky white, brushed back from his temples, quite striking against the sour cherry color of his brocade dressing gown and matching slippers.

"I was expecting Suzanne," he said, his accent distinct but unfamiliar. He blinked at us. "You'll have to assist me; I fear I have left my glasses out back."

"I am not Suzanne," Phillip laughed, entering as though invited.

"Who—" The man peered in the direction of Phillip's voice. "—Hogarth?"

"And a friend." Phillip crooked his finger beckoning me inside. "She's not Suzanne, either."

Oliver sighed and closed the door after us. "Suzanne, if you must know, is my physical therapist."

"Is that what you kids are calling it these days?"

"That is what we kids have always called it." Oliver chuckled and motioned us to follow him toward the rear of the house, guiding himself with one hand along the wall. "So tell me friend of my tormentor. Do you have a name?"

Phillip raised his hand to stop me from answering. "If she doesn't tell you hers, I won't have to tell her yours."

"Mine is on the door."

"Your real one."

"Ah. Yes. That would be too much an intimacy for first meetings. Tell me, friend of Phillip, do you know the difference between a lawyer and a whore?"

237

"Must you resort to that one every time I visit?"

"I am reminded of it only when you visit." He gestured us through an archway into a small library. As I passed him, he took my shoulder, his grip stronger than he looked capable of, almost painful; he pulled me in to whisper, "A whore will stop fucking you when you're dead." His breath smelled of clove and he was wearing cologne of Oriental fragrance. He tightened his fingers before letting me go, waggled his eyebrows with glee. Finger to his lips, he instructed silence, making me his coconspirator. He then shuffled over to his desk and indicated we should sit. We did not.

The library was what one would expect from a man such as Oliver: rich but worn, faintly decrepit. Fragrances of lemon oil and leather melded with tobacco. The heaviness of the drapery and antique furnishings combined to produce that sense of Old World lassitude that American movies use to convey evil. Here, up close, it seemed more a case of severe boredom. He had seen it all before, over and over again, so many times, that the sequence of days blurred, overlapping into a sort of non-history. It would be difficult to get a sense of where you were on the time line from Oliver or this room—if not for the fax machine and phone blinking frantically for attention.

Phillip was playing with the globe next to the window, spinning the world this way, then that. "Do you remember Sophia, Oliver? The young woman who helped us out in resolving your predicaments?"

The man had his lenses on now, thick bifocals. "I'm losing my sight, Phillip, not my memory. Who would not remember Sophia? Vibrant intelligence. Makings of a first-rate researcher. She went on to good things, I hope."

"Better things than this. Right now, she may be in some distress and we need to find her. Quickly."

"What sort of distress? Legal? Financial? Romantic?"

"Distress is distress, Oliver."

"So this is a mission of mercy? That would explain . . ." He turned to me, his eyes magnified to flylike bulges behind the glasses. "Normally, Phillip does not come in the company of witnesses. You would be a friend of Sophia's, too?"

Phillip jumped in before I could speak. "We're here to get information; not to make donations to the well."

"One must give to get. I need something to seed the system. A penny for the wish, so to speak."

"I have her social."

"Aha. Keys to the kingdom," said Oliver, telling me where Phillip had picked up the phrase. He picked up the phone. "Will you write the number down for me? So much easier for me than by hearing them. These tiny numbers on the pad. Impossible."

"I'll provide what you need when it's needed."

Oliver waved his arm in frustration. "Everything we've been through and still no trust." He put the phone to his ear, turning away from us, speaking into the receiver in what sounded like a dialect of Chinese. I went over to where Phillip had gone back to tracing his way around the world.

"Doesn't he have some sort of security personnel?" I whispered. "I've only spent three minutes with the guy and I want to hurt him."

"Other people would mean other eyes and ears. He'd rather lose his life than lose one of his secrets."

"Why let you in then? Are you one of his secrets?"

"May as well be."

Oliver cleared his throat to get our attention. "Numbers, Phillip, or I can do nothing for you."

Phillip went to the desk, where Oliver had laid a pad and pen. He wrote something on the pad and when Oliver reached for it, Phillip grabbed Oliver's glasses from his face and tossed them at me. I barely made the catch.

"That was simply uncivil," said Oliver, sinking back into his chair, sulking as Phillip punched the series of numbers written on his palm into the phone's keypad. Almost immediately, the fax machine glittered to life and began to print. Phillip took the receiver from Oliver and hung up the phone.

"This may take a while," Phillip said to me, moving to collect the pages as the machine fed them into the bin. I went over to return the lenses to their owner. Oliver took them and pulled the pad over so that we could both read the *fucked again* that Phillip had written. Oliver glanced over at Phillip, before smiling up at me and speaking very low. "Man goes into a bar and asks the bartender, quite politely, for a glass of water. The bartender pulls a revolver and points it dead in the man's face. The man swallows, says 'thanks' and leaves."

"Excuse me?" I leaned in, trying to hear him better.

"Humor an old man. What happened between the customer and the bartender?"

"Don't talk to him." Phillip's tone was stern, bordering on anger.

"He's talking to me," I called back and then, softly, to Oliver. "I don't know. What happened?"

"Leslie!" I heard Phillip realize his mistake before my name was fully out of his mouth.

"Ah, so this is the infamous Leslie? That was sloppy, Phillip. I

240

would have thought you better by now." Oliver grinned and pulled me closer. "I shouldn't gloat. A man is never weaker than the moment after he believes himself victor."

"I'll try to remember that." I leaned in further. "So, what happened in the bar?"

"Hiccups. The man who went into the bar had the hiccups. Barman pulled the gun to scare them away. It worked. Hence, the gratitude."

"The water might have worked. He could have tried that first."

"Yes, but it is overwhelming sometimes, is it not, the instinct to go for one's gun?"

Behind me the fax continued to grind. Oliver and I considered each other, his grin broadening. He had known whom I was when I came in the front door with Phillip, before he could actually see me. We'd been expected. I leaned in even closer. "You certainly are well informed."

"I'm in the business of staying informed."

"But why information about me? Who am I to you?"

"It's always useful for the exiled to keep accounts on those who operate the gates." He gestured toward Phillip.

"But why me?" I pleaded.

"You're of interest to Phillip."

"But me? I'm no one."

"Everyone is someone. Everyone has value in my work."

"Aw, that's so sweet. But me?"

"Obviously."

"And Sophia?"

"Yes."

"Sophia Mallory?"

"Of course."

"And Nate?"

"That goes without—" He pressed his finger to his lips and then wagged it at me. "I am not to be trusted around women."

"You needn't worry about that." I got up from the desk, went to the fax machine, where Phillip was paging through the printouts so far.

"We've got tax returns and bank statements; credit cards should be up soon."

"Nice," I said before hitting the cancel button.

He grabbed at my hand, too late. "Shit, Leslie!"

"Oliver is doing this for us only to buy Sophia some time. She's already been here. She wanted help finding Nate. He knows where she was headed when she left."

Phillip glared at me then at Oliver. "He told you that?"

Oliver shook his head in sorrow. "I'm afraid she left angry. I could not help her."

"I don't believe that." Phillip shook his head. "You could have helped her but you didn't."

The old man shrugged. "She wouldn't help me. Suzanne is so late this morning, and I ache."

"Christ—"

"Christ will forgive us all, Phillip. It's in the contract."

"But you do know where she went?"

"She may have mentioned something about . . . alas, I am an old man. I forget the particulars. No cure for old age."

"I'm sure we can find something to relieve you in the short term," I said and started toward him.

"Phillip will not allow you to harm me. That's in the contract, as well."

242

"He's right, Leslie. *You* cannot do that." Phillip pulled me aside and began to unbutton his cuffs. I smiled at Oliver, who cowered in his chair before Phillip's quickening advance. You would think, for a man who prided himself on information, Oliver would, especially at his late age, be better informed than to think man can tell woman, who has lived in exile since her creation, something she doesn't already know about men.

their eyes and the house

trigger

I drove, lurching us through the first few intersections as I regained my clutch-shift-release skills. The gears protested occasionally, and I would look over to see Phillip wince, although that may have been due to the swelling and bruises on his knuckles. He'd changed into one of the fresh, pressed shirts he kept in the trunk of the car. He had not said anything since we'd left Oliver at his desk—hunched and a bit bloodied, but unbroken of will. Phillip turned down my offers to get ice or aspirin in such a way that told me he wanted the pain.

"I knew that wouldn't work," he said, finally, mostly to himself, scolding. "I knew it."

"We don't need him. We have these addresses from what did print out. The ones on the taxes give us plenty of places to start."

"I could have killed him, Leslie."

"But you didn't."

"I could have." His voice was wistful, his expression a confusion of wonder and regret. "I could have done it."

I let go of the shift, reached over to run the back of my fingers over his cheek. I wanted him to feel the reality of me there with him, the fact of the event being over. "But you did not do it. You stopped. You stopped yourself."

He laid his injured hand over mine. "I wanted to."

"Of course you wanted to stop."

"No, Leslie. I wanted to."

The highway entrance was up ahead; I had to ease my hand out from under his so that I could shift into proper gear. "But you didn't."

He looked around as though just awakened. "Where are we going?"

"Those addresses on the tax statements? We know she didn't meet Nate until after she was fired from the firm, and we know when that happened. The next year's return has her address as being the same as it was three years before she came to the city. She lists her income as next to nothing. Where does a struggling grad student who has been disgraced on the job go?"

"Home." He took the papers from where I'd stuck them in the sun visor and saw the location I'd circled. "That's a full day's drive. We won't get in until tomorrow morning."

"Which is why we're driving fast." I merged into traffic and started navigating for the far-left lane. "Get some sleep."

"Don't think I can. Do you have any idea how disbarred I am?"

"That won't happen. You know enough, remember?"

"Not enough to make a difference this time."

"More than enough," I said, patting his knee. "You know Oliver, and now, Oliver knows you. My guess is he won't say a word to anyone. Old man with vision problems; he fell down the stairs. The more boo-boos for Suzanne to kiss. Therapeutically, mind you."

"You're the last person I would have expected that sort of fairy tale from, Leslie. That's not how it works."

"He didn't even try to protect himself. He let you do that to him. He welcomed it."

"Donald Oliver is not suicidal."

"Didn't say he was. He wanted the contact; he was willing to die to get it. He's sort of in love with you, I think."

Phillip's eyes widened and then he broke into a genuine laugh. "Okay, *that* is the fairy tale I'd expect from you." He settled back against the door. "Thanks for the bedtime story, darling; I think I will take a nap." He closed his eyes, yawned, and chuckled again under his breath. "You *are* unhinged. You know that?"

"Yes, dear, I know," I said and resisting the urge to touch him again, I reached instead for the headlights in preparation of dusk now ascending on the horizon before us.

Phillip took over the driving right before we reached the mountains. We climbed into night, the solid dark of slopes rising massive only to fall into void on either side of us, stars in a narrow band above us; and when we'd round a bend in the optimal direction, glimpses of the new crescent moon hooking the edge of the peaks, anchoring the sky to the earth. We didn't talk much; he was distracted, edgy. We came into a touristy little village on the outskirts of the ski area, he pulled over and asked if I would mind taking the wheel again; his hands were hurting. We got out to change places and I stopped him in the beam of the headlight to get a good look at the damage. His left hand was bruised, but the swelling in the right hadn't begun to subside and an eggplant colored lump ridged his knuckles.

"What? Did Oliver have a steel plate in his head? This hematoma looks bad. You're still bleeding."

"I think I broke something. At least, this is how it felt the last time I broke it."

"The last time?"

"Punched a wall. Found the stud."

"I never heard about that."

"Yeah, well, you were the reason."

"Way to share the pain, Phillip."

"It did hurt. Does hurt."

In apology, I leaned down and kissed the bruises, gently, just brushing them with my lips. Instinct or impulse, it was without any consideration of what he might read into the act. My usual way of screwing things up. I raised my eyes to see him smiling sadly, head turned away. "We'd better find someone to take a look at you," I said and pointed him toward the passenger side. We continued on into the village where we found a roadside bar. A waitress, dressed as an alpine milkmaid, told us of an urgent care facility further up the road toward the ski slopes. She put some ice in a plastic bag, gave it to Phillip along with a clean bar towel and volunteered to call ahead to let them know to expect us.

The doctor, an athletic-looking blond, was waiting outside the sliding door, holding it open by standing in the sight line of the automatic eye; she took Phillip right into x-ray while I filled out forms on a clipboard, sitting alone in the empty waiting area. I reached the "relationship to patient" line and didn't know what to write. I finally decided on "friend" because any other descriptive noun would have required explanations I couldn't make. But truthfully, "friend" didn't cover it, didn't even begin. The doctor came out as I was finishing the forms. Phillip's hand wasn't broken, but they were setting him up with a sling for comfort's sake.

"What did he hit?" She was assessing me with quick up and down glances.

"You mean 'who'?"

"That's what I mean."

"Not me."

"What condition was 'Not me' in when you left him?"

"He'll live."

"That's good. Where are you two headed?"

"Phillip must have told you."

"I'm just making conversation."

What she was doing was getting ready to alert the system that she had a guy with battered hands but no indication of any return blow. Truth was the only chance we had. "We're on our way to Bellwood. We are trying to locate a friend of ours. She may be hurt."

"Who hurt her?"

"Not me."

Her posture relaxed. "I'm supposed to call something like this in."

"I know you are. Former cop, here."

"And he's a lawyer? Fun."

"We're not. Having fun."

"Obviously. It is possible, I guess, that we could get very busy and I could forget to make that call. Unless, of course, something should turn up in the paper or on television that would trigger my memory." She took the clipboard from me. "We'd better get you back on the road." She gave me one last frown of warning and then went back into the examination room, leaving me alone.

I thought to close my eyes, relax for a few minutes because I would be driving the rest of the night. Just as the thought came to me the clinic doors slid open, remained open, as they had when the doctor had waited for us. No one came inside; no one was there. I stood and moved closer to the door. Saw no one. I went out into the night, into the parking lot. I could see the rapid, steamy puffs of my breath. Nothing else. And then way up the road, speeding in this direction was what at first I thought to be the single headlight of a motorcycle. But there was no sound. The light came on faster, leaving the road, heading for the building. Not a vehicle, but a person on foot, running hard, impossible speed taking shape from my recognition of him. It was the boy, running right at me, head down charging. He hit the first round of lamp light falling on parking lot and then the next and then, faster, he was charging directly at me; I could not move; he was still gaining speed; I braced for the impact but at the last instant he vanished—or transformed, because something hit me; a blow of rage crashed hot into my chest, knocking the breath from my body, moving through with claw and tooth and a roar so terrible that I covered my ears, wanting to cry out for the pain but unable to speak, to breathe—and then it was over, or made to be over by Phillip, who was standing beside me.

"Leslie?" He pulled my hand away from my ear.

I could only stare at him. "What was that?"

"What was what?" His face had the slack blankness of the recently medicated. "You okay?"

"No. I mean, yes. I mean I don't know what I mean. He was a kid when it happened."

"Who?"

"James. He thought it was his fault. Kids always think it's their fault. You have to tell them it isn't. Over and over, you have to tell them. They still don't believe you, but you have to try. No one told James—no, worse. Something worse."

"I can't follow—what are you talking about?"

"He was a child and they made him believe. They beat belief into him."

"Belief of what? Are you okay? You're bleeding."

I reached up and felt the trickle of wet from my ear. I moved back toward the building, closer to my reflection in the window, dabbing at the blood with my fingertip. "It's only a scratch; must have done it to myself." I tried to catch the light at a better angle, and saw the stripe of red at my jaw line. Red stripes. "Tigers."

"Leslie, you're going to have to be more specific; the codeine is making me kind of—"

"Tigers. He wrote about tigers but he means the welts, the stripes that were raised on his back by his father's belt strap. 'Pain makes a man think.' That thing about the stallion."

"Now we're talking about horses?"

"The tigers taking down the stallion. A black stallion. It's in his papers, his *fiction*. It doesn't matter if he's making it up, that part about the stables; it's true all the same. James wants his father dead for what he's done. The beatings, the lynching, God knows what else. James wants to rip his father to shreds—"

"Leslie?"

"—but of course he can't do *that*. He can't kill his own father. He can't endure the man any longer, either. So he runs away. In the papers he left, he says he ran away into the countryside . . . into the wilderness. That's what the illustrations are about. *The Wilderness* is James's way of destroying his father. The poem itself must have meant something in particular to Dad." I could see James in a booth at the coffee shop. I could see the horror registering on Nate's young face as uncle explained to nephew, listed detail after detail, the violent events he's managed to

253

outline in seemingly innocuous drawings: He took me to a lynching; he beat me with belts; we were grieving, grieving what? Something else the father had done? There were twelve pictures to be made here, at least. *I saw the man* . . . How had that girl come to be buried broken, in the pond? James would have told Nate this in order to explain why he had to get the books back. The contraption he had designed to stop his father had instead carried that violence forward into the general population. The book and hence its curse were James's fault. All of it delusional, yes, but Nate being predisposed, would have embraced the delusion.

"Leslie?"

"There are always more." Was that a statement of hope or threat or resignation?

"Leslie? Can you even hear me?"

I thought about the ransacked state of their house, Nate's inking his presence from the photograph, Sophia's smashing of her own work, James's cutting himself out of the picture of one terrible night in a life of terrible nights. Erasure. "We'd better find them soon," I said and headed over toward the car, "or there will be nothing left to find."

greg

The house is the same house. These mullioned windows. These foot-worn stairs. This thin lamp light. That threadbare rug. The scuffed paint on the baseboards. The wallpaper in the entry with its painted swallows winging away, garlands of laurel in their beaks.

It is Leslie's house. The place of her girlhood where so much went wrong. She slept in the room where Molly sleeps now, buried in her blankets and held down with the help of a tiny white pill. Emma has the room Leslie's sisters shared, keeping their secrets and their distance, leaving Leslie more alone than they could have realized, leaving her no choice but to invent ways to fill in the spaces.

And our bedroom, the one that was once shared by her mother and father, and then by her father and others and then no one. I had suggested rearranging the house, at least rearranging us in the house, but she had said no, already resigned to a past she could neither embrace nor betray. These are the rooms that hold the answers she will never have to the never-ending why, why, why of her life. She needs to be close to the possibility of answers, as close as she can get without ever touching them. When it seems those answers might reach out in return, she runs.

She doesn't leave us; I understand that. Nor is it us she comes back to. I wonder if she will even notice that when she finally comes back this time, we are no longer here. Will she wander about, calling for us like the family ghost she is? Or will she steel herself further in another layer of armor against her own heart? The woman prides herself on her ability to be left behind without bending to weep.

The suitcases are packed; I'm not sure where we're going. I have the hours between now and the girls' waking to decide that. I will leave a note, a number. Leslie would throw herself in front of locomotives, off skyscrapers, into the whirlwind for any one of us; I know that. I do not know if she'll pick up the phone and call. And if she did, what would either of us say? I cannot in good conscience keep our daughters here any longer. I cannot in good conscience leave Leslie alone in this, her house, what with the threats it holds for her. I need to do something, the best thing, the only thing I can do. Between now and the time we leave tomorrow morning, I am taking down the cupboard door, the one beneath the kitchen sink, replacing the board, and filling in that goddamn eye.

trail

We arrived in Bellwood before daybreak when the stars were thinning and the world was without color. The community had tucked itself in among the embattlements of the foothills. The residential roads were steep and narrow, making access difficult. I imagined the Mallory family had moved up here shortly after their son's death. Bellwood was the sort of place you went when under attack.

Phillip was still asleep when I found the Mallory home; a split-level ranch on a street of split-level ranches designed to accommodate the slope. The house was dark, except for the front porch light that shone above the wrought-iron numerals of the address. I parked on the roadside, left Phillip in the car, and headed for the front door. I knocked, rang the bell, but got no answer. The neighboring houses were in various phases of awakening: Lights came on, garage doors opened. I started back for the road to decide which of these homes looked *up* enough to approach at this hour. A van rolled by, its driver-side window down for the arm throwing plastic-wrapped newspapers, one onto each driveway or lawn. No paper for the Mallory house, though.

I checked the mailbox. Nothing there. I was about to wake Phillip to tell him we'd struck out when the front door of the house across the street opened and a man in a plaid flannel robe stepped out, proceeded by a large tabby cat that ran, tail erect, into the bushes. He didn't see me until after he'd bent down to retrieve his paper from midpoint in the dew-soaked grass of his yard. He stood, rubbed his hand through dark hair and smiled before starting toward me.

"Nice car."

"It's not mine."

"Never are, are they? The nice ones. You look lost."

"I'm trying to find the Mallorys. Are they out of town?"

"In a manner of speaking. What would you be wanting from the Mallorys at this time of day?"

"We're friends of Sophia."

"Not very good friends or you'd know that no one lives over there anymore."

"They've moved?"

"Moved on. Passed."

"Sophia's parents?"

"Douglas went several years ago. But Mrs. Mallory left us last autumn. Keep thinking Sophia will put the house on the market, but . . . she's the last one. I guess it's hard for her to make it final. She pays someone to keep the grass cut, look after things. We keep a watch in general." He pulled his bathrobe tighter against the early-morning chill. "Why don't you tell me what you and the fancy car and the sleeping guy are up to here?"

"We're looking for Sophia."

"She's not here now."

"We didn't expect her here. But we thought someone—maybe something in the house could give us an idea where she might be. We need to find her quick."

"Got that. Want to know what for."

"We're worried," I said, explaining what I could, the only way I could. "We're very worried. We don't want to lose her."

He considered me and swung the paper back and forth in its plastic bag as though it were a decision-making oracle. "I was afraid it was something like that. My wife and I have thought Sophia was having a bad time of it for a while now. We have a set of keys; I'll let you in." He headed back for his house, and I went to rouse Phillip, who as a rule did not wake up happy.

The neighbor, who had introduced himself as Henry, would not leave us alone in Sophia's house. He said he hadn't seen her since her mother's funeral, but that his wife had spoken with Sophia when she came by the house to arrange upkeep on the place. Even though no one was living there, she had a housecleaning service come in weekly. The furniture was dusted and the carpets bore the tracks of recent vacuuming. Ready for return. We'd done that too, my sisters and I. For a few weeks, we'd been extra good, helpful, tidy, thinking we could lure our mother home, thinking it had been the household pandemonium she'd fled. We could fix the disorder around us and thereby fix the disorder in her. We had believed that we had that kind of power over time and space and other people. It had not worked, of course, and with failure the world-altering behaviors fell away before a sharp word or a dirty sock under the couch, back to normal, order crashing in slow motion as the facts sunk in. She had not only left the house; she'd left *us*. That Sophia was grieving her mother's death on top of everything else meant that she was in avalanche condition more than I could have guessed.

Phillip and I looked room to room; Henry, vigilant, stayed with us. We found a portrait of Sophia that Nate had done hanging in the dining room. So, if she had not brought him here, at least her family knew of him, her mother approving of the man enough to display a gesture of his love for her daughter publicly. On the wall opposite were framed photos of Sophia. In time lapse, Sophia grew up, lost teeth, rounded into chubby adolescence and out again as the elegant woman I knew. In the living room, all along the bookcase shelves, I watched photos of her parents date, wed, grow old, and then her mother growing even older alone. Photographs of the three of them together, their poses ranging from relaxed to valiant, lined the hallway. No pictures of a boy, her brother, Joseph. That was to be expected; those who have been stolen from learn not to put their treasures on display. Sophia would have noticed how open to predatory forces they had left her.

We found the pictures of Joseph in what must have been her mother's bedroom. Arranged in silver frames on the table beside the bed, Joseph would have been her first and last sight each day. A discreet little shrine of baby pictures and school photos, including the one I'd seen online, centered around a votive candleholder that, when lit, provided light for a portrait of Jesus in prayer at Gethsemane.

Grownups pay for their own sins. "There are no pictures of Sophia in here."

"None of the husband, either," said Phillip. "Just the boy."

Henry cleared his throat. "If you knew what happened to that boy—"

"We do. Know," I said. "I meant that I'm getting a clearer sense of what's pushing her. She's a daughter. A grownup daughter."

Phillip nodded. "She's trying to save her family."

"She's trying to save the world."

"World can't be saved." Phillip sighed and lifted his sling-bound arm as a reminder of Oliver. "Keep trying to explain that to everyone. To her. To you."

"Yeah, but you aren't the little girl who has been making herself crazy in order to prove to her folks that she is worth their—"

"Crazy?" Henry raised his hand to stop me. "Sophia is the brightest child I've ever met. I'll have you know that the Mallorys were extremely proud of that girl. They saved every report card, every piece of writing, every scrap of paper that child produced. Full-scale braggarts. They adored her."

"I don't doubt it, but adored isn't the same as . . . I'm amazed that given everything she's taken upon herself . . ." The unlit Christ gazed up at us, pleading for mercy. "Did you ever meet the boyfriend?"

Henry tugged at the belt on his robe. "That Nate fellow? Naw, I heard about him, though. Nothing disparaging. Mrs. Mallory liked him well enough, but too much history there to get comfortable, if you know what I mean. She kept her peace when Sophia was around, but privately she wasn't shy about her opinions. Thought the situation was dangerous."

I looked at Phillip. "Dangerous?"

Henry's expression grew suspicious. "Mrs. Mallory used to say that most young couples give off a shimmer of happiness, gratitude for having lucked into each other; but Sophia and Nate gave off a gleam of triumph. Like they'd been looking for each other specifically, like they willed each other into being. Trajectory, she called it; like they were a thing propelled, she said, and when they peaked, when they hit the inevitable downside, they wouldn't be falling in love any longer; they would just fall."

"They're falling now." I felt sick with the certainty of descent. "Is there any chance you know exactly when they met? Where?"

"Exactly? No. But—" He went to the dresser and opened the top drawer. "When she got bad toward the end, I'd bring her mail in every day." Henry pulled out a white paper box. "Sophia's letters. Mrs. Mallory wanted them organized by date. My wife helped her with this." The box was stuffed with envelopes, grouped in packets; each packet tied with a hair ribbon, a different color for each month.

"Keys to the kingdom," said Phillip.

"We're talking about a person, Hogarth." I took the box from Henry. "There is no kingdom."

Henry smacked his tongue in distaste. "Hogarth?"

"Look, I'm doing my best to make it up to her."

"I should hope so. Let's get on with it then."

Between Henry and Phillip's knowledge of Sophia, we were able to narrow down the dates to a few months, but when I went to untie the ribbon around one of those packets, Henry laid his hand on mine. "Better let me do this. I can approve of what you're looking for, but there are most likely private, family matters in these."

I let go of the packet, motioned to Phillip, and we left Henry alone to read. We wandered down the hall to a closed door on which a painted name plaque hung from a nail. SOPHIA. I looked back at Phillip. "Should we?"

"Might help." He reached from behind me and opened the door. I found the light switch. We stood in the doorway, looking in. It could have been my room, the room I left behind when I left home. Sophia had always favored blues and lavender, it seemed. She had a collection of perfume bottles. Her shelves full of books; the bed crammed with stuffed animals. The walls decorated with posters, but unlike mine of rock bands and movie stars, Sophia had fallen asleep each night beneath the watch of Martin Luther King and a close-up of a broken, rusted shackle above the word DREAM. We stood there on the threshold looking a long time; I wasn't aware of Phillip putting his arm around me, only that I was being held.

"I know what you're afraid of," he said in my ear, "but we'll find them. We have to."

I nodded, leaning into his warmth before switching off the light and pulling the door shut. We sat down on the carpeted floor of the hallway to wait for Henry. When he came out of Sophia's mother's bedroom, he was holding one of the hair ribbon ties and a piece of pale blue stationary, which he handed to me, bypassing Phillip's outstretched hand. Phillip craned his neck to read over my shoulder. I recognized Sophia's carefully crafted lettering:

. . . *thought I had "official" family permission to have open-ended access to the materials, but that seems to have fallen through. The new arrangements are that I may have only one day in the house to sort through all that garbage. AND a designated family representative must accompany me. Just to help me out. What a thoughtful gesture. Not restrictive in the least.*

They're sending a nephew of James K. Nathaniel, I think his name is. And get this. He's never been there, either. So how much help can he be? Obviously, the Kendricks have found out what I'm writing on and are sending an errand boy to report back—and of course, make sure I don't steal anything.

"Where is this place?" I offered the portion of letter back to Henry. "What house is Sophia talking about?"

He folded the sheet back along its crease lines, put it in the pocket of his robe along with the ribbon, a yellow one, half of which remained hanging over the pocket's edge. "I wish I could tell you. I recall Mrs. Mallory speaking of Sophia as being excited about finding a place where someone had lived, about it being a regular pigsty—one of those places where the owner never throws anything out, stacks of newspapers, mail, bags of rubbish. If she said where that was, I truly don't remember. Next thing I heard was that Sophia had taken to Nate. Mrs. Mallory was in a tizzy over that, I tell you. The whole love-at-first-sight malarkey. But that's the young. Everyone wants to be Romeo and Juliet, as if the ending will be different for them."

" 'Deny thy father and refuse thy name.' " Phillip pulled back the sling to check his knuckles. "Cannot be done."

"No, it cannot," said Henry.

"Doesn't stop them from trying," I said, my mind starting to fixate on the end of the yellow ribbon swinging against Henry's robe. "They have to try." I could imagine Sophia and Nate laying eyes on each other the first time, the sense of recognition. If violence and madness are predisposed, why not love? Why not love especially? That's how we saved ourselves from the violent and the mad, wasn't it? We found some one or some thing to love, some way to raise concern for another's pain above our own, lift ourselves by lifting the other? I went back to Sophia's

264

bedroom. I could hear Henry asking what I was looking for and then his protesting the trespass. But I knew. I knew before I opened the door and turned on the light. The boy was sitting on Sophia's bed, waiting for me. He removed his cap, turned, and lifted his face to look at me. I had to look back. I had to see him. He was everyone I'd ever known.

I turned off the light, closed the door; I ran my fingers over Sophia's name on the plaque, marveling at the way the lines of individual letters could be made to intersect into larger beings. "They must have known each other. James and that little girl. She may have been his friend during the lonely summers. I don't think James had many friends. He must have loved her and then been forced to witness . . . that's why he had to stop his father. Not because of what his father did to him, but because of what his father did to her. Deny thy father; refuse thy name. He tried."

"Wouldn't it have been easier to call the constable than bury the story between whatever layers of symbolism make up that book?"

"You are thinking like a lawyer, Phillip. What ten-year-old boy is going to turn in his father? The father who has beat obedience into him? And even if he had, you saw that postcard. Did it seem to you that anyone would have cared one iota? The guys who were supposed to care were the guys who did it."

Henry cleared his throat. "Sophia showed you the post-cards?"

Phillip and I exchanged a quick, guilty glance. "We saw them," I said.

"How human beings can carry such terrible notions, let alone carry them out . . ." Henry shook his head. "Has she found one yet?"

"Not yet. Not as far as we know. James probably destroyed each book as soon as he found it."

"Book?" Henry said, confused. "She never mentioned any book. Last I heard she was looking for the irons. The branding irons?"

The axis of the planets slid. In a vertigo of realization, I saw James's spiders working their molten webs. "Branding irons?"

"The brands on the bodies? How each club took credit for its kill. They started out as slave hunters, but when slavery was made illegal, the livelihood became sport. Sportsmen. That's how they thought of themselves. Started charging big money to join in the game. There were quite a few chapters. Spread out over the country. They held competitions. The brands kept the counts honest, you see? Each had its own insignia—I thought you said you saw the postcards."

Sophia in judgment: *You did not look.* "One was a peacock."

"Not a peacock." Henry patted down his robe. "Don't have anything here to write with."

Phillip offered a pen to Henry, who took my right hand. "Now, this is from memory, mind you," he said, as he drew, ink on my skin, the simple shape of a bird with a fanned tail, it's head turned back, as though its neck had been broken. "Looks like a peacock, I guess. It's a sankofa bird. West African. Properly drawn, a sankofa is turning her head to tend to an egg she is carrying on her back. The future she left behind her. It is not considered taboo to go back and fetch—"

"What you forgot." I studied the bird drawn into my skin. "Sophia said that yesterday."

"I guess she was trying to tell you then. The clubs used African symbols as a means of covering their tracks. The brands were

266

African in design. Make it look like we were lynching our own."

I held my hand up to show Phillip. "The other symbols? A comet. An oak tree. Ants?"

Henry nodded. "A shooting star. A baobab. Termite. Whatever could be rendered in iron. Sophia has pictures of them in those postcards."

Phillip pulled my hand closer to look. "Why have I never heard of this before?"

"Who's to say you haven't?" Henry stifled a yawn. "No one I know is keeping it a secret."

"They took their *insignia* from that poem." The planets skewed again. I was very much aware of the walls, and the floor, the ceiling above us, the shingles, mist, clouds, stars, silent forever, above that. "If James's father and his club are behind the publication of that book?"

Phillip released my hand. "Then it's not a confession. It's a field guide."

"Worse," I said, "it's indoctrination. For kids."

molly

When Molly was very little and Emma was a baby, Mom and Dad took them on a vacation trip. Molly remembers it mostly in a jumble of random, disconnected images, but some of it has held together in spite of the disruption, like when you return a completed jigsaw puzzle to its box. Here's a section of the long boring car ride. Here's a bit of how hot it was; she sits in the backseat watching drops of sweat roll down her father's neck. This is the diving board at the hotel swimming pool. One large segment remained intact: they went to visit a park that had big caverns with great toothy rocks jutting from the floor and ceiling. The teeth were lit up so that they shone in rainbow colors. The ranger guiding the tour wanted to show off the echo, so he had the whole group get quiet, then he asked Molly to shout "Hello!" Molly had been too scared or shy to do it, so he'd asked some other kid. And then, to show what real darkness was, he turned off the lights—all the lights—for exactly one minute. Everyone screamed and then laughed and then got as quiet as it was dark. The lights came on again and then the tour was over, everyone blinking as they climbed back into the sun.

After the cavern they had gone to another part of the park called Mystery Ridge. Here your car appeared to coast uphill; for five bucks you could sit in the car and be amazed. Next they went to a strange house in which everything was leaning side-ways, beds, chairs; but if you put a pencil at the base of the sloping floor, it would roll back to the top, just as the car had. Dad said it was a trick, but Molly can still remember feeling pulled for the rest of the day. Even after they left the park, she felt as though she leaned in impossible ways.

Molly can name the force pulling her house off-center this morning, but watching Dad trying to keep his balance makes her sense that one more question about Mom might push him all the way over. She had been awakened by the phone ringing very early this morning and through the muddle of sleepiness had listened to the low reverberation of Dad's voice coming up through the walls. It might be Mom; it might not. Molly hadn't any need to hear the words. Thunder is thunder. It always means the same thing. She tries to keep her sister from being lightning bait, cajoling her into being extra cooperative, extra smiley, extra fast and extra out-of-there early for a Saturday morning. Rita, who knew how to read the Stone family weather from a distance, calls for Emma to come play, offering movies and gossip, an exit. Emma takes it without looking back.

At lunchtime, the suitcases are sitting by the front door. Dad hasn't said why, but Molly doesn't really want him to say anything. After they eat, he takes her over to the Swifton convalescent home for her job. He says he'll pick her up in a couple of hours like he usually does, but before she can get out of the truck he reaches over and tugs at her ponytail.

"You might want to tell them that after today you may not be able to come in for a while."

She says, okay, and then gets out. He waits until after she is inside; she waves to him; he drives away. In the reception area, she runs into Zeke, who is in jeans and a purple T-shirt instead of the white jacket they require aides to wear. He pushes his hair out of his eyes and waves a slip of paper at her.

"Last paycheck, Molly. I am so outta here."

"You quit?"

He turns his arm to examine his elbow. "Christ, yeah, I quit. You're only here once a week, but damn, what a drain from day to day."

"What are you going to do?"

"Find something else, I guess. Right now, I'm going back to my place and sit out on the roof in the sun, drink a few beers, and be glad I'm not here. First decent day we've had." He lowers his mouth to her ear, his breath is hot and it sends a tingle down her neck. "Want to join me?"

One minute. The ranger, his finger on the control panel, had said it would be dark one exact minute. "Yeah," she says, thinking she hears her voice echo. "Yeah, I do."

Zeke pulls his head back, confused. A soft smile curls into his soft features. "Cool." He makes a gallant flourish of a gesture toward the front door. "Let's go."

want

Henry wouldn't agree to let us stay in the Mallory house unsupervised, and he had to go get ready for work. He did, however, invite us to make use of his home for as long as we needed. Henry's wife insisted on making breakfast for us. She bustled about her kitchen, voicing her concerns for Sophia between recounting memories of the Mallory family. I had called Andrea and given her Sophia's license plates as well as a rundown on Nate's probable condition based on what I'd seen at the Willet house. I had also given her my intuitions, best as I could outline them, and told her Sophia may be in need of intervening care as well.

"How many bodies are we looking for, Leslie?"

"None. Please. Don't find any bodies."

"You could have called earlier, you know?"

"And you can lecture me later. Just APB them, now."

"Remember when I said how much I missed the old you?"

"You were lying."

"Like road kill. Where can I reach you?"

Phillip wanted to stay put, but I insisted we head back. I had a one-word argument for getting home right away: Greg. I had given Andrea the number on Phillip's cell phone. On hearing his name she tut-tut'ed me in feigned disapproval before promising to get back to us as fast as she could. We passed the promise for information along to Henry and his wife, thanking them for their help and the meal. Phillip, still in pain but far more alert, said he'd drive. I helped him undo the sling from behind his neck. We set out into the bright, cloudless morning.

I tried to call home on Phillip's phone but the mountains were blocking the signal. "Probably for the best," I said, returning the phone to its charger. "I can wait a little longer to hear that he's leaving me."

Phillip sighed and shifted up to the next gear. "Do you want kindness or honesty?"

"Must it always be a choice?"

"Greg should have kicked your butt to the curb years ago."

"Thank you."

"It would have been better for him; better for the girls. Much, much better for you. He should have been an absolute bastard and given you one sorrow in this life that you couldn't hold yourself solely responsible for."

"Was that the kindness or the honesty?"

"It never ceases to amaze me the amount of ruin that follows on the determination to be *good* rather than just human."

"And it would have been human to toss me out?"

"You, darling?" Phillip took his eyes off the road and gave me a long hard stare. "Hell, yes."

"Thank you, again."

"Remind me to show you my X-rays. And the repair bills for the wall."

I turned away, focusing on the tiered ledges of granite cut through for the road. Phillip gunned the engine; we were gaining speed, taking the curves too fast and passing the slower vehicles by swerving into the oncoming traffic lane. He was trying to get something from me, but I wasn't giving. The scarier he drove, the more resolute my silence. We passed the peak elevation sign, immediately beyond it was a scenic view and picnic area. He had to slam on the brakes to make the turn into the parking lot. We skidded to a stop. Phillip wrenched the key to shut down the engine, got out of the car, strode over to the passenger door, flung it open. He grabbed me by the wrist—in his sore, bruised right hand—as he bent over and hit the release on my seatbelt with his left; breathing hard, he yanked me out of the car, pulled me along behind him; we went past the visitors building, past the picnic tables splattered with bird droppings, past the concerned appraisals of the other travelers; he pulled me up the slope into the trees, maples and birches, shimmering with new leaf. He pulled me along until we reached an escarpment of sheared granite, and he could pull me no farther. Not that he stopped; he swung me around, forcing me backward so my shoulders were against the rock, forced my hands over my head; I heard my rings scrape on the rock, heard him groan against the sting of the rock scraping against his already battered knuckles; he brought his face fractions of an inch from mine and stayed right at that fraction, both of us gasping for air.

"Once and for all," he said, his eyes searching my face, "what do you want?"

I couldn't answer; I had no voice. Between trying to breathe and trying to slam down the sudden racking sobs in my chest, I couldn't answer. He saw me fighting hard, but not with him. The fierceness in his expression gave way. He released the pressure on my hands. "Leslie, you must know—" he began, but I couldn't bear to hear it. My hands came down around his neck, and my tongue slid in between his lips, and then his hands were in my hair and under my sweater and in my jeans and then in me and then he was in me and I laid back on the wet earth, staring up into the shimmering birches, not crying, not fighting, not anything.

It was chilly there on the ground, wet, muddy, reeking with the sweet fumes of spring decay. We didn't linger for more than the few minutes it took to get back our breath. We said nothing about pasts or futures. What can you say about the flow of the tide? It leaves. It returns. It will leave again. You adjust your travels accordingly or learn to be content to go when and where the tide takes you. Phillip helped me back to my feet and we walked down the hill, neither together nor apart.

When we returned to the car, Phillip checked his phone messages while I pulled the winged samara of maple seeds from my sweater. Andrea had called only minutes earlier. The SUV had been found, parked on a country route that saw little traffic. No sign of trouble. No Sophia, either.

"So much for the romantic nostalgia theory. Somebody must have picked her up," said Phillip, as he got behind the wheel, "which is flat out wonderful, because I was afraid we were going to end up with only these two we couldn't find. Now we have three. Huzzah." He turned on the ignition.

I hesitated getting back into the Jag, just to let the sun hit my face a bit longer, dry the wet in my hair, memorizing this place, this moment, the way lovers who will never see each other again try to memorize that last kiss as though it were the first. "Where exactly is the SUV?"

"Andrea didn't say. Only that they are getting ready to tow it in."

"They're together. Sophia and Nate are together." I crawled into the seat and grabbed the phone. "Drive."

Drive he did, descending at such a speed, my ears ached. I hit redial for Andrea, willing her to pick up, letting the line ring until she did.

"Don't tow it!" I shouted over the weak connection.

The static-broken signal garbled the first part of her response, but then cleared. ". . . so, let's review our basic legal terminology, shall we? *J* is for jurisdiction. Two counties over? They're only going to laugh extra hard before hanging up on me. It's already in transit. Done deal, sweetheart."

"Where did they find it? Where exactly?"

"I'll check." She put me on hold, and I got to listen to pre-recorded safety tips set to a peppy tune that in itself might be a form of correctional punishment: sixty days *or* the safety tape. Andrea came back on. "I'm looking at a county map. The only thing we heard is that the vehicle was found, abandoned, about sixteen miles down old Route 27. No signs of forcible anything. Just empty. They're hauling it in before one of the local pot growers decides the universe has gifted him with a brand-new delivery van."

"Sixteen? What else is out there? Sixteen miles down?"

"Sorry, it's Animal Control's turn to use the supersecret spy satellite this week. My guess? Mile sixteen is a lot like fifteen and seventeen. A whole lot of nothing."

"One soul's nothing is another soul's ground zero."

"Should I write that down, Leslie?"

"In gold ink. Put lots of little stars around it. Who owns the property?"

"I'm looking at roads here. Let me track that down and get back to you."

"If you could. Phillip and I are headed out that way now."

Phillip growled in misery. "We're headed where?"

"Look for the name Kendrick in the deed."

"I'm not researching titles for you, Leslie. I have my own job—"

"Thanks, Andrea."

"Well, if you're sure there's no other way I can fail or disappoint you."

"Not at the moment."

"You're welcome." She hung up, laughing, before I could.

Phillip glared at me. "And?"

"I'm not wrong."

"You? Never."

"Sixteen, Phillip. Sixteen miles down the road. There's a line in the poem about something being sixteen feet deep. That can't be a coincidence."

"Of course not. Sixteen is such a rare, underused numeral—"

"That's where Sophia met up with Nate. He was waiting for her."

"In the middle of nowhere?"

"In the middle of nothing."

"Meaning?"

"Whatever it means. I have to see what is out there. Sixteen miles down old Route 27. The place they met. Or agreed to meet." The roughly notched walls of granite around us channeled streams of water from the melt-off. It was still cold enough at this elevation to freeze the finer trickles into veins of ice along the stone. "I'm starting to think it went down exactly as Nate told her. I think he may have killed his Uncle James exactly in the manner, exactly for the reasons, he said he did. To avenge Sophia."

"Because he loves her?"

"Because he loves her."

the sun and man

curse

Sophia had not been deliberately covering up for Nate; of that I was certain. She was providing him a false alibi through fabricated memories. It had been her own denial she had been outlining when she had offered her reasoning for Nate's refusal to accept he had seen James at the coffee shop. She needed to believe he had been sleeping at her side every night that month. Her words, her voice, incredulous, kept coming back to me: *How could Nate kill anyone?*

She had shunted her mind away from Nate's actions by lasering into her work, which focused on Nate. Sophia's need to get to Nate before the authorities did was as much about protecting herself from what she knew as it was protecting Nate from being found out. She kept backing right into the truth she sought to run away from. Such was the way it worked with decent people. Bad guys would deceive with a smile and unblinking eye contact, shoulders down, fingers still, palms dry. The good would dart their eyes between the ceiling and the floor or fix their stare on the moth carcass on the windowsill, a smudge on the doorknob, anything but the questioner, as they flat-out lied to no one but themselves, their words telling you all was fine as their body language screamed *help*.

Sophia wasn't lying. She was relaying those facts that supported her fantasy. Fact: No mention of homicide had been made in any official report concerning James's death, but that did not make it any less so. An itinerant man of such advanced age, found under those conditions, who would think, who would care to look for anomaly? The knocking at the door that James had written about was earlier than he had come to expect, had that knocking been Nate? Had James been happy for his nephew's visit or had he surmised Nate's mission the moment he opened the door. Had he been frightened or grateful? Was it Nate who had cut his uncle out of the photograph, put him in the stove to burn but had not lit the thing due to a sudden, better idea? And the peacock drawing? When in the night had Nate done that? Had James, barred from the house, perhaps welcoming of banishment, stood at the window and watched his nephew commit an old, coded horror in heavy strokes of deep color? Accusation? Explanation? At what point had James turned away and walked himself into the cold and the dark, acquiesced to his fate because in the Kendrick family this was the sort of event one expects?

The closer we drove to the supposed answer, the more these questions proliferated until I was uncertain of even what the word *fact*—applied to anything other than death—was supposed to mean. Mid-afternoon: We reached the county line and the turnoff that marked the beginning of Route 27. I leaned into Phillip's shoulder to watch the odometer turn through the miles. We stopped exactly at the sixteenth; Phillip then let the car roll slowly forward. It was definitely the nothing and nowhere Andrea had promised. These were grazing fields, long abandoned by livestock and interest; the fences left unmended, the earth left to sprout sorghum, sprawls of fat-headed dandelions, clover, and thistle. We rolled on, Phillip looking left, me right.

"There," he said, pointing to where the remains of a stone

foundation poked through the grasses. He pulled as far off the road as the narrow shoulder allowed. I got out. Phillip instructed me to wait for him, but I told him no, that I wanted to go alone. He got out of the car anyway, shielded his eyes, and studied the distance, pretending not to be watching me as I crossed the road in front of him.

A paved break in the roadside grasses pointed to the path of a driveway. I followed the rutted macadam, noting the bent stalks of wild onion and newly crushed dandelions that betrayed earlier footsteps. Nate or Sophia or both. I reached the foundation, fieldstone falling away from crumbled mortar. Smallish in dimension. A quick scan of the surroundings revealed no indication of other buildings, no barn or stable nearby. The house had been built too close to the road to be of use to a farm family. This had been a secondary residence, for relatives or tenants, perhaps.

The cellar space had been filled level to the exterior ground; no timbers or debris lay about in the weeds. No artifacts that would be expected from the haphazard work of natural decay or collapse. The building had been taken down as a whole and the remnants hauled away. But when? Perhaps the foundation was only a marker, a milestone, literally. That could cement at least one line of *The Wilderness* for Nate and Sophia: *I saw a house, sixteen foot deep.* Yet, that might only be their personal reading. A private coincidence that they used in private context. What did that make of other lines? *I saw the sun and I saw a cloud*— constants of weather around here in the summer months? That made four references to the poem. *I saw a well?* A place way out in the country here would have to be using a well. Five.

I stopped my general survey and started looking for more

specific physical connections that would lock in this location: oak tree stumps sunk among the grasses; sankofa birds—that to the deceived eye might look like peacocks—carved into a rock; shards of mirror that might make for the Venice glass. The need to find specific links between this land and that poem kept tripping over my own skepticism. Even if I found all twelve symbols here, including a view of the sea and the sudden appearance of a comet overhead, what would I have proved? I could go down thousands of roads and hit a house at mile marker sixteen. Where could one not find sun and cloud and wells? Ants went about their work in any damn location they pleased. The sea made up most of the planet. The sky was to be seen everywhere. Put the words in place here or anywhere and I'd still be reading a significance I had imposed onto constellations I had created. The symbols had no context outside the poem, and within it, they would not sit still long enough to generate context. Kendrick and his club members had chosen it for that reason. It was nonsense that served an armature to infinite interpretations; only those capable of such obscenity as James's father would be able to read obscenity into it. Had they put the damn book together as no more than an inside joke? Had James, the family artist, been asked to render the brand symbols into colored ink suitable for small children? As the spiders had done in his little horror story, had James woven webs into innocuous shapes?

He must have figured out that the words in and of themselves were designed to be meaningless. Pictures, however, with pictures he could illuminate the malignancy. How long had it taken for him to realize he had succeeded only in giving the evil a larger reach? It didn't matter whether you wanted to attribute the effect to supernatural forces or to the neurochem of sociopathologies. Those images allowed horror to be inlaid as the subliminal fretwork of reason in already receptive minds. *Fiction makes a man think* . . .

In 1928, when *The Wilderness* first surfaced, James would have been in his mid-twenties. A damaged child hiding in the shell of an adult. He would have thought like a kid: Tell only enough to keep yourself safe. But truth cannot be halved or apportioned in comfortable doses. Tell it all or you've told nothing. His half-telling had not turned out the way he had planned and the subsequent crimes associated with the book had galvanized his childlike sense of accountability. *Having once created pain* . . .

Sophia, of course, would have had this locked down long before she contacted me. I still could not say I had been lied to. She had never misrepresented herself or her intentions, but like the Kendrick ghost she was chasing, she had not been straightforward for reasons of protective self-interest. The woman was cleaving to her version, her facts, because she needed, desperately needed, to get her hands on that book, the one that had stolen her brother and with him her parents' ability to risk loving her fully. Sophia had pinned her faith to some future moment when, having excised the unknown and its threats from the world, the world would return to forward motion; the past would be officially passed and then slowly, very slowly, moment by moment, memory by memory, what had been *might* become bearable.

The weight of the past on Sophia's narrow shoulders had altered her carriage, had chosen her path without her prior consent, had defined her meaning before she had been old enough to have a grasp of meaning itself. That weight was not the amassing of recorded events, but that of learning left behind. Events fell away, particulate in the slough of time; the learning stayed coiled in our cells, a kind of experiential DNA. That learning was passed along with all the other traits of our being to the next generation and the next by way of stories, yes, but also by way of the tone of voice a sibling takes around certain holidays, the solidity of a parent's embrace at bedtime, the way certain rooms had to be lit to a certain brightness, any shadow avoided. We then spoke and embraced and turned on lighting to those levels for our own children, knowing this was the way to do it, the way it had to be done.

It was an undertow; the deep pull of rituals we perform against fears we aren't even aware of having, fears that something we cannot name might happen again. I baked bread when I couldn't sleep because my mother, who left while I was sleeping, went through a frenzied stint of bread making each November. November had been the month that her mother, my grandmother, had stopped—after decades—baking her own bread because the cancer had become inoperable and the woman felt it was time to indulge in the luxury of store-bought. You could understand the impulse; but fighting it was impossible. You went with the undertow until it released you or you drowned.

Whatever had befallen the Kendrick household at the end of that last winter, whatever grief or insult had sent James's father into his murderous battle of wills with his God, the learning of that event was relaying itself, a power surge, through the entire family still, generations on. Nate was embodying these terrors because he had learned them in the gesture and whisper that served as sublimated edicts. It had to be awful for him, but held against the lessons Sophia was trying to keep true to? Those of her own life, those of her family's losses plus those of an entire culture *here* and before *here*—and now, Nate and the part she would say she had played in his breakdown—the full measure of her grief was beyond my comprehension. Maybe that was the difference between each of us, what it really came down to, the question of how densely the past had written itself into our code of apprehensions, how much we were expected to carry forward and by whom. Sophia, even if she could, was not about to lay one element of her burden aside. She would carry it, all of it, to the end or until it killed her because she expected no less from herself.

Phillip, apparently tired of watching me stare off at nothing, had hiked out to join me at the foundation wall. "What do we have?"

"Just what it looks like."

"Then why would they come *here*?" We both turned at the sound of an approaching engine. A multiple-row tiller was passing by at the stately pace of maybe five miles per hour. The machine was massive, the driver in his cab towering above the road, chugging along on bulbous tires. The teeth of the tiller blades flashed sun, as did the elbow joints of the arms, gleaming green, bent up close to the chassis like a grasshopper preparing to spring. The driver waved to us as he went by. Phillip and I waved back. We watched it jostle away.

"Amazing," said Phillip, "you'd think something that size would sink into these wet fields."

"You'd think." I looked again into the filled cellar space. The ground was nearly level to that we were standing on. I stepped over the foundation, into the house. There was a definite sense of down as the soil, wet, sank beneath my foot. I stepped out again onto solid, compacted earth, which took my weight without give. Water seeped into the footprint I'd left in the house; the cellar backfill was still settling. The house had been razed a relatively short time ago, and it had been done fast.

"Sophia had been given only one day in the house with the materials. Nate was coming out to represent the family," I said, as much to myself as to Phillip. "This must have been that place. Nate was supposed to supervise. Why Nate? Wouldn't an older family member be able to deflect her questions? Put her off the trail?"

Phillip gave me a lawyerly nod. "That is precisely why *Nate*. He was sent to obstruct her, stop her from taking materials from the house. So much the better if he really doesn't have any answers because he really doesn't know. You've seen Sophia in action. No man or his army could stop her from getting what she wants. She didn't find what she wanted here because Nate didn't know what to tell her."

"But she found Nate."

"For the good that did her."

"He does know, Phillip. Even if he can't explain it. You don't grow up in a nest of secrets and not know. When James told him whatever he told him, Nate believed it. Why would this educated young man immediately buy into the ravings of his crazy old uncle? He believed because he already put it together on a level that had no language until James gave him the words. I wouldn't be surprised if Nate had seen copies of the book, maybe here, maybe on that day he met Sophia, without realizing what he was seeing."

"Nothing here now, Leslie."

"No. But Sophia would have known that. Nate, too. Sophia got here first; she was up here at the house when Nate arrived. She ran down to meet him, got in his vehicle. That's why she left hers. They didn't expect to find anything here, except each other."

"Then where are they?"

"I don't know. It depends on whether or not they have the book."

"Why?"

I shook my head and started back toward the Jag. I had no inkling of where we should go. Andrea would get in touch soon. I prayed to the deity of good luck that in spite of not being able to locate the petting zoo's history of ownership, this land and the house that had once been here were indeed traceable to the Kendrick clan. We would have names and addresses. Be able to run them down, chat them up, garner denials or admissions, collect more data that would open up more paths to the same conclusion: Sophia and Nate were lost to everything but each other. It was as though they had been fused with the instant of their meeting; she was sworn to find what he was sworn to protect her from. It was not that they had come back here; they'd never left.

If they did not have the book, they'd keep circling their moment, caught in each other's gravity. If they did have the book, and I feared that they did, the exhaustion and sorrow and futility would collapse the distance between them, leaving each no escape from the other. Nate would be forced to show Sophia what she wanted and then she would see—be forced to see—that the past would never be set right or made sensible. Nothing was going to be recovered or regained. No one was going to rise from the ash or the ice. *The Wilderness* was, in the end, only a book; if it led anywhere, it would lead to only more graves. Seeing that certainty in each other, that glimpse into the truth of their lives, might be more than either of them could manage.

Phillip caught up. We had nothing left to us but to wait for a phone call. I told him to take me back to the Aberdevine Motel, back to Willet, to my car. I wanted to go home to my husband, to be looking at him straight on when he told me it was over. I wanted to take in my daughters' disappointment in me. I wanted remorse and guilt to rack my heart. I wanted to admit that I loved them to the limits of my being and let them tell me that it was not enough. I wanted the truth of my life.

greg

It is a common mistake to think that the dark knots marring otherwise clear wood is damage, a scar left by injury or infection. A knot is the place at which branching occurred. You can trace the knot down through successive boards to the pinpoint emergence of change, an emergence predetermined by species or sometimes in response to injury or infection, an acknowledgment of damage. Trees take their shapes from necessity. The grain line in a board is the map of the necessary for that tree; the way that tree had been forced to grow to get enough sun, to get enough purchase against the wind, to cast its seeds broadly enough that at least a few took root outside the circle of its parent's shade.

The rings tell how as a sapling the tree survived the blow of a hunter's boot heel or the inconvenient reality of a boulder's presence where as a seedling it had been breaking through the soil. The years of watershed and drought. An infestation. A fire. What gives wood its beauty is its full telling of what it had to do to keep going, each year a new circle that must take its shape from what went before as it adapts to what is.

I am trying to do the same, circling the house, skirting the suitcases where I left them in the foyer, reciting necessities as I go: pack the truck, call about storage, pick up Emma, pick up

Molly, decide, damn it, decide. What about work? School? Leslie? How do you walk away from someone who so obviously needs a center to stabilize her orbit?

Leslie's mother did that. Walked away. Disappeared in the middle of the night when Leslie was five. No one has heard from the woman since. My parents could not escape their system of dependent resentments; they split up but stayed close enough to spend the rest of their lives lobbing hatred at each other, brimstone raining down on those stuck between them. Injury and infection. Leslie has not been faithful, but then from moment to moment Leslie is neither here nor there with anyone. She is always just passing through. Because she is always temporary, she believes we are beyond being hurt by her. She pleads the past; she points to her necessities, hell-bent on showing the world what it has taken to keep going—branching so intricate it would be mistaken for blight—whether the world wants to see it or not.

I finally stop circling; I stop in the now blind kitchen, where the smell of fresh varnish from the repaired cupboard door drenches the air, wet and oily. The new board is almost the same shade of yellow as the pages of this phone book. I am looking up numbers for self-storage facilities. We have so much junk between us, and Leslie's sisters are not going to let the house stand empty. They'll put it on the market within a week. I have no idea where we are going, but the act of reading the ads gives me some sense of control over the rudder until I hear Leslie's car pull up in the driveway. The car door shuts quietly. A few seconds later, I hear her key in the lock. She stands on the threshold, blinking at me as though I'm one of her mind's

292

projections. I can see it in her face. I'm not the only one who is changed.

She comes into the house where neither of us belongs, her keys jangling against her palm, and says, in genuine surprise, "You're still here."

break

"You came back," Greg said and set the open phone book on the counter.

I caught the odor and sniffed my way toward the source. "You fixed the cupboard."

"It's one of those things that never gets done until it's time to move—don't touch it. Still wet."

"The girls?"

"Emma is down at Rita's. Molly has another hour down at the center. I'm going to get her."

"And then?"

He shrugged and rubbed a varnish-stained thumb at his unshaven cheek. "I'll need to leave the workshop here until I can find a suitable space. I'll pay your sisters—you—some sort of rent."

"Greg—"

"The guy who does scheduling down at the hardware store phoned to see if you planned on coming back to work. He'd appreciate a call."

"It would be ridiculous for you to give up this house. The girls, your work, everything is so settled in here. I can get my apartment back—"

"It's your house."

"Yes, but it will be so much easier if I—"

"It is *your* house, Leslie." He shifted his red-rimmed gaze toward the phone book. "I'm looking for a place to store our crap. Unless you want to divide it up first."

"I'll take what I usually—"

"Aren't you even going to try to convince me I'm mistaken? That you and Hogarth aren't back together? That I'm paranoid or stupid or just wrong?"

"You're not stupid."

"Try."

"Or paranoid. I tried earlier."

"Try again."

"You did a great job on the cupboard."

He worked his fists; his brow tightened into that familiar knot of muscles in defense against his own emotions. This brought an involuntary squint to his eyes that forbid my reading him too well. "Please, Leslie. Try."

I exhaled and stared at the floor. "I can't."

"You won't."

"I won't lie to you, no."

He laughed the way a man laughs when he'd rather hit something. "I guess I had this coming, didn't I? I'm the one who said 'choose.'"

"This isn't about you, Greg."

"The hell it's not." His voice edged up in volume. "This is my entire goddamned life we're talking about."

"Yeah. It is." I took a step toward him. He backed up further. "What didn't I do, Leslie? What don't I do?"

The anger couldn't quite disguise the panic in those questions. I hadn't known my husband when he was very young, but that was how I saw him here: the mystified little kid who, having done the very best he could, was being told he had not proved himself worthy. I was suddenly every teacher, every coach, every boss, every accusation of disloyalty from his slyly vindictive parents because Greg, boy hero, had been determined to love them both no matter what. His whole life had been an escalation of those heroics. Yet, every dragon slain bled only doubt about his ability to face down the next one. He didn't want our marriage as much as he wanted to know he had not failed. Greg was announcing departure so that I would be the one to tell him not to go. He wasn't asking for my love or my fidelity. He was asking me not to dismiss him. I could not find words that were both honest and kind. I said nothing.

He took the silence as confirmation of his fears. "You can't say I haven't tried."

"No one could say that. No one will."

I watched the significance of the future tense of my assurance alter his posture. The fight he had braced for was not coming. He nodded and then made for the door with quick heavy steps, pausing to stare me down—anger or hope?—before pressing past. He muttered something before he pushed on out the door. I didn't pick up the exact words, but the tone was pure *fuck you, bitch*.

The pickup pulled away, the sound of the engine traveling along the interior walls. This house knew how to listen for leaving. When it was quiet again, I headed for the stairs; I wanted a shower before I faced our daughters, wash away as much scary stuff as I could. I wanted that more than I wanted food or sleep. I stopped to count the suitcases; he'd used every one we owned.

I went upstairs to the bathroom, gathered the used towels from the floor, and put them in the hamper, straightened the disarray of little-girl cosmetics on the counter. I turned on the taps—the water up here took half of forever to heat—before going to find something clean to wear. In the bedroom, my clothing had been dumped from the drawers, pulled from the closet, and heaped in the corner. Much of it damp with various wet smells of my husband. A bottle of whiskey, cap missing and label peeled away, was on the table beside the unmade bed. The contents, half-drained or half-set aside? No optimistic way to read this one. The photographs on the dresser had been scavenged clear of those with my image. Scraps of torn photo paper led me to find myself ripped up and buried in pieces among my urine-scented, semen-sticky clothes. I had never seen him do anything like this, ever; Greg did not lose control of himself. Even drunk, he would have raged very quietly, so as not to frighten the girls. This frightened me. It had frightened him, as well. That's why he had packed without any idea of destination, why he had to get out of here. But he had not cleaned this up; he had wanted me to see the full scope of his fury. Anger and hope, can't have one without the other.

I picked a few wearable pieces from the bottom of the pile and hurried to the bathroom where fingers of steam curled from beneath the door. The fog inside provided a screen between the mirror and myself. I was grateful; I did not want to be naked and see myself alone here. The shower stream was needled and as close to scalding as I could stand, soaping and scrubbing and rinsing, letting the water sting down on my closed eyelids, into my open mouth. I groped for the taps, and in the grip of a desire to hurt myself in ways Greg would not, I cranked the hot higher, open all the way. My skin screamed for the half-instant before I twisted the hot water shut. I stood, icing over, in the sharp, cold spray until I couldn't take it anymore.

I dried off as best I could in the steam and finger-combed the tangles from my hair before the useless mirror. I finished dressing before unlocking the bathroom door. Steam rushed out ahead of me. I had only a few minutes before Greg would be back with Molly and Emma for one last chorus of "things are going to change a little around here." I imagine we'd already played that one to death for them—beyond death. The kind of refrain that makes you hate not only the song but also the singers, the composers, the radio, the very idea of music. It was no doubt stuck on an obnoxious infinite loop in their minds, never shutting up, and no escaping it. It sang them.

But I needed to talk to Andrea before Greg came back with the girls. Surely, she would have to have property owners' names and maybe some information about Sophia and Nate. I hoped not; any news on Sophia and Nate coming through official channels was going to be bad. I went down to use the phone in the kitchen, skirting the suitcases as I passed them as though they might attack.

The squad secretary caught Andrea as she was leaving. Andrea came on with a fatigue-heavy sigh. Sorry, no word on Sophia or Nate, no Kendricks to be found anywhere in the documents she was able to track down on such short notice.

"I can't even offer you an alternative version worth interest, Leslie. Most of that stretch of land was deeded to a private banking concern. The property was divvied up between creditors after the bank went bust in 1929 with everyone else."

"Less than a year after the thing was published? The entire country collapsed a year later?"

"What thing?"

"Do you believe in curses?"

"The only thing I believe right now is that I'm going to start charging you by the hour. From what I can tell, it seems from 1929 on out that land was divided again and sold and resold several times. Now developers are buying up the whole area. That is who owns mile sixteen at the moment. Some residential development group."

"Is there any indication of when the house was leveled?"

"No record of when the house came down, or who did that work under whose orders. My guess would be the developers. Keep squatters out."

"And crazy old men?"

"That you will have to find out for yourself. May I please go home now?"

"Death certificates. Did you come across any notices of death in the Kendrick family? The year would have been 1913."

"*A*, they don't list deaths with property transfers. *B*, you know that."

"Can't you check?"

"Can't you?"

"Yes. Sorry. I'm just tired. I owe you."

"Add it to the list. I'll be in touch. One way or the other. Promise." She told me to get some rest. I thanked her again, and was about to hang up when I heard her shouting my name and "Wait."

"You were going home."

"Still am, but I forgot to tell you that although it's not Kendrick-related I did stumble on a bit of an interesting coincidence."

"I'll take anything I can get."

"You know Happy Andy's? That property is deeded to M. N. Hoffman."

"Beat you to it. Already in my notes."

"Well, here is the interesting stuff. Your leveled house sits on a chunk of land that belonged, back in 1940, to an Andrew Hoffman. It was sold in '47, bags o' money going to a daughter, Millicent Noelle—"

"Hoffman."

"So, I went to look. M. N. bought what would become Happy Andy's in 1947 for the grand sum of, wait for it, one dollar."

"That has got to mean something."

"When you figure out what, let me know, okay?"

She hung up, leaving me to the ordinary silence of my ordinary kitchen. All that land for only one dollar? It sounded like either bribery or blackmail. You find a body on your property, in a culvert, buried under a tree, a taste in the groundwater. You know something of local gossip. You do not go to authorities, instead you contact the previous owner, who, wanting only your comfort, offers to compensate you for the inconvenient dead by buying you out and replacing your loss with bigger, better acreage. Only a dollar to make it official. Afterward, your amenable blackmailee informs you that your new place may come with more inconvenience, and this time, should you complain, he may have to point out to authorities the suspicious pattern of your finding dead bodies in succeeding backyards.

Millicent Hoffman had been the sharp-tongued old bat that had owned and run that petting zoo. I remembered the finger curls plastered with Dippity-Do, never uncoiling no matter how much she sweat. Her patched overalls. Her thick saggy arms bare and flecked by overlapping years of sunspots. The way she watched us, her paying customers. The way she let those pea-cocks wander and attack. You could tell she hated the place, hated us. For some reason she had to stay. For some reason she could not bear to be there alone. Unnerved, I, out of habit, glanced over at the cupboard to double-check what the Eye might be seeing. I had forgotten it was gone. Greg had taken out one ghoul only to have more threatening presences replace it.

It seemed essential to keep moving. To stand still was to invite the threat closer. I needed to stay near the phone. Andrea had promised; she would call. And I needed to be present when Greg arrived with the girls. Being here was important. I found myself pacing the perimeter of the room, running my hand along the edge of the countertop, pausing to tighten the dripping taps on the sink, which continued to drip all the same. James's father had worked for a bank, and a bank had owned that land until the Depression, which had arrived on their doorstep on the heels of what?

The scene unfolded before me: James's father, white haired, tied tight in his brocade smoking jacket, looking very much like Donald Oliver; settled in his leather chair, before a healthy fire, beneath the large and growing-larger canvas of a powerful stallion falling beneath the tigers' remorseless appetite. Kendrick/Oliver examining the newly published guide to his little hobby's nomenclature; examining the illustrations his then-twentysomething son has generously produced; proud and then ill at ease and then looking more closely and then seeing his child's revenge. How like a serpent's tooth. Or a tiger's claw. The hasty note dashed off in shaky hand, Kendrick Senior to whomever: Get rid of the land; get rid of it now. The summoning to that terrible room, the young man who would always be that little boy frozen in a photograph from a nightmare. *What have you done to your father, James?*

What had he woven into those drawings? Names? Dates? Was it a map to the graves? When had James understood that only those who were capable of such cold, terrible violence would be able to break the code? I could see that moment of recognition, the first panicked gathering of whatever copies he could find, the ripping of pages; throwing volumes onto the grate; the room growing hot as peacocks, comets, moons, houses, seas, went up in flame.

I was aware of the heat. My mind came back to my kitchen, to my body that was shaking and hot. Palm to my cheek, I felt fever in my skin. My running about in rain and cold had taken its due. Great. Just great. I went to the cupboard by the phone where we kept the bandages, antiseptics, and several dozen bottles of store-brand analgesics, most of which had expired. After double-checking the dates, I shook two aspirin, then a third, and chewed them for the physical diversion.

Eyes watering, near gagging for trying to swallow the chalky bitterness, I tried to focus on the yellow pages Greg had left on the counter. The book was open to a long list of glorified garages that could be rented for weeks, months, or years at a stretch. I wondered if Greg would even tell me which site he chose. I paged through the advertisements, each promising electronic gates and alarms, guardianship and levels of security that made me think we should move ourselves into one of these places and leave our stuff here for the taking.

Then I saw the tiger. A clip-art illustration leaping out from an advertisement. The very same image Nate had been drawing. It was the logo for one of the region's largest self-storage operations, one of those out by the airport. I'd passed those low fortresses of concrete and roll-up doors so many hundreds of dozens of times, I stopped seeing them as distinct, stopped seeing the billboards offering first month's rent free in climate-controlled units. Nate had been drawing it because Nate had seen it, too; he knew this is where they had stored everything from the house out on Route 27. He had been trying to tell Sophia everything without telling her anything. The Kendrick family MO—

"Stop it." I slammed the phone book shut. "You don't know that. How could anyone know that?" It was a guess; an attempt to make an answer out of thin air; a reason to run away from the confrontation with Greg and the girls; *something* I could do as an antidote to the sickening helplessness I felt. In admitting to helplessness, I found a far more viable mission. I could prove myself wrong.

I opened the phone book again, found the page, picked up the receiver, and dialed the number. A recording told me the business office was closed for the day, but one of the advantages of storing with Tiger was twenty-four-hour-a-day pass code access. If this were an emergency, leave my number and they'd get back to me within the hour. The recording thanked me for calling and reminded me that Tiger Self-Storage would protect me like nobody's business. *Roar.* The voice mail beeped. I said nothing; just stared down at the tiger logo, listening to the hush of expectation on the other end. I listened and listened until the hush broke with a sudden squeal of feedback—like metal shearing in collision—so shrill and terrible I dropped the phone. I knew that sound. I pivoted to see the peacock, as giant and merciless as it had been when I was a child; it lunged across the kitchen, beak open, shrieking, its tail spread, electric with iridescence, but its eyes—its eyes were as dead as ice. I could not move to protect myself or fight back. Because I was, had been a child.

I came back. The phone was at my ear; line disconnected and beeping busy. I was wrong. No way, could I know this. But what if I were right? We could get somebody out there. No harm in checking. I called Andrea's number. She'd already left for the day. I forgot. Sorry. No, no message. Not yet. No one but Andrea would trust me enough to even try to get a single squad car out to go door to door through scores of storage units because I had seen drawings of tigers—let alone do so without warrants. Calling the owner wouldn't work; they let me in and the lawsuits would flatten the business. I set the receiver back in its cradle and began searching for a pen to leave a note. I found one, had it poised over the paper. But what could I say to Greg anyway? *Had to go; peacock problems?* I dashed off a *Back soon, sorry*—before running for my keys, for the car, knowing that my note was meaningless reassurance for any of us. By the time I got back here, no matter what, my husband, my daughters, would be gone.

molly

"So this is the poem thing," says Molly, finishing the last line with a period. It's hard to read her writing, because the only paper she could find was a brown deli bag and the pencil lead doesn't show up well and she's using her thighs as a desk. She hands it to Zeke, who is lounging next to her on the "couch," which is really a camp cot pushed against the wall, backed with bed pillows. He has a television set and a portable CD radio deal that is playing acoustic music, sad guitar and cello that Molly would never have guessed to be Zeke's taste. He inhales from the joint, offering it to her as he takes the paper bag. She says, "No, thank you." And that makes him laugh softly. "Cool." He tries to get the bag at a good reading angle, tilting it in the sunlight glaring through the tall, narrow window.

Zeke's tiny apartment is above a laundry that does the wash for hotels and restaurants. The vibration from the dryers hums in the floor and the air smells like bleach—or did before he lit the joint. He gives her the paper and then goes back to making lazy spirals down the arch of her spine, which is what he was doing when Molly decided she wanted to tell him about the poem.

"I don't get it," he says.

"It's not hard. See? Everyone thinks it's the description part that should get moved around. But it's not. You can't move those around very much. Those are the rhymes; they have to stay together. They have to be moved in pairs. And this one with the

305

period has to go at the end. Move 'I saw the sun' down to 'saw this wondrous sight' and you have six *s*'s in that one line. The letter *s*? Two sets of three. That's the double *s* at the end."

"The end of what?"

"The word 'wilderness.' That's how you can do it. Make thirteen out of twelve. Sets of three. Three letters. You match up one letter from the *thing* to two letters in the description of that thing. Like only one of the *things*, the well, starts with a *w*, that's the first letter of 'wilderness' so it has to be in line four and the description with the most *w*'s is 'swallow up a whale.' Since those two go together, 'brim full of ale' has to come right before or after. To keep the rhyme together. See? Here, I'll write it down the way it should go."

"Yeah, but it still doesn't make any sense. The sun can't see anything."

"Homophone."

"Whatever." His fingers slide up under her T-shirt, light and airy against her curved backbone. More circles. The circles shiver up and down her in such a way that it makes her toes itch. She straightens her spine away from the sensation; his fingers follow her.

"No. Look, Zeke. If you change it to the other word, *s-o-n*, then it makes sense. The son saw a wondrous sight. Lots of homophones in this thing—*w-h-a-l-e* can be *w-a-i-l*; *a-l-e* is also *a-i-l*, like in sick?—and if you change them all, once it's in the right order, here, I'll write it out." She takes the pencil, pushing it hard into the paper, into the tensed muscle of her thigh. "I saw a blazing comet. Sixteen foot deep. That's the *T*. The only *h* is 'house' and 'weep' is the only rhyme for 'deep.' So, the next line has to be 'I saw a house full of men's tears that weep.' It's only two *h*'s, but—"

"The exception that proves the rule."

"What?"

"What that is." His hand slid around her side, his fingers fitting between her rib bones. "Right?"

"Yeah. I guess. And then, the 'Venice glass'—whatever that is—is 'full of ale.' Or the *a-i-l* that I said a minute ago. The first spelling gives you the three *e*'s for the *e* in '*The*.' The second makes it about a sickness, maybe."

"Seems pretty tricky to me. You could make anything out of these words. How do you even know you've got the answer right? Is there a prize or something?"

"No, there isn't a prize. I'm not sure this is right, but do you see any other way to make this work?"

He laughed. "Yeah. I do."

"Really?"

"Yeah." The tip of his index finger edges up under the band of her bra.

"Well, let me finish writing the—"

"I don't get it, Molly."

"Let me finish."

"I don't get why you wanted to come up here."

She puts the pencil down. "I don't know."

"I think you do." His finger stretches the band of her bra outward, lets it snap back softly against her skin. He pulls his hand back until his palm is flat against her spine, slides down, to the gap between the small of her back and the waistband of her jeans. He stops there. It doesn't feel invasive, more an invitation. As though he can feel her considering her options. He says, "I'm sure you know why you're here."

Yeah, she does. She turns to look at him. He's smiling

307

but serious. She returns his serious look. "I wanted to find out."

He nods. "So you've never?"

"Nothing."

He rolls his eyes. "But me? This place?"

"Why not?"

"Good question." His fingers close over her waistband, pulling it, pulling her back against him until he can get his arm around her. He stretches back to tamp out the joint—she can smell his deodorant and the clean cotton fragrance of his shirt—and he then moves forward so that he has his arms all the way around her. "So we make a deal here, okay?" He loosens her ponytail so that her hair is sagging soft against her neck. "As soon as you find out what you wanted to find out, you say something and we'll stop. Deal?"

"Deal."

He extends his little finger in front of her face. "Pinky swear?"

That makes her giggle, and while she's laughing he kisses her, his mouth soft. Choruses of alarm clocks go off inside her, panicked alertness, but her mouth, unheeding of the bells, softens itself to meet his. He pulls away. "All right?"

"Yes." Feeling like she ought to shout to get her voice above the bells.

"Keep going?"

"Yes."

He shifts a bit and produces, as though from thin air, a small square packet of red plastic through which a rigid circular shape is visible. "You know about these?"

"Yes."

"Never without one of these. Never."

"I have to leave in a few minutes."

"Cool," he begins to move away. Molly stops him, pulls him back.

"I can stay for a while."

"So, basically shut up and get on with it?"

"I'm ready." She closes her eyes, as his body increases his weight against hers. "I want to know."

"What comes next?" He is lifting her T-shirt. "In the poem deal. After the glass?"

She wants to ask why he is asking, but then feels his mouth. "The well. 'I saw a well swallow up a whale.' And then 'I saw a pismire big as the moon and higher. I.' That's the *I*."

"Aye-yi-yi. You really are beautiful, you know that?"

" 'I saw a cloud all in flame of fire. I—' " she has to catch her breath—" 'saw a sturdy oak drop down hail,' or *h-a-l-e*. Looked that one up. Had to. It means healthy or haul. An old-fashioned word for 'haul.' Something was hauled up into that tree."

"Molly, baby? If you want to stop, tell me now because—"

" 'I saw a peacock with a fiery tail.' Or *t-a-l-e*. That's pretty obvious, huh?"

"Okay then."

" 'I saw a raging sea with ivy circled round. I saw the man creep upon the ground. I saw their eyes even in the midst of night. I saw—' " She can't continue. Her breath is coming too fast. Zeke is breathing hard, too. How can someone be so close and yet feel so far away? What if she does have it all wrong? "I want to know," she whispers and lets her self sink beneath the reach of ringing alarms, unblinking eyes, and the endless spinning, spinning, spinning of words.

answer

I reached the access road at the dark edge of sunset; when the sky was shutting down the spectrum, making the world of things into a world of shadows. The runway lights glittered, and up ahead the glass and steel box of the airport terminal cast a hard-edged gleam against the dusk. The sensors on the streetlamps were kicking on; the blue-white pools on the roadway brightened the farther I went, trying to find the entrance to Tiger Self-Storage. The number of personal warehousing facilities out this way was astounding. Animal logos were the theme and an indication that in spite of the differing names, the places operated under the same management. King Storage had its cartoon lion, crown askew; Beher Brothers its arm-in-arm grizzlies, Stop-N-Store its grinning cheetah complete with cloud of speed-raised dust. Each facility offered the same concrete bunkers behind barbed fences. It was Happy Andy's reimagined for secrets.

Had the Kendrick family been aware of why, given the many places to choose from, they'd chosen this stretch of warehouses, let alone this petting-zoo echo? Did they tell themselves, truly believe, it was the cost or the security offered, when really it had hit the subliminal tuning fork? The tiger logo came into view up ahead: a lighted sign, posted high to be visible to traffic. I realized that I must have just passed the sign, just caught it peripherally, when the boy had appeared on the overpass ledge.

The hallucination had been the work of my subliminal tuning fork as well.

I pulled up to the barred gate and stopped beneath the entrance lamp. The plan, such as I had one, was that someone would be out here, loading or unloading something or other, and I would talk my way into getting the gate open. So much for plans; apparently no one had need of his or her stuff this evening. Nothing stirred among the rows of storage spaces; the metal slatted doors shut tight, each lit with its own spotlight like a stage curtain. The idea of giving up then did venture a weak presence, but I could see a row of parked, darkened vehicles at the far side of the buildings. Not knowing what Nate would have been driving—*how do you know Nate had been driving?*—was reason enough to ignore common sense.

Improvise. A card swipe and keypad controlled the gate. A phone box was mounted to the lamppost; the word EMERGENCY stenciled across the door. An adhesive label fixed below that announced direct access to the security firm servicing the site. Patrols were made regularly it promised. The fence around the property was ten feet tall; warnings of prosecution and fines were posted at regular intervals. Any attempt to climb the fence or break in would summon interference—and maybe necessary help for Sophia or Nate. *If they are even in there*, protested an increasingly distant rational voice. No matter how security was summoned, it would take a good ten, fifteen minutes to get out this far, and I didn't want to waste time trying to explain the situation to a dispatch person. Better leave them no choice but to respond.

I backed up the car, repositioning it so that it was parallel with the gate and as close as I could get without scraping the door. I shut off the engine; got out and climbed up the hood, onto the top of the car, and hoisted myself to the top of the gate, throwing one leg over and then the other, turning myself around so I could hang by the rail, getting my feet as close to the ground as possible before letting myself drop. I hit the ground; the impact sent immediate notification to my brain that this was not appreciated. I let my knees drop to the pavement and then my hands, crouching before the pain.

Trucks rumbled in the distance and jets boomed and whined overhead, but no alarms. I'm sure I had broken the gaze of an electronic eye. A business like this wouldn't want to advertise a break-in with competitors so close by; alarms would be silent, a light flashing on some remote console. A jet, taking off, roared above me; I watched it gain altitude. I had a thought to sit down there, wait for someone to show up. Whatever virus was wending through my veins had stiffened my joints, scalded my throat. *You are not well*, complained rationality, fading out completely to be replaced by the mechanical command of will power: *Get your ass up, Leslie, and get moving.*

Moving. I limped up to the first door of the first row: 1A. Knocked. Tapped, really. Called their names. No answer, of course. Next door. Next. I reached the end of the row and leaned to rest against the hood of one of the stored vehicles. Too dark to see the interior. I'd left my flashlight in my car, which was stupid. I needed to think, to try to think, but the only logic I could process ended with images of Sophia and Nate in death behind one of those sturdy doors.

Up again, moving faster. Down one side of the next row, back up the other side. With each successive door, with each successive lack of answer, it seemed my head cleared and the correctness, the inevitability of my finding them gained solidity. The notion that I had invented this connection because I had needed it seemed more and more wrongheaded. It was either run through the gathering night, knocking on strange doors, or give up hope. Not this time. I was going to get hope out of this one alive.

I began to work more furiously, faster. Third row. I went down one side, pounding at the slats with the heel of my hand. Not asking that they answer me, but demanding it. Shouting. My voice strained, fracturing. I reached the end, started down the other side. And then the fourth row and the fifth. Halfway down the fifth row, I paused; I had to, to catch my breath. I leaned my forehead against the cool metal door, feeling my heartbeat transfer in vibration. That's when I heard the laughter. From inside? I pressed my ear to the door. I knocked. *Nate! Sophia!* Nothing, but I knocked, pounded again, harder this time. The laughter was outside, moving. I moved away from the door to look down the long corridor of closed storage bays. The laughter was coming closer, lightening, becoming girlish and then becoming a girl, the little girl from Willet. She was running down the corridor toward me, coming and going from the world as she entered and exited each of the spotlights. She wore the white dress and boots and peacock ribbons of my first imagining. No acknowledgement as she ran past me, but she was giggling with playful delight. Fast behind her, came the boy in the cap. He too was laughing, calling for her to wait. A name; he said a name, but the word garbled in my ears. They ran to the end of the row, taking a turn for the next, out of my sight, but I could still hear them laughing, running up and down the rows. Another roar sounded, swallowing the laughter. It was awfully low, too low; I raised my eyes to find the airplane—but the sky above me was empty. The roar continued. It was on the ground.

I took up running again, this time, harder. Not knocking at doors, but kicking and shouting: *Answer me!* Up and down the rows. I would get glimpses of the children, just passing the edge of that corner, just cusping that circle of light, running hard, no longer laughing. This was no longer a game. In the spaces between the lights, something large was on its feet and moving with us.

Up and down the rows, chased or being chased, I couldn't say. My throat was so strained with yelling and sickness that I could hardly make any sound. Row, nine and ten. Somewhere between my breaths I was aware of sirens in approach. Eleven. Twelve. The roar was punctuated now with the high, keening wail of a frightened child. Peacock. I told myself as I beat my fists against another door. It's only a peacock. Or is that what James's mother told herself when she heard her son crying for help. Row fourteen. Where was thirteen? I went back to the end to double-check. The numbers on the doors jumped from twelve to fourteen. Superstition was built in here, as well. No thirteenth row unless you were actually counting what was really there, which is what I did. That's where the children had stopped running, a couple doors from where I now stood. The thirteen on Nate's drawing pad. Telling without telling.

The children looked at each other and then again at me. The little boy shook his head, took his friend's hand, and led her to and through the metal of the door. It was then that I noticed the knife's-edge sheen of light coming from beneath the door. Behind me, I heard the approach of a vehicle of some sort; I could imagine the searchlight flashing down the aisle; any second it would find me. I ran up to this last door and threw my body weight against the metal, slapping and kicking.

"Nate! Goddamn it. Sophia! Answer me!"

It was not that I was oblivious to the sound of male voices yelling at me to stop, to freeze, immediately. I could not. Stop. The noise of all the shouting and pounding, the door rattling on its rollers was very far away. I was more aware of the gaps of silence; I had not noticed the echo before that. My head rolled back; I could see where planes banked and twinkled, roaring indifferent mechanical roars across the sky as hands clamped hard around my arms and arms clamped hard around my middle, pulling me away, me fighting, slow, spongy muscles, them half-dragging, pulling me toward the car with its revolving colored lights and rasping radio voices. I had to shout to make them hear me, shout the word that worried me most. One of them chuckled—I felt his chest vibrate with amusement—and yelled above my yelling, "Worry is the way pessimistic types do their wishing." And the other laughed back. "If wishes were horses . . ."

It was then, then that I heard the hallelujah racket of the door ratcheting on its rollers and Sophia's voice, groggy, confused. "What?" She was squinting through the floodlight, the breeze tugging at her long blue skirt as she shifted from one foot—only in socks—to another. "Leslie?"

"You're all right." I wrestled myself away from the security guys, whose grip seemed to melt at Sophia's emergence. I hurried, half-stumbling back to where she stood. "Is Nate here? You're both all right?"

"Yes. Of course. We're all right. I made him take his meds. He's much better—so, I'm much better. He told me where they'd stashed James's old stuff—"

"I figured that out. I knew that was why you'd be here."

"—he told me he'd known all along. We've been working for hours, going through James's pack-rat collection, trying to find—"

"You understand how tiring that sort of thing can be," Nate said, coming out of the garage behind Sophia, yawning. He draped his arms around her, the same pose as the portrait back in Willet. But now there was the tattoo. I could see the word: *gone.* "We must have fallen asleep. What time is it?"

"Not late," I said and shooed away the patrol guys, who turned back to their car with no further interference. "Did you find the book?"

"The question is how you found us?"

"It was easy. You wanted to be found."

Sophia raised her head, arching her neck to exchange a meaningful glance with Nate. "As long as you're here, you may as well see. Quite the vault, James had going. It's a mess, but we'll sort it out. It will make sense. Eventually. Come see for yourself."

And so I followed them and they showed me what they unearthed. The book, of course. I asked them to show me the map in the illustrations—I really wanted the book to make a map; we *would* find the lost; we *would* learn their names; we *would* bring them peace. I had to ask to see the painting from James's father's study, the one of the tigers and the horse. I also had to ask to see the photograph from which James cut himself free. The oval that contained James was now a void within the picture.

However, the image around the void evolved along with my theories. I saw the photograph being taken, a moment committed to history in a flash that burned red on the retina even from a great distance in time. I saw what was being taken: James at the location of the lynching or posed in a nursery; at a graveside; there are other children in the picture; the little girl is there; James and his father are alone. The images changed each time I imagined it because really I was only *imagining*, and at the time, hunkered down and glowering in the back of the security patrol car—feverish, delusional—I kept recycling the fantasy to stay ahead of the dead-end fact that most likely I never would know what had become of any of it.

Once the security agents believed they had me calmed down, they called dispatch, which wondered if it ought to call for an ambulance or backup. The guys were considering this, and I took the moment to offer them one of my possible futures: My ex-husband was being a prick about certain family heirlooms; I had decided to get them back any way I could. Sort of let my anger get the best of me. Sorry. I was really sorry. The guys were kind, kinder than the situation required. Said this sort of thing happened more often than I would believe. They escorted me back to my car and let me go with the advice to consult a lawyer and a warning that if I showed up again, they'd have me prosecuted. Torn between worry and wish, I drove back to Swifton to wait for whatever was going to happen.

Greg's truck was gone, but the suitcases were still next to the front door. I called for Molly or Em. The house was empty. The message light on the kitchen phone was flashing, red pulses. I hit the button to hear Andrea's recorded sigh. "Aw, Leslie, I'm sorry, but we have some bad news."

witness

Sophia's injuries, the ones Nate had inflicted, were so serious that at first the doctors refused to hazard future tense in terms of prognosis. But she regained consciousness after nearly two days and had steadily, if slowly, improved. They anticipated keeping her in the hospital for at least a week longer.

She had been found after authorities were alerted by an anonymous 911 call, the recording of which no one seemed to be able to locate, although the operator who had taken it continued to swear the caller had sounded like a child over a bad connection. Nate's body had been curled around Sophia before a cold hearth at the lakefront cabin they'd rented several times before over the years. Nate had liked to paint up there, the owner had volunteered. It had been the site of their "whatever moon" portrait they'd taken together. Nate had nearly taken her life, coming close to crushing her larynx.

That, along with her other wounds, was healing but Sophia was not talking much. She had offered no information in any form about what had transpired. I knew this because as soon as news had reached Phillip, he had hustled himself into defense position between Sophia and the questioning hordes. He would phone daily to keep me apprised of her condition. She could barely raise a voice above a whisper. Her preferred word being *no*: no visitors, no memory, no reason for what Nate had done to her.

"And you believe her?" I'd asked.

"No." He promised to let me know if anything changed and said good-bye. We did not discuss matters beyond that. He called my cell number to avoid getting Greg, although I always told Greg what Phillip had told me. I slept, when I slept, with the phone beside my pillow in the sewing room.

It was the ringing that woke me. The chime was right at my ear, and I slapped about in the dark trying to shut it off. The bell did not stop. I finally opened my eyes, fumbled around for the switch on the bedside lamp. The light came on. The bell went silent except for the echo in my ears.

I sat up, looked for the phone, and realized that the ringing had not been a call coming in. I recognized the still-fading sound as the doorbell from Willet. A dream, I decided. The travel clock beside the lamp was humming its battery-driven hum. Nearing three, the second hand sweeping. More alert, I was aware of how very warm the room was, stuffy. The window was open, but there was no breeze. Outside in the humid dark, rain was gathering.

The sewing room door had been shut. Normally, I kept it open a crack when I went to bed in order to encourage ventilation. Who had closed it? I got up to crack it again. Greg must have left windows open elsewhere, because suction from the hallway fought my efforts. I had to tug to get the door open, holding it there while I looked around for something to keep it ajar.

The hallway light we always left on went dark just as the doorbell downstairs rang. Rang again. Long, louder, someone leaning into the button. No stirring from Greg in his bed or the girls' rooms. Only I was hearing this.

Not much of a choice before me. Try to ignore it and the

neural disorder would only become more chaotic in the escalation of inarticulate panic. Answer it and find some horrid little association that my waking mind was willfully avoiding. Better the pain that at least served a purpose. I switched the light on again. The bulb popped, arced a blue-white flash, and went dark. The doorbell picked up again.

"This is my house." I said it as loudly as I could and made for the stairs, dragging my hand along the wall, in part to steady myself and in part to keep in physical touch with the real. "My house. You cannot come in here." Distinct drafts glided around me in opposing directions at differing speeds. The rope pull to the attic swayed slightly while stronger currents circled my ankles. When I reached the top step, I grabbed the banister and lowered myself to sit on the riser. "I'm not letting you in." As though it were not already as far *in* as a thing could come.

The bell stopped and was immediately replaced by knocking. Insistent and without pause. I covered my ears, but the sound, because it was coming from inside my head, was not muted in the least. Had it been like this for James?

And Nate? Had this persistent visitor followed him from Willet? "Stop it." Had this been what finally drove him to reunite with Sophia before ending the torture the way he had ended it for his uncle? "Please." On that request, the banging got louder.

How much of this could a person take? I could imagine Nate's relief on making the decision. Of course, for the execution to make sense, it would have to be based on James's crime. Sophia would have to die as the little girl had died. But Sophia had done what the child could not, she had fought. "Stop it now." Nate must have believed he had killed her. There before the cold fireplace.

The banging stopped. I lowered my hands. If Nate had sought to re-create this in all its troubling detail, then he would need all the details.

"He would have to write out a confession. He made James write out a confession." That was why Sophia wasn't providing any information. "And then he would hide it." She had fought and survived Nate at the end so she could get back up there for his version. And maybe the book. And that child's name.

I glanced to my left and wasn't startled in the least to find Greg sitting beside me on the step. He took care not to touch me, leaning away into the shadows; he was more body heat and sorrow than a visible presence. "It's getting worse, isn't it?"

"How long have you been sitting here, Greg?"

"Since you started shouting 'stop.' Has it? Stopped?"

"No. Not yet. Did I wake the girls?"

"None of us are awake, Leslie. You are only shouting inside your head. This is you hoping I would wake up and keep you from going to the lake."

"You aren't going to do that, are you?"

"As if I could."

I nodded. The sensation of warmth and body faded. I was alone at the top of the stairs.

struggle

The cabin's location was listed on the preliminary forensics report. Andrea had sent me a copy without my having to ask. I appreciated the gesture; the detached descriptive listings provided a mental discipline, a means of arguing down the elaborate speculations that rose in the absence of fact. For me, especially. I appreciated it all the more as I drove toward the lake with the report in one hand, trying to read it while I steered.

The report identified the scene as the name of a road, a direction, and a unit number. These meant nothing to me. Turns I chose took me around the lake, but no closer to it. I rounded a bend to find an older couple out walking with their dogs. After clarifying that there was no Jenkins Road but there was a Jenkins Chase, they pointed me to an unmarked rutted lane through the woods. I bumped along Jenkins until it gave out into a grassy clearing where I parked. The lake was only a few yards farther, where a broad path followed the steep rocky shoreline. Any stretch of this could have served as the backdrop for Nate and Sophia's self-portrait. I walked along the water, which was calm in the still, heavy air. The rain had already passed through here and the wet earth steamed up a thin mist that only intensified the odors of mossy decay. Early sun glinted off the windows of dwellings on the far shore. Cries of hungry nestlings and bug buzz nettled the peace.

I carried the report with me. Andrea had stapled grainy copies of some of the scene photos to the report. That helped because the cabin at the end of the path bore no identifying numbers, although the band of crime scene tape, already busted and looped loosely between the porch pillars, would have been sign enough. The cabin was closer to the water than I had imagined, the rear of the structure barely falling in the shade of the woods behind it. No ornamental landscaping, except a stone-edged path down to the wobbly-looking pier. The same sort of stones outlined the narrow, untended flowerbeds that ran around the perimeter of the foundation. Small and plain, the place seemed beneath Sophia's more moneyed tastes. The privacy and beauty of the view may have made up for those.

The cabin appeared to be many decades old. Patches in the floorboards of the porch, although well made, were pale in comparison to the older planks. None of the work had been done recently or looked to have been disturbed. The front door was locked shut with a padlock. I'd expected as much and had debated approaches to entry on the drive up. Stealth wasn't required here. I kicked in the door.

The interior was standard rental functionalism. Straight-lined and spare. I tried the porch light switch. The electricity was on, but I wouldn't need it. The front door was centered between two sets of windows. More windows made up the rear wall. The overhang of the porch shaded the front of the house but abundant natural light filled the entries to the few other rooms. The effect felt more consoling than cheerful.

The air reeked of bleach. The furniture had been removed, no doubt unsalvageable. Small kitchen. One bedroom. One bath. If it were not for the suspicions behind my trip up here, I would have brushed aside the similarities between the cottage at the petting zoo and this place. No giant peacocks on the wall, however. Such a thing would have been written up in the report, but secretly I had been hoping someone had overlooked that detail. Perhaps Nate had planned to replicate the drawing, but Sophia's lack of cooperation had upset his plans.

I stood looking into the fireplace. The hearth and firebox had been vacuumed clean by the aftermath people. Temperatures taken at the scene indicated the fire had not been lit that night. The ashes had been analyzed. The last items burned in the grate had been photographs and some other paper items that left traces of ink and photography chemicals. Whatever it had been, the flames had been fed with an accelerant to make certain that everything was reduced to powdery nothing. The papers I had come up here to find? The book? I doubted it. Sophia would not have allowed that to happen. Had that intervention been the source of the violence that followed?

The exact order of events was a matter of speculation that only Sophia would be able to resolve with any concrete definition, and Sophia was as determined in her silence as in any other commitment. What counted was that at some point in the proceedings they had struggled. *Struggle* was the official term, but from what I'd seen of the reports, the term was too polite. They had battled, slugged it out in dazed fury, notions of love gone dark before the will to survive. Under debate was whether Nate had relented because he thought he'd finished her or Sophia had gained the upper hand and done what she had to do. Either way, at some juncture the struggle had ended; Nate had closed his bleeding body around hers and succumbed.

The floors and walls had since been scrubbed, but the photocopies of the crime scene pictures showed without judgment or compassion how badly they had damaged each other. If a clue to hidden things had been left, it was gone from the present around me and unreadable in the images from the past. The scent of cleaning agents became all the more distressful for the thought of what might be lost to this antiseptic erasure. I could not very well dismantle the entire structure based on a hunch. The combination of futility and fatigue drained my remaining strength; the chemical odor became increasingly nauseating. I went to raise the window. The frame resisted, jammed. I yanked. It came up suddenly, to its full height, the counterweights dropping with a bang. Fresh air from the lake, ripe with green smell, rushed in through the screen. Relieved, I rested my forehead against the cool glass, closed my eyes. No good to be done here. No good to be done anywhere. May as well go home.

I straightened my thoughts as best I could and started to close the window. That's when I saw the letters. Someone had carved, in very tiny, uneven print, the word SEA into the wood beneath the brass pull on the window frame. The scars were pale, recent. When shut, the letters would have been hidden by the sill. If you didn't open the window—

—They had nailed the windows at the petting zoo closed. I unlatched the panel on the left. It rose easily. Beneath its handle, carved into the wood: PISMIRE. The windows on the other side of the door, more lettering: The left panel had been given GLASS; the right panel was WELL. The windows that looked out onto the lake had been given the poem's references to water. Nate or Sophia? Which one of them had done this?

I went to the windows that faced the woods on the other side of the room and raised all four. CLOUD, OAK, EYES, HOUSE. Yes, from this window in this house with my eyes I could see both the woods before me and the high thin clouds above the trees. I felt as high and thin as those clouds, numbed yet revving on both adrenaline and dread. My legs were mechanical as I steered myself toward the small double-paned windows over the kitchen sink. These were of a newer casement style. I cranked them open. The woodwork was blank. The casement panel in the bathroom was blank as well. That left the bedroom.

The bedroom was in the front corner of the house with windows that looked directly onto the lake from one wall and farther up the shoreline from the other. I raised the lake windows. SUN was indeed shining down on MAN from this vantage. The floorboards bore long rectangles blanched white from years of suns pouring in at this angle. That meant the last two objects of the poem had to be etched into these final two windows. Certainty that those would be marked COMET and PEACOCK unraveled my motivation to open and see because unlike the views offered from the other windows, I already knew that neither comets nor peacocks would be seen from anywhere inside this little cabin. Or outside of it for that matter. Those were not feasible here. I could live without yet another demonstration of meaning implied but held out of reach.

Still, I'd come this far. Up went the windows. COMET was on the left; PEACOCK was on the right. The windows offered only a stretch of empty shoreline through one and the edge of the woods through the other. Everything was right in front of me and I understood none of it. In an attempt to outrun failure, I toyed with the romantic idea of a secret compartment in the windowsill under PEACOCK and pried at the framing with my fingers. Solid. I wasn't going to find anything in this house; these clues at windows only pointed me outward to the world at large. To ask where to begin to look out there was to become Sophia. Or Nate. Or James. I had enough crazy to deal with on my own.

I shut and latched the windows, tried to make sure the front door would stay closed in spite of the broken lock. I wanted to take one quick look at the outside of the place. I didn't want to give up. I made my way around the perimeter of the house, following the narrow band of a flowerbed edged in a neat row of rounded stones. Someone had hauled those rocks up from the lake, sorted them for size and similarity, aligned them with care, and then apparently tired out by that effort, had let the bed go to weeds.

I was coming around to the front of the cabin again, ready again to admit defeat, when I caught the sound of rhythmic splashing. A young man was standing, his back to me, at the edge of the water. Skinny, his hair matted, his clothes stained red. I did not call to him. I recognized this Nate from the crime scene photographs. *There are always more.* He appeared to be skipping stones outward, but as I watched I realized the reverse was happening. The water was expelling the stones, skipping them back to him. He'd catch each and place it in the pile growing at his feet.

The stones that edged the beds. Nate had done this? These were too big for skipping purposes. But still. They had covered her body with stones. I turned back and began to mentally line up the stones with the centers of the carved windows. I got on my knees and lifted away the stone that matched up with GLASS. I dug with my hands, clawing past earthworms and pebbles and roots through the rain-softened soil. An involuntary chortle of triumph escaped my throat as my fingers hit plastic, tugging until I pulled free a ziplock bag. I brushed aside the earth clinging to the plastic and held it to the sunlight; I didn't want to take the object out of the bag until I knew what it was. Inside was a heavy piece of shaped metal, dark and pocked, iron. About six inches in length, four wide, it resembled the outline of a water jug. There was an extension that seemed to be fitted for another piece such as a handle.

I knew what it was then. I considered the row of stones beyond me. To answer your question, Henry, apparently someone had found the branding irons. Sophia would not have done this. She would have trumpeted the find and forced witness to the suffering that had been endured beneath these. It was in the Kendricks' interest that these be lost along with all traces of *The Wilderness*. This had to be Nate's doing; Nate, like James, would have been torn between family fealty and moral rightness. Had James given him these or had he found them among his uncle's junkyard possessions on the day he and Sophia had met? Had he even told her he had them or had shame prevented him from speaking? Nate, like his uncle, would want to destroy the incriminating evidence and yet leave signs as to how to locate it in order to incriminate the culpable. He had carved the words into the window frames for himself in case an absence seizure kept him absent for good. This was Nate the artist, tattooing history onto the world.

I placed the branding iron back in the ground and scooped earth over it, packing it tight before sliding the stone back in place. Sophia had to know these were here; it seemed essential to her recovery to leave them for her to unearth. Perhaps she had tried but Nate had stopped her. Perhaps that explained the blood authorities found on the steps and in the yard.

The splashing picked up again. If I looked, Nate would still be there. He wasn't going anywhere until I'd fulfilled my own greed for answers. To end these hallucinations, I had to find whatever it was that Nate had been willing to kill his uncle and his lover and himself to keep out of eyesight. Nate still needed to be found.

The sun was brighter on the far side of the house, the warmth felt good on my back as I set about digging under the peacock window. Nate had gone deeper with this one. The soil was tougher. I hit the edge of a rock and the tip of my thumbnail bent back under the force. A few choice swear words later, I shook the pain from my hand, glancing up as I did so. Nate was standing over me, his arms limp, his face passively sad, watching.

"I take it this is the right place then," I said. "You can go now." When the hallucination did not end for the disruption of my voice, I went back to digging, harder. "You are not really there, Nate. You are too much coffee and not enough sleep. I don't need you here to prove anything—" I snuck a peek at his mud-caked bare feet, the place on the ground where his shadow ought to be "—but see, I am so fucking tired that I can't even make you—" my fingers grazed something slick and angular.

A few more clawings of dirt and I could make out the upper edge of a box. It had been planted vertically. I dug and wrestled until it came free. The box had been wrapped in the dark green plastic of a garbage bag before being sealed in a large ziplock. I cleaned the dirt from my hands as best I could, wiping them on my sweatshirt before opening the bag. Weight shifted inside as I removed the garbage bag to find a battered wooden cigar box, obviously very old. The cover of the box was stamped with an open fan of Spanish design on which the word ALCAZAR was lettered in an arabesque of a font. A worn paper label on the side carried the picture of a handsome black horse and ALCAZAR in the same ornate script. An alcazar was a sort of castle. The fan looked like a peacock's tail. Was this black horse James's black horse? All that fanciful storytelling had been to describe a cigar box in which he kept a vengeful tiger? Is this what James gave you, Nate, that afternoon in the coffee shop? The gift you were buying for your heartbroken lover only to discover you could not bring yourself to give it to her? That a larger gesture was called for?

The horse appeared on the label on the interior lid as well. A blurb assured that that these cigars were NOW UNION MADE. The price was listed as two for a nickel, although under that I was told that these were WORTH MORE. No doubt.

The sankofa-shaped iron weighted down the other item in the box, obviously a book, wrapped in white linen. I thought of burial shrouds first and then as the shape of the bird's head registered, I thought of the white of the little girl's dress, at least the one I imagined, and then the white of her bones on the tray in forensics, the crescent of char seared into them now as clearly the sankofa bird's head.

The terrible fact about facts is that they are what they are. Put them at the center of your story or ignore them altogether; facts cannot be altered by a telling or a not-telling. Imagination is the blind spot of consciousness. That blind spot could make the moon disappear. Just as easily it could make the moon the only thing that ever was. While we teetered between extremes, the real moon rose and set, unmoved by any eye—king, poet, or priest—that watched it. What had happened to Nate and James and Sophia and all these other grief-mad minds was not the shutting out of reality; it was having been shut out of any possible escape from reality. Facts had overwhelmed the blind spot. Light poured in. They saw everything and could not get away from it. *They don't like it when you shut the doors.*

I lifted the book from the box, opened its cotton cloak. Hardly any size to it in length, height, depth. The size you'd give a small child to entertain herself with in a crib. The peacock on the cover glared at me in warning from atop its perch on *The Wilderness.* "I thought it would be, I don't know, bigger," I said to Nate, but he was no longer there. For that I smiled down at the peacock. "Oh, go ahead. Curse me some more."

The pages were gone. Rather, they'd been replaced. The originals had been pulled free and in their stead were pen-and-ink drawings on new, heavy stock, stuck among the torn edges hugging the spine. I recognized the cracked-mirror lines from Nate's ice drawings, but these were much more densely rendered, edge to edge covered in complex, endlessly regressive lines. It was as though he were drawing into the page rather than on its surface. He had used no words, only page after page of ornately fractured detail. Taken individually, the drawings meant nothing, but one following upon another, these took on the quality of trail markers. The path of story was unmistakable. This is the way it went:

Once upon a time, there was a prince and a servant girl who were great friends in spite of the king's objections. One day the king found his son and the girl together in the royal stables. He had made her a crown of peacock feathers, and she was thanking him with a kiss, as children will. The king fell into a rage. He dragged the prince out by his collar and bolted the stable door, shutting the prince away from his friend, shutting the king inside alone with her. *Terrible noises came from within the stable, the horses whinnied and snorted, hooves pounded the walls. After too long a time, the king opened the stable door. The girl lay limp in his arms.* This is your doing. *He dropped the body at his son's feet.* You would not obey.

He ordered his son to accompany him on a long ride into the countryside, where after nightfall they built a fire. The king heated the family signet in the fire and marked the girl's body, a warning to the other servants. They lay the girl's body at the bottom of a shallow pond. At his father's orders, the prince found rocks with which to weigh her down.

The next morning, the girl's father knocked at the castle door to ask if anyone had seen his daughter. The king sent word that he was not to ask again. The day after that, the father returned, deeply troubled because he could not find her. Do not ask again, *the king shouted from his throne. But the man returned the next day, weeping for grief.* Have you seen my child? *The king was furious for having his command questioned and summoned the man before him.* I told you not to ask. You have not obeyed. *With that, the king had the girl's father arrested. He was beaten and hanged from a tree until it was certain he would ask nothing of anyone ever again. The king ordered the body taken down. As his men began this task, a peacock flew up on the branch and began to scream. The king ordered the bird to silence, directing an archer to shoot the bird dead. The next night, however, another peacock alights in the tree. Another archer kills this other bird. The next night, the same thing. And the next night. No matter how the king attempts to silence the bird's wrenching cry, it keeps coming back. There are always more.*

The final drawing was complex in perspective. The viewer was looking through an open window into an oval mirror in which a reflection of the king in his crown, squatting on his haunches, his hands over his ears, looking at his reflected self, his jaw dropped in horror. I had no way of knowing if these pictures were James's illustrations deciphered or Nate's re-creation of what his uncle had told him. It didn't really matter, because what I had before me was all I had, and what I had, for its fairy-tale trappings, was clearly true. In this last drawing, you could not see the peacock. The way it was drawn implied exactly who was seeing this wondrous sight of a king in chaos. This was the wilderness and here was the peacock, who, seeing what he really was, could do nothing more than scream.

the wilderness

sojourn

Sophia was discharged from the hospital on schedule, and after being pronounced legally clear of any malicious intent in Nate's death, she went into seclusion without letting anyone in on her plans. I tried to call, write; did not hear back. Although I had a pretty good idea of where she'd gone and what she had found there.

We, the survivors, went forward into April, the month already renowned for its seasonal cruelties onto which Greg and I dog-piled our own. The suitcases were waiting by the door, still. The girls had hauled their stuff back upstairs, but Greg's remained. The suitcases lay opened, the contents rifled through for necessities. He slept on the old sofa in the front room. I was back in the sewing room. No one used our bed. The marriage was over and leaving had begun.

It can take a very long time to figure out how to get out of your own house. The circles beneath his eyes, his posture, made clear the effort he was putting into what might be misinterpreted as ambivalence. Greg was a careful man, a devotee of the "measure twice, cut once" school of insurance against his own mistakes. He'd measure three times just to make certain of his certainty. Who could say how many times he would have to assess this decision before he made it? How sure he would have to be before taking the blade to his own heart? The closer he came to knowing the cut had to be made, the more he held me responsible for the outcome, the impending agonies when metal tooth first caught flesh. We were done, and somehow in ending we needed each other more than ever. That we couldn't be friends to each other at a time when friends were so necessary was more of a loss than the marriage.

Emma and Molly, aware of the new finality in the house, did not try to amend matters or us with their behavior. No extra diligence with the chores; no requests for reassurances. They did not want to talk about it with us or hear us talk about it or hear us not talk about it. Emma rarely came home from Rita's before bedtime and then slept in her sister's room. Rita's mother, Lillian, kept me informed about how my daughter was holding up. That Emma had taken a sudden liking to a series of young adult books that featured the doomed love stories of pretty girls with terminal diseases told me plenty.

Molly tried to stay gone, out of the drama as much as she could. She spent afternoons at the library or volunteered more hours at the convalescent home. The day I had gone up to the cabin and without advance word to anyone, Molly had cut her hair. Since preschool, she had worn it long; braids had bounced down to her mid-back for all her girlhood. Getting her to indulge the occasional trim required Geneva-level negotiations. Her hair now framed her lovely, serious face in a dark graduated fringe that closed like a curtain—"watch this"—around her when she lowered her head. When she lifted it again, I had no choice but to look her directly in the eye. She turned away but let me touch the edges, let me feel how soft it was. I teared up, apologized for being one of *those* moms. She then handed me a plastic bag that contained the braid, banded at both ends, which the stylist had made of the length before lopping it off. I looked at the bagged rope of my daughter's relinquished childhood. Before I could ask her why, ask her forgiveness, she had left the room.

That's how every room in the house felt, as though it had been recently vacated. Even when the four of us were together at the table, I thought we were missing a person, waiting for the return of one who stepped out for a moment; the warmth of a presence was still palpable but dissipating as the waiting grew longer. I tried to explain the sensation to Frank at our first session, an appointment I'd made from the first pay phone I came across after leaving the cabin. I'd left dirt on the dial buttons.

"You think it might really be a ghost?" I'd asked him, laughing.

"Ghost. Loneliness." He'd answered, not laughing. "Same thing. What is that you have there?"

I pulled the elastic band off the packet of postcards. When I'd returned home, I found the mail had brought a battered padded envelope, addressed to me in Sophia's handwriting, postmarked from the town nearest the cabin, dated the day before Nate died. "These belong to Sophia. She sent them before . . . well; it's as though she guessed how bad it might get. Nate was burning everything. It was her way of saying this needs finishing, you know?"

"You should allow her to finish it then."

"I don't know how to get these back to her. Besides, I'm not sure she can manage it alone."

He went through the cards slowly, shaking his head. "Leslie—"

"Don't try to tell me, Frank. Tell them. Tell them you think it's okay to let this go."

"*Them?*"

"The ghosts. Their ghosts."

"That's what I meant about loneliness—the longing for what cannot be done or undone. The only ghosts we have here are the ones in your mind, Leslie."

"Tell *me*, then. Look me in the eye, and tell me it's all right for me to know this happened and walk away."

"You wouldn't be walking away. You'd be accepting that not every story is your story."

"That 'it's not my problem' crap is the problem out there. You are a very smart man, Frank, but you're wrong on this one. Absolutely wrong."

He rubbed his forehead. "Have I told you how much I've missed you?"

My sisters had joined forces in hyena mode. Joanne and Denise decided that it was way too soon in the ongoing Swifton property boom to sell. Divorce had a way of screwing up profit margins. Phone calls burned the lines back and forth between both sides. Greg or I would talk to them, and without invitation but with knowledge, the other parties would be on the extension listening in. It was family business, money that would be coming to me, money that I would split with Greg.

Joanne called again the night of April 14. Wednesday. It was very late; she had a way of forgetting the time difference. The girls were in bed; Greg and I were working on getting our taxes filed. He in his room; me in mine. We had been making occasional trips to each other's space to request receipts or check stubs. At first, these favors were asked the way one might approach a dying man about a blood donation, but after a couple hours we had fallen into a kind of easy mutual hatred of the tax code. The mood had lightened. We were making jokes about Rita's parents getting the child credit for Emma. Then the phone rang. Greg answered downstairs. I heard him say "Jo," and I went into the bedroom to pick up. In those few short seconds, they were already swatting at each other. Being Joanne, her taxes had been filed back in January, by her accountant, who she had since consulted about selling the house at this point in time. Greg was making his usual arguments; Joanne was punctuating his reasons with her usual sighs; he finished; she went into the speech she'd obviously been practicing. "Local property values are still going up, Greg. 'Skyrocketing,' I believe, is the term used in the papers. I keep up, you know. My accountant—"

"You know it gets to a question of greed, Joanne."

"This is my retirement fund, Greg. Denise's."

"I wouldn't sell short, Joanne. It's just—"

"Why should you have to uproot the girls, Greg? Again? Why should you have to accommodate *her* again?"

"Leslie would not be living here, either."

"I should hope not. She's too unreliable and—"

"I don't want to talk about—"

"And selfish, ungrateful—"

"You forgot 'insane.'"

"I knew you were there, Leslie. I heard you breathing."

"Good, then I hope you're able to hear common sense now. We're selling, sister dear."

"I'm handling it, Leslie."

"It's my family, Greg."

"I would remind you both that we have a contract. It's legal. Binding."

"Are you threatening us, Joanne?"

"I'm only saying that if Denise and I have to, we'll exercise our rights. It would mean attorneys. And you don't want to bring yet *another* lawyer into this, do you?"

Greg made a sound of disgust before slamming down his receiver. I heard the door slam seconds later. "Nice work," I said, biting the syllables. "You've been saving that one, haven't you?"

"I'm not the one who is out sleeping around, Leslie."

"Shut up, Joanne," I said before hanging up on her. I went downstairs to find Greg standing in the foyer, his back braced against the front door.

"One of us should leave tonight," he said.

"Sounded like you did."

"What I meant." He cleared his throat to cover the emotions in his voice. "What I meant is that you should leave tonight."

He wanted me to say that I didn't want to leave. If I said that, we would have fought to near death for the rest of the night and maybe the next day, fought as long as it took to exhaust ourselves, to leave ourselves no energy to move, let alone change course. That was what we did; that was how we kept going. We'd get here, to the borderlands, get a glimpse of the unknown beyond, and immediately sell off another piece of ourselves in return for a map—always, always forgetting that you can only map the places you've been. We would slice off another bit of our souls for the directions that could lead us nowhere but here, again, to the border. Each time we arrived we had less of us to offer up in trade. I knew what Greg wanted me to say because I wanted to say it. But I couldn't. I was used up. So was he. "All right, Greg. I'll go." I turned around and started up the stairs, behind me I could hear him kicking the shit out of his suitcases.

The drive into the city was long. Traffic was not so bad but it seemed as though my destination was being inched away from me out of spite. Oncoming headlights blurred through the tears that were in a blatant violation of my prohibitions not to cry. Bootleg weeping; the sobs came harsh and searing in my throat. I reached Phillip's apartment building at around twelve thirty and sat in the parking lot until I got myself under control. I called up; he buzzed me in, met me at the door of his lawyer-swanky place with its great view of the park and the spacious rooms softly lit and the leather furniture and the specimen trees up-lighted on the balcony. I had awakened him; he was bleary, yawning, trying to figure out how the belt on his robe was supposed to work. He gave up on the robe, letting it fall open over his bare chest and pajama pants. More alert now, he studied my face, his eyes traveling down to my sneakers, back up to my ripped-knee jeans, my baseball shirt, my eyes. He took the suitcase from my hand and gestured me to come in. "Is that my shirt?"

"Probably. I've stolen a lot from you over the years."

He set my bag beside the couch. "It's different this time."

"This is different."

"You need someplace to stay for a while?"

"Tonight. What's left of tonight. Tomorrow—"

"Tomorrow is a long way off. Do you want to be by yourself?"

"Being by myself is getting tiresome."

He took my hand and pulled me gently into motion, leading me back to his bedroom. The bedside lamp was on, a book flattened on the pillow beside his. He sat me down on the edge of the mattress, kneeled in front of me to take off my shoes. These he placed next to his before peeling off my socks, tucking those into the shoes, before taking my left foot in his hand to rub and flex it. He smiled up at me; it seemed like forever since anyone had offered that simple evidence of being glad to have me in the room. The lamp provided only light enough to find the edges of Phillip's face, his hair, the shifting of his body as he lowered my left foot and took up the right, his fingers sliding under the hem of my jeans, up my leg, the pressure against my muscles increasing.

"Do you want your stolen shirt back?" I said.

He laughed. "Don't worry about it."

"I mean do you want it back now?" I lifted the shirt up, exposing my middle.

"Leslie. No." He stopped my hand, took the fabric from my grip, and smoothed it back down my body, held it there.

"I guess it is awfully late. I'm sorry—"

He shook his head at me. "What I meant was no, Leslie; let me." He ran his palms up my sides, rising up on his knees as he went, forcing the shirt up with him, up my arms, over my head until it was off. The neck opening came free of my hair, which fell over my eyes. He brushed it aside, stroking my face, moving down my throat. "You know," he said, "you don't have to be by yourself. You could let someone in there with you."

"I've got plenty of *someone* in here with me already." I had not meant to whisper.

"Then what's one more?" He whispered back.

I nodded. He smiled and tapped his index finger against the middle of my forehead. "Knock, knock."

When I woke, daylight was hard in the window, bursting into the room to lay in a wanton glow over the bed. Phillip was in the shower; I could hear him singing a jingle for a local used-car lot, off-key. I dragged myself out of the sheets and went to join him. He allowed me to warm myself in the spray before handing me the soap and a washcloth.

"You know, Leslie, as an officer of the court I am sworn to prevent criminal action whenever I am able."

"Prevention would put you out of business." I lathered the cloth and circled it along his back, down the muscles, to his ankles, back up again.

"Yes, well, prevention can only go so far." He turned his back to the spray to rinse off. "If you were to move in here, with me, all that stealing would be more of a borrowing situation."

I snorted a laugh so sudden that water went up my nose, down my throat simultaneously, which set up a coughing jag. When I could speak again, I choked out the obvious, "Us living together would never work."

He steered me around so my back was to him. "How do you know? We've never tried it." His soapy hands slid over my backbone and around front to cover my breasts before sliding downward in tandem. I grabbed at his wrists to stop his progress but he slipped right on through.

Secondary defense: I pivoted to face him—"I've never tried driving a roofing spike through my eye, either"—and left his hands on the small of my back, which he brought together to pull me up against him. I snuggled my belly up against his erection. "Some things a person just knows."

"You're afraid."

"Of you?"

"Of being happy."

"Leslie Land is a long way from happy."

345

"What are you right now, Leslie? Right at this moment. What are you?"

I blinked through the water up into his streaming face.

"That's what it is, Leslie. That's all it is. Not a reward. Not some recognition of inherent goodness. It's just a moment, every now and then. You don't get happiness because you deserve it." He shut off the water. "You get it because you were paying attention when it walked through the room. Want to go for two in a row? Double or nothing? And yes, that is a dare."

"Double dog?" I kissed his sternum.

"Triple. Should it come to that."

It did not come to that. I moved in with Phillip the first weekend in May. Greg took Molly and Emma out of town; this heart transplant process was gruesome enough without having to worry about the trauma caused by children watching. That was the agreed upon rationale, but I sensed that he also wanted them out of reach should I get into my head they were a part of my belongings.

Once moved, I needed income to continue my search for the little girl's identity, but I wanted a job that promised only the mundane, manageable sort of sorrows. I took a position doing investigative work for Phillip's firm, tracking down bank accounts and business records. The sterile safety of numbers. That meant another meeting with Regina. She remembered me, too. The woman was cordial enough during the intake interview, but her manner suggested the unfailing mistrust of any animal, mineral, or vegetable associated with Phillip Hogarth. It was clear that I was already entered on her short list of shady employees. She walked me to the elevator—probably to make sure I got on. While we waited, she asked if I realized I was taking on Sophia's job—her way of telling me what she knew and what she suspected about how I'd come by my new employment.

"This isn't exactly the sort of work Sophia did."

"Let's hope not." The elevator doors opened, she waved me on, indicating I was to leave. "That man's luck can't hold forever."

Phillip's luck—or the threat of his talking—held for the time being; Oliver had filed no complaint about the assault. He did balance the ledger, however, flooding Phillip with the tax foulups, immigration problems, and ugly divorce cases for what Oliver called his "practice" of physical therapists. These women with dance-trained bodies and wardrobes from lingerie catalogs would sit in Phillip's office for hours, diamonds dribbling into their cleavage, as they—at Oliver's obvious instruction—regaled Phillip with tales not only of Oliver's prowess, but his relentless appetites. They brought video records. Phillip would come home from these meetings and head straight for the shower.

Greg and I spoke when required. We kept to the bullet points of formal agendas. Who had the girls; what bills needed paying. He had stayed in the house after all. The only rational thing to do given finances and jobs and school. More so after my sisters' attorney sent a list of legal options available to them in consideration of back rent and breach of contract. When Greg wasn't working on his job at the professors' place, he was reworking our—what had been our—home. Wallpaper was coming down, new paint going up. He was refinishing the rest of the kitchen cupboards. Floors would be next. He said he wanted to get it done, get the place on the market, sell it, and get out. But what he was getting rid of was *Leslie*, sanding me out of the woodwork as one would any other scar.

In mid-June we signed formal separation agreements, going for the no-fault option because we were all blamed out. With the papers signed, the divorce finally on the horizon, we found it easier to talk. Inmates paroled from the same prison on the same day. We didn't exactly know each other, but we shared a history all the same. We made tentative efforts to catch up on each other's lives. How was work? Did you get the storm out your way? Did you read in the paper where . . .? Our conversations were awkward, defensive in advance expectation of hurt, but we were trying to foster the bonds forged from the new information between us, the growing amazement that this wasn't going to kill us.

It was during one of these exchanges of personal current events that Greg told me Happy Andy's had been sold. The same commercial retail developer building at the end of the road had taken the whole property. No official site plans as yet—although a cineplex and go-cart park were rumored. The property would be cleared of structures later in the year; building was expected to begin soon after. Apparently there was a way to dig up the whole countryside while simultaneously burying it.

I was sitting on the floor before the sliding glass door watching clouds roil and sink, the rain falling scattershot. I had arranged the postcards, as I did almost daily, in a long line along the base of the window. What had first appeared as random wounding had become quite plainly symbols etched into the victims flesh. How could anyone *not* see? The terrible images lay, some by almost a century, beyond the reach of kindness and yet desperately in need. I could do nothing for these men who were gone before the camera caught them. Our kindness, our concern, was of no use to them at all. They were gone. This could not be undone. I heard a knock at our door, and called to Phillip to answer it. He did not hear me, and the knock sounded again. I got up, still calling to Phillip, went to the door and found Sophia, preparing to knock again with the handle of her cane. Before I could say hello, she said, "We're not going to leave her there."

It was a beginning, Sophia said. We could take the girl's remains out of their storage box marked with a number in a basement warehouse, hidden away as though she were a secret. We could make an open declaration of her short life as being larger, more significant than what her death said about us. She had a name; whether or not we ever learned it; whether or not we could stand on top of the rocks as James had and call for her across the fields or repeat it silently in prayers when we asked blessings upon her soul, forgiveness for our own. She had been loved; she had been given a name. That small kindness we could offer; we could love her as a child rather than as an idea or a cause, love her as we would one of our own, and admit that we had failed her.

Phillip drafted the paperwork. The county didn't put up a fuss. Sophia took custody of the little girl's remains on the morning of the twenty-first of June and drove them to Bellwood. I had made arrangements with a funeral home for a child's casket, white. Andrea and Kim met us there with flowers, a spray of tiny pink roses. We followed the hearse out to the cemetery where Sophia's family has laid itself back into the earth for generations. She had land waiting for her there beside her brother. Sophia had told them to dig in her spot, to put the child with her.

It was early-summer hot that Monday; baking heat with thin humidity. Phillip wore a suit, and I, my one good dress, of charcoal gray knit. Greg brought Molly and Emma; the three of them kept close together and avoided making eye contact with me. Sophia had invited the minister from the church her parents had attended. The minister, a plump, contented-looking man, had been told the details. He smiled at each of us and then said only one word above the casket: *Listen.* From then on, we were quiet; no one tried to say anything meaningful. No one said anything. The silencing of ecumenical chatter in favor of the cicadas, the questioning of the doves in the shade, the maternal shushing of the breeze did seem most appropriate. We watched as the tiny white box was lowered. It seemed as though we should do something else, but nothing was left to do in that place. We'd have to leave and take that sense of the unanswered with us. Sophia wanted to stay behind a bit longer. She said we'd get back to work soon, and then she returned to the graveside, her thoughts her own.

Phillip and I walked to where we left the cars. The representative from the funeral home, the one who had driven the hearse, was waiting. He said the marker would be installed in a couple weeks—he'd let us know when—and gave me the form to double-check the wording. Not much to check. The polished granite had space for three lines; Sophia had requested the top one be left blank. Beneath the blank, where we would one day— God help us—place her given name, Sophia had asked that they engrave:

DAUGHTER

LOST IN THE WILDERNESS

Molly and Em gave me quick good-byes. I thanked them, thanked Greg for making the trip out. Andrea waved farewell. Kim blew a kiss from her index finger. I had insisted Phillip and I drive up separately. No explanation offered, but he had quickly surmised my intentions at the request. He didn't want me going out to the petting zoo alone; he had said so, knowing that it wouldn't make a difference. Phillip's great gift was that he knew when to stop arguing. I drove up to Willet. In the trunk was a box with some cleaning supplies, a few tools, a change of clothes, and my video camera.

It was late afternoon when I arrived. The property of the petting zoo, now posted against trespass, was lush with grasses still tender, softly green from the wet of spring. It would be bristle-brush stiff a month from now. I carried the supplies up to the cottage, weaving my way around the opened, always-opened cages. A new latch had been bolted to the cottage's doorframe, a padlock clamped through that. I'd expected something of the sort; I pulled the bolt cutters from the box and snipped the lock free.

The interior had been stripped of Nate and Sophia's belongings. The floors had been swept, but not thoroughly. Bits of paper and fluff stirred about the open rooms. The sulfur stench clogged my nostrils; under that was a mildew odor. I changed my clothes there in the entryway; absently reaching to hang my dress on the coat hook; but it too was gone. I put on jeans and one of Phillip's baseball shirts that I'd taken from the bedroom that morning because it carried his smell, which I tried to concentrate on. Socks. Shoes. Ready.

I carried the video camera back outside. It was one of the heavy, cumbersome models from a couple decades earlier, but I had a tripod for it and it recorded directly to tape. The tripod had not been used in such a long time that the chrome on its adjustment wheels was pitted with rust, difficult to turn. I got the camera screwed on tight, and set about changing the focus in order to get the widest view of the cages; made sure the time stamp was on and then hit Record. The camera clicked and whirred as the tape engaged. The battery lasted six hours max; at least it had when it was new. I stepped around in front of the lens and rattled off the spiel I'd been rehearsing for days, which basically boiled down to *the following is a test of the emergency broadcast system.* I wanted to know where my story ended and theirs began. I turned around and closed the cage behind me. And then the one beside that. I moved through the yard, closing up the cage doors even outside the range of the lens.

That done, I went back to the cottage, back inside, careful not to look back, not to jostle the camera, which would record what it might. The camera didn't choose what it saw; it had no personal stake in reality, no blind spot. I took the box of cleaning supplies into the front room. The peacock was still there, faded and smeared, but still there. I opened the box of rubber gloves I'd purchased for this task, slipped them on, and then opened the canister of mineral spirits, soaked one of the rags, and began to scrub. The peacock lost its form, becoming more an aurora of color than a shape. The rags saturated with diluted color; I tossed them aside like bandages when one is attempting to staunch a serious injury. The fumes made my head swampy and my stomach ill; the solvents made the fingertips of the gloves tacky, slowly melting through. But I kept at it. Rag after rag, until the colors were pale on the cloth, and then gone. The peacock, the words, came down. The light in the window grew lower. We had turned into the early side of evening. Didn't matter. I had plenty of light left. This was nature's most generous day. As of tomorrow, we would be on the wane.

I tugged off the gloves and tossed them on the pile of rags. Not only was the wall clean of colors, it was just plain clean; the plaster gleamed. I left the supplies where they were and, dizzy with fumes, went back outside to check the camera. The sunlight stung my eyes; the fresh air hit my lungs like water hits raw thirst. I took greedy breaths, sniffling, chemically induced tears wetting my face. Beside me the camera whirred. The cage doors were open again.

My breath was coming fast still, but for a different reason. I pushed the Stop button on the camera, and then Rewind. The motor puttered up to speed, the tape spooling backward, the zippering noise accelerating until the solid *thunk* of it reaching its end, its beginning. I looked out across the yard, up toward the rocks, from where I would see the pond, the fields, the sky that had witnessed all and revealed nothing. I thought of Nate, winding through the ether. I thought of the little girl sleeping in what would one day be Sophia's bed. We were going to be lost for a while. I repositioned myself so that my view was shielded from the indifferent sun, steadied my resolve, and pushed Play.

acknowledgments

My unending thanks to those who wandered with me as this novel found its path: Elizabeth Sheinkman, agent and friend; Karen Rinaldi, for whom I am running out of ways to say thank you; Lara Carrington, my editor, whose faith is as great as her vision—a bouquet of pancakes for you. Everyone at Bloomsbury, bless you. A fireworks display for Lorraine Berry, in honor of her uncanny sense of research direction and brilliant courage in truth telling. A friend will read your manuscript; a true friend will call to tell you it isn't *there* yet—and then dive for cover. To Amy Small-McKinney, who writes the poems and asks the questions that serve as a calculus for the heart, thank you for the poem and the question that set this wheel in motion. Kristan Ryan, long-distance guardian angel to one half of what I hold most dear in this world; the future—not to mention this writing nonsense—is easier because of you. Judy Hershner, thank you; just thank you.

To Barry, KC, and Robyn: Thank you for putting up with the sound and the fury and all the frozen pizzas. To my family: I love you, wherever you are.

author's note

The ability to see the world in its complex entirety is the basis for locating what is true in events and in us. For that reason it is important to delineate the elements in this novel that preexisted its writing and continue outside its pages as fact.

The poem "I saw a peacock, with a fiery tail" is traditional and was officially first published in the *Westminster-Drollery* in 1671. All manipulation and meaning the novel's characters invest in the words are of my invention. The dates provided in the grounding of these inventions are accurate. The story pulled out of the poem is fiction. The history on which the story is based is true.

The postcard souvenirs of racially based murders are documented among the ongoing photography exhibits at Musarium.com. *Without Sanctuary: Photographs and Post-cards of Lynching in America* (http://www.musarium.com/ withoutsanctuary/main.html) will show you more than you may want to see. Yes, these went through the mail. Yes, these are real. My gratitude goes out to Alan Dorow and the staff at Musarium.com for their steadfast insistence that history demands witness.

Each of us has a blind spot in our vision. To *see* that blindness compensated for with images invented or denied is both humbling and instructive. You may learn more on how your blind spot works, see it in action, and map its dimensions at the wonderful site called Serendip (http://serendip.brynmawr.edu/bb/blindspot1.html). At Serendip, literature and science meet in vibrant creative alchemy. Thanks to Jeffery Oristaglio and Paul Grobstein for lending visibility to the part of us that cannot see.

A NOTE ON THE AUTHOR

Karen Novak is the author of *Five Mile House* and *Innocence*, both Leslie Stone novels, and *Ordinary Monsters*. She lives in Mason, Ohio.

A NOTE ON THE TYPE

The text of this book is set in Linotype Sabon, named after
the type founder, Jacques Sabon. It was designed by
Jan Tschichold and jointly developed by Linotype,
Monotype and Stempel, in response to a need for
a typeface to be available in identical form for
mechanical hot metal composition and hand
composition using foundry type.